CLEAN COPY

R.R. BROOKS

Published 2021 by Next Chapter

Edited by Brice Fallon

Cover art by CoverMint

ACKNOWLEDGMENTS

The author acknowledges the useful criticism of two groups in honing this thriller-science fiction tale with an espionage plot. Authors Rob Jacoby, Frank Robinson, the late Lenny Bernstein, and Tom Hooker of The Appalachian Roundtable critique group provided detailed feedback on characters, plot, dialog, and pacing that slowly and surely helped craft the story. The Blue Ridge Writers Group heard sections read, providing diverse feedback. My wife Sherry read the manuscript after it was re-worked. Her suggestions, as usual, fixed and improved. Her encouragement and support never wavered. The author thanks all these people who helped improve the novel.

The novel is dedicated to scientists who do the hard work of day-to-day experimentation, as well as those who design next steps and try to make sense out of the results.

PROLOGUE

Jun Wu, a petite woman in her thirties, had just stepped from her post-breakfast shower and wrapped a towel about herself when the phone rang. She left wet footprints on the tan bedroom carpet and picked up the receiver. When it turned out to be her boss, Jun tried to sound dignified.

She rubbed the towel end over her short black hair and listened as Peter Valois explained the unusual call at such an early hour. After a moment, Jun said, "I'm fine, Peter." She paced around her queen-sized bed and listened to more explanation from the phone. "A premonition? About what?" She glanced at the clock and pulled the red bedspread straight. "Danger? Well, I'm not in any danger as far as I can tell," Jun said in a calm voice. Except for catching pneumonia, she thought. "Everything is normal, it's a beautiful April day up here, and I'm getting ready to leave."

Jun lodged the phone between her shoulder and ear, dropped the towel, and went to the dresser. "Your premonition makes no sense. You don't know what the danger is or where it lies. Maybe it's something in the lab." From the closet she grabbed the day's outfit and threw it onto the bed and then shifted the phone to her other ear. "I'll be extra careful, but I'll be an hour or so late. I have to see an insurance agent."

She hung up, wondering what that was all about. The boss had called her at home before, but never at this early hour. Strange. A thought crossed her mind. Was there a connection between Dr. Valois's intuition and her not-so-pleasant conversation with the insistent guy from the Chinese Scholars Association? She, like any other educated person of Chinese descent, knew the Association was one of many dedicated to transferring technology to the motherland. Jun didn't feel her position in a company doing classified work for the U.S. government allowed her to consort with agents of the People's Republic of China, and she said so. Insistent guy had asked her to collect technology and wasn't happy with her answer.

Two men sat in a black Suburban parked in front of the vacant lot near Jun's house in the San Diego hills. Most of the lots in the new development had FOR SALE signs, so it was possible the occupants were considering a purchase. In fact, Yingyi, a wiry Asian with a cheek scar, and Morgan, a big-fisted, muscle-bound Caucasian, watched Jun's small bathroom window and the front door.

Both men were employees of Xianxingzhe Group of Beijing, a leading R&D outfit in China. The conglomerate competed with Jun Wu's employer in robotics and needed something from Jun's boss.

"The bathroom light just went out. Ms. Wu, she of the small but shapely ass, will soon emerge on schedule as usual," Yingyi said as he lowered the field glasses. "Seems a shame to waste such fine assets without putting them to some use."

"Shut up," Morgan said. "I don't think you could fuck the broad and still make this look like an accident. She just passed the front window. Mighta noticed us."

"So what. We're prospective buyers looking at real estate. We're just part of the normal scenery, and if Ms. Wu is alarmed, that's a real shame. A frightened rabbit is more fun for the hunter." Yingyi donned reflective sunglasses and smiled. This operation, part of a larger plan, was his boss's idea, and he was glad at last to be doing instead of planning. There'd been months of that. He finally felt alive. He interlaced his fingers and stretched his arms.

"Too bad it's bright and sunny," Yingyi said. "Rain and wet pavement would make an accident more believable."

Minutes ticked by as the two men drank the remains of their lukewarm coffee. They dropped the cups into a plastic bag when Jun emerged from the house and approached her compact, beat-up Toyota.

Jun smoothed her tan skirt and adjusted her sunglasses, smiled in the direction of the Suburban, and got into her car. She started the motor and lowered the windows, took time to maneuver the rearview mirror, studied the men in the black vehicle, and then backed from her driveway.

"Punctual as usual," Yingyi said. "And neatly dressed."

Morgan let Jun get half a block away before he started the Suburban and followed. He stayed back at a non-threatening distance until they reached the steep, twisting road that led to the main highway. When the switchbacks began, Morgan drew close. Jun glanced in her mirror and swerved off the pavement.

"That's just normal driving for her," Yingyi said. "Let her be nervous."

Morgan got near the Toyota, as if he wanted to pass. Up ahead was a stretch that had no shoulder.

"We're coming to the place," Yingyi said."

Jun accelerated, but Morgan kept pace, and then retreated. Yingyi saw the woman reach over to something on the dash. Distractions cause accidents, he thought.

The next section curved around a steep hill. A cable strung between metal posts separated the narrow shoulder from a rock-strewn ravine. Morgan had made sure the cable was slack and low, too low to prevent a car from flying over the edge. And Jun was on the downhill side. The Toyota's tires squealed in a hard turn.

A yellow sign indicated an S-shaped curve and recommended twenty miles per hour. Jun slowed some, and Yingyi waved Morgan forward. Now the woman might suspect that her pursuer was not just a bad driver. The little Toyota kicked gravel as it strayed off the pavement.

The Suburban kissed the Toyota's bumper. Jun left the road again with another blast of tire on rocky dirt. This time she yanked the wheel to the left and took her foot off the accelerator. Morgan nudged the smaller car with the brush bar on the front of the Suburban. Jun went off the road but somehow managed to maintain control. The SUV backed off and sped forward again. This time it did not contact the rear bumper. It swung into the opposite lane, came alongside, and pushed Jun to the right. The much heavier vehicle shoved the Toyota off the blacktop, and as the road curved, the smaller car faced open air.

Jun screamed as her sedan flew past the cable barrier. The undercarriage caught the wire, and the Toyota held for a moment. With a screech, the vehicle broke free, and the rear tires rolled over the cable. The front end bounced once on the slope before the drop-off, and then the car somersaulted into the abyss. Wheels spinning, the Toyota landed roof-down with a crunch of metal, its feeble horn wailing. A few rocks bounced off the undercarriage, and then there was silence.

The Suburban pulled to the side, and the men strode back to the now flattened guard rail. Morgan took off his dark glasses and gazed at the belly of the Toyota far below. "What do you think?" he asked.

"Either dead or badly injured," Yingyi said. "Must have dozed and lost control on an unfortunate section of the road. Fiddling with the radio probably distracted her."

"Miss Wu won't report for work anytime soon. Someone will have to take her place." Morgan walked back to the SUV. "Let's get the car taken care of and tell the boss how the accident went."

The men returned to the Suburban and drove off as a single, pumpkin-sized rock loosened by the crash finally let go of its perch, rumbled down the slope to the edge, and rolled off. The smell of gasoline tainted the air. Crows, silenced by the screech of metal, resumed their bickering. The sound of a small engine interrupted their caws. A moment after the SUV departed, a Honda cycle bounced from a narrow path on the uphill side of the accident site and stopped near the guard cable.

A leather-clad, helmeted rider dismounted from the motorcycle and gazed into the ravine. Seeing no movement and hearing no sound near the overturned car, the figure cursed and pulled out a cell phone. There was no signal. The rider remounted the bike and, after another glance into the ravine, rode off.

PART 1
OPPORTUNITY

In revenge and in love, woman is more barbarous than man.

- FRIEDRICH NIETZSCHE

1 / ANTOINETTE

In January, three months before Jun Wu's murder near San Diego, events unfolded in Langley, Virginia that sealed her fate. At the Central Intelligence Agency, Antoinette Dai-tai Marino worked as an analyst, a job she'd had for almost two years. Her Italian and Chinese heritage explained an unusual beauty that featured Mediterranean olive skin and ebony hair from her father and Asian eyes from her Chinese mother. More than one man had called her striking.

The CIA was her third employer—she'd spent two years after college working for a biotech company and four years in the army. Known as Andy to her colleagues, she had a reputation as competent and tough. What her intelligence co-workers didn't know was that she had an agenda of her own.

She had to find out why her brother Tony had died. The CIA job meant access to documents about his death, but she couldn't let her search be obvious. Dogged pursuit of information on this topic had nothing to do with her assignment and might threaten her career. Despite the risk, she again entered Records to access a Nicaragua file. Her professional attire—knee-length skirt, white blouse, and picture identification card—gave her every right to be there. She pushed open the door and marched in as if nothing were amiss.

Andy strode across the gray room: carpet, government-standard furniture, and walls were shades of gray. Pictures of the president and the Agency head decorated one wall, and overhead fluorescent lights gave no-nonsense illumination. An ozone taint in the dehumidified air almost made her sneeze. She suppressed it and nodded to the desk clerk who continued watering a pathetic philodendron, a protest of the room's rigidity. A thick-necked man, white collar choking his red face, occupied one carrel, engrossed in a file. He ignored her.

Andy took a corner carrel and pulled a yellow pad from her folio. She sat, eyes closed, and took measured breaths. The voice in her head said investigating her brother's death was not her assignment. But it's something I must do, she thought. For her sake, for Tony's sake.

A shuffling noise from the red-faced man brought Andy back, and she turned on the light under the bookshelf. On the pad she wrote a number and took it to the counter. The clerk disappeared and returned a minute later to hand over a manila folder.

Back in the carrel, Andy turned over sheets in the file with a steady, deliberate pace, rechecking contents seen before. The material from Army intelligence was its version of what happened. It seemed insufficient to tell the real story. Terse field reports, Tony's cryptic letters, and her own research, including an off-the-books trip to Central America, left her unsatisfied. Her mind wandered over what she knew.

Tony had left the army and was recruited by the Drug Enforcement Agency, which wanted experienced men disrupting drug routes in Central America. That he was killed in an ambush in Nicaragua leading trainees through a supposedly secure area was clear enough. He had been ordered to take that route. But why?

She shook off her sadness and again tried to understand what lay beyond the anemic facts. Willing calm, she selected the page with a post-event investigative report. The team reported finding twenty bodies—nineteen Nicaraguans and one American—one fewer than the twenty-one supposed to be in the unit. Perhaps the original information on unit size was wrong. The possibility that a man had escaped or been captured was recognized. Andy wondered if the twenty-first man was the enemy. The report said nothing of attackers and motive. American-made spent cartridges were left behind and not much else. Tony's body was shipped back home. Andy knew every sad detail of that part of the story.

A pot-bellied co-worker with a wrinkled tie passed the carrel, his glance lingering a second too long. Her skirt had moved well above her knees, exposing several inches of thigh. She lowered the skirt, muttered an expletive, and went back to the page.

The report raised the possibility that Taguro, the Nicaraguan unit commander, might have betrayed the group. His allegiance was suspect, but no reason was given. Andy knew the name, for her brother had mentioned him in his letters where he described Taguro as dedicated, loyal, and dependable. Why would he have anything to do with an ambush?

She needed to see the intelligence report that authorized the path they were on. If faulty intel caused the unit loss, there should be something about the source and its error. She stared at the page that first mentioned Taguro and her eyes drifted to the footer, a line that usually contained the file save date and the preparer's initials. These were present, but in parenthesis after the information was a six-digit number preceded by two letters, possibly a file ID, perhaps a file that contained more information about something on the page.

Feelings of sadness, regret, and sorrow fell prey to a new emotion: anger. Without any evidence, she felt certain that the file in front of her did not contain the whole story, that the death of Tony Marino and the Nicaraguans was not just an accident of being in the wrong place at the wrong time.

She wrote down the footer number. Her knowledge of the Agency security protocols told her the unusual coding of the file made it unavailable to her clearance level. She had no official reason to access the document. If she asked for it, a report would reach her boss.

She returned the folder to the records desk, stopped herself from requesting the file, and left, thinking how she could get access.

John Caro's office was spacious with a mahogany desk and matching bookcase that warmed the room. The fortyish section chief was not the flower type, so Andy assumed the vase of fresh flowers had to be his secretary's work.

"What's up?" he asked, continuing to scribble on a pad. "Just let me finish this sentence."

Andy watched him scrawl several more words. He still had a full head of brown hair and was good-looking in a pinstriped brown suit and red tie. He smiled, showing a chin dimple, got up, and came around the desk. He put his hand on her shoulder and steered her into a chair.

"It's good to see you," he said. "You always brighten this office. Now what can I help you with?"

She gritted her teeth. "I want to ask about that security upgrade."

Caro sat in the other visitor's chair, his knees an inch from hers. He reached to loosen his tie, revealing a gold watch on a tanned wrist. "It'll happen in due course. What's the rush?"

"I think time has run its course. I've been here two years and came with an exceptional track record in army intelligence. Any man with that background would have started above my current level."

"Would he?" Caro asked, his jaw muscles tightening.

"Wouldn't he?"

"Why do you need a security bump? Is there something in your assignment that requires it?"

"Nothing specific, but more than once I've had to check something in another file and had to stop what I'm doing, interrupt you, and maybe get back to that job a day later. Not efficient. And not necessary. I should have that upgrade."

Caro leaned back and folded his hands. "Well, I never mind your interruptions. It does get lonely in here. But I'll see what I can do. Wouldn't want you charging gender discrimination. But keep your nose out of what doesn't concern you. Now get your ass back to work."

Andy left wondering if Caro was watching that part of her anatomy as she left.

Her bitching worked, but Caro made her wait. Twice she reminded him and twice she was told to be patient. After a week she was about to make like the squeaking wheel yet again when the upgrade notice reached her.

2 / THE FILE

THE DAY HER SECURITY CLEARANCE WAS UPPED, ANDY REQUESTED the mysterious file from the Records clerk, who glanced at her computer terminal and said she wasn't eligible to view such material. With barely contained anger, Andy prodded the clerk to confirm her new status. The woman did so and, without saying a word, retrieved the requested file.

Andy grabbed the folder and retreated to a corner carrel where she sat, staring at the prize, willing her racing heart to quiet. The anticipation of learning from the CIA perspective why her brother died blurred her vision. She wiped the tears and at last opened the report, which consisted of a short, official document and an appendix. She skipped the usual subject-and-security coding at the top and perused the body, a concise account of the number of dead men and their names. It identified a joint task force of the DEA and the CIA as the agency that had authorized the mission and the route. It referred to a standard operating procedure, or SOP, for the intelligence gathering and claimed the area had been quiet for a month. The region had been scanned by a chopper-flyover the day before Tony took his men into the jungle. The summary attributed the massacre to the unexpected infiltration of a force from the drug cartel whose shipment was going to be stopped by the unit. No evidence was cited.

The dry report contained an appendix, labeled as an eye-witness account from the one survivor of the attack. This was the missing twenty-first man. Why hadn't the main file made this clear? Maybe he hadn't shown up until after that first document was prepared. Andy noted that the appended material was labeled as having been typed by the witness and unverified. She started to read and realized the tone of the text was unexpected, something written by an educated, intelligent person. At times, the material was almost poetic.

Lieutenant Tony Marino led us along an overgrown jungle path on Nicaragua's Mosquito Coast, between the Rio Grande de Matagalpa and Rio Prinzalpolka at the end of the rainy season. We tromped through festering, wet jungle, the homeland of the Miskito people, and wiped sweat from our faces under a midday sun. Tropical plants tried hard to engulf the narrow path, and we hacked them back, seeing no reason to be quiet or cautious. We were in the pacified zone from which both drug-shippers and those unhappy with the present government had been driven.

Things seemed normal. Above the insect buzz, raucous birds protested, and somnolent lizards swished leaves in scurried retreats. We hacked foliage, scattering snakes and lizards. The lieutenant stopped to wipe his forehead and watch a scarlet macaw take flight. A green anole with rosy dewlap whose bright color worked against any camouflage jumped in front of us.

"Mating first, invisibility second," Lieutenant Marino said. He pointed to another lizard decorated with prominent red spots. "Another survival ploy. Garishness that says only a foolish predator would even come close to such poison."
When we moved, the lizard's protuberant eye followed with a jerky movement, like the spasms of a loading Ferris wheel. I tell you this detail to show how relaxed we were, relaxed enough for biology.

Andy blinked away tears. The dialog sounded like Tony Marino, the brother she knew, one interested in everything around him, always with a theory. She forced herself to read more.

We walked single-file, close together, rifles hanging from shoulder straps. No one was particularly alert. The territory was safe. We expected a quiet stroll to a village for a few days of R and R, perhaps some gecko soup, as a reward for a successful training mission. The lieutenant was pleased with our accomplishments and felt that Taguro, our leader, was ready to take on a significant role. If the lieutenant could convince his superiors. Diplomacy and political awareness were not Taguro's strong points.

Andy remembered Tony telling her he had received more than one communication from command indicating misgivings about Taguro, although nothing specific was ever cited. Tony figured he did not have the intelligence rating for such sensitive information. All he was eligible for was risking his life in a bug-infested hell.

The sound from a zul, a native flute, stopped us. It had to be from an outlying farm, for we weren't near the village. Suddenly the music stopped and the jungle quieted. The men tensed and raised their weapons.

The next sound we heard was not of the jungle. A single rifle shot rang out and Taguro screamed and fell. The men reacted by firing into the trees at what they thought was the source of the shot. The tat tat tat of automatic rifle fire sprayed bullets everywhere. Around me men dropped with cries of pain or the silence of instant death. Blood splattered over giant, green leaves and dripped to the spongy forest floor. My leg took a bullet, but I was lucky. I fell behind a downed tree trunk and stayed quiet. Covered with blood, some mine and some the lieutenant's, it was easy to play dead. Thank God the shooters didn't come closer to finish the job. My leg wound was minor, and I managed to limp away after the attack.

Andy shuddered and closed her eyes. She imagined her brother's last thought was a question: how could the intelligence report be so wrong?

If the attack aimed to eliminate Taguro, why? Did Taguro have unacceptable allegiances? It was not unusual for Central American leaders to be in bed with drug lords. But where was that data? She also wanted to know the intelligence that cleared the path to the village.

From Records, Andy went directly to John Caro's office. He

pretended to maintain an open-door policy, but Andy knew he hated to be interrupted. She didn't care.

"John, I need your help on something." She sat. "I've been looking at a file on my brother's death. I need to know why the rebel leader he was training was under suspicion."

"Why the hell are you wasting your time on that? Your brother's loss was tragic but put it behind you." He wore a brittle smile.

"I'm not satisfied I have the full story. My brother was gunned down and there is some reason for it."

Caro came around his desk. "You have got to let it go. Focus on getting ahead in your job. Just curb your anger and be more pleasant."

Andy took a deep breath. "If I can get to the bottom of this, maybe I can move on."

"There are some files that even your new security upgrade does not open. Try putting your energy into fitting in. Use your assets to create your career path."

"What assets are you talking about?"

"You are a beautiful woman. Like any organization, the CIA runs by more than rules and regulations. People call the shots. If you want to get ahead, be friendly to those who control your future." Caro sat down and placed his hand on Andy's thigh. "I might answer your questions if you were friendly enough."

She was stunned. And then it all became clear. He didn't just want her to be friendly. He was looking for favors. It happened fast. In one fluid motion, she jumped up, and her hand came around and slapped her boss. His glasses went flying. Caro's face reddened.

He grabbed her hands and pressed himself against her. She reacted without thinking and brought her knee up into his groin. He rolled away, clutching his genitals.

"You bitch. That's ground for dismissal."

"So is sexual harassment." Andy's analytical brain took over and came up with a stark conclusion: she had to quit. She'd run into a brick wall in investigating her brother's death. Caro could fire her, and she didn't want that on her record. Working for Caro disgusted her. The course was clear. "But I'll save you the trouble. I quit."

"Good riddance. Clear out now. I'll have security give you a hand.

And don't plan to work for the government again. I'll see that your attitude problem is well known."

Andy glared at Caro, wishing she could hit him again. She suppressed that impulse and left the office. A security man showed up with a carton as she cleaned out her desk. Without saying goodbye to anyone, she let security lead her to the exit. She walked stiffly to her car across the icy asphalt, avoiding the patches of snow and feeling the chill of the winter air that matched the black cold in her heart. That her predatory boss should remain employed while she was out the door enraged her.

She deposited the box in the trunk, sank into the driver's seat, and was about to stick the key into the ignition when the glint of sun on chrome caught her eye. Caro's new BMW, polished and shiny, was parked four cars away. This was his new toy, and he'd made it clear how much he cherished the machine. Andy loathed the BMW as she loathed Caro.

She eased open her car door and slithered out, crouching to stay hidden from the lot security camera, and crept to the BMW. Without hesitating, she ripped a key along the side, leaving a satisfying scratch in the black mirror coat from the front wheel well to the rear door. For good measure, she unscrewed the rear tire valve cover, tossed it, and depressed the valve stem with the key. Air hissed out and the tire grew soft. When it was almost flat, she crept back to her car, got in, and drove away feeling better.

3 / OPPORTUNITY

AFTER LEAVING THE CIA, ANDY MARINO HID IN HER APARTMENT, trying to find a job and thinking. Today, still in pajamas with her second coffee, she sat staring at an old family portrait, remembering growing up in the Midwest with her brother Tony. The children of a career army father, a cold and abusive man, and an intimidated mother who ignored her kids, the brother and sister had learned early to rely on each other. Now, Tony and her father were dead, and her mother was in a home.

Getting away to college had been a blessing. She'd stayed close to Tony during her University of Maryland years, and they would often walk on campus and try to resurrect, or manufacture, the good times of being kids. He'd been the one who comforted her when her boyfriends turned out to be pawing bores and a college advisor made a clumsy pass. Only later did she learn that he'd also popped the guy, breaking his nose.

Andy got dressed, stopped thinking of her brother, and mulled over what had become of her career. At twenty-nine, she had none. She'd run into sexual harassment yet again. Did she invite such behavior in some way? Her middle name Dai-tai did mean "leading a boy in hopes," so maybe her inadvertent, genetics-dictated behavior sent out the wrong message. Bullshit, she thought. The wreck of her intelligence career galled her, not just because she liked the field, but because she'd lost the means to find answers about her brother's death. Pissed off and frustrated she couldn't do this one thing for her brother —or was it really for herself?—she obsessed on how she might punish John Caro.

Getting the final paycheck from the CIA made finding a new job critical. Or else there was no affording the apartment or the car, let alone sending support money to her mother. She had worked for a couple of years doing biological lab work in a drug-discovery company in California. If she applied for a job in that field, she didn't need a letter of recommendation from the CIA, although an employer would most likely call them. She landed a few interviews but got no offers. She revised her resume and started again. Still nothing.

By the third week, her attitude morphed into a blend of anger and fear. She had begun to consider unskilled jobs. Anything for income before she had to give up her apartment. She was prepared to widen her search, to try for something in another city, to loosen her criteria. She considered a loan to tide her over. She thought of suing the CIA for sexual harassment and wondered if she could tolerate asking fat customers if they wanted fries with that.

Morning became afternoon as Andy made phone calls that got her no closer to employment. Later in the day she was sipping the final glass from her last bottle of cheap Chablis and thinking of going for a run when the call came. It was after business hours, so it probably wasn't job-related. She stared at the ringing phone, thinking it couldn't be anyone from the CIA. No friends there or elsewhere. It rang five times before she answered.

"Is this Antoinette Marino?" asked an accented voice.

"Speaking."

"My name is Mr. Wu. I work for the China Internet Information Center. We assist companies in meeting specific technology needs, and there is a client that has a special position, one matching your background."

"My background? Just what background are you referring to, Mr. Wu?"

"Training in biological science, your military career, and recent government service."

Andy imagined that they knew very well that the latter was kaput. "How did you get my name? And just what is the job we are discussing?"

"For security reasons, I can't give that information on the phone."

"What is the name of your client?"

The man hesitated. "I can only say that it is a large company of great history, Miss Marino. I can say more in a face-to-face meeting. Would lunch tomorrow be convenient?"

Andy suppressed instinctual alarm. The man seemed quite mysterious, but he did say he had a job that used her background. All of it. "Lunch? Yes, that's possible."

"Fine. Tomorrow, then. Noon at the Hilton?"

Andy agreed and immediately went to her computer, glad that she had not had to cancel her internet service provider. She searched the China Internet Information Center, learning that they were a Beijing-based, nongovernmental organization with U.S. offices. It was affiliated with several other state agencies, including the Chinese Association for the International Exchange of Personnel. She didn't how she was supposed to feel about this intermesh of internet, state, and personnel organizations, but the Information Center seemed to function as a legitimate human resource organization, recruiting foreign experts for Chinese companies with interests in pharmaceuticals, robotics, and control systems software. She wasn't sure how someone with intelligence expertise fit into any of those areas and went to bed filled with questions.

4 / THE XIANXINGZHE GROUP

The Xianxingzhe Group occupied a modern complex in a science and technology park outside Beijing. In an office atop the main building, Sun Yingyi remained quiet as his boss paced past large office windows that overlooked the glassy towers of Zhongguan Plaza. Zheng Liu, still muscular in his fifties, paced the perimeter past the executive desk, conference table, and guest chairs while Yingyi waited near a line of potted grasses and ferns. His boss wasn't happy, but at least he was no longer talking.

For an hour, the man had probed every detail of the plan, interspersing tactics, strategy, and philosophy, with sporadic referrals to the evil consequences of failure. Usually the source of pressure, Zheng made it clear that he was stressed. "Others" would not tolerate failure. Yingyi presumed the scheme was condoned by and would be monitored by the Ministry of Defense. Maybe by the Central Committee.

Zheng leaned fist-down on his carrier-sized desk. "When will she be here?"

"Her flight landed at ten, sir," Yingyi replied. "She has instructions."

"You should have met her."

Yingyi bowed. "This man did not want her to be seen with a

company employee. The agency has handled her travel arrangements, and she must first register at the technical fair."

Zheng's eyebrows arched. He grunted and resumed his pacing.

Antoinette Marino and three hundred gritty-eyed passengers on a Delta flight from Dulles entered the immigration lounge at Beijing Capital International Airport. Having flown business class and gotten several hours of sleep during the smooth trip, Andy appeared unstressed. Ruly black hair, a tanned face, sunglasses, and her Michael Kors outfit gave her a fit and relaxed mien. The job possibility had rejuvenated her spirits and restored a natural optimism and confidence. But nerves made her check the time periodically on a gold-banded watch.

She pushed through the crowd of bustling Chinese residents to join the line for nonresident immigration. The reflection in the immigration booth plastic caught her attention. A thirtyish American man behind her stared at her legs where she wore a gold anklet. His gaze rose, and he expanded his chest and leaned forward.

"This is my favorite part of the process," he said. "Is this your first trip to the land of the sleeping dragon?"

Andy half-turned her head. "Yes." She stepped forward.

The man followed and leaned close. "How about a drink to celebrate our arrival? Maybe a little party."

Andy rotated and considered the man for several seconds. Her eyes lasered his smiling face. "Shove it, buddy, before I call security."

The man sputtered and then adopted a John-Wayne drawl. "Well thank you very much, little lady, and y'all have a nice day. Bitch."

The "bitch" curtsied as a female voice announced in three languages a British Air flight to Osaka. The line grew shorter when two uniformed immigration officers ushered away a hapless passenger, perhaps one lacking some essential paper or proper answer. Still third in line, Andy willed patience as she recalled the events that led her to Beijing.

During the lunch in Washington, Mr. Wu, the agent for the China

Internet Information Center, said the position was delicate and therefore not advertised. In fact, she should tell no one of the trip and would learn the name of the company only upon arrival in Beijing. Her purported reason for visiting would be to attend a technical fair, one of many held around China throughout the year. They attracted foreign visitors, so she would fit right in. Her travel arrangements would be handled by another Chinese agency in New York. Her plane reservations came from the local office of Triway Enterprises in Falls Church, VA. The recruitment effort impressed Andy, who figured it at least implied that the company was legitimate with connections.

When she'd pressed for more information, Wu said the position was one that required technical training provided by the company, but that also depended on her background in intelligence. The objective was to acquire technology. Wu further said that she'd work in the field independently, free from "patronization, condescension, and harassment."

That, of course, struck a chord after her experience with her CIA supervisor, who'd provided plenty of all three ingredients. Not for the first time did she wonder how the recruiter knew she would respond to such a job description. In the end, the appeal of working on her own, her desperate financial situation, and the prospect of power made her accept the invitation.

"Time to move your shapely butt forward, young lady," John Wayne whispered.

She considered a groin shot with her briefcase, but decided it wasn't worth the fuss. At the counter, she handed the immigration agent her passport.

The uniform looked at her passport picture and then at her face. "Please remove your sunglasses. How long will you be in China?" The man spoke in English.

"Perhaps three days," she guessed and took off the glasses.

"And the purpose of your trip?"

"Business meeting. I'm attending a technical symposium."

The agent stamped her passport and directed her to the baggage carousels. She worked around passengers struggling with immense pieces of luggage, grabbed her bag, and headed for Customs and then the exit. Before she reached the door, however, a uniformed driver identified himself as from Triway Enterprises. He led her outside to a waiting car, put her case in the trunk, and held open the door. A short drive along the Airport Expressway brought them to the northeastern Third Ring Road at Sanyuanqiao, and then they were in Beijing. The driver left her at the Beijing Foreign Experts Building, a large, modern hotel devoted, as its name indicated, to housing visitors.

In a comfortable room, Andy changed into a Calvin Klein charcoal suit. That and a Kors shoulder bag produced a business-success look that had vaporized her savings. She had lunch, and followed the next step in her instructions, namely, to register at the technical conference, which had something to do with artificial intelligence. She expected to be contacted there by the company that was paying for all this. Surely it would happen right away, because she had no training to absorb anything theoretical or practical about AI.

She made her way past the few blocks to the conference center, signed in, and received a note telling her a Mr. Sun would see her in a second-floor room. He was waiting for her in the hallway when she exited the elevator.

"Hello, Miss Marino. I am Sun Yingyi," he said in perfect English. "Welcome to China. I hope you had easy travel." He shook her hand.

"The trip was uneventful, Mr. Sun, and I am ready to learn of the company that wants my service."

"I see you know how we use our family names. But we will be working together. Please call me Yingyi."

They descended a vacant, back staircase to a parking lot. Yingyi ushered her into a small sedan and drove her northwest at a sluggish speed familiar to the Washington, DC motorist. They passed Peking University and entered the Haidian District, an open, modern area with industrial sites, office buildings, and shopping facilities.

"This is Zhongguancun Science and Technology Zone," Yingyi said, gesturing to the many buildings. It contains seven parks, all dedicated to industry."

The name rang a bell for Andy, and it took her a moment to remember that a major technology program at the University of

Maryland had some affiliation with the Z-Park. The connection made her feel more comfortable.

"There are over twelve thousand technology enterprises here. Companies like Google and IBM have facilities." Yingyi pulled into the front drive of a blue-glass-and-steel, multi-story structure at the center of an array of buildings, parking lots, and landscaped islands of greenery. "And here is your host company, the Xianxingzhe Group."

Andy heard it pronounced "Zan-zin-she" and imagined a wine conglomerate. Zinfandel was one of her favorite California wines.

Yingyi led the way into a grand lobby, serenely lit, with a large stone Buddha in the center. Background flute-and-bell music, indirect lighting, and wall-hugging potted bamboo conferred a temple atmosphere. Beyond the statue stood a reception desk whose shiny red finish contrasted with the black marble floor. Yingyi gave Andy's name and, after she surrendered her cell phone, led her to the elevator bank.

"My superior, Mr. Zheng, is in charge of foreign talent recruitment," Yingyi said as he keyed the elevator with a reader. "He will enjoy meeting you."

At the top floor, they passed several secretaries and entered an office that seemed far too grand for a Human Resources functionary. It was sparsely furnished for its size, with one wall covered by windows and one with black, lacquered shelving containing a few books and statues of a lion, a bird, and a snarling dragon. White tapestries with black calligraphy coated another wall.

A man with broad shoulders, a thick chest, and a shaved head came around a desk, introduced himself in English, and offered his hand. Andy shook, feeling the strength in the man's grip. Zheng directed her into a black leather chair with wide arms.

Zheng thanked her for accepting their invitation and asked if she needed anything. When she said she was fine, he did something she thought was out of character for the Asian. Without preliminaries, he plunged into the business of their meeting, lecturing as he walked. She listened with increasing amazement to references to higher purposes of a corporation and the need for a global community.

"We follow the teaching of Zhang Zhidong who gave us the principle of *ti-yong*." Zheng then quoted from the man's 1878 essay:

"'Keep China's style of learning to maintain societal essence and adopt western learning for practical use.' This principle has allowed China to take great strides forward, largely by using the information that is so widely available in books, journals, patents, abstracts, and company documents."

Andy cleared her mind of the thought that Zheng was following Zhang. She was well aware that China had many organizations devoted to acquiring, analyzing, digitalizing, and indexing all aspects of technology. The China Society for Scientific and Technical Information or CSSTI employed thousands. On the surface, only open-source materials were gathered. But Zheng's next remark showed he wasn't talking about items in the public domain.

"Some things, however, remain hidden, things essential for peace and global understanding. Such information must be shared," he continued. "That is why we offer you this opportunity."

Realizing what Zheng was really talking about, Andy grew angry, stood, and removed her jacket. The room was too warm. Certain that her action breached protocol, she decided she didn't give a damn. She sat down and held up her hand. "Let's cut the crap, Mr. Zheng. You're talking about espionage. As I told Mr. Wu, I didn't like coming here without more information. It's clear now that I should have insisted. I don't know why you picked me, but this is out of my league, and I'm not interested. We'll just pretend this meeting never took place, and I never heard of Xianxingzhe or you. I'll be going."

Zheng's face reddened. "I would ask you to think differently on several points. It would not be in our interest to let you know the company name before you arrived, precisely because of the nature of the job. We picked you precisely because you are most qualified by background and abilities. Pretending the meeting never took place is impossible. And you will not be going."

Andy stiffened with the realization of her position. She was supposedly attending a technical fair, had not known the name of the company until she arrived, and had not been seen in public with Yingyi. She had been asked to leave her cell phone in the lobby. No one knew she was here. She'd told no one where she was going and had no friends who might wonder. Her only relative was a mother in a care facility who wasn't with it enough to miss her. Zheng was a hard ass who seemed quite able and willing to keep her prisoner. At least the statement that she was qualified for whatever scheme they imagined for her was a positive. The wise thing seemed to be to listen and learn. To play along. She feigned relaxation.

Zheng moved in front of the chair. "I think you will find our offer most inviting." He managed a questionable smile.

Andy held the man's gaze. "Tell me about it," she said.

5 / THE OFFER

ZHENG RETREATED BEHIND HIS DESK AND OPENED A FILE FOLDER. He examined the contents and seemed to be in no hurry. "Ms. Marino, you must realize your position. You have no power. You can't really learn why your brother was killed, you have been harassed by men and have no recourse, and you are poor. I am offering to change all that. Now, you must listen patiently to what I have to say. I respect women and their contributions. They can reach objectives not accessible to men. You are here because of your background, everything in your background, including that unfortunate incident in your boss's office about the Nicaragua file."

"How—"

Zheng held up a hand. "We have details—names, dates, even photographs—that show how and why your brother died. We know who was responsible."

Andy straightened at the mention of her brother. "What about my brother?"

"Patience. You think you are motivated by the simple need to know what happened. But that is not what you want. The need for justice, even revenge, drives you. We will show how the U.S. Department of Defense caused your brother's death. You can then exact justice and revenge."

The speaker's words fascinated her. She was in over her head but wasn't sure she wanted to swim to safety.

"You must perceive what vulnerable means. You are helpless facing the U.S. Army, the U.S. government, even the male hierarchy at the CIA. We offer a way to overcome your frustrating weakness. I'm offering a trade. We get your background, capability, and motivation. You get information and power."

Zheng touched a deep truth that Andy had not realized lay within. Her frustration was rooted in her inability to avenge her brother's death. Knowledge alone was not her quest. She wanted revenge. That was an epiphany.

"From mutual benefit flows cooperation," Zheng said. "We work, in the last analysis, for ourselves. You must see your alternatives clearly. Either you continue as an ineffectual gnat, or you can become an irresistible pathogen."

"Fine," Andy said. "I get the point."

"Another point, Ms. Marino." Zheng opened a desk drawer, extracted a large photograph, and passed it to his guest. "This woman depends on you."

Andy stiffened. The photo captured her mother's vulnerability. It showed Xianxingzhe's power—their knowledge of her mother and ability to photograph her.

"We know of your mother's illness and her need for your financial help. Success in this task will pay handsomely."

Andy met Zheng's eyes.

"Good, we have an understanding." Zheng touched a switch that activated a large flatscreen. A picture of the campus of Xianxingzhe Group appeared. "This company is an organization of great scope. Economic success makes it a surrogate for the Chinese people. I must do today what will guarantee our future, Xianxingzhe's and China's." The man, whose grey business suit bulged with muscles, moved to the windows and gestured Andy to follow.

Andy looked down on neat modern buildings guarded by parking lots. Pairs of strolling workers appeared as black specks from the high perspective.

"Do you know the origin of the Xianxingzhe name, Ms. Marino?"

Andy shook her head.

"It is the name of China's first bipedal, humanoid robot, a machine that stood one hundred forty centimeters tall, weighed twenty kilograms, and could walk two steps per second. The Chinese characters of its name mean 'forerunner' and signaled the beginning of robot creation by China. We were proud of that creation, that great event, but the Japanese called it Senkousha and ridiculed it, calling it a military weapon, saying the bulging plastic joints at the crotch was its cannon. They made internet games based on the crotch cannon and showed the thrusting of its hips to fire the weapon. But Xianxingzhe was a major achievement, and this company is named for that first robot. We do not intend to be ridiculed again."

Andy analyzed the situation. Given what had been done and what she'd already heard, she doubted she could walk away. Even if she could, Chinese authorities would see nothing amiss in a company stealing technology. It was the national pastime. Her only option was to learn as much as she could. "You are truly a visionary leader, Mr. Zheng. Perhaps we can develop a mutually satisfying relationship, but I need to know exactly what you want me to do."

Zheng gestured to the chairs. "Some research must be widely shared to ensure world stability, equal competitiveness, and peace. Tea?"

Andy nodded. "Research on what?" She suspected the references to world stability and peace were propaganda, perhaps megalomania, but she played along.

Yingyi picked up a red phone and spoke briefly in Chinese. Moments later a striking woman entered in a short-sleeved, ankle-length red dress decorated with strands of white and pink flowers at the shoulders. along one side, and at the bottom. Andy thought it both formal and serviceable. The servant set cups, tea, and almond cookies on the table between them, poured, and waited for Zheng to taste the offering. He nodded and she left.

Andy sipped tea, sampled a cookie, and waited.

Her host said, "The area is robotics, but our interest is derivative: neural recording."

"I have no background in neurobiology."

"We can fill the gaps in your education. Neural recording research is going on in government-sponsored laboratories because of its military potential." Zheng put his tea down, rose, and picked up a remote. The first picture to appear on the screen, a flow diagram of the process of recording a brain, set Zheng off on the technical aspects of the project. Then he struck a somber note. "We have not come up with the biochemical scanner or the data-processing software, which depends on algorithms that balance speed and accuracy."

Andy heard the tinge of sadness in Zheng's voice. "What are the applications?" Andy asked.

"One word: transcription. Transfer of a human brain file into a biosynthetic brain. The resultant android would not only have its own analytical powers, but also human knowledge and relational capabilities. In sum, a superior organism."

Andy immediately thought military. "Are you saying robot brains can absorb a human brain?"

Zheng smiled and refilled the teacups. "Precisely, Ms. Marino. It is no more difficult than inducing in sufficient neurons—or what serve as neurons in an artificial intelligence—the proper binomial state—firing or not firing." He advanced to the next image and continued.

"If you accept that a biosynthetic brain can be programmed, you must expand your thoughts to the next step: programming the natural brain." He let the concept hang.

Andy's mind raced. Was this some kind of joke? Is this the evolution of brainwashing? Was it mind control by computer? Svengali with new tools?

"I see you are amazed. Now think of behavior modification. Substance abuse, sexual deviation, personal violence, criminal activity are society's ills. If one had an accurate copy of a brain, one could modify that copy in a constructive fashion, strengthening pro-social patterns and inhibiting antisocial ones. Then the revised brain file could be returned to overwrite the original, defective copy."

Andy finished the thought. "Thereby relieving society of the burden of controlling antisocial behavior. Freeing up valuable resources for more productive activities."

Zheng smiled.

"Aren't you afraid of a society of ants, programmed drones?"

The smile became a grin. "You exaggerate. That is a remote danger, and the potential reward well justifies the risk."

Andy stood and went to a window, letting silence grow. She asked, "Where do I fit into all of this? You said that this technology had necessary components that remained undiscovered, problems no one had yet solved."

"I said *we* had not solved those problems."

The implication was clear in an instant. "You mean there's an organization somewhere capable of brain recording and transfer?" she said.

"Precisely."

"Where? Who?"

"That is information you will have when we come to our agreement. You will procure the blueprints for the scanner and a copy of the software."

"Why me? I have no experience in field espionage."

"That is one of your strengths, in fact. You must penetrate an American company that has taken great security measures. For you to be hired by that company, your clean background is not only an asset, but a necessity."

"I see. But what makes you think success is possible?"

A plane heading west from Capital Airport passed low over the Xianxingzhe Group complex and softly rattled the windows.

"The materials are well protected," Zheng said. "But the system is not impenetrable. The weakness is people. You will identify and exploit the weakness to obtain the materials."

Andy circled the office, her mind going over the information so suddenly dumped before her. "How does my independence and power come into this?" she asked.

Zheng paced after his guest. "You will be in charge of this operation. The items you seek are being developed under a United States Department of Defense contract. Getting them will not only strike a blow for world peace but will pierce the heart of the organization that killed your brother."

Zheng picked up a piece of paper from his desk. "It is time to formalize our agreement. We will provide you with training and resources. When you deliver what we need, we will pay..." He pointed to a figure on the paper he put before her.

The amount staggered her. It was enough to give her mother the best care and leave plenty to make Andy a wealthy woman. She fought unsuccessfully to feign calm acceptance of the new information. "This seems commensurate with the risk I would be taking."

"We will deposit the money in a numbered account, Miss Marino. When you have the materials, but before we take possession, you will be given access to the account to verify the balance. Then you will be allowed to change the password. Thus, our relationship is terminated, as if it never happened. Based on that fee, can we sign this agreement?"

Andy took the paper, a simple fee-for-services contract, and thought over the payment procedure. She would make sure they were in a public place in the U.S. when they made the exchange. There was really no debate left about the pros and cons of getting involved with a dangerous, illegal, albeit lucrative venture, because there was no way out. Zheng was not opposed to using force and violence. It was agree or die. Strangely, that stark choice did not disturb her. Her brother had never had a choice before he would up bleeding to death on the jungle floor. She sat in Zheng's desk chair, a choice he eyed with a frown.

"Fine. Let's do it."

6 / *AGREEMENT*

After signing the contract, Andy returned to the chair in front of the desk. Zheng joined her and signaled to Yingyi, who emerged from the potted bamboo in the corner and took over the briefing. He fidgeted at first but grew confident once he got into the slides.

"This is Cybernetic Implementation near San Diego," Yingyi said, pointing to a picture of a campus-like industrial setting. "Our intelligence indicates they have a working scanner and software to control and analyze the state of the brain. Although confined to animals, their work may have already advanced to modify behavior by brain-file manipulation."

Yingyi's English had a TV-newscaster flavor, and Andy suspected that he'd used it in the United States. "And what's the security weakness that allows us to acquire the materials?" she asked.

A new slide showed a middle-aged, white male in a jacket and tie. "This is Dr. Peter Valois, perhaps the foremost expert in this area. He has privileges and a lot of freedom at Cybernetic Implementation. With the proper inducement, Dr. Valois will provide the scanner blueprint and the software."

"What inducement?"

"You will devise one," Zheng said. "We will pay you a large sum to solve this problem. You have seen the inner workings of the government intelligence community and are aware of techniques that compel action. We will not presume to tell you how to do this job."

That non-answer meant she was to improvise. The money meant that anything was permissible. Ethics were of no concern. Her mind jumped to tactical aspects of the problem. "Who did your surveillance and when?"

"Yingyi was involved, and surveillance continues," Zheng said, confirming what Andy had surmised about his presence in the States.

She examined him as a horse-breeder might a potential stud. "May I use him?"

"Certainly. Would you like more manpower?"

"I might. Not Asian."

"Yingyi will provide files."

Andy considered what that meant. "How do I make contact?"

Zheng tented his fingers. "That will be your first problem. It might be best to become an employee, but Dr. Valois has no opening for a technician."

"But if he were to lose a technician..."

Zheng nodded. "If a position should open, you would have an advantage for filling it. You have laboratory experience, and Dr. Valois has hired only female technicians."

"I will need information on the Valois staff—names, ages, where they live, their schedules."

"I knew you would take this challenge. But let us understand each other. The reward for success is a large sum of money, enough for a lifetime if properly managed. You will be told exactly why your brother died, and you will be given the tools for revenge. Should there be failure, it would be necessary for Xianxingzhe to sever all ties and eliminate any trace back to us."

Severing ties would be easy, Andy thought. Just sever my head from my shoulders.

"To protect our interests," Zheng continued, "we will monitor your operation. You will be in charge, but you will be watched."

Andy considered the implications for a moment. Did that mean that they would have another agent in the shadows? Maybe, but what difference did that make as long as he didn't get underfoot? "Of course," she said.

The meeting ended on that note. Zheng indicated that Yingyi would arrange her training. The woman who'd served tea showed Andy to her living quarters: a small but comfortable apartment on the top floor of the Xianxingzhe building. Her bag would be transferred. A selection of white lab coats was displayed on the bed.

When they were alone in the office, Zheng asked Yingyi if he was satisfied with their choice for the job.

"She has the background we need, including the biology and espionage—"

"Plus the fortitude to do whatever is needed," Zheng said. "And motivation—she blames the United States government for killing her brother, and she wants revenge. This is a Defense Department project she is infiltrating."

"Can she be trusted?"

Zheng pondered the question. "She knows what's at stake and understands the power of Xianxingzhe. It's your job to watch her."

Yingyi nodded. "I find her most attractive."

Zheng crossed his arms.

Over the next weeks, Andy posed as a new company representative who needed technical training. She learned the science of brain recording by lectures, demonstrations, and hands-on work. She acquired theory and methods, covering computer systems, brain recording, and animal surgery. In the process she learned the status of Xianxingzhe's research, holes and all.

Yingyi covered Peter Valois and his family. In the process, Andy got to know Yingyi very well and decided to use him to fill a gap in her living arrangements.

Late on a Friday afternoon, Andy told him she needed more information on the Valois family. "Bring what you have to my apartment after dinner."

When he arrived, Andy came fresh from the shower wearing only a robe. Music with strings played in the background, and the lighting was subdued. "Come in, Yingyi. Wine?" she said.

Yingyi stared too long at her before nodding and settling onto the Western-style, white couch. "I've brought the materials on the wife and the son. His situation is most interesting."

Andy returned with two glasses and sat down, letting the front of her robe fall open. "I admire your facility with English. How did you become so proficient?"

"I was born in the United States. My parents spoke Chinese, but I learned English, American English. I returned to China as a teenager and realized I should serve the mother country. I have been back to the United States for several assignments."

"That explains a lot," Andy said and sipped her wine. "So, you probably know a bit about American women."

Yingyi nodded. "They are as mysterious as Chinese women."

"Let's just relax for a moment. We can do business later."

Yingyi dropped the papers on the coffee table and leaned back, a thin smile parting his lips. He breathed faster.

They drank, and Andy studied her visitor. Her mind tabulated the pros and cons of what she was about to do. In the pro column was the fact that Yingyi was handsome and available. He could satisfy a need that she'd neglected for the entire two years she'd been with the CIA. Of course, there was the obvious con that they had to work together, and this dalliance might spoil that. Another pro pushed that con away. This job gave her power that she'd never held before. Using it would prove that she had it. Sex had been used against her, but now she would use it for her purposes. And she did need some stress relief.

"What are you thinking, Yingyi?"

Yingyi let his eyes move slowly from her bare legs to her face. "You are beautiful."

"Since we will be working together, I think we should get to know each other." She demonstrated her meaning by leaning over and kissing him, rather like a wine judge switching to a new vintage and taking the first swallow. She placed their glasses on an end table and slipped from her robe.

PART 2
CYBERNETIC IMPLEMENTATION

Men were not intended to work with the accuracy of tools, to be precise and perfect in all their actions.

- JOHN RUSKIN

7 / THE SCIENTIST

Peter Valois emerged from his San Diego ranch house at seven a.m. for his short commute to work. The calendar said April, but it was already warm enough to make him feel damp in his sports coat. He approached his Jeep and noticed the new crease in the bumper. *Damn kid drives with his eyes closed.*

The lawn had not been mowed, and the uneven growth marred the precision of his wife's landscaping. Warm weather and a bit of rain had forced everything along—the goldenbush and honeysuckle, the boxthorn below the picture window, the western azalea at the lamppost, and the out-of-control grass.

Seventeen-year-old Dan Valois slouched through the front mahogany door with a backpack and a skateboard.

"Dan, look at this lawn. It needs attention. I've asked twice before. Since you are no longer playing basketball, can you spare an hour today to cut it?"

"Sure, Dad, I'll get to it." The boy shrugged into the backpack and continued hurriedly down the front walk.

Peter stretched his shirt collar with his finger, wondering again why his employer insisted senior technical people wear ties. Probably for meeting visiting contractors and Defense Department brass on equal footing. All visitors seemed to come from cooler climates. He eyed the grass again, muttering, before he yanked off his blazer, tossed it and his briefcase into the passenger seat, and loaded his two hundred pounds into the car. The Jeep coughed to life, and Peter gunned the engine and threw the car into reverse. Backing up, he rolled over a clump of Pam's daylilies.

A back road took him to Cybernetic Implementation, a glass-and-steel, modern facility surrounded by parking. Beyond the cars lay trimmed lawns, a reflecting pool, and flower beds. Peter nosed into his regular spot near his office window and opened the car door. When the outside air seemed cooler than the Jeep's feeble air conditioner output, he leaned his head against the steering wheel, listening to slamming car doors, a distant mower, and the gurgle of the pond fountain. He pulled himself from the car, carded his way through the main employee gate, and signed in.

He'd been a Senior Cyberphysiologist for years, having single-handedly developed brain recording and sold it to the Department of Defense. That meant the big DOD contract was his, and his ass was on the line when progress wasn't timely.

"Good morning, Dr. Valois. A bit later than usual today," the guard said. The jovial Mexican was probably near sixty and still had a full head of black hair.

"A few delays on the home front. Guess I'll have to work overtime."

The guard waved him through, and Peter went down the blue hallway to the restricted research wing. The security checkpoint, a small counter with scanning modules and fronted by a scale platform built into the floor, guarded the steel door that separated routine work areas from the top-secret, defense-related projects. To enter the restricted space, he had to satisfy the humanoid securibot manning the checkpoint.

"Please step to the scanner, Dr. Valois." The securibot was short, intelligent, and rigid about what had to be done.

Peter went through the whole procedure, including scans of retina, weight, and height. He passed the voice recognition check, and the door opened. A green-and-cream hallway with recessed fluorescent lighting led past offices and laboratories devoted to code creation, animal testing, and parts fabrication.

In an isolated corridor, he punched in the office-door

combination and entered, again annoyed by the cramped space that housed his small desk set, a single file cabinet under the wall shelf, and a guest chair. At least there's a window, he thought. The pane vibrated as a mower worked the strip of grass between his window and his car.

Peter hung his tweedy sports coat on a wall hook beneath his Stanford diploma and donned his short, white lab jacket. He unlocked the file cabinet and grabbed a notebook and a thumb drive.

Across the hall his junior research associate, Lisa Macquire, was busy in the lab with syringes, catheters, and clamps. Tall and fit, with shoulder-length, strawberry-blond hair, Lisa was generally quiet, even mousy, but would occasionally smile if provoked. Peter's years of handling rats, even talking to them, probably made him think of her as mousy, a notion helped by a scattering of freckles that could be mistaken for whiskers.

"Good morning," she said. "I brought Horrible Harvey up from the animal quarters and I'm just about set up." She pointed to a plastic container with a white rat near her.

"Fine. I'll load the log-in software." Peter sat in front of the computer, loaded the encryption shell, and initiated the recording program.

The Department of Defense project required two techs. Jun, his senior tech, had been enough to begin the project, but success allowed him to hire a second assistant who left after six months to be a full-time mother. Lisa was her replacement.

Lisa's resume had reached Peter's desk the very day the approval for continued DOD funding came through. With a degree in biology from Michigan State and two years relevant experience, she'd turned out to be an enthusiastic learner and worked well with Jun.

Lisa was the sole child of a policeman and his homemaker wife. Peter's gentle, persistent questioning uncovered the two retirement hobbies of Lisa's mother. She painted feathers and other natural artifacts that needed no adornment, and she badgered her daughter about marriage and kids.

Peter glanced at the wall clock. "Where is Jun this morning? She's never late. Did she call?"

"No, and she didn't say anything last night."

"Unusual."

As Lisa hooked up leads to record blood pressure and heart rhythm, Peter scanned the recent notebook entries and Lisa's overnight animal report.

"The new scanner unit my friend in fabrication made seems to be doing the job," he said.

"You designed the Computerized Transference Tomography unit yourself, didn't you, Dr. Valois?" Lisa picked up the ion-sensing end of the COTT device, a two-inch cylinder half the size of a lipstick.

"Yes. That's my bioengineering side. The COTT unit is key for recording the conscious brain. That's what we'll do with Harvey today. We've seen some stress in animals after recording their brains, and I'm convinced the new sensor will remedy that."

"Stress? You mean, like, death?"

"Only a couple of rats died. Probably had nothing to do with being scanned. Could have been due to old age." It sounded as though he were trying to convince himself.

In fact, Peter knew it wasn't recording, but the second secret procedure he'd put the rats through. Transferring a brain file back into a rat wasn't in the letter of the protocol, but he could argue that it was implied. That was the problem the new COTT module would fix.

"When the Defense guys come in, I want brain recording done in ten rats and maybe in a few dogs," Peter said. "We want the brass to be comforted."

"And if they're not?"

"They could cancel the contract...and you...and Jun. I'd wind up on some other project shuffling papers or in early retirement." He stood still when the premonition that something might be amiss with his senior technician hit. "Speaking of Jun, I'd better call her."

Peter made the call from his office, fighting off a sense of doom. It took a moment until he felt calm enough to dial. Jun answered and assured him she was just fine and would be a bit late because of an appointment. The message should have assured him more than it did. He'd worked with Jun for several years, and their relationship had been both as friends and colleagues. Jun knew his moods and often worked magic to get him out of a funk and back on tract. He liked her and was still shaking off his premonition when his boss called to say he wanted an immediate meeting.

Peter told Lisa he'd be back and headed for the office he called The Swamp. The designation could be due to the ferns his superior loved, but the real reason was that he called his boss The Frog.

8 / THE BOSS

PHILLIP LYERSON HAD AN OFFICE FOUR TIMES THE SIZE OF PETER'S. Peter pushed open his boss's glass-paneled door to view a six-foot oak desk, matching bookcases, and a conference table with six beige-cushioned chairs. The furniture did not crowd the space, even with the hanging and potted plants.

Big frog, big swamp, Peter thought.

Lyerson had a pale, round face with slightly protuberant eyes and tended to smile a lot. As usual, his nails were manicured and his red hair coiffed. Peter sat at the conference table, and The Frog plopped down across from him and folded his puffy white hands over the customary yellow pad before him. He leaned back in what Peter read as feigned relaxation, something he'd picked up at a management course that taught behavioral modification. He seemed to like courses that taught manipulation.

Lyerson wetted his lips before he spoke. "Peter, I wanted to talk about progress on our Department of Defense project." The voice dripped with concern. "You've missed a couple of benchmark deadlines, and the military guys will be in soon for a formal review."

Peter caught that the project was a joint affair, but that the missed benchmarks were his alone. "We just didn't have enough data to meet those decision points. I wouldn't want to risk our credibility—your credibility—with partial data."

"Let me worry about my credibility. So, what's the delay?" The freckled face smiled.

"Experiments don't always work."

"Mistakes." Lyerson didn't make it a question.

Peter considered a judicious reply. The Frog held an advanced degree but hadn't been in a lab for years and wouldn't know where to stick a thermometer. His two papers published years ago suggested the lab training was a waste of time. "No. We've learned some things and made adjustments. Designed a new COTT scanner and expect smooth sailing."

"You were late with that interim report. Let me see the next report in plenty of time to go over it before DOD arrives. I don't like surprises."

"Right. That should be no problem," Peter said, hoping it was true.

Lyerson drummed his pudgy fingers on the yellow pad. "Good. You know how important this project is. Not just the big bucks DOD is paying now, but future contracts. Management is really keeping an eye on this, and if you can't produce in a timely fashion, they will have to reassign the project."

The iron fist peeked from the green velvet glove. Froggy didn't have to complete the litany. If he had no project, Peter might not have a job. Scientific accomplishment was evaluated with the money ruler. Years of work and insight counted for naught, and one scientist could be plugged in easily for another.

Peter stood, nodding. "We've just started a set of critical experiments to go in the next report. When they are complete, I'll draft it and get you a copy." He knew that was the last thing he'd do. It would be like dumping gasoline on a smoldering fire. He left before Lyerson could respond.

En route to his lab, Peter wondered if he should curtail his extra work transferring recorded brain files back into rats to boost productivity. He rejected the notion. Transference had to be done near the time of transcription to avoid problems with brain changes over time. Besides, he did that work after hours.

"You left the log-on device in the machine," Lisa said in greeting.

"My mistake. Don't tell anyone."

"That's a no-no."

Peter eyed the clock. "I just remembered that Jun told me she had a meeting this morning and would be late. Has she called?"

"No. Could be stuck in traffic."

Peter moved to the Plexiglas cage at the end of the bench and peered in. "So, how's Horrible Harvey this morning?"

Harvey provided the answer himself by rearing against the back wall and hissing.

"How nasty you are, Harvey. Just perfect. Did you have a chance to review last night's video on the rat's behavior?"

"Yes. Harvey is not much of a gentleman among rats. Consistently aggressive. He's just a grouch. That makes him a good test case for whether biosynthetic brain laws can control a recorded consciousness, at least in a rat." Lisa hooked up the oscilloscope to the COTT control panel and flipped on the switch marked "Self Test."

"What do you mean 'in a rat'? This theory is solid for all mammalian brains."

"But we are still struggling with getting a reliable recording of a natural rat brain."

"Were struggling. Now we're past that bump in the road. The new COTT unit will give us an accurate picture of electrical activity, ion movement, and connectivity."

"What exactly is connectivity anyway?" she asked, pushing an unruly strand of hair behind her ear.

As if cued by a stage director, Peter went to the white board where he drew neurons with extensions reaching out to almost touch their neighbors. "Connectivity's the third parameter that fixes the state of the brain at any given moment, the others being location and firing state. It measures who a neuron is talking to. The COTT unit tickles the surface of the cell to see what electrical contact it has, and the computer averages things out and extrapolates."

The two continued working in silence for several minutes. "Did you figure out which car to buy?" Peter asked.

"Not yet. I plan to discuss it with the security guy Carlos, the one who thinks he's hot. He's owned a lot of cars, and I'll be complimenting him by asking." Lisa filled a syringe with the relaxant ketamine and put sterile tubing into an infusion pump.

Peter leaned back against the lab bench and surveyed the scene. "Well, don't get too friendly with security."

"Worried that I might let it slip out that you wrote that letter to your friend in China without clearing it with security?"

"Well, I..." Peter cleared his throat. "There was nothing in the letter but generalities and good wishes. I learned more about what was going on in China than he learned from me."

"Nevertheless, rules are rules."

"It won't help to have a security audit right now, so stick to cars. Besides, the letter was of a personal nature, dealing with my family and how I live." Why would she even mention the letter, he wondered.

As Peter checked the rat-recording data, not paying full attention, a pattern emerged, the sort of thing that pops up only on casual examination. Tapping his pencil on the computer screen, he said, "I don't know why, but male rats seem to endure the recording procedure better than females. Probably has to do with the more systematic organization of the male brain. Maybe we'll uncover differences in male-female wiring."

The room was quiet for thirty seconds before Lisa said, "I look forward to reading that paper."

Peter stuck his hand into a rodent-handling glove, opened Harvey's cage, and reached. The rat jumped and sank its teeth into his thumb. The glove blunted the effect, but the incisors still penetrated enough to cause Peter to yelp. Harvey held on and squeaked, maybe in fear at becoming airborne or in the satisfaction of revenge. Peter grasped the incensed rodent by the scruff of his neck.

Lisa rotated Harvey to expose his belly, inserted the ketamine needle, and administered the relaxant. Harvey squealed and released Peter. Lisa took the animal to the recording harness.

Peter cursed as he removed the glove. He ran tap water over his bleeding hand and left to find the nurse.

Lisa watched him depart, glanced at the computer with the running COTT program, and shook her head.

"Just a slight nick," Peter announced on his return. "Paperwork took longer than the treatment. I blame the accident on being distracted by the meeting with our leader. And I blame the rat. You'd think he'd be grateful for living here. Our procedures are noninvasive, we provide fresh cedar chips daily, he gets regular food and the best veterinary care, and he gets to play with other rats. What more could he want? At any rate, if Jun had been here, she would have been the victim. Maybe she's late because she had a premonition."

"Jun never gets bitten."

Lisa placed the limp Harvey in a harness. She attached pin electrodes, positioned the scanning unit, and began the twenty-minute run to establish all neuron positions in relation to optic nerves and the cerebral aqueduct. Servomotors hummed softly as a three-dimensional image of Harvey's brain appeared on the color monitor. Six columns of numbers scrolled on the second monitor while a bottom line showed more slowly changing brain coordinates and reported what percent of the brain had been scanned. Only when scanning passed ninety percent completion did the infusion pump deliver a supplemental dose of anesthetic. When the scan was complete, Lisa freed Harvey from his holder and put him on a bed of cedar chips in his cage.

"Just about lunch time," Peter said. "Harvey should be good as new in about an hour. Have Jun put him through the maze test while you find the rest of those references. I have a meeting this afternoon with the Space Utilization Team."

Peter turned off the computer and removed the COTT security drive. "Harvey should have a formal gross observation to see if the simple process of reading his brain has any effect. I'd better get on the phone and see if I can locate Jun. Her hour appointment has turned into half a day. She's never been AWOL before."

As Peter entered his office, the phone rang.

"This is Mark. I've got some bad news, very bad news." The caller was the Cybernetic security chief.

A dark premonition, like the earlier one he had about Jun, swept over Peter, and his breath fled, leaving a hallow chest pain.

"There's been a car accident on the mountain road. The sheriff's office just called because the victim had a Cybernetic ID. It's your technician, Jun. I'm sorry to have to tell you she's dead."

9 / THE COMPANY

It was after dark when Andy Marino, dressed in black, visited the rented house in a San Diego barrio. She slipped through a side door that led to the kitchen where a single below-cabinet light fought the gloom. Yingyi was waiting at a small wooden table. Andy dropped a manila envelope before him.

"Here's the resume," she said. "Get it to your contact in HR and have her deliver it to Valois without his noticing. Tell her to slip it in with other files and use in-house mail. Got it?"

Yingyi picked up the envelope. "Should be no problem."

"Has to be done immediately."

"Just like the accident that befell Jun Wu."

Andy tapped a long finger on the table. "Exactly. And just as clean. I checked on the site where she drove off the road. Nothing to contradict the verdict of an accident. Now, let's cash in on that success. Let me know when the resume gets planted."

She pulled her black gloves tight and left.

The period after Jun's death was filled with grieving and saying goodbye. Peter took time off to assist Jun's parents in arranging their daughter's final services and burial, and he made sure Human

Resources expedited the paperwork for handling the company life insurance benefit. Not much got done during those weeks.

Lisa and Peter found it hard to work in the space that Jun had occupied and commanded. Peter knew he had to do something about the loss of his senior technician, for without help, they would never have enough data before the DOD review. With immediate authorization to hire a replacement, he'd collected resumes and interviewed two prospects. Neither seemed the right fit.

Finding someone qualified occupied Peter as he drove to work. As he plodded into the building, the Frog caught him at the door.

"Morning, Peter," his boss said. "You seem distracted."

Peter opened his mouth to say something, but The Frog continued.

"Can we get together this morning? I want to discuss things."

"Things? Right. Sure. Let me get started in the lab and I'll be down." Peter grimaced.

Peter reached his office and grabbed the COTT software. He crossed to the lab and found Lisa turning pages in her notebook.

"Morning," she said. "The six rats recorded with the new COTT unit look fine. All are functioning well after the brain scan."

"Great. Today we begin the next phase, transcribing a real rat brain file into a biosynthetic rat."

"Roborat is certainly ready," Lisa said. "What rat file do you want to use?"

"Do the last experiment first. We'll use Horrible Harvey's file."

"Really? Maybe we should start with a quieter, calmer rat."

"No, we need to make up lost time. Do the baseline recording on Roborat while I'm chatting with the boss."

The Frog skipped preliminaries. "I haven't seen that draft report yet, Peter."

"We've been slowed down. Missing a technician, I've had to help in the lab. We need more data before I finish the report."

His boss frowned, looked at his notes, and cast his eyes at Peter without raising his head. "It's your responsibility to hire a replacement," he said.

"You met the two we interviewed. They lacked relevant biology skills."

"Someone must have the skills. Get on this hiring thing full time, overtime. There are no spare techs to plug into your operation, and if I'm forced to shoot another project in the foot to rescue yours, it will not look good come evaluation time. You are responsible for your own shop."

The Frog began his prepared litany of how to find a technician, most of which were simplistic, irrelevant, or already being used. Peter's mind wandered, remembering Joseph Conrad's observation that a man must take his contentment from social standing, the job he was forced to do, or the leisure he was blessed to enjoy. Peter felt there was another category: doing the job one loved to do. He liked being a scientist. His promotion path from Staff Scientist to Senior Research Scientist occurred as a loner, but further advancement wasn't likely. He didn't have the people skills to be research director. No big deal. Bosses in that career track changed jobs every eighteen months as if this were a consumer business, instead of the most advanced robotics R&D organization in the West.

Peter dragged his eyes from the window overlooking the lush green lawns as The Frog intoned the final benediction. Maybe he needed to cut the guy some slack. It wasn't his fault that he didn't know the details of how the research was going. That was Peter's responsibility. Not every superior had to serve as a mentor.

"You may have worked out the science," his boss said, "but we are on a deadline and need results. Get a tech."

Peter agreed. Cybernetic used the what-have-you-done-for-me-lately rule. He'd be downsized out the door if he didn't impress the Department of Defense reviewers. He had to have a technician.

"Be innovative," the Frog said. "Relax your criteria. Get someone in and train, train, train. Now hop to it."

"Right." Peter hopped up, like an acolyte frog. The image of decapitating a frog with hedge shears flitted through his brain. He left wanting a donut, big and jelly filled.

. . .

He relaxed as he entered the cafeteria, a beige-carpeted, pastel room filled with tasteful blond wood tables. Two landscape murals conveyed peace, and the full-length windows framed the manicured lawn and the reflecting pool. The setting and indirect lights created a bright, cheery gathering place that offered quiet islands of privacy among leafy potted plants.

Guilt came with the donut. Not quite six feet tall, he'd let his weight creep up over two hundred and was sporting a midlife bulge. His once jet-black hair, what remained of it, was graying. His longish face and bushy eyebrows tended to scare small kids at Halloween. His back ached in the morning and his heart thumped after the walk from the parking lot. Peering into the twilight of life, he did not relish the view.

Cybernetic Implementation, his home for over twenty years, offered modern and well supplied laboratories, good benefits, and a chance to study what was important. From that standpoint, it was a good place to work. One negative was the threat of downsizing. It hadn't affected Peter, but there wasn't another promotion for him on the technical ladder, and he didn't fit on the management ladder. Executives were handsome, tall, and outgoing. He was plain, round, and introspective. They'd probably let The Frog join the club just for the sake of amphibian diversity.

Beyond the foliage two tables away, a young technician sat, her short skirt revealing long legs. The girl was probably intentionally showing off. His own sex life had dwindled to the occasional physical blips of middle-aged married life, small blooms of activity scattered on a dry plain of ennui. He wondered why this didn't bother him more.

"Hi, Peter," said a passing brunette in her late thirties. Marcia, a Cybernetic survivor, smiled as she conducted a tour group along the prescribed public relations path. Why visitors would care what the Cybernetic staff ate was incomprehensible, but he sat up straighter, sucked in his stomach, and smiled.

The aliens eyed Peter as if he were the new dinosaur exhibit. Others sniffed at philodendrons and touched hanging air ferns, perhaps thinking that the environment and its decorations said much about Cybernetic and what was going on there.

"Can I talk to you? I'll hand this group off to the next guide and be right back." Marcia's smile had disappeared.

"Sure, I'll wait."

Marcia herded her flock of glassy-eyed, disinterested sheep to the exit. The divorcee had told him about trouble with a rambunctious teenaged son, and he'd recommended a strong hand and setting high performance standards. He thought of Dan and winced.

He tried positive thinking. He'd discovered how to record the state of a neuron and a whole brain. He'd designed the scanning and sensor mechanisms to get the brain data into a computer file. These results won big contracts for Cybernetic Implementation. But he'd had only two promotions in twenty years, had but a small laboratory, and now only one assistant. At least until he found a new one. Maybe it was time to take more risks.

Marcia returned and sat. "It's my son. He's been to two rehab sessions and is slipping again. I'm at my wit's end."

"Rehab? I hadn't heard."

"Drug use. Peter, what am I supposed to do? You've had first-hand experience because of your brother."

Peter struggled to control sudden emotion. His brother's drug problem had not been helped by several bouts of rehabilitation. And suddenly his brother was gone. Dead of a heroin overdose.

"My brother was years ago. They must have made progress in treatment by now."

"I wish that were true." Marcia wiped at her eyes with a tissue.

Peter put his hand on her arm. "You can't sit back and do nothing, hoping for a miracle. You have to get professional help and act on it. He is still your charge, and you have clout. You can force compliance."

"You mean more rehab?"

"Have you considered some underlying problem? Like depression? Maybe he needs more medical help and less program help. I'm sure my brother was depressed."

Marcia stood. "Thanks. You've given me something to consider."

With a glazed look, Peter watched her leave. He had to squelch the sad remembrance of his brother's smile and mischievousness. He forced his mind back to the DOD work, thinking of the ultimate goal—routine brain recording.

Problems encountered with some rats—cardiac arrhythmias and death—would be fixed by the latest ion beam device. He'd already recorded several rats and results looked good. More data would cover his ass for the DOD review.

He opened a reprint, a Russian paper on transference theory, and sipped coffee. The Russians were working the problem from the same angles as Western scientists. In contrast, the Japanese emphasized development and manufacturing. They attended meetings, presented peripheral papers, and asked questions about practical issues. The Chinese—the dozen relevant papers all came from the same government research institute—were a mystery. They played their cards, not just close to their vests, but inside them. What was published revealed less about their work than the top of an iceberg revealed about its submerged bulk.

A group of men and women in lab coats entered, trailed by his boss who cast a meaningful glance at Peter and then turned his attention to the glazed donuts. It was time to leave. He deposited his mug on a tray and watched a duck enter the pond and glide to the center. A glint of reflected sunlight from a cemetery beyond the road caught his eye. He focused on the spot but saw only gravestones and flowers.

10 /THE RAT

PETER ENCOUNTERED A FIVE-FOOT TALL HUMANOID UNIT IN A WHITE jacket at the tray-return station near the cafeteria door. "I hope you enjoyed your respite," the android said. "May I take your cup, sir?"

The robot was an early model in the human-replica K-series designed for domestic use. It was life-like, but the short stature and odd speech pattern—only a machine would say "respite" rather than "break"—distinguished it from the real thing. Peter's work on the project produced this potential money-maker for Cybernetic Implementation. As a result, the Valois house had the latest, much improved version in the K-series to field test.

Peter placed his mug in the outstretched hand, and the robot returned an eerie smile.

The vacant bench in Peter's lab that should accommodate a second technician reminded him of his boss's words. His peripheral vision glimpsed Jun in a white lab coat, her face smiling and alive. When he turned to the ghost, she was gone. The police hadn't explained Jun's death to his satisfaction. Jun was a careful person in all things, not the sort to be distracted and drive off a cliff.

Jun had been more than an employee—she'd been a dinner guest, a tennis partner for Pam, and an instructor about all things Chinese. He never tired of hearing about proper Chinese attitudes and behavior, this despite her having been in this country since her college days. She still had contacts in the "mother country," as she called it. She'd been a friend whose loss he would make official if he hired someone to take her place. Maybe that was why he dragged his feet on finding a replacement.

The project needed two assistants. With Lisa alone, progress inched forward at half pace. Peter was working his way through a pile of resumes, but choosing took time. He had to find technical expertise, efficiency, and a companionable personality. Plus, any candidate also had to pass a security clearance.

Lisa came back from her break. "Are you all right, Peter?"

"Yes. Just thinking. What's the bottom line on Harvey?"

"He passed all behavioral tests. Recording his brain didn't change him in any way we can measure."

"Good. Let's process Roborat." Peter turned toward the end of the bench. "Over here, Robo."

There was a movement on the counter. A white rat appeared from behind a pile of computer printouts and ran to Peter, looking up with pink eyes.

"What a great job the fabrication guys did," Peter said. "The plastic face even has tiny tension fibers to produce characteristic rat snout expressions. Amazing!"

"The real rats still know he has the wrong smell. Maybe Roborat will have sympathy for his animal compadres after he experiences their brains firsthand."

Peter grunted. "That's what DOD really wants—a way to transfer human training and experience into a synthetic being, one more expendable than a soldier." He turned to the artificial rat. "Time for the restrainer, Robo, to keep you from moving during the transfer. You'll also need your circuits dampened." He inserted a needle into the robot's neck and administered a bionet relaxant. Use of a chemical agent showed how advanced the synthetic neuronal circuits had become, requiring more than a computer command to dampen activity. He waited seconds and then fitted Roborat into the recording chamber.

"You always talk to Robo. Surely it doesn't understand human speech." Lisa placed the COTT scanner over Roborat's left eye.

"I think the sound of my voice is a calming signal."

"So, we're about to transfer the brain file of real rat Harvey into android rat Robo. How exactly does that work?"

"Roborat has way more neural storage space than Harvey, so all of Harvey's brain recording will fit in. And the bionet control center will examine the rodent brain image to see if there are any anomalies and pathways that may lead to aberrant behavior based on its understanding of how rats work. I expect Robo to manage Harvey's aggressive personality without adopting those traits." Peter started the transfer of Harvey's brain into the robot.

The brain hologram appeared on the computer screen and became denser. When the entire file was in place, Peter injected a stimulant and the robot made extensor movements with each leg. It righted itself but remained in a scrunched-up position. After a minute, it raised its head and began to look around with normal rat movements.

"Over here, Robo." The robot didn't move.

"I guess that's the first positive result. No response." Peter reached to pick up the rat.

Lisa grabbed his hand. "Gloves? Robo has teeth and claws."

"Let's see his response to a bare hand." Peter used the hand without the bandage, and the robot did not protest or struggle. "I guess we score that one as a success. Biosynthetic brain constraints seem to have Harvey's aggressive personality under control."

For the discrimination test, Peter placed Roborat in a plain, white square chamber with two levers, located at opposite corners. Lights near one lever glowed red. Robo moved to the lighted lever and pressed it. A pellet, a chemical concoction that provided energy, dropped from the shoot. Roborat swallowed it. The chamber then went dark, the light over the opposite lever came on. The robot rat went to the lighted lever and pushed. Ten minutes later, Robo had eighteen correct responses out of twenty tries.

"Robo was always perfect on this simple test, but Harvey never was. The two mistakes mean that the Harvey brain pattern has had some effect on Robo." Peter entered some identification data and saved the file.

"Good thing Robo relishes fuel," Lisa said. "Else we couldn't reward him."

Peter eyed the clock. He exited the COTT program and removed the log-in device. He slipped it into his coat pocket, mumbled to himself, and left.

In his office, Peter dropped the security software into the top desk drawer and picked up the phone. He dialed and listened to half a dozen rings before Pam answered. "Hi Honey, it's me. How are things on the home front?"

"All is quiet. Will you make it home for dinner? Your schedule hasn't made you very reliable in recent months."

"Yes, I'm about to leave, but I have to duck back in here tonight. Did Dan cut the lawn?"

"Dan hasn't gotten back from school yet."

"I can't say that's a surprise. If he shows for dinner, we will talk. See you shortly."

That evening Peter returned to the laboratory. Roborat's behavioral tests showed the robot had accepted the brain file of the aggressive rat. The real question was whether the bionet could condition it. The off-protocol part of Peter's research involved reverse transfer of a brain file into a live rat. The bionet brain had a wonderful property: it could find and fix disorder in the brain. It could suppress circuits that put the body at risk. Subtle and minor changes would improve behavior, which he could measure by testing rats before and after the procedure. He'd done this several times on previous evening visits to his laboratory, but this would be the first experiment with the new COTT unit.

He re-recorded Roborat in full view of the security camera. There was no reason to hide what would appear to be usual activity, and the security guys couldn't tell legitimate from illegitimate. What's more, the videos were only kept for two weeks. The recording went well, and the robot recovered function without incident. Peter started the program that used powerful algorithms to extract the Harvey components—hopefully slightly modified—from the brain data. This recovered file would go back into the donor rat.

For the next procedure, Peter arranged an electronics rack and the data monitor to shield his activity from the camera. He brought Harvey's plastic cage into the laboratory and grabbed the animal firmly with his gloved hand. He brushed off clinging cedar chips and injected relaxant and anesthetic before arranging the subdued rat in the scanning apparatus. He invoked his own subroutine of the COTT program, a modification that vastly improved the fidelity of transfer. Slowly, the file taken from Roborat was inserted into Harvey. This was the hard part of the evening visits, the sitting and waiting, fearful a colleague would drop in and ask what he was doing. When the transfer was almost complete, Peter was startled by a knock on the door.

He jumped, feeling a spasm grip his heart. The face of a uniformed guard was framed by the door's glass panel. Thankfully, the man required only a wave and a smile to convince him that everything was all right. When he left, Peter trembled.

He administered a stimulant to Harvey and tried to relax while Harvey recovered. The wall clock unhurriedly clicked off thirty minutes. Peter rose with nervous excitement and approached the rat's cage. When he peered through the stainless-steel grid, Harvey looked up with bared teeth. Perhaps more time was needed for neural integration.

He picked up the thick, gray handling gloves. When he removed the cage cover, the rat reared. But he didn't lunge. He wasn't friendly, but few laboratory rats were. Peter put his gloved hand in and gently lifted the animal. Harvey squealed and clamped onto the glove, but his heart did not seem to be in the gesture, and he took his mouth away as if the fabric were a foul piece of cheese.

Mentally, Peter gave Harvey a moderate score for aggressiveness, although he admitted that the recent exposure to the COTT cocktail could account for the improvement. Harvey showed the usual excitement, but he could go through the discrimination test, scoring much higher than normal. That result had to be due to the Roborat's influence.

Satisfied, Peter made entries in his notebook and removed the altered COTT routine from the computer. He returned the laboratory to the usual neat condition favored by Lisa and delivered Harvey to the animal quarters where Lisa would find him in the morning. If she noticed that Harvey's aggressiveness was reduced, he would attribute it to getting used to being handled.

Back in his office, he was filled with exhilaration. This was success. A biosynthetic brain had conditioned a mammalian brain to produce useful behavior modifications. He was elated as he locked up the memory stick with the modified COTT routine.

He came back down to earth when he eyed the pile of resumes on his desk. He had to find a new technician. They needed success with whole brain recording in more rats and in something bigger than a rat in time for the DOD review.

He plopped wearily into his chair and prepared to rank the dozen candidates who'd passed his first screen. Not thrilled with any of them, he committed to getting the top ones in for interviews. Personnel had already done a preliminary check to clear these applicants. He had to find the best fit, the one with both skills and a compatible personality. The list had to be in the hands of Human Resources in the morning.

He put a blank yellow pad on his blotter and took the top folder from the stack. The name on the file was unfamiliar. That surprised him, for he'd studied every one of the applications. Could he have missed this one? Or forgotten a name? Reading the file revealed the perfect candidate. Education, job history, and skills were ideal. Almost too good to be true.

The file had the authenticating Human Resources date stamp, but Peter was sure he'd never seen it before.

PART 3
THE VALOIS FAMILY

Correct thy son, and he shall give thee rest; yea, he shall give delight unto thy soul.

- PROVERBS 29:1

11 /DAN VALOIS

Dan Valois lifted his lean, seventeen-year-old body from its nest of sheets and flailed at a buzzing alarm clock. The alarm woke him, and the blast of sun in his face from the parted drapes finished the job. He sat on the edge of the bed, his feet planted on a manure-brown rug dotted with socks, undershorts, jumbled jeans, and balled-up tee shirts. The thought of straightening up crossed his mind as he gazed at the books and papers around his backpack.

He lifted his eyes to the wallpaper scenes of baseball, football, basketball, and every other conceivable ball. A design Mom had chosen. Once it had pleased him but now seemed infantile, reminding him of earlier, simpler days when he had some credibility as a student-athlete. The track trophies atop the cluttered bureau made him feel as if he'd lost a friend.

As he headed for the bathroom, a lone sneaker tripped him. His shoulder banged against the doorframe, and he muttered, "Damn." Rubbing the injury, he headed for the bathroom.

Under the shower he discovered only a few soap fragments in the tray. Shampoo solved the soap problem. As water pounded his head, he urinated and tried to ignore the buzzing in his brain. He needed a hit. He shoved open the curtain and planted one foot on the floor. The other snagged on the tub. He pitched forward, catching himself on the towel rack and yanked one end from the wall. He shoved the screw back in and grabbed the towel, thinking he could fix the rack if he had the time or the motivation. He dried off, checking his physique in the full-length mirror and grew hard, wondering if Megan O'Rourke were doing the same thing.

The girl he'd grown up with was another painful remembrance of lost good times. They'd enjoyed dating, and he'd fantasized about more.

He brushed his teeth, combed his hair, and decided not to shave. His parents' voices drifted from the kitchen, so he risked stepping bare-assed across the hall. In his room he found clean underwear and rummaged on the floor for jeans and a polo shirt.

He made his way to the front door, listening to his father's loud voice. Demanding and getting your own way, he thought. He stepped outside into morning warmth, high for April, and walked to the corner of the house. He checked to see if his departure had been noticed. The ranch in the center of the large lot was quiet, the perfect suburban home. His mother's horticultural touch was everywhere: the eye-pleasing beds of narcissus, hanging fuchsia by the large living room window, and the potted geraniums guarding the front door.

The neighbor's dog barked a couple of times but seemed to lose interest as Dan walked to the back corner of the lot and disappeared into a hole in the thuja trees. A tree yielded a hidden joint, which he lit and sucked on as a haze built over the neighborhood. It would be hot. Tar blobs in the driveway were already shiny. He should probably wash his mother's car.

His father often lectured on the importance of time management—planning, setting priorities, and working on the important. The lectures echoed in his head. The grass needed cutting yet again, and his father expected him to mow, even though the robot could handle it. But Peter Valois didn't like showing off Kayten to the neighbors. Dan took another drag on the joint and mused that he didn't like cutting grass, only smoking it. So the lawn wouldn't get cut today. He crushed the remains of the joint into the dirt and headed back.

When the front door closed, his mother called from the kitchen, "Dan, are you going to have any breakfast?"

"Not hungry, Ma." He added a "quit buggin' me" under his breath, thinking how his mother always focused on stupid, unimportant things. Having a good time and feeling good was important. That didn't require juice and cereal.

He climbed the stairs, intending to grab his backpack and leave for school. He stopped at his parents' bedroom, listened again for the kitchen murmurs, and entered. In the top dresser drawer lay his father's wallet. It held about a hundred in cash, so Dan felt comfortable filching the twenty. He grabbed his school bag and crept down the stairs toward the front door.

His father's voice caught him. "Dan, if you don't put fuel in the tank, the car won't run."

"Right, Dad. I'm late for school. I'll get something from the cafeteria. See you later." Dan closed the door, sucked in his breath, spoke softly to himself. "Putting fuel in the tank is only important if the car is going somewhere, Dad."

Of course, his father expected the car to go to college, beyond college, to a professional degree. He'd made his expectations clear and wouldn't abide doubts, uncertainties, the possibility of failure. Dan acquired his skateboard and aimed it toward Seneca High.

12 /PAM VALOIS

When the door slammed behind Dan, Peter banged the paper on the table. "Damn! You can't tell them anything at his age."

The domestic-service android known as Kayten refilled two coffee cups. The unit was designed to look and act as a human and appeared to be in his late teens or early twenties with a slender athletic build. Peter had modeled Kayten using his son as a template and had been so successful that even his wife had mistaken Kayten for Dan when the android was clipping bushes in the backyard. To the few outsiders who glimpsed him, Kayten was a medium-height human who happened to like domestic work.

Pam, a fit, five-foot-two brunette, squinted at her husband. "Peter, Dan's really changed. He doesn't eat. He doesn't tell us who he's with, where he goes, or what he does. He's dropped both track and choir, his room is a shambles, and his grades have plunged."

Peter placed his cup on the table, still staring at the newspaper. "He just ran into a tough patch in the math and science courses."

"No, dammit. I think he's using drugs," Pam said.

Peter's eyes widened, and his mouth opened, but no sound emerged. Finally, he managed, "Don't go jumping to conclusions without data. Our kid would not use drugs. He knows about his uncle. Probably just a phase he's going through, something we can straighten out when I talk to him." He patted his wife's arm.

"A talk! You're kidding. Be a scientist about this, not an ostrich. I've trusted your judgment on many family matters, but you are way off base here." That meant she handled family problems on her own, something she couldn't do in this case.

Peter withdrew his hand and was about to respond when Pam continued.

"This is way beyond the father-son chat stage," she said. "You don't see Dan as I do. You're so wrapped up in your robot brains that you've lost touch with your son. We need help."

Kayten stopped unloading the dishwasher.

Peter's face reddened, and he slapped his napkin on the table. "You don't seem to trust my judgment now. Damn it, Pam, don't go blabbing your worst fears to your girlfriends. What will they think? If this gets out to Cybernetic, it will become a security issue. I could get fired. If our son's experimented with drugs, we'll handle it and keep it in the family. God damn it, I'll straighten him out!"

He stomped from the kitchen before Pam could answer. When he returned, stuffing his wallet in a back pocket, he said, "My sock drawer was a mess. Were you looking for something?"

Pam stared.

Peter didn't give her the usual goodbye kiss. "I'm late. See you this evening. We'll fix this."

As the front door closed, the air conditioning kicked on, and Pam shivered. She heard the car door slam. He just doesn't want to see the problem, she thought. In twenty years of marriage, she'd grown to know her husband well: he was extremely talented in his field and could be decisive and forceful when the need arose but was amazingly unobservant at home. She wished he could see this crisis for what it was.

Maybe she could do a better job of convincing Peter if she had more knowledge of drug addiction and what to do about it. Dan had a disease and needed professional help. Somehow, she would have to get her husband to drop the denial and foolish concern about gossip. More than talk was required.

Kayten asked, "Does madam need assistance?"

"Not the kind you can provide, Kayten," said Pam, putting the accent on the first syllable of the android's name. She reached for the phone.

After a brief delay, Kayten asked, "Is that because the assistance is of an emotional nature?"

"No, Kayten. You are showing your male-programming bias. I suggest you watch more daytime television and try to remedy that defect in your character."

"Very good, madam." The android went back to the sink.

Near the Valois house, just hidden by border trees, sat a nondescript sedan containing two men. Morgan and Yingyi were the same pair who'd followed Jun Wu and forced her over the guard rail. Morgan lowered the field glasses after watching Peter Valois leave the house and drive off. "From the look on his face, I'd say you were right about the raised voices. There is unrest on the home front."

"Which is exactly what we want," Yingyi said. "The more distracted Dr. Valois is, the easier he will be to deal with. I'm sure that the son is the cause of the unrest. His drug problem must be obvious by now."

"You gotta give the boss credit for coming up with that."

Yingyi grunted. "Right. The son will be a pressure point if the father doesn't cooperate. We probably ought to introduce Dan Valois to the next drug, just to make sure he's hooked."

"How?" Morgan asked.

"Let's find him at the end of his long, hard day. He'll appreciate a free gift then."

Morgan started the car and drove off.

Pam pressed a speed dial number and waited for the pickup that came on the second ring. "Hi, Gerry. It's Pam. I need some serious talk. Are you busy?"

She'd known Gerry O'Rourke since Peter started at Cybernetic

Implementation. He'd had to be cleared by, and then work with, the head of Cybernetic Security, Gerry's husband Mark. The two had consulted on the security system for the new Defense Department research wing and become friends. Gerry and Pam were pregnant at the same time and gave birth within a week of each other, Gerry having a daughter and Pam a son. Subsequently, they became tennis opponents, bridge partners, and confidants.

"What's up?" Gerry asked. "Got a problem with that husband of yours?"

The question did not surprise Pam. They had spoken of such things in the past, including how she'd maneuvered Peter into their marriage, even though it didn't take much maneuvering. It was, by all criteria, an arranged union that had to be pushed, since left to Peter, they would have entered an old age home together as friends. She and Gerry even talked about whether their sex lives needed rejuvenation.

"Yes and no. Primary problem is Dan, but that, of course, includes Peter. It's a bit complex, and probably needs a face-to-face. Can I come over?"

"Sure thing. The only thing you'll be keeping me from is shampooing the carpets. Not a job I enjoy, and the rugs aren't that dirty. If they are sadly neglected for a bit longer, I'll survive, and they'll survive. Mark won't notice either way."

"Expect me in about forty-five. I have to shower and stop at the bank. I'll bring Kayten to do your rugs. Thanks, Gerry."

Pam finished her coffee. The head of a tortoise-shell cat rose above the edge of the table and scanned the plates. Pam rose and lifted the animal from the chair, placing it on the floor. "No!" The cat issued a protesting "meow."

"Would madam like more coffee?" Kayten held the glass carafe.

"No thank you, Kayten. How would you like to shampoo some carpets today?"

"That was not on my schedule, madam. The carpets are shampooed on a ninety-one day cycle and were done sixty-seven days ago. My sensors do not detect any unusual buildup of foreign substances in the carpets. Would madam elaborate on her requirements?"

"Calm down, Kayten. I was referring to the carpets in the O'Rourke house."

The android said nothing for five seconds as if engaged in internal debate. "I was not aware of any increased activity in my circuits that would correspond to human anxiety. So, calming down would not be appropriate. Madam is aware, of course, that shampooing the O'Rourke carpets would require my departure from the house, an event not favored by Dr. Valois?"

"I'm quite aware of what's favored by Dr. Valois, but this wouldn't involve your being outdoors. We would remain for a short time in the O'Rourke house with Mrs. O'Rourke. Only the three of us. No other family members. Gerry knows who you are and what you are, since her husband authorized your presence here. You have been with Mrs. O'Rourke before."

"That is true, madam. And each time Mrs. O'Rourke has been in this house. I regret that I cannot comply with madam's request. I must remain in this house." Kayten spoke with a peculiar hesitancy, the timing between his words off a fraction of a second.

Pam studied the android. She tried again. "Listen, Kayten, this is almost the same as being with Mrs. O'Rourke in this house."

Kayten's head jerked. "I regret that I cannot comply."

"Kayten, this is a direct human command." Pam still didn't believe that the android could fail to follow her orders. Was something going on she didn't understand?

"I am quite aware of that, madam. But there is no human danger involved and I must adhere to my priorities. I am assigned to protect this house and am commanded by Dr. Valois not to leave. I regret I cannot comply."

Pam put her hands on her hips. "Well, damn! You're just full of surprises, aren't you? All right. I'll leave here after I take a shower. Please tend to the house if that is what you think you must do." She left the kitchen shaking her head, leaving the android in a state of analysis that prevented him from returning to the dishes for several minutes.

. . .

Pam stepped from the shower and dried herself in front of a full-length mirror. She was happy with her figure: breasts still firm, a flat stomach, and buttocks that could still interest her husband, even if that happened only infrequently. She wrapped the towel around herself and left the bathroom.

In the hall, she called, “Kayten, I’ll need you in the bedroom to hold the hair dryer, please.”

She entered the master bedroom and, shortly thereafter, Kayten appeared at the door with the hair dryer. He plugged it in while Pam finished drying her body.

“See what you can do about getting my head dry while I dress, Tonto.”

Kayten’s programming allowed him to easily learn new tasks, and Pam had trained the device to dry hair, which she wore in a short pageboy cut that made the process easier. He held the device above Pam’s head at a precise distance, moving when his touch determined that the hair was dry. She donned slacks and a polo shirt and sat on the bed to don socks and sneakers. Kayten followed her with the dryer.

“I have not previously been called “Tonto”. Is this a term of endearment? Can madam enlighten me?”

“Tonto was a faithful Indian companion of the Lone Ranger, a western hero. Tonto obeyed all his commands.”

Kayten considered this for a while. “I am familiar with that story, but in what way am I an Indian?”

At the vanity, Pam applied a pale pink lipstick. “That’s the one part of the meaning that doesn’t apply, Kayten. You have to learn to extract the relevant information from any comparisons and see if that part applies.”

She felt her hair and picked up a brush. “That will have to do for the hair.” She brushed it out as Kayten left with the dryer. Satisfied, she grabbed her purse and headed for the garage.

Pam backed a Ford from the garage into the bright sun. Heat lifted shimmers of warped air from the asphalt, and pollen settled on the windshield. She hunted for her sunglasses, agitated over what she had to discuss with her friend. Talking to Gerry was bound to help. Maybe she was overreacting.

Unable to find the sunglasses, she waited for her eyes to adjust to the brightness. That was when she noticed the white pill on the passenger seat. It had no markings, and she was sure she'd never seen it, or any pill like it, before.

13 /GERRY O'ROURKE

GERRY OPENED THE FRONT DOOR OF A LARGE, RANCH-STYLE HOME and waved to a neighbor picking up the newspaper from his front walk. She watched Pam exit her car and said, "You have worry written all over your face. Come in."

Gerry had a model's look, tall and slender with shoulder-length blond hair. She lacked, however, the pouty, forlorn expression and any inclination to spend time posing. In fact, she always seemed ready to play something outdoors—golf, tennis, badminton, even tag. Her cat-like prowl had an infectious energy that annoyed Pam, but usually sparked her to action. Not today.

"So, what happened to the rug-shampooer?" Gerry asked, when they reached the kitchen.

"Kayten wouldn't come. I thought he had to obey humans, but he claimed my husband's command to stay on the property took priority. Peter never told me about that restriction. Now that I think about it, Kayten has never left the house. Strange."

"Therefore, no rug-cleaner?"

"He wouldn't budge."

Gerry raised her eyebrows. "There's something odd about that fine machine. I doubt anyone, including your husband, really knows how Kayten thinks."

"I thought you said he was a work of technological art?" Pam said.

"That too, but we don't always understand art. Do we really get Dali?"

The spacious kitchen was getting its dose of morning sun. Gerry pointed to the coffee pot. "You'd better straighten this command thing out with Peter. Kayten is supposed to be for your protection, right? Something to do with your husband's defense work. He can't protect you if he's not here."

"I suspect the android is just being field-tested as a domestic, not a protector."

Gerry gestured to the breadbox next to a stack of dishes. "There's coffee cake in there. I have to put in a load of laundry." She disappeared into the utility room.

Pam added the dirty plates to the dishwasher, cut a slice of pecan-crusted cake, and poured coffee. At the table in the breakfast nook, she sat and tried to organize her thoughts.

Gerry returned. "Nice of Peter to provide that android. I'm sure you've forgotten how to wash clothes." She filled her coffee cup and sliced some cake. "If you can get Kayten to leave the homestead, I'll bet he could feed us tennis balls."

"Like a machine."

"Could he learn bridge?"

"He'd play at a master's level and put us all to shame."

"Does he serve breakfast in bed?"

"He would if we asked him, but neither Peter nor I are the eat-in-bed types. Peter could never tolerate the delay in getting up, getting dressed, and getting to it. Type A personality."

"Tell me what's troubling you."

"It's Dan. I think—no, I know—he's using drugs." Pam studied a sparrow pecking seeds from the backyard bird feeder and imagined a teenager snatching drugs. "I told Peter this morning, but he only half bought it. He wants data, not my hunch. If Peter can't measure it and label it, he ignores it. In this case, he says that Dan is just not living up to expectations. Even if my husband suspected something was behind Dan's behavioral changes, he'd say he needed more data. Well, I have enough data, and we have to do something now."

Gerry refilled the coffee cups and waved Pam to the sunroom, a small space just off the kitchen. It also afforded a view of the backyard, including the bird feeder. When they were settled on the wicker furniture, she asked, “What are the symptoms?”

“The classic ones we hear about at PTA meetings. Dan does no schoolwork, has lost interest in track and other sports. His room is messier. He’s dropped his straight, achieving friends and now associates with kids we don’t know. There’s more: he never tells us where he’s going, keeps his voice low when he’s on the phone, and doesn’t eat. You’d have to be as blind as Peter not to notice.”

“Your husband doesn’t want to admit that anything is wrong with his only son, right?”

The sunroom faced east and had three, mostly glass walls. Pam closed her eyes in a beam of sun. The AC kicked on as the room warmed. “He said he’d talk to Dan. But we need more than just a father-son talk. I’m sure Dan will deny there’s a problem, and that’s what Peter wants to hear. Nothing will be done.”

Gerry rose to lower a blind to block the sun. “My nephew Tom went through drug rehab,” she said. “My sister-in-law talked a lot about it.”

“What happened?”

“Tom had all of Dan’s symptoms. Both parents were in denial, and when they woke up, the drug use had been going on for two years. They intervened and got him help. They tried the outpatient counseling approach, but the kid relapsed more than once. Finally, they sent him to an inpatient program, and he came out clean and started to attend meetings. There was a relapse, but he seems to be drug-free now.”

“So that’s good, right?” Pam said, placing her cup on the glass-topped table.

“Yes, but my sister-in-law’s biggest lesson was that both the drug-user and his parents need treatment. Substance abuse is a family disease. It affects everyone in the house. His parents have been involved with a support group ever since. They acknowledge they’re part of the treatment.”

“How are they doing?”

“It’s hasn’t been easy, but Tom seems to be with his program for the moment, and they are all coping. The other big thing they learned is that help is out there. It's available, but you have to look for it."

Pam digested that as she watched a squirrel approach the bird feeder. It sniffed the ground below them and enjoyed the sunflower seeds that the birds had dislodged. Apparently not quite satisfied, the animal eyed the obstacle of the thin, metal pole. It went to a nearby tree, climbed, and found the limb overhanging the feeder. With a fearless leap, it landed on the plastic cylinders with the seeds. It managed to hang from the top as it stretched out and began plucking sunflower seeds from the small holes. Pam got up and moved to the window. The squirrel went on with his theft, ignoring her four feet away.

"I guess that's encouraging. What should I do?"

"You need help. You shouldn't handle this alone. I can get you in touch with Tom's mother."

Pam frowned and shook her head. "No. I have to keep this close to our family."

"Well, talk to Dan and then the school. They probably already suspect Dan is using. This county has an agency that handles substance abuse. They know what to do. My sister-in-law said you can't take half measures like one hour a week of outpatient counseling. Just because Dan tells you he's going straight; you can't trust him. Don't let the counselors sell you on an outpatient program. She suspects they know better but do this to prolong their role. Probably has to do with funding and getting their share of the pie, figuring they can go to the next step later."

Pam turned back from the window, frowning. "Peter is opposed to getting outside help. Thinks it's just youthful exploration that can be treated at home. Wants to keep this quiet and wouldn't approve of my talking to you—especially you—because Mark is the head of Cybernetic Security."

"This is between us."

"Thanks."

"You may have to act alone," Gerry said. "Be open with Peter and try to get him to talk to someone who has dealt with a drug-using teenager. Regardless of Peter's notions, you must use the help available."

"God, I know you're right, Gerry." Pam returned to the armchair and took another sip of coffee. "But should I act without Peter?"

Gerry touched Pam's hand. "This isn't about Peter. It's about your son. Stay focused on Dan, and you can do what's needed. Don't put it off. As a matter of fact, why don't you call the county agency now? You can get some information that may sway Peter. More important still, you'll be doing something."

14 /MEGAN O'ROURKE

DAN JUMPED OFF HIS SKATEBOARD WHEN HE CAUGHT UP WITH TWO girls a block from the high school. Terry Evans, a short, solidly built brunette with a permanent startled expression, walked with Megan O'Rourke, Dan's "maybe" girlfriend. Perhaps "former" was how Megan saw it.

"Hey, Dan. How's it goin'?" Terry asked. "Haven't seen much of you lately."

"All's fine. I've been busy." Dan put his arm around Megan's waist and said, "Babe, you sure are looking good."

"And what am I, chopped liver?" Terry asked.

"No way. You're totally okay. As beautiful as ever."

Terry rolled her eyes.

Megan, the daughter of Gerry and Mark O'Rourke, had known Dan since babyhood. Their family albums contained pictures of early shared events in their lives, like birthday parties and outings to the playground and pool. They went their separate ways once school started and only noticed each other again sophomore year of high school.

Almost as tall as Dan, Megan was slender and athletic with strawberry blond hair, freckles, and a devastating smile. With the smile and greenish eyes that lit up her face, she turned out to be quite the teenage beauty and had her choice of male companionship. For some time, however, she'd been identified as Dan's girlfriend, at least until his behavioral change. As Megan saw it, Dan ended the relationship, and she was sure his new love came in pill form.

She shed his arm. "Cut it out! It's not the time or the place." In an angry tone, she continued. "Busy, Dan? With what? Seems like you're hardly in school anymore. And you haven't asked me out recently. Remember what a date is, Dan? You know, Friday night, the movies, a pizza. We used to do that. Not that I'd want to date the new Dan." Struggling to bring her emotions under control, she asked, "So, tell me. What are you up to?"

"Finding the meaning of life. Learning who Dan Valois is and what's important."

"Oh really. You're so full of crap. Just listen to yourself." She started walking again. "How about June? What happens then? There is life after high school, you know. Weren't you thinking of college at one point? I guess that was when you were getting real grades and still using your brain."

The two had lagged behind Terry when the sidewalk narrowed between hedges and the curb.

Dan spoke in a low tone. "Hey. Now you sound like my father, always harping on college and telling me to make something of myself. Saying if I don't live up to my potential, something terrible will happen. Maybe there are other ways to lead one's life, other things besides grades and college." He stared ahead, as if he were talking to himself.

Megan softened her voice. "Don't get hyper. Just asking about your plans. Like you can't be a high school student forever. Only two choices after high school. More school or a job. Any thoughts, Mr. Philosopher?"

"College is a possibility. But I may just take time to travel around and do some thinking. You know, see this great country. Meet girls."

"Wow. Great plan. You can meet girls at the beach. And you're so rich you can afford not to work? How long you gonna mooch off your father? Or were you planning to work, maybe as a farm hand? You've got no clue, do you?"

"Not a problem. I'm blessed to be an only child. I can sponge off

Dad for years. Think of all the money I'd be saving him by not going to college."

Megan stopped and frowned. "Heavy idea there, Dan. I thought you said you were postponing college, remember? Postponing is not saving. You can't travel and live at home too. Better rethink the whole thing. Have you talked to the guidance office? Maybe there are travel-related careers that would let you see the country and earn money."

Dan shrugged. "I may see the world by joining the army."

Megan issued a dismissive puff. "That's a crock. You haven't thought of the military. You just want me to stop badgering you."

"How about the great Megan O'Rourke? Where will she be after June, modeling, married in the suburbs, hooking?"

Megan winced. "I'll be at the beach July and August, and then I'll be going to a place where I can actually train for a career and a future. I'll be at one of the University of California campuses, depending on who wants me."

Dan lowered his eyes and said, "I want you."

"What a thrill. To be wanted by someone with no plans who is trying to find himself. Someone who's dropped out and doesn't care. Come back when you've gotten your head screwed back on."

When the group arrived at Seneca High School, whose glass and wood doors were consuming a steady stream of students chattering and occasionally yelling, the girls entered, but Dan held back, saying that he had something to do. Megan, eyebrows raised, watched him ride to the next corner and disappear around the building.

Dan parked the skateboard in a school bike rack and ambled a block to a drug store. A six-foot-high, wrought iron fence surrounded its empty parking lot. A grass strip with the occasional bush hugged the fence. Plastic bags, paper cups, and popsicle sticks dotted the asphalt. Pickup would be the first job of employees to make the store fit in with the neat school neighborhood. But litter suited the kind of business he intended to conduct.

He thought of Megan, how her face, framed by reddish curls and always threatening a smile, still made his breath catch. She was probably right about having plans and preparing for the future, even if it did sound like the usual paternal jazz. But Dan had trouble preparing for the next day, let alone some distant future. It just didn't seem important or worth the effort. What he was doing now was important.

He walked to the late-model, highly polished, black sedan parked near the building. The driver's window lowered, revealing a large dark-skinned man at the wheel.

The driver's eyes scanned beyond Dan before he finally spoke. "What's happenin', Dan? Gotta need we can feed?"

The man, dressed in an expensive gray suit and wearing a tie, was in his late twenties. He looked like a successful businessman whose only defect was the scar on his left cheek. His mouth smiled, but his black eyes didn't.

"Man, I have ten for ice and ten for grass." Dan glanced around before pulling his right hand from his pocket. He placed both hands on the windowsill and, opening the fingers of his right hand, dropped a twenty-dollar bill into the car.

"Take a walk across the road. The man will be by." The driver picked up a cell phone and pointed across the street.

Dan sauntered over and stood by the curb. A dark blue sedan turned the corner and rolled to a stop beside him. The driver checked in front of the car and in back before handing over a miniscule brown bag and leaving. As Dan headed back toward Seneca High, a gray sedan matched his pace a block behind.

Dan stood before his locker, considering the need to conserve the newly bought stash, to save it for Friday. This didn't used to be such a problem. Maybe he really couldn't stop when he wanted--if he wanted, which he didn't. He needed a little something to get the day started, forgetting about the joint he'd smoked for breakfast. Life really was a pain. Then another shocking, intense thought gripped him. Maybe it was time to get help. The high school had some kind of counseling team. Megan would know who they were. He opened the locker and, his hand shaking, put the brown bag on the shelf.

"Hey, you cut it close. Get a move on." Megan slammed her locker shut. "You sure have changed, Dan. You're using, aren't you? What kind of shit are you in to?"

"Don't freak."

"You've got a problem. You used to be someone worth knowing, someone with a future." Then, as if she had read his thoughts, she added, "Dan, there is a faculty crisis team here at Seneca. Mr. Wilson is on it. You should see him." There was anger in her voice.

"Thanks for the advice, beautiful. How about getting together this Friday for a movie?"

"Sorry, I'm not interested in the new Dan. God, I hate to see you this way." She met his eyes for a second and then hurried off. He watched her leave, admiring her tall, slender build. A strange pain gripped him. He turned back to his locker and held on to the door, hoping his blurred vision would clear.

A student approached a nearby locker, shoved in a book, and asked, "Coming to social studies?" Pete Reynolds had known Dan since the fifth grade, and they'd been good friends when that involved roaming fields and playing ball. "Rumor has it that it's surprise quiz time."

"Yeah, I'll be there in a moment." When Pete started down the hallway, Dan reached into the brown bag and grabbed a pill. Moving his head closer to the locker so that he faced the door hinges, he put the drug in his mouth. He then closed the locker and went to the water fountain.

There was, in fact, a social studies quiz. Most of the questions Dan had to guess at. For some he couldn't even manufacture a pretend answer. But it didn't really bother him. He sat through a Spanish class without saying anything, and the teacher did not call on him. In industrial arts the teacher asked him to stand back and watch other students running the machinery. He made it to math class but did not have any homework to hand in or to discuss. English was held in a class with windows that overlooked the volleyball court. Dan watched junior girls in their gym uniforms playing volleyball.

Yingyi called Andy and reported Dan's morning drug buy. She seemed very interested in the details.

"Sounds like he's only into weed and pharmaceuticals. Can you get hold of cocaine?"

Yingyi conveyed the question to Morgan who was sipping a beer. Morgan nodded and Yingyi told his boss.

"I want you to find a way to give the coke as a gift. Claim it's a reward for being a good customer."

15 /PLANS

AFTER HIS LAST CLASS, DAN WANDERED TO THE SCHOOL LIBRARY, entered the reference section, and selected a volume that he'd looked at before. In the V-section of *American Men of Science,* he located his father's name and read again the list of degrees, accomplishments, and honors, staring for some time until his vision blurred. He wasn't sure why he did this, for he already knew what was there. Without a doubt his father was a big shot, a leader in his field. On one hand, it made him proud to have such a father. On the other hand, it made him feel inadequate. And angry.

He reshelved the book and went to his locker to retrieve the brown bag. The hallway was deserted, so he stuffed the thing in his pants pocket and left the building by the rear door that led to the athletic fields. At the football field, he found a handful of users in the shade of the aluminum stands. Dan sat next to Brock, a skinny kid in a black tee shirt, who hugged his knees smoking a joint.

"Hey."

"Hey," Brock said. "See that guy?" He pointed at a lone runner on the track. "He's a middle-aged fart trying to keep himself young. Bull. He should give up. Or they should sic a dog on his butt to get him moving."

"At least he's doing something." Dan watched the man jog around a distant turn. He shook his head, fished a rolled cigarette from a plastic pouch, and lit it.

Brock let smoke leak from his mouth when he said in a raspy voice, "So, whadaya doing, Valois? To get out of this rat hole?"

Dan eyed the three other students and decided they were far enough away to keep the conversation private. "We'll be out in months. I'll probably go to college in a year. My old man expects it. More like demands it. I'll find some party school to keep him happy and off my back. Then I'll get back at him by having a blast while he pays the big bills." Dan was shocked at how stupid that sounded. He took a drag as a hot breeze curled beneath the bleachers.

"That's bogus. Colleges like good grades. You need to pull a miracle out of your butt to not have a failed course or two on your record."

Dan's face reddened. He didn't need to be reminded about academic shit. "Well, fuzzbrain, who cares! What are you going to do? Become a pimp for your sister?"

"Don't start the crap. I'm gonna join the army. That will get me outta this town and pay me to boot."

"Are you kidding me? Who's gonna take the physical and pee in the cup? Even if you passed the physical, today's army wants a high school diploma. We're not at war, you know. They can be choosy."

Brock studied his joint. "Well, we better find some way to get money. This crap ain't free, and the price keeps going up."

"Maybe that's because our tastes keep improving. Weed used to be enough. Not anymore. Any ideas for getting cash now, before you join the army?" Dan's question was more than half-rhetorical, and he was surprised when his companion took it seriously, as if he'd been already thinking about an answer to the very problem.

Brock lowered his voice. "Actually, dickwad, I do. This is top secret, but I found out they keep the athletic money—you know, the stuff they make at the refreshment stand—in the equipment locker. It's not a lot, but it's left all by itself in a strong box until one of the office women hauls it to the bank."

"Why would they do that?"

"Cause the women don't want to wait around on Friday night to make a deposit."

"Sounds totally stupid."

"No shit. I'm sure they'll close the door after the cow gets out, but we only need a one-time hit."

Dan saw the precipice, but he did not draw back. He needed the money. "Really. Tell me about it."

Which Brock did, probably inventing a plan along the way, making the whole thing seem easy and low risk. Dan, hardly capable of critical thought, didn't ridicule and didn't ask many questions. In the silence the scheme hung there, available for full contemplation.

As the runner thumped past the bleachers, Brock changed the subject. "How are you doing with Megan O'Rourke? The hottie. Gotten into her pants?"

"Nobody gets near Miss O'Rourke. She's not interested in me. Thinks I'm a druggie."

"You are."

Dan winced. "A little recreational use does not a druggie make."

"What else does O'Rourke say?"

"I should talk to the school crisis team." He paused, remembering the intensity in her eyes and voice. "Maybe I should. So should you. Then we wouldn't have to become thieves, and you wouldn't have to embarrass yourself trying to enlist."

"Bull."

A student yelled as a sheriff's car pulled into the adjacent parking lot. Five teenagers ran from the stands like bees from a disturbed hive and jogged toward the far football goalpost. Dan stuffed the bag into his pocket and followed Brock toward the low, chain link fence separating the track from the field next to it. Brock jumped and Dan got ready to do the same. But he miscalculated where his trailing foot had to go and snagged his ankle on the top of the fence, ripping his sock. He hit the ground, rolled to his feet, and limped across the field beyond the fence.

Halfway through the grassy expanse, Brock turned to go a separate way, "Hey. What about the money solution, Valois?"

"I'll think about it."

After field hockey practice, Megan and Terry took their time getting to the locker room. Most girls were done with showers and filled the space with a buzz of voices. The noisy group left quickly, leaving behind the sound of a dripping showerhead. Megan and Terry enjoyed peaceful showers, toweled off, and dressed.

"So, whatya gonna do about Dan?" Terry asked as she buttoned her blouse.

"Not sure." Megan pulled jeans over bikini panties. "Drugs changed him. No more the guy with a future. We had good times before he became a zombie."

"He does seem to be in a haze. Like off in his own world. Dan Valois used to be fun. Not to mention hot."

"That too. I miss our talks and cuddling at the movies. You know, I was considering going further with him."

"Thanks for that, Miss Horny. So you say," Terry said as she stuffed clothes in her bag.

"Hey. We were friends with future benefits. What I miss most is the good friend."

Terry picked up her gym bag. "Well, what now?"

"Not sure."

"He needs a counselor."

"Duh. So I told him already."

Terry led the way to the door. "Hey, maybe you could talk to Dan's parents, get them to see what's going down."

"Not sure I'm up for that."

"They must have their suspicions," Terry said.

Outside, the sidewalk was deserted. They walked in silence for a block before Terry said, "Hey. Your father—he heads security where Dan's father works. Maybe he could do something."

Megan mulled that over. "I don't know."

Terry latched onto Megan's arm. "It's gonna go from bad to worse. Dan is freakin' out. Friends don't let friends drive drunk, and we shouldn't let Dan drive his life into a shithole. Talk to your parents and make a fuss. Remember that session about an intervention for users. We're at that point."

As the girls strolled away, both apparently absorbed in their own thoughts, the sun disappeared behind a gray cloud.

Morgan and Yingyi watched Dan make his way through the grassy area and onto a sidewalk. Morgan drove slowly, keeping the limping boy in sight.

"He'll cross at the next corner," Yingyi said. "There's a quiet stretch in the next block where the houses are hidden by bushes. We can talk to him there."

Morgan smiled. "If his ankle hurts, he'll probably need a pain reliever. Do we have anything like that?"

Yingyi held up a small glass vial. "Just what the doctor ordered."

Dan limped past stores, each fronted by young palm trees in a patch of grass. A gray sedan trailed him. When he turned into a quiet residential street, the car pulled up alongside, and the passenger window slid down.

"Hi, Dan. I got a little present for you." The speaker was a small man who appeared Asian, maybe Chinese.

The driver, a big man in his twenties wearing a polo shirt that revealed thick arm muscles, stared past the Asian and held Dan's eyes.

"Are you talking to me?" Dan asked, without moving closer.

The Asian seemed to study his face before he said, "You're Dan Valois, aren't you?" The guy smiled as he reached into his shirt pocket.

"What of it?"

"As a good customer, we have a present for you. Something to recognize your status." The man held out a small vial.

Dan didn't like this, and he thought of running, but then his ankle twinged. "I've never seen either of you before. I've got to be going." He made no move to accept the vial.

"Come on, Dan. Security. We use different delivery trucks all the time. It's no big deal. If you don't want the present, give it away. Here."

The speaker tossed the vial in an arc, and Dan grabbed it out of the air as the car moved away. The vial held a brownish-white crystal, obviously crack. Holding it made him feel like little bugs were crawling over his skin. The guy claimed to be a dealer, but Dan bought from only one dealer, and he'd never used crack. Were the dealers trying to hook him even more? Again, the precipice loomed before him, and the clear picture of the downward path panicked him. Maybe Megan was right. He tried to focus on the thought that he was in over his head and getting in deeper, but that kind of thinking hurt. When it got too painful, he needed his escape. Which always worked. The problems, the fuss, the fear went away, and everything was all right. For a while, at least. He could even forget the father problem. He looked again at the vial he held in his hand, considered tossing it, and pocketed it.

16 /CANDIDATE

PETER LIFTED HIS HEAD FROM HIS HANDS AND STARED AT THE OFFICE desk. He'd started the day with a headache and still had it. The pain, worse than the usual one from job pressure, he attributed to his son. Dan needed attention, and Peter considered taking a leave of absence. Cybernetic would let him do it, but the project would go to another senior scientist. He might never get it back and then wouldn't have a job.

Then there was the other problem: replacing his technician. He knew who he wanted. He just had to get her into the lab. Expediting that process might require calling in a favor, so he picked up the phone and dialed Mark O'Rourke, Chief of Security. They'd worked together many times, and Peter expected to get quick clearance of his technician pick.

O'Rourke's secretary put him through.

"What's up, Peter?" Mark said.

"I've decided who I want for the tech vacancy," Peter said. "Name's Antoinette Marino. I want her in for an interview. ASAP. I need your security clearance and I need it double-quick."

"Calm down. What's the sudden rush?"

"Sorry, but my boss wants action. He's worried about the upcoming visit from the DOD and wants a good show for them. For that I need data. That means I need a technician to do the work."

O'Rourke sighed. "Spell the name."

Peter did so and listened to a keyboard clicking.

"I don't see that name in the HR file. Where's this coming from?" Mark sounded concerned.

"The file was on my desk. It has the Human Resources stamp, so it must be there. Did you spell the damn name right?"

"Not here, Peter. Nada."

"Well, hell, some idiot down there didn't enter it in the database. Or sent it to me before that step."

"Maybe. You'd better bring it down."

"Fine, but I need this clearance now. Like in twenty-four hours."

Peter grabbed the Marino folder and went through the contents again. Her qualifications seemed perfect. She had a BS in biology and worked for six months at a California contract animal-testing laboratory until downsizing eliminated her job. She'd spent four years in the army and two with the CIA. Given the secret status of the Valois project, this kind of background should be a plus.

When he reached O'Rourke's office, ready to fight for prompt action, the security chief had a visitor. The secretary took the file and his message of urgency. He returned to his office and tried to concentrate on research, entering the latest rat data for statistical analysis. Ten minutes later his phone rang.

"This Marino gal has an interesting background," Mark said. "I'm a little concerned about her abrupt departure from the CIA."

"The CIA connection should be an asset. What's the hang-up?"

"No hang-up. We just need to dig a bit."

"Give me a break here, Mark. I really need the slot filled to meet my project deadlines. The pressure is on. Move the clearance along. Is there anything I can do?"

"Just be patient and sit tight."

Peter began pacing his cramped office. At least he had an office, he thought. New guys got cubicles. He imagined the arguments he might face later from Mark.

Mark called a contact in the DOD contracts office and asked for any background they might have on an ex-soldier. The woman called him back, confirming that Antoinette Marino had served and left in good standing. She also noted that Ms. Marino had a brother in the army who had died in a Nicaraguan operation. He was less successful with his second call to CIA Human Resources. The clerk refused any information, despite the caller being part of a company that did DOD research.

Mark tried a CIA acquaintance who, after a bit of research, confirmed that Marino was a CIA employee who left abruptly. He suspected it had something to do with her brother, with whom she'd had a close relationship only because someone had used the word "obsessed" in connection with the issue.

The death of Tony Marino seemed important. Another contact, an Army officer, knew a man who would answer questions. For money. The Army friend promised to have his source call Mark directly.

An hour later the phone rang. The caller identified himself and, speaking with a Spanish accent, inquired about payment for his consult. He provided electronic routing numbers and said he'd call back when the down payment showed up. He wasn't cheap. Mark arranged payment and again waited.

Ten minutes elapsed as Mark penciled little soldiers with helmets and rifles on a yellow legal pad. The stick figures crouched behind small hillocks and aimed at each other across the page. He laid a ruler along a gun barrel and drew a line. A miss. He'd devised the game in childhood and still found it amusing. He was about to lay his ruler along another rifle to see if a return shot would pick off an opponent when the phone rang.

The voice, apparently satisfied with what he'd learned from his bank, began without preamble. "I was in Tony Marino's squad when he led twenty Nicaraguan soldiers to a tiny village. Quiet, you know, except for machetes hacking in that damn steamy jungle."

"Where were you heading?"

"To El Mica, well within the peace zone where no opposition troops and no village politicos with an ax to grind had been seen.

Everything should have been okay, but I thought the air was too still. No insect buzz or bird calls. I was edgy and didn't like it."

"Was Marino spooked?"

"Maybe, but we didn't have time to discuss it. Suddenly bullets were flying and bodies falling. Everyone was hit, and they all died. Probably wondering why and how the hell we walked into an ambush."

"How could it have happened?" Mark asked.

"I think Taguro, our native contact, irritated the army brass with comments about other rebels we were supporting. Interfered with their plan and pissed 'em off. The ambush didn't just happen. They were waiting. I'm supposed to be dead. Who knows what the army brass thinks, but they're not looking for me."

Mark examined his notes. After a moment of silence he spoke. "Why would everyone be killed if they just wanted Taguro out of the way?"

"They gave the job to trigger-happy hotheads who probably sympathized with the opposition. *Stupido*."

"Thanks for this information. It may help with a security issue."

"I don't give a damn about your security. Just pay me." The man repeated the price and the payment arrangement and waited until Mark confirmed the transfer.

The caller got Mark to thinking. Ten minutes passed as he laid his ruler along rifle barrels and pinged bullets into little soldiers across the page. A fluorescent bulb flickered and finally died. He put his pencil down, still unsure how interested Antoinette Marino was in finding out about the operation that killed her brother. The CIA contact had provided another phone number that Mark dialed. At a home in northern Virginia, an older woman answered with a Southern softness. Mark introduced himself and explained why he'd called.

"I understand security around a DOD contract, Mr. O'Rourke," the woman said. "I did spend a career with the CIA, even if it was only as a records clerk. And if I can help with your prospective employee, dearie, I will."

"Did you know Antoinette Marino?"

"We worked in the same building in Virginia. She had her desk upstairs and I was in Central Records, but I saw her in the halls, always dressed nice. You know, clean and neat. Looked fine, but sort of grim and preoccupied. Shoulda smiled more, that one."

"How often did she show up in Central Records?"

"Hard to say, honey. I wasn't always on duty. But right before she resigned, she made several visits when I was there. Always checked out the same folder. Got special clearance to see it." The woman paused as if to catch her breath, but she could have been refreshing her memory. In the background, a clock chimed the hour. She let it finish the job before continuing. "Now, I didn't normally keep my eye on people—I'm not that sort, you know—and it's the job of the door guard to make sure nothing gets taken out, but I watched her go through nearly one hundred documents. They couldn't be copied, so she had to take notes right there. She spent about forty minutes with the file contents and came back for the folder twice, at least while I was at the desk. Never saw a soul so taken with one file."

"Did she want any other materials?" Mark asked.

"No, the same one every time. She read and took notes."

When he hung up, Mark pondered what he'd learned. Ms. Marino was close to her brother Tony who'd served in a special Army operation in South America, one in which he'd died in a not-quite-explained incident. She had been obsessed with finding out what happened. Mark wondered if there was blame to be placed on the government. He made several more calls, begging favors from government contacts. Late in the day, he finally called Peter.

Little time passed before the scientist stomped into Mark's office. "So, what have you got?" Peter asked, sounding pugnacious. "Are we cleared on Marino?"

"Not yet. For your project, this Marino woman will require almost the same level of security clearance you have. But first the positive. She was in the HR database, misspelled as Warino."

"Good. So, what's the negative? She's technically qualified and even had security clearance in the army and the CIA. All good, right?"

"She left the CIA categorized as 'possibly disgruntled.'"

"Is that a real classification?" Peter asked.

"No, it's my translation. She was upset."

"About what?"

Mark picked up his pencil and tapped it on the yellow pad, creating bullet holes in the stick-figure terrain. "Her boss was probably the proximate cause of her leaving, but there was a deeper, more serious reason. Had to do with her brother."

Peter opened his mouth but said nothing.

"He was on an agency mission in Central America and died in an ambush," Mark continued. "I just spoke with a survivor of the ambush. He claims Marino was instructed to lead his squad to a certain village along a specific route. They were ambushed, either as the result of botched intelligence or as part of some larger plan."

Peter listened to the whole account and said, "There's nothing here but a gruesome war story. Nothing that would make Antoinette Marino anti-government or anti-army."

"She may have concluded the government caused her brother's death." Mark summarized what he'd heard from the records clerk.

"That's just conjecture. I still don't see the problem."

Mark held the pencil horizontally and rolled it in his fingers. "She requisitioned a file not needed for her assignment. The file contained brief summaries of correspondence between Washington and Nicaraguan contacts. I got a CIA insider to look at it. He says you could interpret the file more than one way, including government guilt." Mark leaned forward and his voice became softer. "The papers were accounts of communications with a certain rebel force in Nicaragua, advising them of a clear path to a destination village. The rebel force leader was identified as Taguro. Tony Marino, your candidate's brother, had dealings with this guy. Both died in the ambush. Ms. Marino could have read it as a setup."

Peter jumped in impatiently. "You've got nothing here but speculation. I want her."

"You may want her and need her, but I'm responsible for security. She may be fine, but I need time to gather more information. You'll have to wait."

"Damn it, Mark. We're working under the deadline of a DOD review."

"Give me a chance to delve into Marino. But keep looking for a backup candidate."

Peter left the office sour faced.

Mark picked up the phone and dialed an internal number. "Carlos, I need to see you, Right away."

17 /VETTING

Carlos Oreta entered O'Rourke's office and flopped down in the visitor chair. The handsome, six-foot-one Latino with tanned skin, brown eyes, and curly black hair smiled. Tan slacks and a blue blazer, even without a gold badge, made him look like the law. At twenty-eight he'd earned a degree from Fresno State in law enforcement and worked briefly with a private investigation firm before being recruited by Cybernetic, where he'd been a security agent for almost two years. He earned his boss's praise by doing well on additional FBI training courses and expected to rise to Chief of Security within ten years.

"What's up, Mark?" Carlos asked, eager as a tiger about to be fed.

"Dr. Valois wants to offer the tech job to a qualified candidate, Antoinette Marino, who has some questionable CIA history. I'd like you to assess the woman and the risk she might represent. Here's her file. I've summarized what I've been able to find out on the phone."

Carlos took the folder and opened it. "Anything in particular you want me to see?"

"Nothing definite, just implications and innuendos. You need to talk to her face-to-face and check her story. The DOD will be in to review the Valois project soon. It's bad enough that Peter Valois is having experimental troubles without adding security issues on top."

"How do you want me to go about this?" Carlos asked. His training and interests had focused on project issues, like keeping equipment and files secure. He enjoyed dealing with the nitty-gritty of procedure but was developing skill in personnel matters, like analyzing motivations and personalities.

"You need to find out what makes Antoinette Marino tick," Mark said, thumping his index finger on his desk.

"So, I'm cleared to contact Miss Marino out-of-the-blue?"

"Yes. You don't need a pretext. Tell her it's part of a routine security check for the job. Keep it low-key so that the real Marino surfaces."

"This her picture?" Carlos extracted a three-by-five black and white photo. "Good looking. I'll handle this over dinner."

"Why does that not surprise me? I know your theory of how candidates loosen up over a free dinner, but make sure no company business is heard by anyone around you. Including the wait staff."

"This is not a security review—I do those in house. Just a job interview, really. I always choose a secluded spot and keep voices low."

Mark let his eyes move to the ceiling. "All right, just get me a recommendation by tomorrow."

"Right. The goods." He made a saluting motion with the folder as he rose.

"One other thing. Let's not do dinner at the Dana Point Resort. I have to approve your expense voucher."

Carlos put his hands up in a gesture of innocence.

Later, in his own spartan office, Carlos opened his appointment book and dialed the candidate. "Miss Antoinette Marino, please."

"Speaking."

"This is Carlos Oreta with the Security Department of Cybernetic Implementation. I'm doing the background check in connection with your application for the position with Dr. Peter Valois. To provide a security clearance. I'd like to meet to go over your employment history. Is there a convenient time?"

"May I call you back, Mr. Oreta? You don't have to give me your number. I'll go through the main Cybernetic switchboard. Would five minutes be all right?"

"Of course." Carlos hung up. He recorded the time of the call, noting that Antoinette Marino showed her background in intelligence with the call-back. That would confirm his identity and that he was where he should be. Miss Marino is cautious," he said to himself, nodding acceptance of her tactic. The phone rang. "Oreta, Security."

"This is Antoinette Marino. You were saying?"

"As part of your security check for the Valois position, I'd like to meet with you. To minimize the inconvenience, I'd be happy to see you after hours, say, over dinner?"

"Over dinner? I see." The voice was icy but warmed as she continued. "Yes. I could use the free meal. Where and when?"

"How about this evening? Isn't Mathilda's near your home address?"

"Yes. About seven. How will I know you?"

"Latin guy in tan slacks and a white polo shirt."

"Are there particular areas you want to discuss? Anything I should bring?"

"Nothing but your memory." He saw no reason to prep the witness.

"Seven then."

Carlos hung up and made additional notes, thinking there was a coldness in the woman's voice. But that could be due to stress. "Or something else," he said aloud.

After he left Mark's office, Peter walked with slumped shoulders, his mind grappling with the need for more data and progress on his project. The DOD guys were aware of the benchmarks he'd promised to meet by the next review. The brass wouldn't tolerate excuses, even with another pair of hands. Things had to break his way. How could he worry about lab stuff with the black cloud of his son hanging over him?

With his office door closed, he paced and fretted. To get positive results with dogs, he needed a tech. He pulled out his copy of Marino's personnel file. Her background meant she could hit the ground running. He had to have her. He picked up the phone and dialed.

Marino answered without giving her name.

Peter introduced himself. "I'm calling to say I'm impressed with your credentials, and I'm prepared to offer you the job. However, this is a government project, so our Security Department has to check your background. I'm hoping for an immediate review and decision."

"I will see a Mr. Oreta this evening," Andy said. "Should I be prepared for anything in particular?"

"You will be questioned about two topics. One is your reason for leaving the CIA. The other is your feeling about your brother's death."

"I'm very interested in the job, Dr. Valois. Is there anything more you can tell me to get past the security hurdle?"

"Oreta is a young guy with minimal experience. He specializes in safeguarding the classified projects. He's got a reputation for appreciating the fair sex, so charm him to calm his concerns."

"I'm not sure how to take that," she said in a strained voice.

"I mean you should smile."

"Right. Thanks for the heads-up. I'll do my best to convince him that I'm no security risk."

"Excellent, Antoinette. Needless to say, there's no reason to mention this phone call. Good luck. I hope to have you on board ASAP."

As soon as she hung up, Andy phoned Yingyi. "I want you to check out the Cybernetic Security Department guy named Carlos Oreta. Start by looking at his residence and get a feel for the neighborhood. When he meets me for dinner, you be there."

"No problem. Anything else?"

"Yes. Put a tap on Peter Valois's phone."

"Why?"

"Because I said so."

18 /CARLOS

Carlos stepped from the shower, finishing the last bar of "New York, New York" in a respectable baritone. He toweled his fit body, the product of youth, two seasons of college baseball, and a mild, but persistent, physical exercise program, including running, tennis, and weights.

He thought about Cybernetic. The job paid well, gave him freedom to think and act, and he hit it off with Mark O'Rourke. This new assignment meant he had to deal with personnel. Personnel like Antoinette Marino.

As the mirror cleared, he detected movement in the window across the alley. His lovely neighbor was being indiscreet. He softly sang, "If I can make it there, I can make it anywhere." Neighbor Maria stripped off her jogging outfit to reveal narrow hips and a shapely backside. *Is this show intentional? Do I care?* Although he'd taken her out several times, including to the beach, he hadn't seen this much of her before.

He considered pulling the bathroom shade down and wondered again about the previous tenants, a young couple who'd left without leaving any forwarding information. Their sudden departure struck him as strange.

Maria claimed to be a freelance writer, and had quizzed him on his security job, claiming it was for a possible magazine piece. The quizzing seemed serious, and her questions showed understanding of what Cybernetic did, and why the company had tight security, suggesting she'd done her homework. Their several dates had ended with intimacy short of bed that promised more if he could produce info for a saleable article. She wanted authentic inside information, something to give the reader a feel for his career and the company.

Leaking info about his employer wasn't worth the implied reward. Carlos began shaving as Maria disappeared into her bathroom. He had to check his neighbor's background before he got any more involved. If there was a relationship growing, it should not be based on Maria's ulterior motives.

In the bedroom, classical guitar music flowed from tall speakers framing a large window overlooking the rear lawn. Umba, an eighteen-pound, orange-and-cream cat sprawled on the bed atop the shirt and slacks. Carlos deposited the annoyed animal on the floor. Umba yowled, jumped back onto the bed, and began pushing against his master, purring with an arched back.

Carlos ignored the display and donned slacks, shirt, socks, and shoes. Then he lifted the cat above his head and let his arms drop in free fall to the pillow. The cat scooted from the room. Carlos went to a tall bureau where he had a better view of Maria's bedroom window. The lights were off, but when she returned from the bathroom with a towel, she was visible.

"Sweet Maria!" Carlos muttered. "You need a lecture on the risks of parading in front of uncovered windows. I have to talk to you, girl. Modesty confers safety. For both of us."

He sighed, grabbed his watch and wallet, and turned his mind to what he'd have to cover with Antoinette Marino. There was plenty worth discussing, and he wanted his recommendation for or against employment to be based on fact, on a fair evaluation.

The cat meowed from the hallway as Carlos fished a handkerchief from the top drawer of a dresser. A photo collage on the wall caught his eye. The top photo was of last year's girlfriend, who'd dumped him, saying he lacked the ability to commit. Sour grapes, he thought, but maybe not totally off base.

His ex-girlfriend looked like Antoinette Marino. Maybe dinner could be both job-related and personal. If it was time to settle down, he had to seriously consider prospective mates. He winced. Was pairing supposed to work in such a cold, analytical fashion? What happened to the bolt out of the blue where one encountered one's soul mate?

He headed for the kitchen. Halfway there, Umba grabbed hold of his left leg and wailed anew. "Okay, okay. You get fed before I leave. Get your claws out before I pull your tail and rub your fur the wrong way."

He filled Umba's bowl, all the while holding the anxious animal at bay with his leg. Even before the pouring operation was complete, Umba muscled his way into the food bowl, eating as though he'd been left untended for days.

He'd ask Ms. Marino how she felt about animals. Attitude about cats and dogs was a required topic, since Cybernetic used animals in its research. They followed every state and federal regulation and guidelines for the humane care and use of animals. Not that those facts mattered to an activist with an agenda, but he certainly didn't want to let said activist into Cybernetic.

"Perhaps you'd enjoy it more if you ate it slowly. And perhaps if you had more manners, women would like you better. Be a shame to get rid of you because a future Mrs. Oreta finds you objectionable," Carlos intoned solemnly. Umba continued eating in his hurried fashion, quite oblivious to his master's goodbye and departure.

Maria was rolling a garbage can toward the curb when he emerged. "Hi, Carlos. Big date tonight?" she said, smiling.

"Just some dining. Strictly business," he said.

"I'll bet." She scanned his slacks and polo shirt. "Does what you're wearing qualify as a business suit?"

"This is business casual. By the way, Miss Maria, learn to keep your shades down when you strip." Carlos looked her over appreciatively.

She placed her hands on her hips. "What's the matter, Mr. Carlos? Don't you like what you see? Or is it too much for you to handle?"

Carlos smiled. "I like it just fine, but not everyone in this neighborhood is as noble, pure, and safe as I am. I'd strongly recommend using the shades. *Buenos noches*, Maria." He settled into his crimson Dodge convertible.

"We'll discuss this some more, neighbor," Maria said. "As well as that security article. I've found a good market." She waved him off.

Carlos smiled and pulled away from the curb. A half block from his apartment, he noted an unfamiliar, dark sedan. A driver with a baseball cap pulled low slouched in the driver's seat. The man sat up and glanced quickly before turning away. Carlos didn't recognize the vehicle as belonging to any of his neighbors and didn't expect visitors to lurk in parked cars. He noted the color, make, and model.

19 /DINNER

Carlos hit the freeway, fighting the California haze and setting sun in his windshield en route to Mathilda's Levee. Thirty minutes later, he pulled into the lot to find Antoinette Marino in a cream-colored blouse and dark skirt leaning against her small car. She looked even better than her black-and-white photo. Sunlight glistened off large gold earrings that drew attention to a classic Mediterranean face, oval and olive-skinned with a smooth complexion and suspicious brown eyes.

The security man nosed into an open space, got out, and walked to her, smiling. "Ms. Marino, I'm Carlos Oreta. Thanks for seeing me so promptly."

Andy studied his face for a beat before taking his offered hand. "Good to meet you, Mr. Oreta. I'm very interested in the job, and Cybernetic seems like a good place to work. I'd like to get started as soon as possible if Dr. Valois chooses me."

"Please call me Carlos."

"All right. My friends and associates call me Andy."

"Andy? Interesting."

"Well, it wasn't that my parents wanted a boy. They already had a son, and in fact it was my brother who stuck me with the nickname."

Carlos nodded and led the way up the plank steps to the restaurant deck. He held the door open, and they entered. "I've eaten here. Good atmosphere and great food. The blackened redfish is their specialty."

The hostess said their table would be ready in fifteen minutes, so they settled on stools in the Jolly Roger Bar. They spoke in low voices over crowd buzz and a country song from a neon jukebox.

"Your background makes you a good fit for the Valois project," Carlos said. "The army and CIA experience qualifies you for high security, defense-related work."

"I hope so."

"This is a routine check. Two applicants for a related project several years ago had excellent science backgrounds. But we found minor flaws that we knew would make the Department of Defense nervous. Couldn't hire them."

"Minor flaws?"

Carlos lowered his voice. "Anti-war protests, relatives with ties to foreign corporations with interests in the same area as the DOD project, unaccounted-for time, stuff like that."

A long-haired brunette in a short skirt came up behind them. "Carlos, how are you? You've been kind of quiet lately. Haven't seen you in any of the usual spots. What's happening?"

Carlos rotated the bar stool and smiled. "Carol! Good to see you." He introduced the women, identifying Carol Sands as an old friend and Andy Marino as a new one. The women exchanged appraising looks and shook hands. "Did you get that job?" he asked.

"Yes, I'm a full-time travel agent now. Come and see me, and we'll plan your next vacation. Something for two, perhaps." Carol nodded toward Andy.

Carol slid a business card onto the bar before picking up her drink. She raised her glass toward Carlos and smiled as she left. "Keep in touch."

"Sorry about that," Carlos said, feeling embarrassed. "Carol worked for a lawyer Cybernetic hired as a consultant. I suspect the law office was too staid for her. She wanted contact with people other than businessmen in trouble, and I put her onto the travel agency. The travel business may be a good choice."

"She seemed nice," Andy said as if it were a question. "Obviously grateful for your help."

The hostess arrived and led them to an alcove table that viewed the beach. The setting sun splashed orange over the white sand where late sunbathers were packing up. In the distance, surfers danced over blue-green waves.

"Great view," Andy said before turning to the menu. Still scanning, she asked in a hushed tone. "So, what aspects of my background need review? The job history section of my resume was accurate."

"Why exactly did you leave the CIA? They gave you a good recommendation, and you seemed to be doing well."

Andy waited until the waiter took their order and then said, "It was time to try something different, a new environment."

Carlos studied Andy's face. "That was all there was to it?"

Andy seemed to be ordering her thoughts. She closed her eyes, bit her lip, and then rushed her story. "I had a question about a file that I needed help on from my boss, but our relationship was troubled. The source of the trouble was sex—his demands, my refusal. I'm no stranger to sexual harassment. I guess the first time I had a real problem was when I had to fight off a lecherous prof in college."

Carlos leaned closer. "What happened?"

"I naively accepted his invite for extra credit in his lair, where he turned every remark to sex. And he kept touching. When he took a break and came back in his lounging pajamas, I wised up, kneed him in the groin, and left."

"I was asking about the CIA."

Andy sipped water as the waiter delivered a relish tray, rolls, and butter. "Right. My CIA boss was subtler, but his objective was the same. He wanted to sleep with me."

"So, what did you do about needing your boss's help?"

Andy sat back as the waiter served two salads and refilled their water glasses. On the deck outside their window, the hostess seated a lone man in big sunglasses. He looked briefly at Carlos and Andy before studying the menu.

"He gave me what I needed," she said, "a security upgrade to check a file with some information about my brother's death." Andy buttered a roll and stabbed an olive.

"We are aware of the Nicaragua file."

"It was no big deal, just curiosity."

Their entrees arrived. Both had chosen the blackened redfish with wild rice. Carlos tasted the fish and said, "As good as I remember. What did you learn from the file?"

"The army account suggested a friendly force was sent into an unforeseen ambush," Andy said. "There was no explanation of how that happened."

"Your interpretation?"

"Interpretation? An unfortunate accident. It was a chaotic situation. My brother's last letter indicated such. He'd even had to correct reports that misstated rebel objectives and practices."

"You were close to your brother?"

"Yes. He visited me in college even while he was in training for the Central America operation. We would take long campus walks and talk, mostly about the future, rarely about the past. Tony wouldn't say much about his army assignment, but when he was leaving Fort Bragg for Nicaragua, he called to tell me. The Army never explained why it became his final destination."

Carlos studied the woman. "Why did you keep returning to the file?"

"Really just curiosity. The army never fully explained the exact circumstances of my brother's death. I kept expecting I'd find something."

Carlos processed that for several seconds. "Did your boss have anything to say?"

"He told me to drop the whole thing and find a social outlet for my pent-up emotions."

"Like what?"

Andy took a bite of fish. "He said I needed to be friendlier."

"What did he mean?" asked Carlos, between forkfuls of rice.

"Are you sure you want to hear this?"

"Just give me enough to convince my boss your move was justified."

"He said, 'Have dinner with me, share some social time, use your assets.' He'd slithered next to me on his office sofa and touched my thigh. I decided that wasn't appropriate. I believe my exact words were, 'Excuse me, Mr. Caro, but you can take your invitation and shove it up your ass.' I slapped him hard across the face and knocked his glasses off."

"So, you resigned?"

"Correct. I walked out the door, slamming it."

"Quite a story. How do you feel about the incident now?"

"To be honest, I still hate the bastard."

They finished their entrées and ordered dessert. Carlos steered the conversation back to the issue of what Andy felt about her brother's death. "You still haven't gotten a good explanation of the ambush, right?"

Andy touched an index finger to her lips. She brushed hair from her eyes, leaned forward, and blinked. "I've let it go. Taguro, the man Tony referred to in the last letter, may have been the target. Tony's description of the man did not quite match what was in the CIA folder, but that was probably just a matter of perspective. Regardless of what happened and why, Tony is still a hero in my eyes."

Coffee and fried ice cream appeared. Carlos pressed. "Any thoughts about why they were ambushed in what was supposed to be a safe zone?"

"Probably just faulty intelligence."

"And that's where you left it?"

"Yes. Not that it makes much difference. Nothing will bring him back."

"And how do you feel about working on a Department of Defense project?"

"I'd love to do that. There are many fine men and women in the army who depend on the progress from DOD research to protect their lives. I was in the Army and I'd be proud to work on such a project."

Carlos asked about what Andy had been doing since leaving her CIA job. She described her trip to China to a technical fair, and her unsuccessful efforts of find a science job with a Chinese company. That caught Carlos's attention, and he had a lot of questions about names and locations of her search. She had ready answers that accounted for her visit and the unsuccessful search for employment."

"Was this your first visit to China?" Carlos asked.

"It was, so I spent some time just sightseeing. Also found some good restaurants."

After ten minutes of back and forth, Carlos was mostly satisfied with her trip abroad. He would check on the companies she's mentioned.

At the end, it was Andy's turn to ask a question. "I understand that this kind of security review is usual for Cybernetic. Do you handle all of them?"

Carlos's voice was low enough to keep the conversation only at their table. "Your check is related to the job for which you are applying. Dr. Valois's project is funded by a government agency. Other labs and projects do not warrant as much concern."

"So, the Valois project is your bailiwick?"

Carlos hesitated. "To some extent."

"And I might see more of you if I get this job."

"Maybe. I like to keep an eye on things, Andy. In the security field, one works to avoid having anything exciting happen. Most of my time is spent on routine checking of paperwork and how our employees follow security procedures. If you keep the routine from going amiss, you avoid the big news items like break-ins, theft of company property, and unexpected behavior."

"Unexpected behavior? You mean like someone going berserk? I thought your careful pre-hire screens would minimize that risk."

"Well, in general, that's true. But people change. Circumstances arise. So, besides being careful at hiring time, we keep our eyes open." Carlos signed the charge slip, and they rose. He took Andy's arm as they left the restaurant, and they walked into the warm night air and a buzz of insects. Carlos stopped and studied a sedan sitting in the row near the road, thinking he'd seen that car twice already this evening.

"What's wrong?" Andy asked.

He quickly recovered and said, "Nothing. Thought I saw a neighbor's car."

Andy glanced toward the empty car and shrugged. "You looked as if you saw something suspicious."

Carlos shrugged.

"What kind of neighborhood do you live in?" Andy asked.

"Sedate. A schoolteacher, a civil servant, a banker. The only one slightly out of the ordinary is my next-door neighbor, a journalist who used to work for an escort service."

"Sounds dull except for the last."

"Dull is fine."

"So, when can I expect a decision on the tech job?" Andy asked as they reached her car.

"Not my call, but I'm sure you will hear very soon."

She thanked him for the dinner and declined his offer to escort her home. With a wave, she slipped into her car. Carlos watched her back out and drive away. He turned and went to check the tag on the car he'd spotted. It was the same sedan he'd seen near his house.

He went to his car mulling things over. Antoinette Marino had been candid about the men who'd harassed her, the discrimination she'd faced as a woman, and her interest in her brother's death. Her time in China needed checking, but Carlos couldn't find any reason to deny her clearance.

By the time he parked in front of his house, he'd come up with a sufficient list of good reasons to clear Antoinette Marino for work at Cybernetic Implementation. He would hit the sack with a clear conscience. He went inside without noticing the gray sedan from the restaurant pull into a spot across the street.

Hours later, Morgan and Yingyi drove in silence to the Valois neighborhood. Morgan shut off the car lights before nearing the house where a single light glowed. Adjacent houses were dark.

"How long will it take you to put on that tap?" Morgan said.

"Five minutes. Less, if there's an outside test jack." Yingyi rearranged items in a small, black case the size and shape of an MD's bag. "How did the restaurant interview go?"

"Smooth, as far as I could tell. A lot of smiling at the end. The fact that there was an interview suggests that planting her file into the HR Department was successful," Morgan said.

"Even if our contact misspelled the last name in the database."

Morgan shrugged. "She was nervous. At least she used the HR stamp and got it on Valois's desk."

"We need results, not mistakes, in service of the mother country." Yingyi zipped his tool bag closed.

Morgan scanned the area on both sides of the street. The light in the Valois house went out. "Give them a few minutes more. I haven't noticed any dogs here, have you?"

"There's a German shepherd three houses away, but they put the dog inside after dark. It's quiet after eleven."

In the Valois house, Kayten placed a light blanket over Peter Valois. The scientist had fallen asleep reading in a living room chair; not an unusual occurrence. The android turned out the lamp and stood motionless for several minutes. He'd noted the arrival of the car and considered its significance.

The presence of the car activated deep levels of programming dating back to the earliest moments of Kayten's existence, directives that defined his true purpose in the Valois home. He was there, not primarily as a house servant or research tool, but for security. Cybernetic Implementation wanted to protect both its intellectual property and its scientist from unnamed threats. Protecting Dr. Valois, and by extension, his family, was in accord with normal biosynthetic precepts—humans came first. But the android had to weigh this obligation with securing company property, some of which Valois kept in his workroom.

As far as Peter Valois knew, he was just field-testing the ultimate domestic robot. He wasn't aware of any security directives. This minor deception disturbed the android, and biosynthetic intelligence experts might even have traced some of the Kayten's personality quirks to the subtle conflict that secrecy imposed. Up to now, however, there had been no occasion for his security role to take precedence.

The car was hardly a basis for alarm, but the fact that he had not heard a car door open and close after the motor was shut off left an unanswered question in Kayten's mind. His memory banks suggested the possibility that this was a case of "parking," a human social practice that was a part of normal inter-gender relationships. This much he had gleamed from conversations with Dan. Kayten knew of no one in this neighborhood, other than Dan, who was likely to engage in "parking." He decided to extend the scope of his usual evening security check of doors and windows to include the car.

He went to the window and looked out at the questionable car. The robot could not read the license plate, which was in heavy shadows. Scanning with his infrared vision, Kayten observed one person in the driver's seat. His sound sensors detected a small noise on the north side of the house, perhaps another person on foot.

The robot hesitated as he weighed several courses of action. He considered alerting Dr. Valois, who was sleeping soundly. Waking the doctor might cause harm, something incompatible with his programming. There was a second choice: to disobey Peter Valois's command not to leave the house. Satisfied that disobedience was the way to protect the family, Kayten checked Dr. Valois again and then moved to the rear door.

He stopped to scan the rear lawn and patio, hesitant again to violate a direct human order not to go outside without permission. But he needed more information. Inaction would allow the threat to exist or grow greater.

Satisfied with the decision's logical consistency, Kayten went out the back door and listened for noise near the house. He heard something, perhaps human footsteps moving away, but the undulating cacophony of insect sounds assaulted his auditory sensors and obscured the sound. The heavy smell of rotting ginkgo seeds filled his chemical sensors as he avoided small bushes, a garden hose, and a soccer ball. He rounded the side of the house and saw no one. A car door opened and closed. He made his way through two yards, avoiding a wagon, a tricycle, and a sandbox, and turned between two garages toward the street. The parked car was only a house away.

Kayten's observation and analysis was interrupted. As a nearby heat pump pulsed to life, a dark shape came hurdling toward Kayten. The growling German shepherd did not give the impression that it could be swayed by human speech. It slowed as if to assess the nature of its foe.

Kayten reduced power levels to minimum and dissipated his surface heat, becoming a motionless, aberrant sculpture in a residential museum. The dog held his position, perhaps considering the chameleon behavior of his quarry. He crept closer to the apparently inanimate intruder, thoroughly sniffed, and backed away.

But a second thought seemed to grip the animal, and he returned, raised a leg, and urinated. Apparently satisfied that there was no threat and that he'd proven his dominance, the canine woofed and left.

Kayten held his pose as he recorded the car, its license plate, and its occupants. The dog, perhaps hearing subtle sounds of mechanical switches, returned once and started to again lift its rear leg, but Kayten, having been marked quite sufficiently for one outing, emitted a high-pitched tone that sent the discomfited dog off with a whimper.

Still statue-like, Kayten watched the vehicle drive away with lights off. The dog had disappeared, so Kayten went to where the car had been. He examined and recorded the faint impressions left in a wet spot near the curb. Satisfied that he had acquired all possible information, Kayten returned to the rear door of the Valois house and entered.

The empty living room chair contained only a rumpled blanket, and Kayten wondered if Dr. Valois had made any attempt to find him. He decided the doctor had just gotten up and gone to bed.

The android opened a wall cabinet near the fireplace and placed an index finger into a socket. The panel was a control station for a sophisticated security system that Dr. Valois had designed. Kayten confirmed that the adult Valois were in the rear master bedroom and that Dan Valois was in the front bedroom. All doors were locked, and the Valois cat was inside. Satisfied, Kayten joined the cat in the laundry room and deodorized his leg.

As she got ready for bed, Andy considered her interaction with Carlos Ortega. The guy was sharp but seemed to accept her account of the China trip. Carlos's admission that he would have further interest in the Valois project meant he could be a problem. He would bear watching. Any signs that he was interfering with the operation would be dealt with. If she wasn't cleared, she'd have to go to plan B.

20 /CRISIS

Pam Valois intended to delay dinner until her son got home but gave up waiting when Dan didn't show: an event not unusual in his new lifestyle. Kayten set tray tables in the den, a spacious room whose sliding glass door opened onto a multicolored flagstone patio, bordered by a cactus garden. The setting sun lit the scene and colored horizon clouds orange and pink. The scene should have been soothing and serene.

Pam and Peter watched the evening news without saying much, leaving gloomy silence despite the TV babble. After they finished eating, Kayten removed dishes and served coffee and a cheese plate. Peter gazed at walnut paneling while the final news story dealing with the war on drugs aired.

Despite his conviction that Pam was acting on irrational maternal panic, Peter finally conceded she should call the local drug abuse agency, provided she didn't give her name. He feared being the butt of gossip among friends and coworkers. Now he learned that she'd already made the call.

Peter punched off the TV. "So, what did they say again?"

"First step is patient evaluation." Pam rose and went to a side table and rearranged flowers before continuing. "They want to see Dan. To find out what he's using and how much."

"Then what?"

"They treat only patients who voluntarily seek their services. If Dan refuses to deal with the agency, then we have to take a different approach."

Peter squeezed the chair arm and leaned forward.

"An intervention followed by inpatient rehabilitation," Pam said. "As parents of a minor we can admit him, willing or not, to such a facility."

Peter sat back and closed his eyes. "Forcing Dan doesn't bode well."

"We don't know how Dan will react," Pam said in a soft voice.

"What's the success rate for the uncooperative patient?"

Pam went to the patio door to let the cat in. "Each case is different. Dan has to want to change. For some patients, that comes only when they hit bottom. We've always protected our son, so he doesn't feel real consequences of his behavior."

"Dan has to get worse before he can get better?" Peter slapped his hand on the armrest.

Pam jumped at the sound and turned to face her husband. "Dan will face reality when he is confronted. He's smart. He'll get the message."

Kayten stepped into the den and asked if they needed anything. Peter shook his head and sat back, eyes closed. The sun slipped below the horizon and the evening concert of crickets and tree frogs began. "What are we supposed to do?"

"Learn what's going on with Dan and be supportive. This disease affects both the patient and his family."

"You mean we're to blame for Dan's problem?"

"Calm down. Not at all. Families often feel guilt. That's why they encourage family counseling. We should go in together and talk to them."

Peter turned red, opened his mouth, and then closed it. He let half a minute pass before he took a deep breath and said, "You're right. I have to get my priorities straight. There's no reason to be angry. I just hope we're not overreacting."

"Overreacting? I don't think so. The counselor said that Dan's symptoms mean he's into drugs, something that doesn't go away without help. Dan is sick and needs treatment." Pam went to the sideboard and poured two glasses of Benedictine. She carried one to her husband.

Peter eyed the offering before accepting the glass. "Thank you." He sipped. "What about Dan and alcohol?"

"They asked, but I had no answer. I got the feeling that, with drug use, alcohol is usually part of the problem."

"Sounds like it could go either way with Dan."

"Pessimism is natural, but the counselor warned not to imagine only a poor outcome."

"So, we talk to Dan tomorrow and get his reaction to making an appointment. Where is he tonight?"

"It's Friday. Probably at the Y for music. Should be back about midnight."

"I've got some reading to do, and then I'm calling it a night," Peter said. "Since Dan no longer cuts the lawn, I'll have to do that tomorrow morning." He grabbed a magazine and left.

Kayten came in a few minutes later and found Pam still sitting, apparently lost in thought. The android asked if she wanted anything, and Pam lifted her empty glass. Kayten took it and gathered the plates, cups, and Peter's glass. Pam picked up the pile of pamphlets on addiction and began to read.

When the phone rang at ten forty-five, Pam had moved to the living room with a book. She took the call on the first ring and listened, saying little. She hung up and went to the master bedroom.

Peter sat with a pile of reprints. He looked up immediately and apparently read the bad news on his wife's face. "What's wrong?"

"That was the desk attendant at the YMCA. They just asked Dan to leave. He was drunk."

"Where is he? Let's go get him."

"I don't know where he went."

"We have to do something. He really needs a straightening out, that damn kid. I'll kick his butt."

"Calm down. At least he doesn't have a car."

"How do we know he doesn't? I should have sat him down and

talked to him before." Peter rummaged in a dresser drawer for his wallet. He'd managed to tie his sneakers when the phone rang again.

Neither Pam nor Peter moved. On the third ring, Pam picked up.

She listened for half a minute. "We'll get him. Thank you for calling." She put the phone down and said, "That was Megan O'Rourke. She said he's downtown in front of Jordan's. She'll try to keep him there until we arrive."

Megan sat next to Dan on a step in front of a closed retail store. He was moaning and repeating, "I feel like shit."

"Hey. Take it easy, Dan. You'll survive."

"Yeah, right. Just lemme alone. I'm fine." Dan spat the words in a slur.

"Whoa. Nice talk from someone who just puked all over himself." Megan handed him another paper towel. "Keep wiping. Why do you do this, Dan?"

"Why not? Life's a sock... I mean a crock. It sucks."

"You don't mean that."

"I'm crap. Like the old man says. Specs me ta be like him," Dan croaked. He wiped his damp forehead with his sleeve. "Ya know, smart. What the fuh? I wanna good time."

"Dude, do you hear yourself? Those sorry excuses are your bag, not your father's. Your self-assessment sucks. Maybe you can't see that on your own. That's cool. Get help."

"Yeah, sure. Hafta barf." Dan scrambled bent over to a nearby parking lot.

Megan turned her head as he vomited. When he staggered back in her direction, she interpreted it as a positive sign.

Peter grabbed the car keys with his mind awhirl as it bounced from fear to concern to anger. Kayten met them in the hallway. "Do you need my assistance, sir?"

"Yes. We have to go pick up Dan. You may have to make a medical evaluation."

Kayten hesitated as if performing a difficult calculation. "I could check on Dan's condition when he returns, sir. I understand that his problem is an excessive ingestion of ethanol. That should not put him in any immediate danger, and thus my assistance at his location should not be needed. I will stay here, sir."

It was only later when his attention was not diverted by the crisis that it occurred to Peter that Kayten's refusal to obey his command was unusual. Even his definitive statement of intent at the end was out of character—a positive decision rather than his usual suggestion of an alternate course of action. He and Pam lurched from the driveway.

Thirty minutes later the car returned. Pam got out first and opened the rear door. Dan emerged, using the door to steady himself.

Peter rounded the car. "Get into the house and go to bed. We'll talk tomorrow."

Pam had insisted he postpone any conversation while the patient was under the influence. Kayten waited inside the front door. When Dan stumbled, Kayten grabbed the boy's arm and kept him from falling. In the process, he leaned close to Dan's face.

Voice thick, Dan said. "Hafta go to bed."

"We have things to discuss tomorrow, young man," Peter said. "Plan on it." He slammed the door. Pam glared.

"Drop those clothes in the bathroom," she said.

Peter turned to Kayten. "Medical assessment?"

"I can base my assessment only on evidence of Dan's speech, motor performance, breath, and his blood pressure and pulse. Pressure and pulse are elevated somewhat. Moderate ethanol intoxication could account for the observed clinical picture. He seems to be in no danger."

"You're sure he's basically all right?" Peter asked.

"Probability of correct assessment exceeds point nine nine, sir. Dan is in a neural-depressed state, but general central nervous system parameters are acceptable. All cardiovascular signs are good. Even after sleep, he will show effects. I believe the term is 'hangover.'"

Peter nodded. "That is the term. You'd better station yourself near Dan's room to keep an eye on things."

Pam and Peter, nerves too jangled to consider sleep, went into the living room. They were silent while the grandfather clock announced the hour.

Finally, Pam said, "We need professional help. Forget about how this will look to friends, neighbors, coworkers, whoever. Dan has a problem. Can we stop keeping our heads in the sand?"

Peter nodded. "Yes, he needs help, but I don't have much faith in rehabilitation. Jack's boy went to rehab. He was clean for only a few weeks after he got back. Now he's dropped out of school, living on his own, and using regularly. Carl's daughter is totally out of control. She's been through two rehabs and has been busted for dealing. At Dan's age, there is not much reason for optimism."

"But there are successes, Peter. Gerry's nephew made it. And we really have no choice. We'll get him into a program."

"Well, we can't do it tonight." Peter took his wife's hand and led her toward the bedroom. "Try to get some rest. I'm going to sit for a while and think. I don't know what we've done wrong, but we've lost contact with that kid."

"We'll make some phone calls tomorrow, right? We need treatment, too. I didn't tell you because I knew you wouldn't approve, but I went to an Al-Anon meeting on Monday. It helped."

PART 4
SOLUTIONS

Employers and business leaders need people, who can think for themselves—who can take initiative and be the solution to problems.

- STEPHEN COVEY

21 /TWO SCHEMES

PETER WENT TO THE BAR AND POURED ABOUT AN INCH OF mahogany liquid. In his favorite chair, he found himself thinking about the time he and Dan had gone on a camping trip when the boy was about nine.

Daylight had begun to fade, and the temperature had dropped by the time they found the campsite. Together they managed to erect a small tent in a light rain. The meal of beans and franks tasted great, and the tent kept them warm and dry. Afterwards, they played the card game radio rummy for an hour before turning in. The next day, sunny and warm, they'd spent fishing, caught half a dozen bass, and had a wonderful time.

Peter regretted there weren't more great father-son times in recent years. His son was no academic performer, at least not of late, but had accomplishments. Dan sang in the choir for school concerts. Not as a section leader, but as a strong voice. Dan competed in high school track, not a super athlete but a swift runner. He'd contributed to several exciting wins, including a victory of the Seneca High team over a longtime rival. After the meet, the Valois family had gone out to dinner to celebrate.

Now Dan Valois had dropped out of choir and track, and the good times seemed long ago. What had gone wrong? Peter wiped his wet cheeks.

Dan's problem went back to his sophomore year. He'd entered the grade with an excellent academic record, motivation, and work ethic. He talked about a medical career. Peter had pushed all kinds of opportunities that required hard work, but yielded fulfillment, at least to his way of thinking.

Then something changed. The homework Dan brought home went from plenty to hardly any. That seemed strange. Pam decided he was doing it in study halls, which never rang true. As far as Peter knew, Dan wasn't passing a single course today, never cracked a book, never worked on a school project. School had become just a place to go during the day to get away from home, to avoid the hassles of dealing with parents.

Peter finished his drink and slowly made his way to bed.

Next morning, Peter sat in the den across from a queasy-looking teenager. Peter had been up for an hour, and Pam had been on the telephone. Together they roused Dan and sent him for a shower. He wasn't interested in breakfast.

"How bad is your drug use, Dan?" Peter asked.

"Everything is under control, Dad."

"Doesn't seem to be. What I see is a mess. You're flunking courses and have dropped all extracurricular activities. You've become a stranger to your mother and me. We don't know where you go, what you do, or who you see."

Peter fought his anger. He'd been coached by Pam to remember this was a disease, and Dan was the patient. He had to stick to the facts. Dan stared straight ahead, his eyes focused on something beyond his father.

"Now you've been kicked out of the Y for drinking," Peter said. "Look at you. You're a mess." Peter knew the last comment did not stick strictly with the facts. He tried to remain analytical, but he wanted to rage.

"Hey, Dad. I'm sorry I am what I am. I can handle it. Just give me some room."

Peter breathed deep and said, "We've made an appointment for you on Tuesday at the Drug and Alcohol Abuse Agency. We'd like you to go. Will you?" Peter hoped he'd made the proper statement of legitimate parental requirements.

Dan seemed surprised and didn't respond at once. Maybe he was mulling over his options and realizing there were no attractive ones. Peter waited.

"All right," Dan said at last. "I'll go. I need to lie down." He left.

Peter wondered what Dan might be thinking. Probably the boy's biggest worry was that his drugs would be confiscated. He probably figured he could play along, and nothing would change. After all, he didn't have a problem. These imaginings saddened, then angered, Peter. This is bull, he thought. Sending Dan to counselors for such a monstrous problem was just bull.

Dan kept the Tuesday appointment. It lasted two hours, and he was walking home when he encountered Megan O'Rourke. She looked her usual, wholesome self in white shorts and a green polo shirt. Her appearance cheered Dan, although he wondered if the meeting was a coincidence. They walked together on a wide sidewalk along a quiet residential street.

"So, how'd it go?" Megan asked, as they passed ranch-style houses with Spanish roofs and big lawns.

"Hey. How did what go?"

"Don't play stupid. The DAA session. Everyone knows what happened Friday night. When your mother let slip to my mom that you had an appointment, the grapevine knew what that meant. So, spill."

"OMG. Like where's my privacy?"

Megan got in front of him. "Remember the old days when you were clean? We knew who the users were, didn't we? Well, the same info network is still in place, and you're on it. What did they say?"

Dan's impulse was to put on a false bravado and bluff his way through the conversation. "The usual bull. I use. My bad. They fix." Then he made the mistake of looking in Megan's eyes, and realized that only the truth would carry with her. He elaborated. "It was two hours of grilling, not very pleasant. They know bullshit when they hear it and don't put up with it. The picture they projected for my future was crappo."

"You didn't expect easy street, did you, hotshot? What goes down next?"

A car cruised past. Dan thought he'd seen it before.

"Uh, hello, Romeo. Still with me?"

"I'm cool. What's next is hard. It's my decision, my choice. Sorta. My parents have a big say in this."

"Dan, I think they mean that you get to choose the pot you stew in. They're not all the same, so you have to pick the best one and stick with it."

"Whose side you on?" Dan sucked in his breath and closed his eyes. "Okay, you're right. I guess the session did what it was supposed to do."

"Well, it's a start. Like it's complicated and a toughie, but other kids have made it. You can, too. And remember, there are friends to help." Megan pulled Dan close and hugged him. "Hang in there, Dan. See ya later."

Dan watched her hurry off. The familiar car passed again. It took him a moment before he recognized it as the same one that had delivered his "gift" of cocaine.

His parents were waiting when he entered the house. He was noncommittal about his DAA session. They didn't press but left, announcing that they had an appointment at Drug and Alcohol Abuse to get the Agency's report. Dan knew that they would recommend outpatient treatment as a start.

Peter and Pam got the report and then spent the next two days mulling things over until they ran out of new thoughts. Both agreed that outpatient treatment was like treading water in a flood. They needed a boat, whatever that was.

"I'll be at Gerry's for bridge," Pam said and left.

An anxious Peter sat in the den clutching a cup of coffee. His head filled with jumbled and chaotic thoughts that morphed into a dread that the situation was out of control. He abhorred not being certain. The report had not been good. In an hour-long session that seemed to deal more with the parents than with the patient, the counselor reported that Dan was into more drugs and using greater quantities than they'd imagined. Alcohol was one of them. The Agency recommended an outpatient treatment but did not rule out an inpatient approach. Dan had waffled about regular visits.

Peter had his own summary: Dan needed help, the help available was probably ineffective, something more had to be done.

Maybe he was wrong to imagine the worst. Or he was being realistic. Dan's self-destructive behavior would not reverse on its own. Hell, if drugs didn't take him down, he might wind up in a car accident. Maybe he'd become suicidal.

He quelled his anger. Drug abuse was a disease, not strictly intentional, and not a judgment on parents. That seemed to let the user off the hook and denied the role of choice in the problem. Peter couldn't swallow the solutions offered by the drug agency. In this age of biosynthetic brains and mind transfer, counseling and group therapy seemed primitive. He suspected those methods were least effective in the young.

As Peter raised the cup, he spied his briefcase. The grandfather clock chimed ten, and the seed of a thought germinated, quickly grew, and bloomed with all the major pieces as the tenth gong sounded. He began pacing. In silence he considered his scheme, plugged in a detail here and there, reanalyzed it, and listed possible defects. For an hour he assumed the role of the critical experimenter, designing a complex protocol.

Twice Kayten entered the room, but did not speak, observing Peter's movements briefly during each visit, and then departing.

Finally, as if the last piece in a jigsaw puzzle had been laid, Peter sat down, muttered "Bloody insane," and closed his eyes.

When Kayten looked for the third time, he found Peter Valois asleep. The android covered him with a nearby blanket and turned off the lights.

22 /THE DOG

ANTOINETTE MARINO SMILED AS SHE MADE HER WAY THROUGH THE corridors of Cybernetic Implementation. The go-ahead for hiring had been given after the dinner with Carlos Oreta. On the day after the interview, Peter Valois had called her with the news, and then had pressured his "girlfriend" Marcia in Personnel to fax the official offer immediately. That was several weeks back.

Valois was happy on two counts, both of which he made clear on her arrival: her qualifications were a fit for the position, and she was immediately available. Valois had expedited her mandatory orientation sessions, including safety and security training. Andy had paid particular attention to the latter. Her interest was, of course, in learning what was in place to prevent theft of company property.

Valois had walked her around to get her employee photo and badge, lab coats, and computer clearances for access to animal rooms and laboratories. He also arranged for her to skip what he called the "totally useless meet everyone" sessions. That was fine with Andy. She wanted to get into the lab as soon as possible.

And she had. Now she was a trusted member of the Valois laboratory. It had all gone without a hitch, although Valois was still having a hard time calling her "Andy."

She emerged from the elevator into the Cybernetic animal area and punched in a combination to open the animal room wing.

Another door gave access to the holding rooms. She donned a lab coat and booties. Wide hallways accommodated large cages moving from the cage wash to the animal quarters. Good airflow swept smells from the rooms that were cleaned daily. The facility had received compliments from United States Department of Agriculture inspectors.

A chorus of yelping and barking greeted her in the dog room. She strolled past the row of large cages, placed neatly along one wall and connected to an automatic watering hose. As she spoke to several of the occupants, wagging tails thumped against the stainless-steel cage sides, establishing a background beat. "It's not quite time for your morning exercise session. You'll be in the runs a bit later." Five of the room's six residents shared a friendly enthusiasm for the human visitor. When she stood in front of the last cage, however, the occupant snarled and lunged, causing the cage to shake and rattle.

"Calm down, Conan," Andy said in a soothing voice. "Be a good dog. No one's going to hurt you."

The dog eyed Andy as she copied a number from his cage tag. "Here you are, guys. A little treat for you before you go for your morning walk." She reached into the pocket of her lab coat and took out some small dog biscuits, depositing one in each food hopper. Even Conan condescended to accept the gift, although he did so growling.

In the hall, a ponytailed man in his forties with a load of pan papers greeted her. "Mornin', Ms. Marino," he said.

"Good morning, Sam. I'll need this dog upstairs at one." She handed him a piece of paper. "And be sure to use a muzzle."

"Yeah, I know that one. He's got a bit of a temper, but we'll take good care of him. I think he's beginning to like me. Maybe the cheddar cheese has something to do with it. I'll be up with him in a transport cage right after lunch."

"Thanks."

Andy returned to the entry hall, removed her booties, and hung up the lab coat. She moved to the elevator and was about to punch the button when Carlos Oreta rounded the corner carrying a clipboard and looking very official in a button-down blue oxford, tan slacks, and matching tie. He smiled and saluted.

Andy returned the salute. Carlos pressed the button on the elevator panel.

"I wanted to thank you for my positive security review," Andy said.

"How do you know my report was positive?" Carlos asked, one eyebrow raised.

"I got the job."

"Perhaps they overrode my strenuous objection."

"Based on?"

"Your feelings about the U.S. Army."

It took a moment for Andy figure out where this remark was coming from. "Well, when I prove unfit for the job, you can gloat. Just what are you looking for in this part of the building, anyway? Rabble-rousing rats? Duplicitous dogs? Or, God forbid, moles."

"I'm scouting for Dr. Valois. He was not in his office, and I thought he might be down here." They entered the elevator. The stainless-steel door closed with a smooth thump.

"Why are you after Dr. Valois? Any problems?"

"Just a routine security interview. I have to schedule a meeting."

Andy studied Carlos's face before she said, "I'll let him know that the police are after him."

The elevator stopped, and Andy stepped off and turned toward the Valois laboratory.

Carlos put his hand out to stop the closing door. "Tell Lisa Macquire that I need to set up a meeting with her, too."

Andy found Peter Valois in the laboratory training a large Irish setter.

"Good dog! Now stay." Peter placed his open hand in front of the dog's face and then walked to the end of the aisle. The dog watched him but stayed put.

"Come, Roverbot, come." The dog trotted over. Peter grinned at Andy. "He's learned his good behavior very well. He can even fetch. I'd say that Lisa's conditioning on this end is perfect and we are ready to use Roverbot for brain recording and deposit. How is Conan?"

"As nasty as ever. Conan's brain file will be a good test for Roverbot.

To see if the biobrain can squelch Conan's bad behavior." Andy put her clipboard on the bench "Do you think you got all the program modifications needed to move from rat to dog?"

"Yes." Not that it was needed, Peter thought. He hoped some lethal abnormality caused the two rat deaths. That would exonerate the recording procedure, modified or not. And clear the off-protocol, after-hours transference procedure he'd done. "Has the blood work come back yet?"

"No. Lisa said it generally takes a day or so."

Andy finished positioning the recording apparatus for a dog as large as Conan. "Looks like everything is set. Have you decided on the best sedative for the canine work?"

"We'll stick with the regular cocktail. All we need is a calm and sleepy dog. Even Conan should be well controlled by the ketamine."

Andy agreed, familiar with the sedative often used in veterinary and human work to initiate anesthesia. It also tended to erase a patient's memory of the procedure. Occasionally, it had an effect on heart rhythm. So, it was Andy's job to monitor cardiovascular parameters during the brain recording.

"By the way, Carlos Oreta is looking for you," Andy said, keeping her tone neutral.

Peter nodded, excused himself, and left. Andy continued with her preparations for the afternoon experiment with their ill-tempered friend, wondering if snooping by Carlos might interfere with what she planned.

After lunch, Lisa wheeled Conan's cage into the lab. Peter helped her ease the sixty-pound, black animal into a sling.

"Take it easy, fella. Everything's fine," Peter said in a calm, even tone.

The dog was not impressed by the soothing words and made several snaps toward Peter's hand. The muzzle served its purpose. His handlers positioned him in the hammock-like sling despite Conan's lack of cooperation. The dog took defeat poorly and howled to remind his human handlers of his wolf brothers. He then focused on his front leg as Lisa shaved an area, inserted a butterfly needle in a vein, and taped it in place. The injection of several cc of a cocktail with ketamine and an anti-anxiety drug relaxed Conan visibly as Andy positioned the electrocardiogram leads.

"I need a little blood, Conan. Just to check that you are doing fine." Lisa collected her sample from the line and then attached a blood pressure transducer. She injected the blood into the blood gas analyzer and, seconds later, announced that oxygen, carbon dioxide, and pH were normal.

"By the way, Lisa, Carlos Oreta is after you for a meeting." Andy made a notation on the chart paper. "What does he do in his security reviews anyway?"

"He checks to see we are following protocols to protect hardware and software," Lisa said and tossed a stray lock of strawberry blond hair behind her shoulder.

Peter positioned the dog's head in the scanning restraint. "Blood pressure and heart rate are stable. Start scanning."

Andy threw a switch on the control panel to begin the recording unit's defined movements over the canine skull. From the hallway came the rattle of an animal cage being rolled to the elevator as a holographic image of Conan's brain began to emerge next to the computer. The density increased as the scanning proceeded.

"With the new program changes, I estimate this should take about forty minutes. We can record some of Roverbot's pre-transfer characteristics in the meantime as we have him fetch and sit." Peter got up off his stool and took a red stick to the end of the aisle and sequestered it under one of several mats on the floor.

"Come, Roverbot." The Irish setter rose from where he had been lying in the corner and trotted to Peter. He showed the dog a duplicate of the stick and gave his commands, "Find. Bring."

The biosynthetic dog began a search in the vicinity of the mats, quickly found the hidden stick, extracted it from under the mat, and returned with it. Roverbot released his catch, then sat and raised his right paw.

"Well, where did you learn that?" Peter shook the dog's paw and patted him on the head. "Good dog."

"Roverbot has been watching me work with several of the friendly pooches. He has seen the response that a paw shake gets out of me." Lisa smiled with pride.

Conan seemed to be sleeping peacefully while the scanner continued its precise movements, forming a complete holographic image of the dog's brain on the display screen.

"Dr. Valois, look at this," Andy said, pointing to an empty area perhaps a centimeter in diameter, near the optic chiasma. "Looks like our friend here has something he shouldn't. We'll have to check the disk file to see what the boundary readings are, but this area isn't being read as functioning neurons. It may be a nonneural tumor. Did any hint of this show up on the CAT scan?"

Lisa came over to look. "The latest CAT scan on Conan was done three months ago, when he arrived from the breeding laboratory. I don't remember anything suspicious."

"Well, we may have missed it with a low-resolution scan," Peter said. "Won't know what it is without a necropsy."

"Maybe we should start with another dog, one without any anomaly in its brain scan," Lisa said.

Peter did not answer immediately. He finally said, "No. Another opportunity to do the last experiment first. Our work is aimed at fixing behavioral abnormalities. Conan has exactly what I'm looking for: a behavior that departs from the social norm. Proceed with the protocol. This will provide information on how the biosynthetic brain handles an abnormality.

When the computer screen indicated that scanning was complete, Peter helped Lisa remove Conan from the sling and place him in his transport cage. The black dog yawned, lay down with his head between his paws, and closed his eyes. Peter summoned Roverbot and positioned the dog in the scanner restraint. "No movement, Roverbot. Duration forty-two minutes. Begin transfer."

Andy asked, "What if the biosynthetic controls are inadequate to control Conan, Peter? Maybe we should do some restraining. Look, Roverbot's eyes seem to be widening."

Peter examined the dog's eyes, not sure that any disturbance in the biosynthetic brain would be reflected in changes of the orbit musculature of a manufactured dog. "You're imagining things. I have full confidence in the power of a biosynthetic brain, and we don't want to impose new and untested environmental conditions on Roverbot. We need to see his reactions under exactly the same conditions as his training."

The transfer continued without any further changes in the robot, at least as far as Peter could discern. The transfer of Conan's brain file into Roverbot was completed without incident.

Peter removed the scanner restraint and put his hand on Roverbot's neck. "Resume activity, Roverbot." The android looked at Peter with a questioning expression in his brown eyes. "Let's try some simple tasks. Would you man the camera, Andy?"

"Let Lisa handle the camera, Peter. She has a steadier hand. I'll take over at the computer keyboard."

Peter nodded and walked to the end of the laboratory aisle. He then turned and looked at the android canine. "Come, Roverbot." Roverbot stared at Peter. The command was repeated in a slightly louder voice. Still, the android did not move. Suddenly, Roverbot lay down on the floor, placed his head between his forepaws, and looked at the scientist.

"Well, that is certainly aberrant behavior." Lisa focused the camera on Roverbot in his new position.

"Not unexpected," Peter said, crouching down so that he was closer to the dog's eye level. He motioned with his hand for the android to come to him. Roverbot looked, lifted his head, and waited several long seconds before responding. He slinked to Peter who patted him on the head.

"Good boy, Roverbot. Very good. Let's try that again. Stay."

Peter walked to the other end of the aisle, turned, and said, "Come, Roverbot."

Again, the animal hesitated, seeming to evaluate the situation carefully before closing the distance. He sat stiffly.

"Well, something has changed in his response pattern," Peter said. "We'll put him through the rest of the command test."

Roverbot was subjected to a battery of simple behavior tests, involving fetching, sitting, lying down, and carrying. Their execution required both voice and sign recognition. Although the android managed to complete all but a few of the familiar tasks, he did so with hesitation and at a much slower pace than he had before the brain transfer. Peter's frowned, a puzzled expression on his face. "There seems to be a slowed processing time, at times almost a struggle going on within Roverbot."

"But, wow!" Lisa said. "Consider the burden the android carries. His consciousness has just received all the information and history of another creature. He is being forced to process that new information and integrate it."

"We certainly had no hint of a delayed processing or a struggle from the rat work." Andy sounded worried but hopeful.

Peter spoke. "True, but we're dealing with a much larger and more complex brain. I want you two to put Roverbot through the discrimination tests, and we'll repeat the same thing tomorrow morning to see if he needs time to process things. We'll record Roverbot late today to have something to compare with his previous file."

"At least he's not biting us," Lisa remarked as she led Roverbot into the adjacent small holding room. Peter watched them leave the laboratory and stood for a while holding his chin.

"Do you want me to shut down the program and bring the disk over to you?"

"That would violate our sacred security procedures with the software, Andy. I'll take care of it. You complete the notebooks for today's experiment and record Roverbot at the end of the day. That will free up Lisa to get some more work done on the rat report." Looking distracted, Peter went through the shutdown procedure and removed the storage device from the PC.

In a luxurious apartment atop a Beijing skyscraper, Chairman Zheng of Xianxingzhe completed his exercise routine and bathed. He allowed the girl to towel him off and donned a light robe. His quarters were traditional in design and decoration, including a corner shrine. Ancient swords guarded one wall. Paintings of The Great Wall and landscapes were on another. The atmosphere was one of peace and order.

Zheng took pride in his disciplined exercise and disciplined life. Physical exertions focused his mind. He analyzed his business problem. At his desk he re-read a terse report on the Cybernetic operation. The drug-using son could be used to force the American scientist to comply. Zheng ran through the implications. The problem was really very simple. His company needed certain knowledge to advance and compete effectively. They had not succeeded in developing that knowledge. Thus, it had to be acquired. Regardless of the means.

Marino had infiltrated Cybernetic and reported the scientist himself could not be taken without raising a storm. She said he lacked usual weaknesses. No mistress, no unsavory sexual proclivity, no gambling. The woman was preparing to exploit Valois's weakness, his addicted son. She wanted to know if he, Zheng, had the testicles to risk such an approach. Her words infuriated him. He had already risked murder. What could require more testicles?

With the question settled, he sat and composed an encrypted message for his personal assistant in California. It confirmed receipt of the update. It authorized the plan for getting hold of the missing components. It emphasized that no one must ever connect Xianxingzhe Group with the theft. Any such tie would have to be severed.

23 /CONAN

Peter returned to Cybernetic that evening after seven p.m. and, after greeting a guard who was used to the evening visits, went to the animal holding room adjacent to his laboratory. There he retrieved Conan and wheeled the cage into the lab, all the while speaking firmly to the animal, assuring him that everything was all right. The dog growled, but his heart didn't seem to be in it. Peter slipped on a muzzle and wrestled Conan into the support sling.

Peter shaved the previously unused forepaw. Probably because he'd had it done before, Conan tolerated the procedure and took an interest in the prep, including administration of the pre-scan sedative. Peter adjusted the scanning helmet, checked blood pressure, and began the reverse scan, dumping the Roverbot-conditioned Conan file back into the big dog.

A giddy excitement gripped him. This was the key experiment to test if the bionet could modify a large brain file to change Conan's behavior. When an android received an animal brain, the bionet remained the dominant consciousness—dominance was ensured by keeping the animal file in a separate location. Robotic principles required that any brain file be molded toward "normal" behavior for the species in question. Any such molding should be obvious in Conan.

Physically, the transfer did not have marked effects on Conan, although his heart rate was briefly irregular. When the modified file had been downloaded, Peter removed Conan's muzzle and put him back into the cage. He observed the dog off and on for the hour it might take for integration. The dog remained quiet for fifteen minutes, then stood in his cage and eyed the human.

Peter thought he detected enlarged pupils, but decided it was his imagination. For a moment the dog paced nervously and growled, then ignored Peter's close proximity. The scientist continued his observation, making entries in the special notebook, and decided to do the safest initial test: the remote discrimination protocol.

Peter got the dog into the testing room, an environment Conan associated with food rewards for correct choices. The fifteen-foot-long space contained two hoppers at each end, four in all, each with a light above. A touch-sensitive panel allowed the dog to choose one, and only one, hopper. The animal had to wait until all lights flashed several times, and the one with food remained lit. Then the dog could tap the hopper that remained lit and receive a biscuit. In past tests, Conan picked correctly sixty percent of the time, a score well below Roverbot's score of one hundred percent.

Peter viewed the test through a glass window. Conan made his choices, perhaps more sluggishly than usual, but in the end got eighty percent correct and relished every food pellet.

"Well, Conan, your performance is certainly not worse," Peter said.

He put the dog through several similar protocols, getting positive results, but with the same slow responses. Although Conan scored better after the brain file transfer, Peter wanted more than an IQ test. He needed a check of the dog's behavior and chose the easiest such check: he entered the test area. Conan followed the visitor's slow movement with wide eyes, then sat and yawned.

Peter coaxed the dog into his cage with the reward of a dog treat. He recorded results, cleaned up, and called the caretaker on duty to have Conan taken back to the animal quarters. He advised the fellow to provide the dog with a treat of canned food.

Alone, Peter sat back savoring a triumph. "Maybe this is Nobel prize material, Peter Valois," he said aloud, realizing how grandiose that sounded, especially after the first experiment. Tests with sample sizes of one were almost worthless. Nevertheless, he was glad he'd worked with the difficult dog first. Conan's clear result supported the theory that a change in behavior could be achieved by copying an animal brain file into an android consciousness and then back.

The next day Peter sat at his desk and considered his new lab assistant. Antoinette Marino seemed like a good choice for the lab position, at least so far. Competent and industrious and not prone to chatter. The interaction between Lisa and Andy was more competitive than he liked, and there seemed to be something between the women he didn't understand.

Increased manpower allowed them to finish recording ten rats. Eight had endured both recording and transference, the later carried out after hours by Peter alone. It gnawed at him that two of the ten had died, apparently of cardiac arrhythmia, but both had been recorded with the original COTT sensor. More work was needed to understand the relationship between heart function and brain recording.

The phone rang. It was his boss, the Frog. "Peter, I understand you've started with dog brain recording. Glad to hear that you took my advice to move ahead without fully understanding the rat data."

"Yes, sir. Recording of three dogs went well."

"We need a fatter, better progress report for the military review panel. With your extra lab help, that's possible, right?"

"Yes, sir," Peter said, thinking the rat anomalies could be backtracked and fully analyzed after the review.

"Good. Keep me posted."

Andy and Lisa entered the Valois office to go over latest results and next steps. Roverbot had recovered fully over a two-day period after receiving Conan's file. The real dog also seemed quite healthy. Peter pointed to the white board covered with data and a flowchart.

"Dogs seem to require more time for processing than rats. Probably because the canine brain is bigger, more complex. Integrating the larger file may explain Roverbot's slow recovery."

He wondered how much time it would take to handle a human brain file. Maybe less time than Roverbot took to process Conan's, given the power in Kayten's bionet. He kept that thought to himself.

To his assistants he said, "Size is not a barrier to integration. Both Roborat and Roverbot have accomplished the task, and the dogs, including Conan, are unchanged by the recording procedure."

"I wouldn't say Conan is unchanged," Lisa said, sounding thoughtful. "He seems much friendlier."

Peter wanted to boast that Conan's brain file had been improved by its brief residence in Roverbot, but he changed the subject. "What's this new discrimination task you've taught the biosynthetic dog?"

"Roverbot can now distinguish a cat with a bow on its neck from an identical cat without," Lisa reported with a tone of pride.

"And he learned this while carrying around Conan's brain file, right? Interesting. We'll know how much of Conan's brain pattern remains when we record Roverbot's brain this afternoon." Peter was talking with his head down, pacing a small path near the whiteboard. "Then we move on to another dog. I'll get you started, but then I have a Security Team meeting."

"The meeting wasn't on your calendar," Andy said. "Something up?"

"Just getting ready for the Defense Department visit. Lock up the scanning program and COTT module if you leave the lab."

Andy picked up the small, metal cylinder and touched the wires. "If this is so important for hi-res data on neuron firing and connections, surely we have a backup."

"Maybe," Peter said.

After lunch, Peter watched his assistants get started with a new dog. He adjusted instrument settings and made notes in an electronic notebook before he left.

When the door closed, Lisa started in on a topic she'd raised before: Andy's security clearance. She asked, "So, what happened on your pre-job meeting with Carlos? You've been pretty quiet about it.

Obviously, you passed whatever test he was using to see if you were a security risk."

"He had questions about my previous positions. Which I answered to his satisfaction. Thus, I am here."

"Nothing harder than that?"

"He was thorough," Andy said. "I gave him an accurate picture."

"What do you think of Carlos? Do you like him? Does he like you?"

"Lisa! We had dinner. We talked. We kept our clothes on."

"How nice."

"Your turn will come," Andy said. "Carlos wants to talk to you about security. Maybe he'll invite you out to dinner for the grilling."

"This is strictly business, and I assure you that Mr. Stuck-on-Himself is not my type."

"He likes to handle strictly business over dinner," Andy said, smiling. "But I agree you are not his type."

Lisa recorded the time when the scan was half done. "Really? How do you come to that conclusion?"

"Carlos likes brunettes, not strawberry blonds. As it turned out, we ran into a former girlfriend, definitely brunette. The encounter seemed to embarrass the poor dear."

"You can't decide based on one girlfriend. You know men would date snakes if they had legs." Lisa watched the completion of the brain scan, which had gone smoothly. The dog rested comfortably in its sling as the recording harness was removed.

"Well, good luck with Carlos. Just remember that he's only a man."

The lab phone rang, and Lisa answered. Andy heard only Lisa's side of the brief conversation.

"Sure. I'd be happy to stop in. Now is probably the best time. I'll be there." Lisa hung up the phone and said to Andy, "I have to run down to administration for a few minutes. I'll be back." She removed the COTT program from the computer and put the thumb drive into a file cabinet, locked the drawer, tossed her lab coat on the hook near the door, and left.

Andy touched the COTT device that interfaced the computer with the living brain. So, security is not so tight, she thought. But it seems to be getting tighter due to this impending DOD visit. She spent the next thirty minutes on routine work.

Peter returned as she was finishing. "Well, we are really violating procedures. The Security Committee would have our heads for this. A single person without top security clearance—that's you, Andy—is not supposed to be left alone with the software!" Peter didn't really sound angry.

"The software is locked up," Andy said.

"Or the hardware."

Lisa entered, hearing the last. "God, I forgot all about that. Sorry."

Andy looked up from the notebook. "I guess we need a security refresher course. Perhaps I could get Carlos to arrange one."

"And I bet you'd want private lessons, right?" Lisa whispered.

"I learn best with a low student-teacher ratio," Andy whispered back.

"Well, I have to run. My meeting with Carlos involves a concert and dinner." Lisa smiled. "Turns out that Mr. Security thinks outside meetings work best. See you guys tomorrow." Lisa strode out of the lab.

Andy finished a notebook entry and followed.

An hour later Peter was still in the lab, plotting how to present the dog results for his report. It was hard to concentrate because the new problem—his son—intruded. His mind returned to the solution for Dan that seemed more certain than the slow and difficult counseling approach. The idea had seemed too risky, and he'd shelved it. Conan's changed behavior revived the plan.

Behavior modification was Dan's issue, and that's what Peter's work led to. He was a world expert in animal-to-biosynthetic brain transfer. The Department of Defense protocols only talked about protecting human lives by transferring trained consciousness into an expendable robot body. But it was no secret that the opposite process was equally possible—transferring a biosynthetic-modified consciousness into a human. Peter's clandestine experiments had been doing exactly that in animals, and the few results were positive.

One would have to be blind not to see that the human experiment would be done down the line. Done in a military facility no doubt, but it would be done. He'd just be doing the human experiment early. With the perfect justification--Dan's behavior threatened the boy's wellbeing, and he needed a surer, more effective therapy. The risks were minimal, at least based on rat data. Yes, he needed reinforcement of the good dog results and would get it. Both for the DOD and his son.

Peter pondered how he could transfer his son's brain to Kayten, but the android needed knowledge of Dan's environment to apply bionet influence. Kayten had to know Dan's associations and activities, including patterns of acquiring and using drugs. Then the android could block those tendencies only, leaving the rest of Dan's personality unchanged.

He imagined a solution: Kayten could go to Seneca High. Peter envisioned a way, thanks to the wonders of modern plastics and computer-aided imaging, to bring the robot into contact with Dan's haunts. Kayten could become Dan. Cybernetic Implementation had the finest facilities in the world for the construction of humanoids. All he had to do was to steal a few things and find the courage to use them.

Ridiculous, he thought. Dan was in counseling. It never worked for Peter's brother, but maybe it would for Dan. He had to be patient. The phone rang, and he jumped. It was Pam, excited and panicked.

"Dan's in trouble," she said. "He borrowed the car. He and another student named Brock went back to school after it was closed."

"Brock? Who's that?"

"Don't know and it doesn't matter. Just listen. A caretaker found the boys in the athletic office, apparently looking for something. They ran, and the janitor called the police. The cops found the car off the road in a ditch with Dan and Brock in it."

"Are they alright?" Peter asked.

"I'm waiting at the hospital for the doctor to tell me Dan's condition. Nurse said it looks like nothing but a few bumps, including one on his forehead. Nothing broken."

Peter asked a few questions and was ready to head for the hospital, when Pam said that Dan was being released.

"All right, dear, I'll see you at home. I guess the Drug and Alcohol Abuse program isn't going too well."

He returned the phone to its cradle and gave into anger. Now he'd be paying a lawyer to handle Dan's latest stupidity. Plus, the auto repair shop, the hospital, and maybe his insurance company. And Dan could have been killed.

24 /WEEKEND VISIT

On Saturday, as daylight probed the edges of the drapes, Peter slipped from the bed, leaving the blanket and Pam undisturbed. He showered, stepped on the scale to remind himself he still carried an excess twenty pounds, shaved, and donned casual clothes. Dan had been ticketed for operating a motor vehicle in an unsafe manner. He and Brock had sustained only minor bruises from the mishap. Brock's father was a lawyer who argued that the boys were in the Athletic Office looking for old track records, something Peter found ridiculous. Furthermore, the attorney pointed out, both a rear school door and the office door were unlocked, so there was no breaking and entering. The school administration declined to press charges. The damage to the family car was confined to the front bumper and grill. Peter paid for that repair without bringing his insurance into play. He knew that Dan had again felt no consequences of his behavior. When would his luck run out?

In the kitchen Kayten was spooning cat food into a bowl. "May I be of assistance, sir?"

"I'll have a fried egg, sausages, and toast, Kayten."

Kayten quieted the cat by putting its bowl on the floor. He served orange juice and coffee. Alongside the juice he placed a plastic container. Peter looked up from his paper and stirred a couple of spoons of psyllium into the OJ, wondering how well eating vegetable fiber compensated for enjoying cholesterol-containing egg and sausages at the same time.

"You have risen earlier than usual for a Saturday morning, sir. Do you have something special to do?" Kayten asked as he delivered the breakfast.

"I have to run into the lab. Should be back before noon."

Peter ate quickly and brushed his teeth. With Pam still asleep, he left the house before seven. From the driveway, Peter was followed by a dark sedan until he entered the Cybernetic Implementation gate.

Pam heard the car and got up. In the kitchen, she asked Kayten where her husband went so early on a Saturday.

"To the laboratory, madam."

"For how long?"

"He did not say precisely, although he indicated a possible return time of noon."

"Well, not having Peter in the way will give you a chance to shampoo the family room rug. I know it's ahead of schedule, but I think it's dirty. Come and I'll show you."

"If madam thinks the rug needs attention, I will be happy to clean it."

Pam led the way to the family room at the rear of the house and pointed to the chocolate-colored carpet. "Here's the beast you must tame," she said, "and the dirtiest part of its pelt is near the recliners."

"Beast, madam? I see no animal here or analogous danger."

"I mean the rug, Kayten. I see you are still learning the language. Will you need help to move the couch?"

"I require no help moving furniture. The rug-cleaning procedure is known to me. I will consider your use of 'beast' in reference to the rug as a further example of the extreme complexity of the English language, or perhaps the complexity of the users. My sensors tell me that there is nothing of animal origin in the carpet, so it would not be a pelt. The job will require forty-two minutes."

"Take your time, Kayten. I'll be in the sunroom if you need me."

"I will take the time required for the operation, madam."

Paperwork had brought Peter in on weekends for the past two months. He had clearance, so getting past the lobby security desk was a simple matter of signing a sheet, swiping a card, and saying something innocuous to the man on duty. He headed to the library off the main corridor. Peter's entry brought a glance from a junior scientist reading at a rear table. Peter silently cursed the nerd for his early morning work ethic, then realized he was condemning his own behavior.

He located two medical texts and scanned contents and indices. Satisfied they contained the information he'd need, he was ready to take the next steps. At the library entrance, he checked left and right. The hallway was empty. He turned away from the main lobby and headed to the research wing. The security checkpoint was unmanned, but not untended.

"Please step to the scanner, Dr. Valois," the securibot said. Although the securibot looked like a mild-mannered dentist dressed in blue, Peter knew that this model was equipped with gas weaponry designed to incapacitate a crowd of twenty-five two-hundred-pound men in four point eight seconds. It also possessed projectile weapons and transmitted everything it saw and heard to the central security suite. The floor scale confirmed his weight, and the hologram scanner verified his body volume. He satisfied the retinal scanner, swiped his card, and attempted to pass a voice-recognition test. When he recited his name and employee number, the tone sounded high pitched and quivery, but the computer seemed satisfied and slowly opened the steel door.

"Thank you, Dr. Valois. Have a nice day," the android said.

Peter pocketed his card, drew a handkerchief over his glistening forehead, and strode down an empty corridor, his footsteps magnified by the Saturday stillness. At his laboratory, he stood before the locked door and listened. He heard voices from another corridor, but they weren't coming closer. The keyboard lock accepted his eight-character code, and the door slid into its wall pocket with a soft click.

Cursing his agitation, he told himself he hadn't done anything wrong. At least not yet. Donning a short lab coat, he sat at a bench in clear view of the security camera and pulled a notebook and microdisk from a locked drawer. Perhaps his anxiety stemmed from stepping over the line. He'd been honest for the twenty-five years he'd worked for Cybernetic. No theft of pens, paper, or personal use of the copier. Taking home an earlier version of the COTT software was perfectly natural—he didn't stop thinking and working outside the office. He even rationalized the unauthorized experiments after hours as in the company interest.

He forced himself to keep his eyes from the camera lens as he rolled an electronics rack between the camera and the computer console. After initiating a built-in test routine on the rack's oscilloscope, he let the pattern of fluctuations in electronic current display on the screen to entertain the camera.

Hidden behind the rack, he booted the computer, and inserted a micro drive into the card reader. At the system prompt, he entered his name and password, having to do the latter twice before he got the sequence of keys correct. After copying COTT subroutines from the hard drive to the portable micro drive, he came around to the front of the oscilloscope and hooked the instrument up to a second module in the rack. A diagnostic routine ran as Peter watched the screen for fifteen seconds.

With a pat, he thanked the oscilloscope with a verbal "Okay." On a nearby bench was a black box, the size of a four-slot toaster, that took input from the scanner unit and passed it to the computer. He'd duplicated the multiplexer at home. From the bench drawer, he took a small, wooden box that he carried to the front of the computer, positioning himself behind the electronic rack out of sight of the camera. From the box he removed a duplicate of the COTT sensor, a cylinder the size of a double-A battery. Peter slipped it into a pants pocket just as footsteps sounded in the corridor. He froze.

His peripheral vision detected a security uniform looking through the door panel. After what seemed too long, she moved away.

His hand trembled as he returned the box to the drawer and turned the lock. He began an inspection of the COTT multiplexer, opening a side panel to access several boards, which he pulled out, examined, and replaced. He closed the panel, then moved to the computer, and extracted the micro drive, putting it into his pants pocket.

Trying to pace his breathing, he stood motionless until the thought occurred to him that lack of activity could look as peculiar as the wrong activity. He cut power to the electronics rack, the oscilloscope, and the computer. At the lab door, he glanced left and right in the corridor before leaving.

In his office he leaned back against the door, happy to be out of sight of a camera. After much debate it had been decided that privacy would prevail over security in personal offices. Peter sat at his desk and placed his shaking hands before him.

He could turn back at this point, with no harm and no danger. Why was he doing this? For his son? Or for himself? The company would get back the hardware and software. He was only borrowing it. But if discovered, he was ruined. His career, his life, Dan's life. He worried about Dan's safety and decided the real danger lay in doing nothing.

Peter opened the filing cabinet and extracted a second memory card containing a copy of the master batch file, something needed to control the subroutines he'd just copied from the lab computer. He also took out a square mailer the size of a birthday card. He closed the filing cabinet and locked it. Back in his swivel-based desk chair, he rotated toward the window and moved aside the right drape. A spatula inserted into a crack in the caulking material between the metal frame and the cement block allowed him to extract a ten-inch-long piece, leaving a rectangular tunnel about a quarter inch high and the width of the cement block. Peter had discovered the construction defect months earlier but hadn't reported it to maintenance. Now he understood the reason for his negligence as he inserted the mailer envelope with the two memory cards into the tunnel. He replaced the caulk.

Peter removed his ancient calculator, checkbook-sized and as thick as a pack of cigars, from a desk drawer, turned the black case over, and took out the rechargeable battery pack. From another deeper drawer came the old battery pack and a set of tools, including a coping saw and a small portable vise. He clamped the vise to the edge of the desk, fixed the battery pack securely, and began sawing. A thin layer came away, and he took out the battery. He inserted the COTT transducer into the hollowed-out box and reassembled the shell, securing it with electrical tape. The calculator, a yellow pad, and a stack of reprints went into his briefcase. He wiped a sheen of perspiration from his forehead.

The knock at the door boomed like a struck kettledrum.

He opened the door to find a security officer, a big man with broad shoulders and no belly. "Is everything all right, Dr. Valois?"

"Yes, fine. I'm just handling some data analysis."

The man glanced around the room, lingering on the open briefcase, and then brought his dark eyes back to Peter. "How long do you expect to be here, doctor?"

"Not long. Almost done."

The uniform nodded. "Be careful when working alone. That always makes me nervous. Don't be shy about punching in the emergency code if needed." He went out, closing the office door.

Peter waited five apprehensive minutes and then walked out with what he hoped was a confident gait. Thirty seconds later, the office lights went off as the wall sensors failed to detect infrared radiation.

Now came the most difficult part of the operation, and Peter wondered whether he should have indicated to security where he would be. It might have provided a semblance of legitimacy, but it could also bring an unwanted interruption. He passed under a "Restricted Access" sign in an adjoining corridor and came to a locked door labeled "Fabrication Laboratory." He punched in his manager code and entered.

At the computer console, he passed through several levels of directories and subdirectories until he came to a program file named FABRIC.MASTER. He executed the program and then walked over to a large scanner connected by cable to the computer terminal. He powered it up and considered hauling over another electronics rack, but that might be too much. Instead, he put his briefcase on the laboratory bench and opened it to hide what he was doing. From a folder in the briefcase, he extracted two five-by-seven glossy prints, front and side views of his son, both in color. He'd persuaded Dan to let him take the high-resolution photos when the plan to fix his son first occurred to him. Dan agreed when Peter pointed out that they really had no close-up shots to show how Dan looked once he'd entered senior high school. At the same time, Peter generated a hologram of the boy. The scientist positioned the head shots on the scanner and inserted the flash drive with the hologram file.

At the terminal he made entries on several screens, reviewed the instructions, and hit the return key. Soft sounds issued as the laser optic module began a systematic scan. Ten minutes later he made more keyboard entries, filling in screens dealing with scaling factors and materials selection. The program came back with an estimated fabrication time and invited Peter to accept the information by hitting the return key. He went to the graphics scanner, examined a large, blue cube next to it, and confirmed that the lines connecting the fabrication module to several chemical tanks were filled. He returned to the computer and, with a shaky finger, punched the return key.

He exited the lab and was closing the door carefully, attempting to minimize the noise of the locking mechanism, when he heard a familiar voice.

25 /CAUGHT

"DR. VALOIS," THE VOICE SAID. IT WAS THE SAME BEEFY SECURITY guard. "I was expecting to find you in your own laboratory or in the library."

Peter couldn't help stammering his answer. "Right. I was just checking on a fabrication job."

The security man studied Peter. "You seem a little agitated."

"I wasn't expecting to run into anyone. You should wear a bell."

"Sorry about the scare. These rubber soles don't make a sound. Is there anything I can help you with?"

"No, no. Nothing. I'll just be busy here for another hour or so." Peter's forehead was damp.

"Well, you have the building almost to yourself. If you need anything, just give a call."

Peter walked away, trying to appear casual, wondering if the man had bought his act. The security man watched with a puzzled expression on his face, then turned and checked the Fabrication Laboratory door. He pulled a small notebook from his shirt pocket, opened it, and made an entry.

Peter settled at a library table near racks of journals. I'm making a mess of it, he thought. Leaving suspicious tracks all over. When his breathing slowed, he opened a medical book and jotted notes on a yellow pad. Forty-five minutes later, he scooped up several papers he'd copied and returned unobserved to the Fabrication Laboratory.

At the door, he froze, thinking he'd heard a thump. When no one appeared, he slipped inside. There, a green light labeled "Ready" glowed on the fabrication unit. He positioned his briefcase so that he could open it and conceal the inside. Near the latch mechanism he pressed the side wall. An opening appeared along the bottom. He lifted half the lower panel to reveal a shallow compartment.

Blocking the camera with his body, Peter opened the fabrication unit's door, reached inside, and carefully removed a flexible, eerily lifelike duplicate of his son face. With shaking hands he laid the mask in the hidden briefcase compartment, closed the panel, and covered the bottom with the calculator and reprints. He killed power to the computer, graphic tablet, and fabricator, and retrieved his son's photos. After a last check, he left the laboratory and walked to the entrance lobby.

The main security desk in the lobby was manned by a human. "Hi, Dr. Valois. A shorter stay than usual today, I see."

"Yes, I just had to pick up some reprints and check some lab equipment to be used next week." Peter put his briefcase on the counter with the latch side facing the young security man.

The guard opened the case and glanced at the reprints, flipping through the pile. He checked the cover compartments. The guard picked up the calculator, turned it over, and put it into the scanner. He seemed dissatisfied with what showed on the screen and turned over the calculator to open the battery compartment.

Peter held his breath, trying to think of something to distract the man, but nothing came to mind. The man was reaching to touch the battery pack when another guard came into the lobby. This was an older man, gray-haired, who looked very fit.

"Jim just called. He'll be about fifteen minutes late. He had to get his car jump-started. It that a problem?"

"No. I have nothing scheduled." The guard replaced the battery pack and put the calculator back in the briefcase. He clicked the latches on the case and handed it to Peter. "Don't miss out on this great beach weather, Doctor."

Peter resumed breathing with an involuntary sound and coughed to cover it. The hand that reached for the briefcase shook, and he hoped the guard wouldn't notice. He attempted to sound casual. "Yeah, that's an important part of California living. See you later." Peter headed for the main door.

"Oh, Dr. Valois!" Peter's hand was on the door when the voice stopped him. He couldn't think of an appropriate action, so he stood motionless and awaited his fate.

"I'm glad I caught you," Carlos Oreta said. "The security check we scheduled for Tuesday. Can we change to Monday afternoon?"

Peter struggled to focus his racing mind. "A security check?"

"Just routine. I wouldn't need but a few minutes of your time."

"Yeah, I guess Monday is fine. Give me a call in the morning to remind me."

"Thanks. Have a nice day, Doctor."

Peter left the building and walked into a blast of early morning heat that did not help his inner chill. He thought furiously about the best course of action, struggling to regain control, to apply a rational analysis to these events. Maybe the young security agent had no more than a routine interest, just as he'd said. On the other hand, perhaps he'd singled out Peter for some reason, some slip up. He considered just going straight home, maybe canceling his plan and returning the stolen materials, but then he remembered Dan.

A strip of grass twelve feet wide separated Peter's car from his office window. Along the building at ten-foot intervals under windows were small bushes with orange and white marigolds planted in between.

Peter looked left and right, then walked up to the window, pushed into the bush, and opened his briefcase an inch, holding the top and bottom together with his hand. The small crevice near the window frame was barely visible, even with the bush pushed aside. He grabbed the corner of the envelope and pulled it out, dropping it into the briefcase in one motion.

"Excuse me, what are you doing near that bush?"

Peter dropped his briefcase.

Thirty feet away was a man whose coveralls identified him as the groundskeeper. His face wore a mixed look of puzzlement and irritation.

Peter regained his balance and some composure. "Just admiring your gardening. What kind of bushes are these?"

The man came closer and looked at Peter. "That's a kind of forsythia. It seems to do well here and doesn't require much care. You shouldn't stand so close to the bushes, mister."

"Right. Sorry about that. Just checking if they had a smell. Well, keep up the good work. I wish my home landscaping looked as good as this place." Without waiting for an answer, Peter snatched his case and headed for his car.

Miles away from Cybernetic Implementation, a young woman held a phone to her ear, listening.

"We'd need an update on what CI security is talking to Valois about," a male voice said, seeming impatient.

"Dr. Valois is up for a routine security review, and the fellow handling it seems conscientious, but I don't know that he's done anything more than just talk to employees about the usual security procedures. Nothing substantive."

"The Agency wants you to press a bit. We think there's a scheme afoot, and Valois has the most sensitive project at CI. Find out what's going on."

"You'll be the first to know. Till next time. It's been a pleasure." The woman didn't wait for an answer before hanging up. She then stared intently at the ceiling for several minutes, realizing that this was the part of the job that required intuition and skill. The training she'd received was thorough, and she believed in the importance of her role in protecting the security of a critical project, but the duplicity was more difficult than she'd imagined it would be. And for the first time her thoughts ran along the lines of what else she could be doing with her life, or at least what she would do when she left this job. The idea of quitting the agency had not entered her mind before.

Up to now there'd been no excitement, and she'd only provided phone updates of project security. Now something was afoot. Washington had evidence that the CI project was under attack, even if they didn't know how, or for what purpose, or by whom. And they were pressuring her for answers she didn't have. To get the answers, she would have to work through someone else.

"Well, I guess this is what they should be paying me the big bucks for: to get Carlos to do what I want." She spoke these thoughts aloud, then lapsed into silence as she thought of dealing with Carlos. She had to point him in the right direction.

26 /INTERVENTION

Peter took a personal day on Wednesday. From the breakfast nook, he watched sparrows and finches fuss at the bird feeder as he once again pondered what he proposed to do. Dan was feigning a measure of compliance after the car accident and positive drug test. He'd gone to several counseling sessions, but his counselor labeled him "noncompliant."

The failure of outpatient therapy hardly surprised Peter. An inpatient rehabilitation program could be tried, but Marcia's son had done more than one such program and now was dead. He thought of his brother's death from a drug overdose. He'd attended both funerals. Marcia was so distraught she couldn't speak, and he'd been able only to look on in sympathy. What would he do if Dan died? He'd been angry with his son for so long that he'd lost touch with what underlay that anger: deep love. This was his only child. If Dan died, Peter felt he, too, would cease to exist.

Two things made him uneasy about tampering with Dan's brain recording. First was the lack of more safety data from dogs. The second was the theological issue: he was proposing to play God. Peter's agnosticism allowed for existence of a god, but one who left no proof of its being and a creation that ran by itself. He had no faith that prayer could affect natural law, but he believed in cause and effect. Human decisions had consequences. Therefore, decisions must be intrinsically good or bad with ensuing effects both here and in the next life, if there were one. Playing God might be an evil decision with unwanted payback in both places.

The incident at the school was still under review. For Peter it was the last straw, like salt in a wound. But what pushed him from vacillation to commitment was the memory of his brother.

Having decided to implement his solution, he turned to practical matters. To minimize risk, he would do the transfer in two steps, maintaining Dan's consciousness in the biosynthetic incubator until he'd checked it out. After forty-eight hours of evaluation, he'd reverse the process.

Kayten would be his incubator. The android's resistance to accompany them to pick up the drunken Dan now struck him as peculiar. Would Kayten refuse to participate?

"Shall I refill your coffee cup, sir?" Kayten was wiping shelves in the refrigerator.

"Yes. I'll take another sausage, too."

While Kayten filled the order, Peter thought of another problem. He had to fly solo and not tell Pam what he was doing. Recording and transference might have a small risk, but doing nothing had great risks: overdosing, death in a car accident, suicide. Any intervention carried risk. He could only minimize. This was the perfect time—Dan had no school today, and Friday was a holiday. He'd been invited to spend the weekend fishing with his Uncle Ed before Ed traveled abroad. He'd be absent from school on Thursday.

When Dan showed up for breakfast, Peter said, "I'd like your help with something this morning."

"Can't it wait? Got some packing to do. I wanna get to the lake before Uncle Ed. Maybe do some fishing." Dan gazed out the nook window as Kayten filled a tumbler with orange juice.

"This won't take long. About an hour. I want to record your brain." Peter hoped he sounded casual.

"Record my brain?" Dan poured milk on a bowl of Cheerios. "Are you serious?"

Dan was probably only vaguely aware of what his father did for a living. His curiosity seemed to evaporate at the start of high school.

"It's just a routine scan with the latest piece of equipment from Cybernetic. Works fine with rats and dogs. I just wanted to test it on a larger brain."

Kayten stopped his domesticity and stood quite still.

"What are you going to do with the recording? Analyze it?" Dan's tone was defensive.

"Only to check on the instrument," Peter lied. "You get to relax and do nothing. I give you a minor tranquilizer to minimize movement. It's a short-acting drug that will wear off completely just about the time we've finished."

Dan spooned more Cheerios into his mouth and wiped a drop of milk from his chin with the back of his hand. "What kind of buzz do you get from the tranquilizer?"

"None. It's in and out. You'll be helping a lot by providing a scan of a complex brain to compare with the animal results."

"I don't know that I like being a guinea pig. What are the side effects?"

"No more than from having your picture taken. It's like an electroencephalogram, an EEG. You've seen that on plenty of TV shows. Just a record of electricity."

"How about trying it on Kayten first?"

"Kayten doesn't have a human brain. Biosynthetic brains have already been scanned. I need a human brain." Peter realized this sounded ghoulish.

"Like Dr. Frankenstein, right? Do I get paid?"

Peter hadn't anticipated pay. He opened his wallet and studied the contents. "For an hour of doing nothing, I can offer a twenty."

Dan eyed the money. "Seems cheap. As a research subject, I'd expect more."

When Peter pulled out another twenty, Dan's eyes widened, and he nodded. "Okay, I guess I can spare an hour."

"Great. I'm ready if you are." Peter folded his paper.

"Lemme brush my teeth." Dan drank his OJ in a gulp and left.

. . .

When Dan returned, Kayten asked, "Will you be needing my assistance, sir?"

"Yes." Peter took his cup of coffee and led the way to the workroom. He unlocked the door and stood aside as Dan and Kayten entered.

The room, painted peanut shell, had a mocha, tiled floor and a sheetrocked ceiling with two banks of fluorescent lights that gave the place a clinical air. Shelves lined one wall, and a table in the center contained tools and electronic equipment. A white cabinet stood in the corner next to a cot. Peter had equipped the room as a laboratory, one capable of brain recording, a simple matter of moving the COTT unit over a skull in a precise pattern and collecting a data file on a computer with the right software. He built it himself. Pam knew he was a tinkerer, never entered the locked room, and never questioned equipment deliveries.

"All you have to do is sit there," Peter said, pointing to the recliner. "The tranquilizer is administered intravenously, so you'll have to endure a needle stick."

"You didn't say anything about that."

"No big deal." Peter unlocked the cabinet and pulled out a syringe and needle, and a small vial of COTT cocktail. "Let's see. You weigh about one-thirty?" he asked his son.

"One-forty-two."

"That will be point seven cubic centimeters, sir," Kayten said. "Shall I attach the electrocardiographic and electroencephalographic leads?"

It surprised Peter that Kayten didn't have questions. Of course, the android didn't know what role he would play. "Go ahead. And put the helmet on him. Turn on the computer and recorders."

Minutes later, Dan was wired and the COTT program was loaded. Peter looked at the baseline ECG and EEG. He wiped Dan's arm with alcohol, skillfully inserted an IV needle, and started a saline drip. He loaded the COTT cocktail and was about to inject it into the IV port when he stopped. His son looked so vulnerable, so peaceful. Was he really going through with this? He swept the doubts from his mind and put his hand on Dan's shoulder. "Ready, Son?"

"I guess."

"Just relax. Here goes." Peter injected the cocktail.

Dan blinked and closed his eyes. The electroencephalogram settled into a quieter pattern, one associated with sleep.

"Kayten, this scan will take about an hour. We may have to supplement the relaxant."

The automatic blood pressure cup inflated and slowly relaxed. Peter activated the COTT program, and the scan began. The hologram of Dan's brain started forming near the computer, becoming denser as scanning proceeded.

After thirty minutes of silence, Kayten looked up from the EEC trance and said, "Increased alpha activity, sir. Some elevation of heart rate and blood pressure."

A knock shook the door, and Peter jumped.

"Are you in there with Dan?" It was Pam's voice.

"We're all here," Peter said, hoping he sounded casual.

"What are you guys up to?"

"Just checking some equipment, dear."

"I want to talk to my son. Can you send him out?"

Peter hesitated before answering. "He's in the middle of something delicate. If he stops, we'll have to start over. Give us a half-hour."

Pam sighed and left.

Peter injected the supplemental COTT cocktail and watched Dan's EEC tracing return to the previous pattern of low amplitude, synchronous waves. Scanning continued until a dense image of Dan's brain was completed and the monitor indicated the file had been recorded.

"Remove the scanning helmet, Kayten," Peter said, as he retrieved another small vial from the cabinet. "I'll administer the stimulant."

By the time Dan stirred, he'd lost the IV catheter and all leads. All he had to show for his assistance with a small, round, plastic patch in the crook of his arm.

"All done, Dan. Everything went fine. Scanner works on human brains." Peter took another blood pressure measurement. "You're in good shape, but it wouldn't be a bad idea to sit and relax with a book for a while. How are you feeling?"

"Not bad. But maybe I will loaf in front of the TV until it's time to leave for the two-hour drive. Did you learn anything about my brain?"

"Like all brains, lots of water and fat giving off electrical signals. I'll do some further analysis and give you a report. I may need you to repeat the procedure after you get back from the fishing expedition."

"I guess, for the same fee. Where is my fee?"

Peter handed Dan the money and watched him leave, ignoring a premonition of something bad.

27 /SOLUTION

A MOMENT LATER PETER SAID, "LET ME JUST PUT THIS FILE THROUGH the verification routine." He began entering instructions at the keyboard.

Kayten stepped toward the door. "If you will not be needing my further assistance at this time, sir, I will see to Mrs. Valois's breakfast."

"Yes, I will be needing you. My wife will have to forage for herself in the kitchen."

"Forage? Is that not a term used to describe food-searching behavior of animals?"

"My usage was metaphorically acceptable. Just add it to your lexicon of idioms. You may be adding quite a bit to your learning in a few minutes." Peter looked up when the computer completed the file verification routine, announcing on the monitor that the file contained only values within specifications and that the organization was correct. "Let me explain what I'm doing here, Kayten."

"Thank you, sir. I do feel a lack of information about your activities. This uncertainty inhibits smooth implementation of my biosynthetic directives, causing moments of stasis."

Peter paced the room before speaking. "We're going to put you in charge temporarily of the computer file we've just created. By a reversal of the brain-scanning process you will become Dan Valois for a day. During that time you will explore one aspect of Dan's behavior: use of illicit drugs. You will then exert biosynthetic brain controls over that use. When you have succeeded in regulating—removing—that behavior, I will re-record your brain and then maybe, just maybe, return the new file to Dan."

"Maybe?"

"You may discover how to modify Dan's behavior by changing his environment—places, people, things. I can use the information to help him."

Kayten stood with one arm raised and remained in that stance for several seconds. "What is the purpose of this file transfer? I am quite certain that my biosynthetic brain is capable of controlling any aberrant behavior, if that is the question you are seeking to answer."

Peter had no way of knowing that Kayten's real concern was that the large influx of data might conflict with his underlying special programming. But the scientist knew the biosynthetic brain had immense storage capacity. There would be no problem accommodating both the Kayten intelligence and Dan's within the same neural mass.

"That's what the animal work says. Time for a first experiment with a human brain. But there's more to what I'm doing. First, you must learn as much as you can of the environment in which Dan operates. Second, you must determine how to modify and eliminate undesirable and unhealthy behavior traits, specifically drug use, in as subtle a way as possible, so that when we re-record the Dan portion of your brain it will no longer follow those paths. But in all other regards, Dan's brain will be unchanged."

Again, Kayten hesitated. "Is there data showing that this is a safe and effective procedure? I am concerned that there may be a conflict here with my... parameters."

Peter slammed the cabinet door. "The data has been positive in rats and dogs, Kayten." He hoped his extrapolation sounded like the truth. "This has nothing to do with parameters."

"Has not work been done in a species closer to man, such as a primate of any size?"

"Those experiments are coming, but we do not have time to wait in my son's case. Now it is time to make use of this system to benefit man, Dan in particular. You are well aware of his problems and the threat they represent."

"I am aware—"

"He'll be taking tomorrow off from school to visit his uncle. I haven't called the school yet to explain his absence and won't. You will become Dan Valois, attending classes and experiencing as much as you can of his daily routine, including drug buying and use." Peter waited for the objection. It didn't come. "You must, of course, at all times act and think like Dan. Based on this information, you can provide the controlling modifications to eliminate the drug abuse."

"How will I know what modifications are required?" Kayten asked in an even tone.

"I'm not sure of that answer, Kayten. All that may be required is a slight strengthening of Dan's inclination to help himself. Or you may have to provide stronger positive and negative feedback loops. We can discuss this when you have acquired more data." The computer had completed its file and systems checks and had returned to the main menu screen.

"Does the use of drugs account for Master Valois's unusual behavior in the past year, sir?"

"Year? Do you mean that you have noted a change in Dan reaching back that long?" Peter sounded and looked surprised.

Kayten took a moment, as if he were reviewing an internal calendar, and said, "Exactly, sir."

"So why didn't you tell us about it?"

"I was under Master Valois's direct orders not to reveal his behavior. There was insufficient evidence that harm would result from compliance with this order."

"I see. We may want to discuss this further."

"This procedure will have to be carefully evaluated for compatibility with my biosynthetic mandates, sir. I am noting possible conflicts on this subject."

"I'm sure your further analysis will reveal the need and justification for this procedure, Kayten. Although you will have all the memory present in Dan's brain file, you will not lose your identity as Kayten. Once we've made the transfer, of course, you will have to remain out of sight of Mrs. Valois until we reverse the process. Peter swept the room with his eyes. "Here in the workroom that I keep locked. I'll tell her that you are undergoing an upgrade and will be out of service for at least forty-eight hours."

"Who will tend the house in my absence, sir?"

"Believe it or not, humans are capable of surviving on their own. And Mrs. Valois used to run this house before your arrival. I presume she has not lost those skills, although you can expect a certain accumulation of tasks that will need your attention when you return."

"Mrs. Valois has frequently voiced an abhorrence of doing certain household chores that I now handle. I hope my absence will not be too stressful for her."

"Trust me, Kayten, she'll be fine. Tomorrow morning I'll transport you to the high school where you will function as Dan, and then I'll pick you up in the late afternoon. We'll identify a spot where you can loiter, if necessary, without attracting attention."

"How will I pass for Dan Valois if I look like Cyborg Unit K-10?"

"The same laboratory that created your humanoid appearance has also created a duplicate faceplate in the image of Dan. Peter grabbed the box with the Dan face mask. "I'll make the cosmetic modification while you are still one hundred percent robot. This shouldn't take long, thanks to the superb design of your unit construction. Sit and enter service mode."

Kayten sat and underwent a transformation from the animate to the inanimate. The machine ran its fingers over an invisible junction at the hairline and along the jaw. Although there had been no evidence of a seam, there now appeared a small flap of "skin" outlining the oval of Kayten's face. Soundlessly, the android lifted his face from the underlying synthetic muscle bundles. Peter took the flexible mask and handed Kayten the face of his son. The robot reversed the process, and Dan Valois eerily materialized.

Peter closed his eyes and said, "To help you adjust the facial muscle array to match Dan's, I have the hologram analysis program in the computer." He took a ribbon cable from the back of the computer and brought it over to Kayten who had lifted his shirt and exposed, under another flap of skin, a female terminal that matched the end of the cable. Peter connected the two, and Kayten took over the process of data transfer.

"Perfect. Now let's get your brain on file so that I can reconstitute you as well as Dan. You'll have to maintain minimal biosynthetic brain activity during the process. Any problems?"

"We can commence when you wish, sir. I will remain at minimal activity until you activate my systems."

Over the next hour, Kayten was scanned, and then the computer transferred Dan Valois's file into the robot brain. Peter watched the computer screen with a combination of fear and hope. Everything seemed to go without a hitch and left Kayten holding the copy of Dan's brain. Before he revived the dormant robot, Peter went to the laundry and picked up a pair of jeans and a sweatshirt. Kayten could use his own shoes. Returning to the workroom, Peter stood for several minutes looking at the motionless body of his robot/son before he touched a spot on Kayten's stomach. The eyes opened and looked at him. Time hung.

"Are you all right, sir?"

Peter wasn't sure of the answer, as he wrestled with the astonishment of Dr. Frankenstein. "Let yourself become Dan, Kayten. Refer to me as 'Dad.' Are you having any problems handling the new information?"

"The feelings are most unusual, sir... Dad. It will take some getting used to. But I already have a large body of information about... my drug usage and addictive behavior. I have been in considerable turmoil over it."

"Do you think you will have any problem playing Dan for a day?"

"Probability of success is greater than point nine five. There are many unknowns that preclude a higher probability."

"Well, put on these clothes. After Dan leaves for the lake, I'll go get whatever school materials he has in his room for you to study. I'll also bring you some tapes of Dan's voice. You must modify your voice to sound like Dan. It will also be necessary that you modify the color and style of your hair to match my son's. You'll find what you need in the cabinet."

"Very good, Dad."

"You'll also have to adopt the teenage male idiom. They do not say 'Very good, Dad'."

"I detect in Dan's brain all the information I need about teenage idiom and will immediately commence its mastery. I estimate this to require several hours."

"I'll tell Mrs. Valois the bad news about your upgrade. She can wait for your return or start on the housework by scrubbing the kitchen floor and cleaning all the windows," he said, smiling. "That's a joke, Kayten. Not to be repeated."

Peter left the workshop and locked its door before Kayten could respond.

Yingyi had just received the call from the team monitoring the phone tap at the Valois house. "The boy is going off somewhere to his uncle's cabin for a weekend of fishing."

Andy frowned. "We can't let that happen. I'm sick of fooling around. You and Morgan have to grab him and take him to the holding house. Is it ready?"

"It's ready."

"This is the opportunity. Our boy will be alone. Will his uncle expect him?"

"His uncle won't be there until tomorrow, so he won't even be missed for twenty-four hours."

"Still not good. You have to take out the uncle, so this stays quiet until Saturday night."

Morgan nodded.

Andy glared at the men. "Well, what are you waiting for? Follow him when he leaves the house. You can't know how private the cabin is, so grab him en route. Get your butts in the car and accompany junior on his pleasant, isolated drive up to the lake."

Yingyi stood and flexed his muscles.

That evening Carlos and Andy endured a new movie that had been heavily advertised and that turned out to need all the promotional help given. They stopped for a drink afterwards.

On the way to Andy's apartment, she said, "You seem quiet tonight, Carlos. Is something wrong?"

"It has nothing to do with us, Andy. Work related. I've just been busy with a tough assignment." Blocks of car dealers, fast food joints, and convenience stores passed in a blur of fluorescence.

"Is it something you can talk about? Maybe just talking will help. It doesn't have to do with Peter Valois, does it?" Andy turned toward Carlos and put her hand on his shoulder.

"Your feminine intuition must be working overtime, Andy. Just some loose ends I'm trying to tie up, and my boss has been on my back about it." A convertible sped past, leaving thumping base sounds in its wake. "Everything I've got questions about can probably be cleared up with a simple conversation with Dr. Valois, but my boss doesn't want me to bother him. At least not with the kinds of questions I have to ask. So, I'm frustrated."

"Didn't you already talk to him?"

"Just a brief conversation on Monday. I have other questions." Carlos turned off the garish white way and felt a release of tension when he reached Andy's neighborhood. The dark residential street was deserted, but the row of houses cast cheery shadows onto manicured front lawns. The blue glow of television screens lit several front windows, and night bugs chirped and beeped.

"Well, don't do anything rash. A good night's sleep always improves one's outlook." Andy leaned over and kissed Carlos before getting out of the car. He watched her walk to her door.

In the animal quarters at Cybernetic Implementation, the second dog used to test conditioned brain transference started to convulse. After it collapsed, a slow ventricular tachyarrhythmia began, which increased in speed, finally degenerating into ventricular fibrillation. Minutes later, the dog was dead. Twelve hours would pass before the morning caretaker discovered it.

28 /INCENTIVE

DAN RETURNED TO HIS ROOM FEELING WOOZY, PROBABLY aftereffects of the sedative and stimulant. He stepped around piles of dirty clothes, scattered books, and empty soda cans, and flopped on the bed, planning to rest. The torrid novel a friend gave him warded off sleep, so he was awake when the phone rang.

"Hey. Howya doing?" Megan said.

"I'm awesome."

"Bull. What's happening with going straight?"

Dan sat up and shifted the phone to his other ear. "Workin' on it."

"That's convincing...not."

"I'm thinking," he said.

"Shouldn't be that hard. It's not like you're a ghetto kid with no future. You've got a whole good life in front of you."

"I suppose."

"They're sending you to rehab?" Megan asked.

Dan picked up soda cans and deposited them in a waste can. "Not yet. I have appointments set up twice a week for the next month, and I guess the jail option depends on my progress. They give my parents reports so they can make a decision." He grabbed another soda can and tossed it. With his free hand he began picking up clothes and putting them in a laundry basket.

"If I were your mom and dad, I'd put you in rehab right now," Megan said.

"Thanks for the vote of confidence. Parents are the hard part. Disappointing them, I mean. Even Dad, who had been a real pain in my butt the last year or so, deserves something better than a junkie son."

"Almost sounds like motivation. Hey, if you need someone to talk to, I'm available. Maybe together we can find that incentive you need."

Dan didn't know what to say.

"Want to do something today?" Megan asked.

"I'm heading off later to visit my Uncle Ed and do some fishing at the lake. Be back Sunday. Sort of rest and recreation, maybe even a reward from Dad for my volunteering to see a counselor." Dan did some quick time calculations. His uncle wouldn't reach the cabin till late or even tomorrow, so he could leave midafternoon and still get some fishing in. "But I'll be here for a while just loafing around. I had to play guinea pig for my Dad. Brain recording stuff. He gave me a sedative that's made me sort of sleepy. Want to come visit?"

"Your parents there?"

"Nah, 'rents went off for a couple of hours. My mother went shopping and my father disappeared, probably to the lab."

Megan hesitated. "Okay. In an hour. Get some sleep, so you're not driving with your eyes closed. We can talk some more. Bye."

Dan put the receiver down and got serious about cleaning his room. The call jumbled his thinking and awakened memories of seeing her every day, dating every weekend, talking, necking. The real Megan O'Rourke was a lot more than the public prissiness she pretended. The petting had progressed to some interesting visits to first, second, and third base before he was cut off. He remembered with a sharp pain the time they'd almost gotten caught half naked at the local parking spot. God, how he missed her. It was the drugs' fault. No, it was his own damn fault.

The split hurt. Drugs sure were effective for easing the pain. He'd been clean for a few days, motivated mostly by the need to show his therapist he wasn't dependent, that he could control it. There was also the no-bullshit urine sample. Not getting a daily hit of something put him under physical and mental stress. Megan's voice made it worse.

He tried to concentrate on the techniques of avoidance his counselor talked about. If he'd had something in the room, he would have taken it without hesitation, but he'd cleaned the room as a gesture of good faith. Actually, his mother had, because he couldn't trust himself. What saved him, stopped him from heading to a stash outside the house, was fatigue, the drowsy aftermath of the COTT cocktail. He put the pillow over his head and fell asleep.

Megan arrived wearing pale green shorts and a chopped off tee shirt that left her midsection bare. She bounced onto the bed where Dan slept. "Wake up, sleepyhead. I didn't come over to watch you nap."

Dan kept his eyes closed until she poked him in the ribs. He sat up, feeling rested. "Hey, you came."

"Nobody's downstairs. Even that weird-ass, talking machine is missing. No one to stop me from entering your inner sanctum."

"Kayten should have frisked you. Maybe I should." He put his hands on her bare waist.

She grabbed them. "Down, Romeo. Bare skin doesn't need frisking."

"But covered skin does. You look great."

"Aside from the pillowcase crease on your cheek and the drool, you look better than ever, more like the Dan of old. I'm glad. So, talk to me about how you're gonna stay clean."

"It's hard. Gotta find a reason to stay straight. College, a good job, not being a junkie bum should work. 'Cept when the desire to escape and get high hits."

"Sounds like you haven't quite got a handle on it yet." Megan looked out the window for several seconds, then took his hand and held his eyes. "You can do it, Dan, with help. Remember the good times we used to have. Think of the cool stuff that will come when you're not running after drugs. Hell, think of me. Let that be your incentive."

Dan leaned forward to kiss her and Megan did not turn away. His hands massaged her back. When his hands moved under her shirt, she muttered "No," but did not move away as he unhooked her bra. It fell free, and he covered her breasts with his hands. She pushed against his chest.

"Dan, we shouldn't." Megan's protest evaporated when she pulled off his shirt.

"I still love you, Meg." He continued to caress her breasts as his breathing became more rapid. Dan gently rolled her onto the bed and lifted her shirt, breaking their kiss only to admire what he'd uncovered. Megan watched, said nothing. She ran her fingers through his hair and down his back. She then pushed him back and sat up.

"This feels so nice, Dan, but it's dangerous." But she didn't stop him from scooting her shirt over her head and let him pull her on top of him. He ran his hands over the flimsy fabric of her shorts as she stretched out and pressed herself against him. Their lips met as Dan slipped his hands beneath the legs of her shorts and caressed the line of her panties.

"Meg, you are so perfect. I love you."

"Dan, this is what you can have when you stay clean, stay straight."

"I'm real straight right now, Meg."

She lifted herself away from him. "I mean straight for good, not just horny." She kissed him squarely and he held the kiss while his hands descended into the top of her shorts. "Dan, we shouldn't."

"I want you so much."

"I want you, but no. It's not right. I shouldn't have let it go this far. We have no protection."

Dan held up his hand, then grabbed his wallet from the bedside table. He extracted the rubber he kept in it in case he got lucky. He was feeling very lucky.

"I know it's not fair, but we have to stop." But her will to stop seemed to have fled and soon the bed became a flurry of touching hands.

Dan removed her shorts and dropped his. When they were both naked, Dan slipped on the condom and Megan guided him into her.

"I love you, Dan. Please love me."

"I do love you, Megan O'Rourke, and always will."

His excitement brought a quick consummation. Afterwards, he let his weight fall fully on her. They lay that way until the sound of a lawnmower roused them. Megan pushed Dan away and jumped up, gathering her bra, shirt, panties, and shorts. Dan slipped off the condom and watched her dress.

"You're beautiful, Meg."

She did not reply until done dressing and then stood staring at him for a long moment. With a thick voice, she said, "Think of me, Dan, when you need incentive." She broke their gaze, cleared her throat, and backed toward the door. There, in a lighter tone, she added, "Maybe we can get together on Sunday. I gotta go and so do you." She threw his undershorts at him, then strode from the room.

Dan felt strange, short of breath, his mind filled with images and questions. He dressed and fetched a canvas bag from the bottom of the closet. He threw in underwear, shirts, socks, and jeans. A search for shoes took him to the bottom of the closet. There, behind the gym bag, he found a stuffed elephant—one Dan recognized as his old friend Thumper, whose name was unapologetically stolen from Disney's *Bambi* rabbit. He'd forgotten about Thumper after including him on the stash list he'd given his mom. She'd probably found what was inside as she decontaminated his room of all drug stuff. But why was Thumper on the closet floor? Not like his mom to re-hide the toy.

He picked it up and felt its soft surface, letting his hand move to the back where the seam was split. Knowing what might still be inside, he considered his options, hesitating for a long time before inserting his fingers into the seam and feeling for the contents. Thumper, acting more the mule than the pachyderm, yielded several joints. They lay small and powerful in his palm, and he felt an overwhelming physical attraction to them. Then he thought of Megan and considered visiting the bathroom with the joints. But the old patterns were strong, and he carefully placed them in a small box that went in the bag. He was shaking when he grabbed the bag and made his way to the family wagon. With a wave to his father on the riding mower, he pulled out of the driveway about noon. Half a block away, another car started and followed him.

. . .

Katy Perry's "I Got the Eye of a Tiger" thudded from the car's four speakers as Dan drove east in the fast lane. Until he remembered his unsafe driving citation and the thought that a cop might search his bag if he were pulled over for speeding. He slowed and cruised near the speed limit, making the tailing car's job that much easier. Dan turned the radio off and drove clutching the wheel.

The two cars traveled together, leaving the freeway to head into the hills where Uncle Ed had a cabin on Lake Cuyamaca in a region served by dirt roads. The cabin was one of a dozen or so that clustered on one side of the lake. For some owners, the small structures were fulltime homes and for others a pleasant getaway from the bustle of southern California. Dan had been there many times before and knew some of the neighbors. He was looking forward to seeing his uncle and fishing, but the weed in his pack screamed he'd made a stupid decision. He wondered if he had the strength to undo the mistake.

When the trailing sedan followed him onto the final isolated, two-lane highway at a point still twenty miles from the lake, Dan noticed it and wondered if it were another lake resident. He didn't recognize the vehicle as belonging there. He'd seen the car on the freeway but didn't think it was following him. When the car disappeared for brief periods on the winding lake road, he forgot about it.

A sign announced a parking area ahead. He decided to stop for two reasons: a call of nature and to toss the joints.

He pulled the wagon into a small, graveled pull-off. This was nature's place: a thicket of hardwoods and pine crowded the edge of the clearing. Only the gravel and a large green trash barrel proclaimed man's presence. He got out of the car, eyes closed for a minute, before walking into the trees, making his way down an incline until he could no longer see his car. Behind a tree as wide as the green barrel, he dropped the joints on the ground, intending to urinate on the stash as a symbolic teenage rejection. He unzipped, aimed, and tried to piss. The image of Megan naked on his bed made it a slow process.

Megan's picture also distracted him from hearing the gray sedan pull in beside the wagon, so he was surprised when he found two men were waiting when he returned.

One was a small Asian and the other a big, muscular Caucasian.

Both had hard, no-nonsense looks. The big guy wore gray slacks and a black tee shirt. The guy's arms were as thick as Dan's thigh. Arms crossed, the man stood relaxed, calm, and unconcerned, maybe waiting for something. The shorter guy in jeans and a mustard polo shirt had a look of wiry strength, poised on the balls of his sneaker-clad feet, as if ready to move instantly. He, too, seemed to be waiting for something, but there was an eagerness in his demeanor that said he would act rather than react.

The pair seemed familiar. Dan had seen them before, but it took more staring before the inkling came. These were the guys who who'd tossed him the crack from the same car near the school.

"How's it going, Dan?" the Asian said.

"Just leaving."

"'Fraid not. You're coming with us."

Hours before the events on the lake road, CEO Zheng had acceded to Andy's insistence on kidnapping Peter Valois's son. She'd convinced Zheng that only a threat to Valois's son would make him cooperate.

Zheng, agitated and perspiring, had just explained what was happening to his ancient but still empowered mentor. The man listened without agreeing or disagreeing with the scheme. The older man quietly stated the importance of procuring the missing components. He seemed unconvinced that direct blackmail of Peter Valois over some personal indiscretion of a sexual or financial nature would not work. Zheng told him there were no indiscretions, and they had to act quickly, for there were signs that U.S. government authorities were focusing on Cybernetic Implementation as a potential target of foreign espionage.

His mentor had folded his arms, fixed him with intense dark eyes, and noted that failure would mean dire things for Zheng's honor, respect, and health. Forcing himself to maintain his composure and an air of respect, Zheng repeated Andy's arguments for kidnapping the Valois boy, agreeing the plan was dangerous and indecorous. The older man had neither blessed nor rejected the plan.

Back in the privacy of his own office Zheng reviewed the latest report from Yingyi and considered how Valois would act. The plan had risks, but they were commensurate with the potential rewards. Valois would hand over the materials to save his son. His mentor had, without condoning the kidnapping, demanded that, upon completion of the operation, all ties to Xianxingzhe be severed completely and thoroughly. The meaning was clear.

Anxious and less certain than he'd tried to appear to his mentor, Zheng sat and drank tea, fixed on the real threat to himself if the project failed. The prospects were not pleasant. He lined up three pencils, laying them across two small blocks of black, polished wood on his desktop, and brought the fat of his right hand slowly to the center of the pencils. With a sharp intake of breath, he pushed his hand down and broke all three pencils. Cursing himself for self-doubt and hesitancy, he opened his computer and sent the coded message to his agents in California.

Having acted, Zheng stood up and brushed the pencil pieces into a waste container. Not unexpectedly he found himself in a state of tumescence. He picked up the phone to call his favorite service girl, then headed to the private quarters adjoining his office. He shed his clothes and entered his hot tub.

29 /SCHOOL VISIT

Peter skipped breakfast on Thursday and went to his workroom. He made sure Kayten, now transformed into a replica of Dan Valois, was properly dressed to play his role at Seneca High School. Shortly before seven, Peter led his android son to the car and hid him in the rear seat covered by a blanket. That kept him out of Pam's sight as well as Peter's. The creator preferred not having to gaze at the fake Dan, a reaction that surprised him.

The overnight rain left a shine of renewal on driveways, streets, and shrubs. Birds asserted their rights to begin a day of pecking and gathering. The sun battled haze and smog. Near school Peter said, "Well, this is it, the big test. Can you pull this off?"

Kayten spoke with Dan's voice. "I calculate there is a high probability that I will be able to play Dan undetected."

"Do you have enough information?"

"I have mastered the teenage idiom from Dan's perspective. I have analyzed thought patterns and reaction motifs. I have all of Dan's experiential knowledge from his brain recording. Although there appear to be holes in that record, and some concepts are not supported by factual memories, I have determined that this assignment will succeed."

The vocal mimicry shocked Peter, but he knew it wasn't Dan.

Kayten sounded like a *Star Trek* refugee. Gene Roddenberry had accurately portrayed the gap between the human and the robot playing a human without having a single experimental result on which to base his Data character.

Peter sighed. "Good. You'd better start using the teenspeak you say you know, or you'll wind up in the nurse's office. You job is to encounter Dan's life situation, to learn firsthand about persons and situations of drug use. Not visit the nurse."

Kayten hesitated as if he were finding another gear. "Got it, Dad. I'm cool."

"Better."

Kayten slipped back into robot speak. "But I am concerned about the safety of programming Dan's brain. I sense that you also have uncertainty."

"The procedure is safe. Any risk is minimal compared to continued drug use," Peter said. "Just gather data and keep a low profile."

The car pulled into the no-parking zone near the gymnasium doors. A few early students clustered here and there on the sidewalk and another knot stood across the street.

"I'll be back here at five. If you need a different pickup time, contact me."

Kayten got out of the car clutching several books rescued from Dan's room. He made it into the building without having to speak to anyone. Peter drove off with a feeling of dread.

Inside Seneca High, Kayten paused to relate his present physical surroundings to the knowledge of the building present in Dan's brain. Once oriented, he headed toward his locker. He found it and entered the code.

"Hey. What are you doing here? Thought you had a fishing trip." The speaker was a young smiling female dressed in a blue sweatshirt over white shorts that contrasted with freckled legs.

"Trip was canceled." Kayten had the excuse ready, but having to use it was unexpected. He figured he'd manufactured a reasonable excuse.

He paused, searching Dan's memory file until his pattern recognition system identified the girl. He then added, "You're Megan O'Rourke." When the female frowned, he realized he'd made his first mistake.

"Very good, Dan. Thanks for remembering. Especially after yesterday." The girl squinted at him.

Kayten wondered what the reference to yesterday meant. There was nothing in the data transcribed from Dan that corresponded to any encounter with the girl. "I mean, how are you doing, Megan?" The girl's quizzical look signaled that something was not quite right in that response. He suspected he should have used a nickname.

"Formal today, aren't we? Are you all right?" The girl's voice signified stress.

Kayten had not noticed any particular formality in the girl's manner or speech, so the use of the first-person plural puzzled him. It also left him without a response.

"Did Dan have dessert with breakfast?"

Kayten remembered the human use of sarcasm. That might explain the "dessert." The girl's language and behavior corresponded to sarcasm.

"I'm fine, Meg. Just not awake yet," he said, hoping the more familiar address and excuse would work. Kayten analyzed Dan's brain file about Megan O'Rourke. There seemed to be an important relationship with Megan, some of it involving rather primitive emotions foreign to the robot's experience. He identified feelings of unsatisfied wants, a nervousness, a desire to please, and a visceral self-consciousness.

"Well, you sound a little peculiar. Sure you're feeling all right?"

"Quite, Mego," Kayten said, latching on to another nickname in Dan's repertoire. Using it seemed to fit this informal interaction.

"Wow. You haven't called me that since the time I let you get my bra off."

As Kayten tried to process that, Megan continued, "Have you stopped in at the Crisis Center?'

Kayten found a memory, somewhat vague, of a previous conversation with Megan that involved the crisis team at Seneca High, but he found nothing that would correspond to a visit with a crisis team. "Not yet."

"Gotta go, Dan. They can help. And remember you have incentive to get clean and stay clean."

Kayten noted the sudden dilation of cutaneous vessels that caused a rubescence to settle over the girl's face.

She glanced at the hall clock. "We'd better move it. Mr. Jerome likes to start on time." Megan whirled and headed down the hall.

Kayten stuffed his pack in Dan's messy locker and grabbed his math text and a notebook. He followed Megan first to homeroom and then to math class.

Kayten was quiet, content to observe behaviors of teachers and students. He noted the slow, repetitious instruction and the low level of student attention. In fact, students seemed to be involved in activities not related to math, including interactions of a sexual nature, the transmission of information dealing with relationships, and other behaviors designed to impress, to call attention to self, or to threaten. When the teacher asked for a homework assignment, Kayten discovered Dan's brain had no homework reference. The teacher repeated the assignment and asked that it be left on the desk when class was over. Kayten took a piece of paper, turned the math book to the appropriate page, and rapidly did the twenty-six geometry problems, using his knowledge of Dan's handwriting. Megan O'Rourke wore a questioning look.

This class dealt with oblique triangles, and their determination, given certain parts. Kayten immediately understood the scope and intent of the lesson and listened as the teacher presented the case of having two angles A and B enclosing the side a. She wanted students to find the lengths of the other two sides and the third angle. The group was given some time to consider an approach, and one student started things off by calculating the third angle as the difference between 180 degrees and the sum of the given angles.

Finding the sides proved more difficult, and a silence grew. Kayten did not contribute, finding no evidence that Dan would have known this answer, but the teacher must have mistaken Kayten's alertness for a desire to answer and called on him.

"Dan, how do we calculate the lengths of the other two sides?" she asked.

A direct question was something else. Dan did have a talent for math and might have contributed. Kayten said, "The law of sines can be used. In any triangle, the sides are proportional to the sines of their opposite angles."

Kayten's response was already bordering on the unbelievable but might not have passed into the realm of the astounding if he had stopped there. However, he poked at his calculator as if he needed the device to determine the answer and continued, "So side b is of length 52.502 and side c is of length 53.951."

Students turned alarmed faces at Dan, and he heard the O'Rourke girl mutter, "Wow!" The teacher appeared flustered and took several tries before she could carry on. Kayten realized he must have said something inappropriate and was quiet for the rest of the class. The teacher didn't call on him again.

Kayten relied on Dan's memory and a card taped to the inside of a ring binder to follow his class schedule. In English, the teacher quoted from a student's essay: "If Jim caring for his sister laying on the couch angered him, he didn't show it." She said this was typical of what she had to put up with in student writing and wanted someone to tell her the error.

Perhaps responding to something in Dan's character that tended toward helpfulness, Kayten spoke up. "There are two errors. The possessive should be used before the gerund," he said, "and the verb should be 'lie' not 'lay' to mean 'recline.'" Again, he got odd looks, including one from the teacher.

In physical education, the activity was basketball. During warm-ups, Kayten sank ten free throws in a row before becoming aware that he had attracted the instructor's attention. He promptly missed the next three shots.

As he went through the day, Kayten used his sensitive hearing to monitor student conversations, developing a roster of who was in any way involved in drug usage, who knew Dan Valois, and where drug use and dealing occurred on campus. He also learned how much time, energy, and conversation both male and female students devoted to the human mating function.

Megan and another girl, who Kayten recognized as Theresa Evans, found him at the end of the day.

"There he is, Seneca's new math genius," Megan said, smiling. "Your performance would make your dad proud. Oops, I guess I shouldn't bring up that sore subject. How'd you know the wowzie answer to that trig problem?"

Kayten filed the notion that making his father proud might be a problem area for Dan. He'd already gleaned that parental expectations were an issue. Now he knew that Dan had spoken to Megan about it. "I happened to look at that sort of problem last night and ran it through on my calculator right before the teacher called on me. Just luck."

"Bet it was the first time in like forever that you cracked a book at home, right?" Theresa said.

Megan continued, "You seem quiet today. You usually go off with jerks after classes. How about a change of pace? Want to walk home together?"

Kayten considered how this might fit in with his mission and his pickup schedule. Getting more information from these friends seemed valuable. Exploring the neighborhood of the school would also be good. "Dad wants to pick me up here at five, but I'll walk part way."

They meandered through an adjacent park, touching on subjects that Kayten had to dig deep into Dan's memory circuits for what he thought were appropriate replies. For several, he received looks that conveyed surprise and disapproval.

At the end of the park, Megan said, "Hey, I think I see some of the old Dan coming back. Keep it up. You home tomorrow?"

"Not sure. I may try to get some fishing in by myself. Thanks, Megan. Bye, Theresa."

Kayten started down a path that led back to Seneca High and

disappeared behind high bushes. The girls sat on a bench and watched him leave.

"Well, did you hear that?" Megan said. "Weird. That's not the old or the new Dan. It's some kind of hybrid. He sort of remembers things, but his comments are off. I just wonder if he's all right."

"Yeah," Terry offered. "Like *Body Snatchers* weird. Freaky. Since when am I Theresa? Sounds like a saint. Maybe he's buzzed on something new."

"I don't think so. I watched him all day. Weird but consistent. Seemed more focused than ever. Strange."

"Whatever," Terry said. "Here's another tidbit. He was too polite. The dude kept hesitating before he said things. Like he was figuring things out. Like he was being careful not to step out of bounds. Maybe drugs have fried his brain."

"Bulldinky. He's just struggling, you know. With this addiction thing. He may seem distracted today, but for sure he was quite the old Dan yesterday." Megan hesitated before continuing. "I probably shouldn't tell you this, and you'd better keep your big trap shut, but we were sort of intimate yesterday."

Terry's eyes widened, acting the wolf tossed a chunk of meat. "What does 'sort of' mean? Don't tell me you went all the way."

Megan, already regretting her indiscretion, didn't answer directly. "Well, we touched." She stared straight ahead.

Another savory chunk. "What did you do that for?"

"Don't know. It just happened. We were in his bedroom all alone, and one thing led to another. Next thing I knew he had my pants down. Maybe I was trying to give him an incentive for staying drug-free."

"Whoa. That's a wacko reason for having sex. Think it worked?"

"Who knows? He seemed committed to recovery yesterday and acted like a serious student today." Megan thought she sounded a bit like she was trying to convince herself.

Terry seemed content to chew on that tidbit. "So, maybe I see what you tried to do, and I can support that, even though it was stupid."

"Thanks."

"And what was it like? His thing, I mean. Was it big?"

"OMG. I should have kept my yap shut. You're a sick puppy. Well, maybe not sick. Just horny. Let's focus on why Dan acted weird today." Megan grabbed Terry's arm and yanked her off the bench.

Kayten had remained behind the bush and the whole conversation had been within android hearing range. He considered the conversation and attempted to relate their remarks to his behaviors during the day. His interaction with Megan was clearly inappropriate in light of what may have occurred between her and Dan in the period after recording Dan's brain.

He walked back to the high school, thinking that this was more difficult than planned, that this unforeseen complication could have been avoided by isolating Dan until he left for his fishing trip. He evaluated whether he should reveal the liaison between Dan and Megan to Dr. Valois and concluded that lack of that knowledge would not harm the doctor. It could harm Dan and Megan. His android analysis concluded that keeping the datum to himself would minimize negative consequences to humans.

He emerged from the park and continued along the block leading to Seneca High. An assortment of characters Dan's memory identified as drug users greeted him. He ignored them. No one tried to sell him anything, and he made it to the gym doors.

Once they left the park area, Megan tried to interpret what she'd seen in Dan during the unusual school day. Terry, apparently still focused on how she could get more details about Megan's hanky-panky, was quiet.

Finally, Megan settled on an idea. "I wanna see the new Dan at home, to check on the weirdness thing. I'm busy on Friday and Saturday and he may be off fishing, but I could drop by on Sunday."

"Don't do it."

"What? I wanna see."

"Sure you do. Don't."

Megan persisted. "How about you, Terry? Wanna be an independent observer? Maybe a chaperone?"

Terry replied, "And a chaperone? Depends on what I have to observe. Don't wanna inhibit anything. You gotta promise to keep your pants on and not try any more touchy-feely therapy."

"Why, Dr. Theresa, I thought you'd be panting for firsthand data."

Terry made a sour face. "Sure you're not blowing up this behavior thing? People have strange days, you know. Not everyone is like always in control and cool and collected like Megan O'Rourke."

"Ha ha. Dan was super strange. I need more data. So, what are you doing Sunday?"

Terry plucked a leaf from a hedge and ripped it apart. "Oh, all right. I'll come, but I don't know why. Sometimes you think too hard, Meg. Just go with the flow. Live and let live."

"Take off the rose-colored glasses. Things don't always take care of themselves. We are our brother's keeper, you know."

"Hey. Like I'm Megan's boyfriend's keeper? Shouldn't I know more about whether he was any good?" Terry ducked the punch Megan sent in her direction.

Lisa didn't like it. Not at all. Something was going on. The numbers were so small as to be meaningless, but that was her gut feeling. Mortality records on the rats used for brain recording showed two sudden deaths out of two dozen rats. Not an alarming number, but still above the normal death rate for this strain of rats in this facility. One could argue that these rats were somehow abnormal and suffered because of genetics or effects of the COTT cocktail. But a cynic might contend that the recording process itself caused some error and left the brain in an unstable state.

The dogs were even more troublesome. One of eight recorded dogs had experienced sudden death, apparently cardiac. That was twelve point five percent, higher than the ten percent of rats. It could be that the larger the brain, the greater the susceptibility. The recording process might be causing damage. But only some of the animals died. At least so far.

But why were they susceptible? Lisa was concerned even if Peter Valois dismissed the deaths as coincidence and certainly wouldn't like to hear her negativity. Nevertheless, she was convinced that cardiovascular changes were occurring, and no one understood them. Maybe the pathology report would help.

PART 5
ACTION

Action is at bottom a swinging and flailing of the arms to regain one's balance and keep afloat.

- ERIC HOFFER

30 /KIDNAPPING

As Kayten impersonated him at Seneca High, Dan paced in a small basement, trying to make sense of what had happened. He'd spent overnight in captivity without knowing why. Dan replayed the scene again in his head.

He'd stopped at the pull-off to empty his bladder and ditch the joints. The area was quiet, not even sounds of passing cars. Not unusual for Wednesday midafternoon on a road leading to the mountain-and-lake area. Strange that he hadn't heard the car, though. He emerged from the woods and encountered the two men. When he recognized them as the guys who'd tossed him the vial of crack, his first thought was coincidence. That was stupid. They wouldn't follow him so far from his usual haunts. Pushing drugs in the vicinity of Seneca High made sense, but not here. The meeting was no coincidence.

Dan closed his eyes, trying to ferret out any details he might have missed, some clue as to what was going down. He remembered the two men standing twelve feet apart, not saying anything, watching as he approached the cars from the path. They'd seemed relaxed, intent.

"Hello, Dan," the Asian said.

He'd seen no reason to pretend that this was a chance encounter. "What do you guys want? I'm not buying today, and I don't want any more gifts."

Neither man smiled. Something was up. Dan let his gaze drift to his car as he calculated his chances of getting to it unhindered. Not good. He felt the chill of danger.

"I'm outta here," he said.

The rest of what happened came fast, but he remembered it in slow motion.

"You're coming with us, Dan," Muscle Guy said in a voice that invited no dissention.

"What is this?" Dan's tone was high-pitched.

"You're gonna be our guest for a while. You get a vacation for a short time while certain business with your father is completed. Play it smart and there will be no problem. Play it dumb and you'll get hurt."

Dan couldn't believe his ears. What possible business could these hoods have with his father? It couldn't be kidnapping for ransom. His family didn't have that kind of money. "What the hell are you talking about? I don't have to do a damn thing with you jerks."

Panic displaced caution. When the men came at him, Dan broke for the woods, hoping his track training would save his butt. He couldn't outfist these thugs, but maybe he could outrun them. Chinese guy sprinted after him.

Dan ran into the trees and felt comfort in foliage until the narrow path vanished about thirty yards in. Pine branches slapped his face and arms and obscured what lay ahead. Hardly the conditions of the hundred-meter dash on a high school track. Although it seemed to go on for many minutes, the chase ended when Dan caught his foot on a fallen log and sprawled face down.

Chinese guy pounced, rolled him over, and punched him sharply in the solar plexus. Dan bent double and almost blacked out from the sudden pain. A knee in the ribs followed, bringing a grunt, renewed consciousness, and what Dan thought was something cracking.

"Enough of your shit. Get your ass into the car, Danny boy, or I'll bust your arm and knock a few teeth loose."

Dan stayed curled up on the ground gasping for breath until he was shoved with a foot. The guy acted like he loved to inflict pain.

Muscle Guy caught up and restrained his partner. "Take it easy. Don't damage the merchandise. He's not going anywhere."

"Just making sure the asshole understands the situation. Get up, jerk. We don't have time to fool around with stupid heroics." Chinese guy grabbed Dan by the shoulder, yanked him up, and locked Dan's wrists behind his back with zip ties.

Pain stabbed his shoulder and ribs. Although the man was small, Dan could feel his strength and didn't resist when he was shoved into their car.

The bigger man retrieved Dan's bag from the station wagon and moved the vehicle far enough into the woods so that it couldn't be seen from the road. When Dan made the mistake of struggling against a blindfold, the Asian punched him in the stomach again, and this time Dan blacked out. He came to later as the car bounced on an unpaved road. He had no idea how long they'd been traveling.

When the car stopped, Dan let himself be led into some structure and down a flight of stairs. His eyes were uncovered and his hands freed. He squinted when Muscle Guy flipped on a bulb behind a metal grid. It cast meager light, revealing a small windowless room with unpainted block walls and a cement floor covered with a circular braided rug. A compact desk sat in the corner. There was a bathroom with a shower. Muscles shoved Dan onto a metal-framed cot and took his cell phone. He recited a number and asked if it was his father's cell. Dan nodded, and the guy had left, saying nothing as he closed and locked the thick, wood door.

Dan surveyed his prison. He was a kidnap victim for some reason. No matter. He had to escape. His mind roamed over movie solutions to kidnapping and the possibilities of rigging up an electrocution trap to gain his freedom, but nothing seemed realistic. He wandered about and finally returned to sit on the cot.

Without a watch and no window, he couldn't be sure if he sat for minutes or hours before the big kidnapper returned. The impulse to run vanished when he saw the bulges in the guy's slacks, well-defined pecs, and massive arms. Vintage Schwarzenegger. His face, wanting to be angular if he were thinner, might be considered open and friendly if it weren't for deep-set, dark eyes under bushy brows. The size and strength of his captor quelled any hope of escape. Despair set in. Dan wanted not to think, not to feel the pain. He knew of one sure way to make that happen. These guys might not be drug dealers, but they knew how to get the shit.

"Let me have some stuff, will ya?" he said, standing.

Muscles seemed to have no doubt what "stuff" his captive was asking for. "Button it. You don't need stuff. You'll get food if I see good behavior. Do you want meatloaf or chicken?

"What do you know about what I need? When the hell am I gettin' out of here? Did you get in touch with my dad? What do you guys want anyway? We're not rich. Or don't you assholes know that?"

The kidnapper slapped him, knocking him back onto the cot. His head banged the wall. The pain stunned Dan, and he'd stayed down with tears in his eyes.

"Good behavior means keeping your trap shut. You want to avoid pain, watch your manners. Meatloaf or chicken?"

"Chicken."

Muscles locked the door. Dan rubbed his aching jaw. His lip was bloody. Why was this happening? If not ransom, then what? He started to stand, but pain stabbed his side and kept him on the cot. He fought back panic and fear. At the same time, he craved something to ease his pain, something he couldn't get. What he got when his keeper returned was a meatloaf dinner. He'd eaten it without daring to complain.

At the end of day two, Muscles delivered a meatloaf dinner and watched Dan eat. Same food as on day one, even though he'd chosen chicken again. The guy then told him to empty his bag on the cot and examined everything.

"Should have done that yesterday. You take anything out of the bag?"

"No."

Morgan walked around the room and then went into the bathroom where he lifted the commode tank top. He returned and pulled the bed apart, then went to the desk and took out the one drawer. He dumped two pencils and a pad onto the floor and retrieved the pencils.

He patted Dan down. At the door, without turning around, he said, "Hope you're not lying, kid. Clean up the mess. I don't like mess."

Yingyi read a paper at the kitchen table, He didn't look up when Morgan entered.

"How's our little junkie?" Yingyi asked. "I don't hear him banging on the door."

"He's feeling deprived. Dessert will fix that. Kids like coke, and prisoners are easier to handle when they're happy. By the way, he had nothing in his bag we might have missed." Morgan stared into the fridge. "Has the boss called yet?"

"Yes. She reports there's been no activity at the Valois house. The parents don't know Dan's missing because there's no cell service at the lake cabin, and his uncle isn't due until tonight. Did you get the address from Dan?"

"The cabin's not far from where we took him," Morgan said. "I'll head up there to keep the uncle quiet."

"I'll take care of the uncle. Andy says you call Valois now using the kid's phone. You're the contact because you don't look or sound Chinese."

Morgan opened a can of beer. "Makes sense."

"Get Valois focused on what he has to do and when he has to deliver. He has to follow instructions if he wants his son back."

Morgan fished Dan's cell phone from his pocket. "What does she say about Valois's chances for getting what we want?"

"He has enough freedom to get it. Already taken stuff for his home research. So, we acquire the material. Then what?"

"We deliver it for testing," Morgan said. "To that lab that pretends to be developing clinical test methods. That's its front. It's funded by the company and can authenticate what Valois gives us."

"What do we do with the kid?" Yingyi asked.

Morgan fished another beer from the refrigerator and looked at frozen dinner choices in the freezer. "All we got is chicken in here." He slammed the door. "We move. If the merchandise checks out, we release the kid and disappear, keeping the whole thing clean and quiet."

"And if it doesn't pass muster?"

"Not my decision," Yingyi said. "But I suspect we keep the kid and go after Valois directly. The company can supply Valois with all the facilities he needs to reproduce what's needed. And he'll have the welfare of his son as incentive. Right now we've got to let the staid, peaceful, middleclass parents know we have their darling boy. Valois is no dummy. He's not going to risk his son's life with bogus goods. But you can remind him."

"I'll call on the kid's phone from down the mountain where's there's reception. Seeing the familiar number will convince the doctor we have Dan.

31 /CONTACT

PETER RETURNED HOME THURSDAY MORNING AFTER DROPPING OFF Kayten at Seneca High and took a personal day so he could hang near the phone in case the robot had to make contact. At four p.m. he put down the newspaper and told Pam that he had to run to the lab.

"Have to add an item to that operating committee presentation." He stood and stretched, doing his best to act relaxed.

"Do you really have to, dear?" Pam asked, pushing the crossword puzzle aside.

"I won't be long."

"You should get your work done in normal business hours. And learn how to take a complete day off without any trips to the lab."

"You're right."

"When's the last time we went out by ourselves for the evening?"

"Okay, okay. Maybe we can go out for dinner tomorrow. Something nice, like a fast-food place," Peter said, smiling.

"Oh, wow."

"We should enjoy being kid-less. And later we can figure out another way to celebrate."

Pam narrowed her eyes. "No celebration until I know Dan is all right."

"Damn," Peter said. "I never told you. I got a text from him last evening. He was fine and almost there."

"You forgot? Well, I still wish he would call. Not that he's very good about letting us know where he is and what he's doing. Especially lately."

"You know the cabin has no phone, right? And there's no cell coverage. He'd have to visit that dingbat neighbor up at the lake, and maybe she's not there. And he's probably been fishing all day. Maybe till dusk."

"I suppose."

"Quit worrying. When Ed gets there, we'll get a call, if not from the dingbat's phone, then from another." Peter started toward the bedroom.

The phone rang.

"I'll get it," Peter said, heading for the kitchen.

He grabbed the phone on the fourth ring. The caller identified himself as someone with information about his son's "problem." Alarms cascaded over Peter's brain as he remembered a middle-of-the-night call about his brother's problem; a drug overdose that led to death. The image of Dan lying unconscious in some alley, shoved on a gurney for the ride to an emergency room, and now abandoned behind a green curtain in a treatment area immobilized him.

The voice with a no-nonsense authority repeated his line, sounding like a detective. Peter braced for the worst possible news. That's when he saw the number on the answering machine: his son's cell phone. The police wouldn't call on that phone.

"What are you talking about? Where's my son?" he asked.

"Not over the phone, Dr. Valois. Dan is with me. We need to meet."

"You have Dan? Where? Is he all right?" Peter's voice had a panicky edge.

"Calm down. Your son's fine and will remain so if you do what I say. I'll tell you when I see you at ten this evening. The back of the mall, the small entrance near the loading dock. No reason to be alarmed. Keep this to yourself, and Dan will make it home. Ten tonight. Come alone."

Peter fixated on "your son's fine" and ignored the rest. When the voice's instructions finally registered, they hardly made sense. A meeting behind the mall in the dark? Why? He released the phone and walked numbly into the bedroom to find his wallet. The voice didn't sound hostile, but it wasn't friendly either. Just insistent. *What problem with Dan was he talking about?* Had to be drugs, but somehow that didn't feel right. *Should I tell Pam about the call?* The voice said to keep it to himself. He should tell his wife. But what if she panicked, wanted to call the police?

There was no reason to imagine things. Dan was fine but needed help getting home. He'd find out what to do tonight. Now he had to pick up Kayten and appear calmer than he felt. What he felt was fear.

When he returned, Pam asked, "Was that Dan?"

He couldn't look at her when he answered. "No, one of the guys reminding me of a meeting." Forcing the appearance of normality, he added, "Want me to stop and get anything?"

Pam shook her head.

He kissed her goodbye, picked up his car keys, and left, saying he'd be back shortly.

Pam watched him drive away, then took her book and sat down next to the phone. She was tempted to call the neighbor at the lake but resisted the urge. She hadn't been enthusiastic about letting Dan go off to the lake in the first place, even though Peter insisted there was little danger in giving the boy a break. Maybe, maybe not, but calling to check on her son would show she didn't trust him. Pam continued to imagine bad things that could happen to her son until the phone rang at five o'clock. It was her brother Ed.

"How are you guys doing?" Ed asked, sounding rushed. Without waiting for her answer, he continued, "Listen, something has come up on the business front. I have to leave for my trip now and can't get to the cabin. But Dan's certainly welcome to use the place while I'm gone. Has he left already?"

"He drove up yesterday afternoon," Pam said.

"Damn. Well, the cabin is well stocked, and he won't starve. I guess I really should have a telephone installed. I'll try to call my neighbor up there to get the message to Dan. Sorry."

"I'm sure he'll miss seeing you. When will you be back?"

"Probably the middle of next week. I'm leaving for London this evening and have several meetings Monday and Tuesday. I'll call when I get back. Maybe all of us can spend a weekend at the lake."

"Sure," Pam said, thinking it wasn't likely.

"I'd really like to see you, Peter, and my nephew. How's Dan doing?"

"Fine," Pam lied. "Just going through the troubles of being a teenager."

"Okay. I'll call when I know my schedule. Bye."

Pam put down the receiver, feeling uneasy. There was nothing unusual in Ed's sudden business trip, and her son could care for himself. He'd call from the neighbor's phone when Ed doesn't show up. No reason for alarm.

Morgan reported his conversation with Peter Valois as he put a dinner in the microwave and punched buttons. "The doctor was confused, but he'll do what he's been told. We meet at ten."

"He bought the idea that this was all about the drug problem?"

"Maybe."

When the oven buzzed, Morgan rotated the dinner ninety degrees and zapped it again. Yingyi volunteered to deliver the food.

Dan put his book down when the door opened, and the man he called Chinese guy entered, still wearing the same dark, casual clothing. Like his partner wore. Almost as if both were in uniform. The wiry man wore a constant, menacing facial expression. Although he contrasted in build and demeanor with the bigger Muscles, the two of them had something in common: movements that suggested unused, reserve power. Escaping by means of some Hollywood gimmick wasn't going to happen.

"I'd suggest you eat, kid. Your choice."

Dan did not move but couldn't control his tongue. "Fuck off. What do you guys, want?"

His jailer tensed and moved toward the cot. He stood motionless with folded arms until Dan went to the desk and studied the food tray.

Yingyi reported Dan's reaction to Morgan. "He didn't seem interested. Not sure if he'll eat."

Morgan frowned. "Captivity is getting to him. Probably time to use more pharmacological management."

Morgan descended to the basement an hour later. Dan mouthed off again, and Morgan slapped him. The blow brought blood. Dan wiped his lip with the back of his hand.

"You've got a real problem with that tongue."

Dan kept his mouth shut.

"You need to learn patience. That's the key to survival. I have something here to help." Morgan deposited a small plastic bag on the desk and picked up the food tray. "Use it and behave, and there will be more."

An agitated Peter picked up Kayten. The robot detected the doctor's state and surmised it concerned how the impersonation of Dan went. He examined the man carefully, listening to words and studying body language.

"So how did it go?" Peter asked. "Any problems? Did you pass as Dan and learn anything of use?"

Kayten heard rushed words. "I believe it went well. And the data gathering was useful."

"No one suspected the switch?"

"I believe that the girl, Megan O'Rourke, was the most perceptive of Dan's acquaintances. She seemed suspicious."

"Suspicious? How? What did she say?"

Kayten discerned more emotion than was warranted. "She kept asking how I felt and if anything special was going on. And looking for some response to a memory that I do not seem to have. Furthermore, I perceived she was monitoring me throughout the day."

Peter seemed to mull over this report as he drove. “Then it is certainly not safe to repeat the operation tomorrow. For that reason alone. We’ll have to make do with the environmental information you have collected.”

“That analysis is correct, sir.”

“Is there any reason to keep Megan away from Dan to facilitate his recovery?”

“On the contrary, sir. I perceive that Megan is a source of support for Dan in his rehabilitation. She provides counseling and friendship. Their relationship is amorous and represents an incentive toward recovery. If anything, I would recommend encouragement of a close interaction between Dan and Megan.”

Kayten considered strengthening the emotional circuit in Dan’s consciousness that linked him with Megan. This might assist in eliminating drug use, but Kayten could not calculate how he would do that, what the total effect would be, and most importantly, what the ethical implication was in manipulating the male-female linkage.

“When we approach the house, get down,” Peter said. “I’ll pull into the garage and unlock the workroom. While I occupy Mrs. Valois, you can enter and lock yourself in.”

“Sir, you said that we would not extend the surveillance tomorrow ‘for that reason alone.’ Was there some other reason?”

Peter hesitated, and Kayten detected a loss of color and an accelerated respiratory rate. “No, we just have to avoid feeding Megan’s suspicion.”

32 /BLACKMAIL

Peter finished Kayten's restoration before six. The android fixed a light dinner of soup and sandwiches that Peter ate his without tasting either.

"Oh, Kayten's back," Pam said on entering the kitchen.

"I finished the systems check. Made a few adjustments, and now everything is within specs. Your faithful household servant is back in operation."

"Excellent. I didn't realize what a wonderful device he is. More useful than a vacuum cleaner and more entertaining. He can resume his duties by tending to the kitchen." Pam pointed to the sink. "If we ever lose Kayten, we will have to hire a butler. Or, even better, a maid. She can wear a nice black-and-white uniform and, of course, be about sixty, from Chihuahua, right?"

Normally Peter would have laughed. Not tonight.

Pam examined him and said, "You all right? Sulking about the sandwich for supper? That's all we have until I shop. There's ice cream in the freezer."

He managed a wan smile.

"I have news about Dan."

Peter stopped with the soup spoon midway between the bowl and his mouth.

"Ed called to say he can't join Dan at the cabin."

"Why?"

"Sudden business trip. I should have told you when you first got in, but I was distracted, and you disappeared into your workroom."

Peter suspected Dan was not at the lake, but did not tell Pam, thinking of the caller's instructions about keeping quiet. Not having Ed discover the boy was missing might be a blessing. To keep Pam from calling the police. "Did you call the neighbor?"

"Ed said he would."

That might be another problem, he thought. Maybe Ed would forget. He hoped to have Dan home when Pam returned from her outing with Gerry. *That's what the caller said, right?* He wasn't sure.

"Dan may be back early, or he'll just stay up there fishing until Saturday. I'm sure Ed's neighbor, Miss Marconi, will take care of him," Peter said, knowing none of that was true. The grandfather clock chimed the hour. "The mall is open until ten, isn't it? I need some electronic parts and tennis balls. Want anything?"

"No. I'm meeting Gerry for dinner. Do you really have to go shopping tonight?"

"Procrastination is not one of my traits."

Peter drove to the mall and parked his car as instructed in a shadowy part of the lot near a rear door. Only one other car, an empty Volvo, sat near the building. He was early, so he wandered into a discount department store where he found and bought three cans of tennis balls. He dropped his credit card twice when he tried to pay for them. This activity occupied time but did little to calm him.

The Volvo was gone when he emerged. The dark area was lit only by a distant pole light that flickered and crackled. He started toward his Jeep, and a gray sedan emerged from a gloomy recess. It pulled up near his vehicle and the door swung open. As Peter reached his car, a man got out. Over six feet tall, he looked to weigh two hundred pounds and moved toward Peter, looming ever larger as he closed the gap.

"Dr. Valois?"

Peter jumped, thinking this had nothing to do with Dan, that he was the target. The empty, dark lot was so isolated, perfect for grabbing someone. When the big man stopped, Peter finally found his voice. "Yes. Are you the man who called? Where's my son?"

The man wore sunglasses with large lenses that hid his eyes, brows, and upper cheek. A brimmed hat hid his hair. Darkness cloaked his face, but he seemed to have a beard. "Your son's fine. For now. Do what we want, and he'll be returned."

Peter thought that he recognized the voice as the one on the phone but couldn't be sure. Who else could it be? The man's imposing size made Peter step back. Had he just heard a threat?

"Let's take a ride." The guy put his hand on Peter's shoulder and guided him to the sedan, making it clear that this was more than an invitation.

As they drove, Peter's mind raced, filling with questions, hoping they were going to Dan. That's why they had to take a ride, right? The silence scared him more than words would. They followed a route away from shops and houses and onto an unlit highway. Unable to contain his anxiety, Peter demanded, "What's this all about? Where is Dan?"

The driver pulled onto a graveled lot and parked. The headlights shone on an auto salvage yard surrounded by chain link fence and unkempt grasses. The lights faded when the ignition was turned off, and the place became darker than the mall lot. A dog barked, deep and throaty.

"Time to cut the bullshit, Valois. The way to get Dan back is to pay. Got it?"

Peter turned and looked at the speaker, not understanding.

"Eyes front, Doctor."

He complied, his mind racing. He thought this was about Dan's drug problem. It was more than that. "Maybe you'd better explain what you mean in a simple, direct way."

"Your son is hooked on drugs. And he's gonna get worse unless you give us what we want. You know how drug abuse goes, Dr. Valois. Using grows until the victim is destroyed. Like your brother."

"How do you know—"

"We know."

"What is this, a clandestine rehabilitation program?" Peter asked, still in the dark.

"Are you stupid?"

Only the repetitive rising and falling song of crickets broke the silence as Peter tried to think. "A kidnapping."

"Very good. You're not as dumb as you look. Let's just say we are holding him as collateral."

"Collateral?" Peter's mind raced to several possibilities, ping-ponged off stupid and fantastic notions, and went blank. "I don't have much money."

"We don't want money. We want the COTT program and the detailed specs for the sensor."

Shock gripped Peter and paled his face. He considered playing dumb, but this guy knew what Cybernetic was doing. "How do you know about COTT? That's top security research. The competition doesn't have a hint about it."

"More stupidity."

Peter felt trapped. "Even if I wanted to go along with this... this espionage, there's no way I can get anything out of Cybernetic. That's a top security area. You're out of luck."

The big man slapped him, knocking off his eyeglasses and bloodying his lip. Peter bounced against the door, stunned. He wet himself. The psychological blow was far greater than the physical. He'd never been struck before. The pain should have generated anger, but only fear arose.

"We don't have time for this crap, Dr. Valois. You helped design the security system at Cybernetic. You've already gotten materials past security for use in your home workshop. Getting the program and the sensor will not be difficult for someone with your credentials and capabilities. Get the stuff or Dan will be dead." The man emphasized the "dead."

Peter held a handkerchief to his lip and fumbled to find his glasses on the car floor, astounded his assailant knew he'd removed materials from his employer. Stunned from the physical attack, he blurted, "How do I know Dan is all right?"

"Pictures will have to do. Tomorrow. Spend the time wisely. Get the stuff from Cybernetic. Keep your mouth shut. We want our business completed quickly. You do your part, Dr. Valois, and your son will survive." The guy started the car.

Peter stared straight ahead, seeing nothing. He had to save Dan and that meant acting in a way foreign to the civilized, professional life. He was by nature conservative and risk-avoiding—or was until he started doing transfer of brain files into animals and skirting hiring protocols and recording his son. Still, he expected to sidestep the chaotic disasters that confronted the reckless. Now he had to rescue his son, regardless of... what? Violating some rules. He had no choice. He felt squeezed and helpless.

When they reached Peter's car, Peter had to be dragged from the sedan and shoved into the Jeep. "Needless to say, Doctor, calling the police would be a very bad idea. We'll know immediately if you do, and your son will die. Have something for us in two days. This is the only way to get your son back. Do what we want and keep your trap shut. We'll call tomorrow with delivery instructions."

As the sedan pulled away, Peter digested the man's blunt language. There'd been no ambiguity. They had Dan and would kill him if they didn't get what they wanted. Even the slap now seemed calculated to make a point: they could and would use force. He'd never had to confront such a crisis. His mind bounced from one aspect of the situation to another like a bird in a shaking cage. From somewhere came an answer: prayer. He never prayed, not even when his brother died. He didn't pray because to do so violated his belief that God's existence was unscientific. Nevertheless, he prayed, asking for guidance.

It was minutes before he could move. His hand shook when he started the car, and he drove off, fighting to focus on the process of driving. Only after he'd left the parking lot did he realize that he had not noted the license plate of the sedan, and he cursed himself. It probably didn't matter. The car would be dumped immediately. What he should have noticed was the guy's face. All he remembered was dark glasses.

He analyzed as he drove. Some company or government was after the brain-recording program. Probably not American. Kidnapping didn't seem their style. But the kidnapper was American, maybe just a hired agent. Maybe a freelancer. Regardless, he'd left no doubt what Peter had to do.

By the time he reached his driveway, Peter had ruled out calling the police. Just making some decision made him feel better. He already had the program and could get a copy of the COTT unit blueprints. Maybe they knew that. But the question he couldn't face was whether it made sense for the kidnappers to ever let Dan go.

When he entered the house, Pam said, "Gerry sends her hello.... Peter, you look like you've seen a ghost. Your lip is cut. What happened? Are you all right?"

Even though he would comply with the kidnappers' demands and hoped Dan would be back before Pam missed him, Peter couldn't conceal the situation from his wife. He had to tell.

"Someone's kidnapped Dan," he said, his shaky voice more like a croak. "He wants some stuff from the lab as ransom." He felt lightheaded and sank to the couch.

Pam came over to him. "Oh my God! Kidnapped? Who is it? Is Dan all right?"

"Yes, yes. The guy said they'd contact me tomorrow with proof he's okay. I have forty-eight hours to get what he wants." He couldn't look at his wife. He felt powerless, emasculated.

"What's this about?"

"Industrial espionage."

"Shouldn't we be calling the police?" Pam asked, making a frantic move toward the phone.

Peter forced himself to look at his wife, seeing her tear-filled eyes, and took her hands in his. He fought to stay calm and tried to answer her question. "Absolutely not, Pam. The man made it clear—that would endanger Dan. Absolutely not, do you understand? No police. No FBI. This guy is a professional. He said he would know. No, wait, he said 'we'll' know."

"We're being watched?" Pam jumped up and closed the pleated blinds on the picture window. "And there's more than one?"

"I have to think this out." A haze coated his mind, and he couldn't focus.

"What option do we have?" Pam touched his arm.

"They want the schematic for a sensor unit and a computer program. I can get them. After we get Dan back, we can contact the FBI, and it will be their job to recover the materials."

"Peter, we're in way over our heads. I think we should call the police immediately."

"Damn it, Pam, I told you we would not call the police. That would kill Dan. We must remain calm and act smart. Dan's welfare depends on my getting what they want, not on having police crawling all over the place, which would make it obvious we alerted the authorities. We'll call the cops when I make delivery. Right now, I'll go get a copy of the blueprint."

"What about the program?"

"That, too." Peter stood and held his wife in his arms.

Kayten came into the room and seemed to assess the situation. "Can I be of assistance?"

"No. I have things under control." Peter said, realizing immediately how stupid that sounded. "Have you noticed any unusual activity on the street or around the house outside?"

Kayten was silent for a moment. "Four evenings ago I observed a car not from this neighborhood parked on the street across from the house. It was occupied. I felt it might represent a threat, so I obtained the license plate number. Is that the sort of unusual activity to which you refer?"

"That might be related, Kayten. Let me have the license plate number. It could be useful. I'd like to know who owns that car."

"With your permission, sir, I could attempt to find more information by tapping into the Department of Motor Vehicles database."

"Is that possible?" Pam turned toward the android.

"With the proper knowledge of access procedures, I can find this information."

"Fine. Do it," Peter said. "Then come down to the workroom. He turned to go and stopped. "No, I can handle that alone. When you're done with the DMV, take the jeep out and fill the tank. Fill the five-gallon can as well."

The robot did not raise any objection to leaving the house. "Very good, sir. Perhaps Mrs. Valois could get in touch with her brother's neighbor at the lake to see if she has information."

"I can try Miss Marconi," Pam said.

"It's way too late," Peter said. "You'll scare the old lady. Do it tomorrow. No, don't. Dan won't be there, so all you could ask is when he was there. If he never made it, she'll wonder why we don't know that. Then she'll panic and call the sheriff."

Kayten had heard the conversation and knew company property was the ransom price. His instructions were to protect both the humans in this house as well as company assets. Revealing the kidnapping to Cybernetic Security might endanger Dan. Not revealing it might result in loss of secret materials. He required more data to choose the path with the lowest probability of harm.

He activated the computer and considered his strategy for accessing the Department of Motor Vehicles. He created several macros, logged into the web site, and began to implement his strategy. He was about to start an hour of reiterative, brute force probing when he remembered something in Dan's brain file. The boy had wasted an hour trying to decide what vanity plate he would get for the first car he'd own. In searching for ideas on the internet, Dan found a collection of sites dealing with California license plates, including several that advertised they could find the owner of a given plate.

He found such a site, paid a fee using a Cybernetic Implementation Security Department credit card number, and entered the tag number. The result appeared on the screen. The car was a gray sedan, the property of Hertz.

Peter poked his head in at that point. He checked the computer screen and said, "Hertz. Not surprising. We need a name."

"I could call the company," Kayten said.

"They won't tell you a name. Wait. You can mimic a voice. I know this may seem contrary to your robotic parameters, but I want you to pretend to be a police officer. Tell them the car is illegally parked. Use the voice of that young cop on the show my wife watches when I'm not around."

Kayten decided that the direct order allowed him to commit what would be a crime: impersonating an officer, although in reality he would be impersonating an actor. He found the local number and dialed as Peter left.

A young female voice answered with, "Hertz Central, may I help you?"

Kayten spoke with a deepened voice, slightly accented. "This is Sergeant Carrero with the LAPD. We have one of your cars illegally parked and want to notify the driver. Can you give us the name?"

"I can if you provide the license plate number, Sergeant."

Kayten recited the information.

"One moment." A minute later the girl came back and said, "The car was rented from our John Wayne location by an M. Antonacci. Renter gave Dana Point Resort as an address."

"Thanks. That helps." Kayten hung up.

The android filled the jeep with gas and returned. Dr. Valois had gone into the laboratory, and Mrs. Valois was in her bedroom, but the light was on. Kayten made contact with the CI computer and transmitted a coded report about the car monitoring the Valois house. He did not add any other information.

Yingyi scanned a copy of the *Union-Tribune* as he listened to Morgan's account of the meeting with Peter Valois.

"The good doctor was shaken up," Morgan said. "Had to smack him. But he got the message." Morgan opened the refrigerator. "That makes me hungry. Want a midnight snack?"

"We need to be sure he's getting the materials. And yes to the snack," Yingyi said.

The phone rang. It was Andy, who spoke while Morgan listened.

"Surveillance says that Dr. Valois just drove into Cybernetic. That's a good sign. Contact him tomorrow. Give him proof of the kid's health, pictures with tomorrow's paper. Have a recording of Dan's voice reading the headline. Maybe blubbering."

Morgan pulled out cold cuts and built two ham-and-Swiss sandwiches on rye. "So, we should have this wrapped up tomorrow night?"

"No," Andy said. "Saturday. Valois can get what we want but needs an empty weekend building to do it. He's already used a system to get stuff past security. There should be no problem in bringing out a few additional pieces."

Morgan, holding the phone to his ear, placed the sandwiches and beers on the table. Yingyi tasted.

"Needs tomato, lettuce, red onion, mayo." Yingyi hissed.

Morgan turned away. "Anything else," he asked Andy.

"The security guy Carlos has been keeping an eye on Valois and asking questions. He could interfere with the good doctor's system or with the exchange. Be ready to take him out."

Morgan ended the call and turned back to Yingyi. "We have a cuke. You peel it, slice it, and make yourself happy."

After the meal, Yingyi left the room to send a coded email, updating the project.

Minutes later he received a reply and decoded it. The rental car had been identified, so they had to dump it. As soon as the material was delivered, the authorities might be brought in, even if the boy was not given over. They were to keep Dan and be ready to move to the hacienda.

Yingyi went back into the kitchen. "Have to dump the car. We may get clearance for transport south of the border."

"And we still return the kid if Valois delivers authentic stuff?"

Yingyi saw no reason to disabuse his American partner. "Correct."

"Makes sense. We don't want national news coverage of a missing son of a scientist working for the Defense Department. We'll keep him happy."

"Yeah, though I wouldn't mind teaching the little shit a lesson or two," Yingyi said.

On Friday morning Dan woke in a fog. It took him a moment to realize where he was, and he shivered. Would he ever see his family and Megan again? Maybe he would die in this basement. How would they do it? He hoped it would be a bullet to his head. At last, he rose and put on clothes that were beginning to smell.

Chinese guy arrived with a tray containing cereal and a pastry. And dessert: another dose of what must be some sort of downer. After his jailer left, Dan went to the desk. Nausea had been bothering him, but today he had an appetite. He ate the Wheaties, put on shorts, and started his exercise routine of pushups and sit-ups. Anything to fight the boredom. When he'd worked up a sweat, he eyed the packet of drugs. They would make his problems disappear for a while. He carried the pills to the bathroom. Just as he'd done with the other "desserts," he dropped them into the toilet and flushed. He stripped and showered.

Back at the desk, he reached for the donut with a shaking hand. He ate slowly, reviewing his situation, fighting to hold down a panic that threatened to consume him. He'd been thinking these guys were drug dealers, but now realized that they had set themselves up to look like that. Why? To study him, find his weaknesses? The gift of crack got his guard down, so in a sense, this thing was his own goddam fault. He was the druggie, and his dependence gave these guys the handle they needed. He was used to dealing clandestinely with unknown characters in out-of-the-way places. And his parents never knew where he was for hours on end, so they wouldn't miss him for a while.

So why kidnap him? To get at his father. They wanted something. What could these guys be after? They didn't fit the mold of what Dan thought of as kidnappers after money. Seemed too intelligent. But they seemed to like dishing out physical punishment. Punches left him with several sore spots on his back and in his gut. His ribs hurt.

Dad did defense-contractor stuff, top-secret work. That had to be it. They wanted his father to get them something from Cybernetic, maybe just information. Dan wondered how his father would handle this. *Do kidnappers ever let their hostages go?* He could, after all, identify them. Maybe they were working for a foreign government and wouldn't stay in this country. They could afford to let him live. Then he thought of Interpol and the global nature of police work, how they could track fugitives.

He felt alone and abandoned yet deserving of his fate for being a user. The wonderful session with Megan played in his head until it was driven away by anger and despair at the thought of losing her. He brought his fist down on the desk and kicked at the desk chair, sending it tumbling. A tremor shook his body, and he began to cry.

A Xianxingzhe vice president delivered the latest updates on the US operation to Zheng. He read the report and said, "Things are proceeding well. But I am disturbed by aspects of the woman's plan. The hostage has seen the faces of Yingyi and Morgan. If they are ever caught, that is a link to the company."

"This is true," the VP said.

"If the boy is killed carelessly, the death of a scientist's son will bring investigation from agencies we do not want involved."

"Yes, you are right."

"But the boy could die accidentally. In a way that does not attract attention. By a self-administered overdose. It happens all the time in the United States. He will not be able to identify our agents. That would be the best."

The subordinate's main function was to agree with his boss. But he couldn't stop himself from pointing out that at least Dr. Valois would know he'd been kidnapped and threatened. The police would know the death wasn't accidental.

Zheng frowned. "But they will know nothing about Xianxingzhe. Only the boy will have seen the clearly Chinese Yingyi. He is the one who knows too much."

This time the VP said nothing.

PART 6
REACTION

Don't be gullible, use life before it uses you, understand there are no free lunches, and for every action you take, there's a reaction.

- SYLVESTER STALLONE

33 /DATES

Carlos went home early Thursday to shower, change clothes, and get ready for his date with Lisa Macquire. It was only a date, he told himself. It would not substitute for the security check of the Valois lab. Office stuff would not interfere with his social life.

He dressed, not distracted by his neighbor's exhibitionism, and reviewed what he knew of Lisa. She'd been at Cybernetic Implementation almost as long as he but remained somewhat of a mystery. He found her quite attractive, but she always seemed aloof and distant. Aside from the casual greeting in hallways, he'd spoken to her only a couple of times: for her interview and for the review of the Valois project last year. Nothing unusual came up in either conversation, but he came away feeling there was something about the woman that he did not understand. This relaxed social event would tell him more about the interesting Ms. Macquire.

He knocked on Lisa's apartment door at seven, waited a minute, and knocked again. Lisa appeared in a blouse and skirt that emphasized her narrow waist and long legs. Her feet were bare. He'd need patience.

"Hi, Carlos. Come in. Almost ready."

Carlos entered a sparsely furnished sitting area decorated in hand-me-downs. The focal point was a fifty-gallon, freshwater aquarium that separated the room from the tiny dining alcove. On each end of the tank was a large flowerpot. One held a shoulder-high rubber tree and the other a split-leaf philodendron. In the lighted tank swam angelfish, cherry barbs, long finned black tetras, and neons in well kept, gently aerated harmony. The tank was heavily planted and spotlessly clean. He liked how the arrangement brought nature into the room.

"The aquarium is great," he said. "I've had tanks, but never like this. I'm impressed."

"Thanks." She left him peering at the fish.

Carlos considered the beautiful tank a better indication of the young woman's living style than the neat apartment. Anyone could quickly straighten up messy quarters, but he knew from experience that the aquarium took continued attention.

Lisa emerged five minutes later, unchanged as far as he could tell, other than the sensible, low-heeled shoes. She sparingly fed her finned friends before they left for the concert. The event, the San Diego Symphony Summer Pops concert at Ashford University, entertained them both, and they left happy and hungry. Carlos selected a cozy Thai restaurant where they were seated promptly at the late dinner hour. The waiter took orders for beers and appetizers.

"Really great concert, right?" Carlos said, studying the menu.

"I enjoyed it. But I have a question. This is a date-date, not a business date, right?" Lisa put her chin in her hand.

Carlos made a stop sign. "Nothing business about it. We bachelors don't need an excuse for taking a good-looking woman out for music and dinner."

She smiled as a waiter served the beer, a salad with lobster for Carlos, and Tom Kha Kai soup for her. They ordered entrees. When the waiter left, Lisa said, "Very good, I love flattery. Don't stop."

"So how did you wind up in southern California?"

"Wind up? I was born and raised here. Went to Michigan for a college education, but I discovered with the first two-foot snow that I liked a warm climate. Also found out I had to go to work. Cybernetic was a great opportunity."

They shared life stories. When Carlos was distracted by a noisy table of six people obviously enjoying themselves, Lisa reached over and stabbed a piece of lobster from his plate.

He caught the motion. “Hey! That was the main reason I ordered this dish. I was planning to enjoy it last.”

“Foolish behavior on your part. How can you worry about company security when you can’t even secure your own food? In the wild, wolves eat rapidly, not because they like it that way, but to guard against their brother wolves. You could learn from them.” Lisa spoke behind her raised napkin, obviously enjoying her ill-gotten prize.

“In case you hadn’t noticed, Miss Macquire, we are humans, not wolves. We have dignity and manners.” Carlos moved the plate closer to him and curved his arm around it. He quietly ate the remains of his appetizer, watching Lisa do the same.

“So, this has nothing to do with your regular security review of Peter Valois?” Lisa asked.

The question surprised Carlos. He looked around to confirm that their words could not be overheard by another patron. “Just a date. The other is a Company matter I don’t handle in public.”

Smiling, Lisa said, “Yes, I know. You handled it last year in your office. I’m glad to see that I get a free dinner this year. Did Andy get a date?”

A clatter of dishes emanated from the kitchen when a waiter came through a nearby swinging door. Carlos asked, “Have you never been on a date? No business is discussed. Nor cat fights. Just enjoy.”

“Sure. Anyway, Andy hardly has any experience with Dr. Valois.”

The waiter served the main courses, a steak concoction for him and a chicken dish for her. They clinked glasses to a “Bon appétit” and started on their food.

Lisa broke the silence by ignoring Carlos’s no business dictum. “I like Dr. Valois very much. He’s been a thoughtful, helpful boss, but he tends toward the absorbed scientist stereotype. Been acting a bit odd recently, though.”

Carlos leaned forward as if he were interested. He scooped a water chestnut from Lisa’s plate.

She shook her head. “Guess I deserved that. Have to give you a mark for humor.”

"I can be a funny fellow," he said and lowered his voice. "Anyway, what do you mean by 'odd'? I'll decide if we need to discuss this elsewhere."

"Probably nothing to do with your hush-hush work, but recently, Dr. Valois visits the lab after hours more than he did before. Doing computer work or something. The computer is near my desk, and I know it's been used because of the slight mess he leaves around it. Pencils, pens, pads. Once he even left the key to his file cabinet. Of course, he could be just prepping for the upcoming project review."

He wondered why Valois couldn't use the computer in his office instead of the lab. "Okay. We can talk in my office."

She ignored the hint. "That will be days from now. This could be urgent. I have a factoid. Whether it's connected to anything else is for you to decide. I had to make a brief visit to the lab to do some timed measurements on rats, and I noticed a micro drive was missing."

"What's that?"

"They're low-capacity storage devices. Like camera cards. Good for collecting data from a single experiment. We get them in boxes of ten."

"Right. I remember the contract requires inventory of storage devices."

"Anyway, there was a new open box with only nine drives in it. I couldn't find the missing one, empty or filled."

Carlos sipped his beer. "So?"

"A new drive was used for something but wasn't in the lab. And it's not supposed to be in his office."

"Do you keep track of blank drives?"

Lisa finished her beer and glanced around before answering. "As if they were narcotics. Everything must be accounted for. Our storage devices are like notebooks. You wouldn't let us walk out of the building with a notebook, would you?"

Cybernetic did use point-of-exit security to control what left the laboratory and figured the disks were probably small and represented a risk. "What if the drive was defective and thrown away?"

"They don't get just thrown away. A defective one is entered in the logbook and incinerated. I'm the one who does it."

"Enough business. You're threatening to ruin my evening."

Lisa leaned forward. "Dr. Valois is authorized to take micro-drives home, but he'd take a whole box, unopened. That you can get it past security. And you still sign out for it in the logbook."

His attempt to put Lisa off until they could talk in the office wasn't working. She seemed determined to get this out of her system. "Anything else?" he asked.

"I think our spare COTT scanner is missing."

Carlos sat up straighter and raised his eyebrows. "What do you mean?"

"It's not where it's supposed to be."

"What's it look like?"

"Like a microscope lens. About the size of a double-A battery."

He sat back and tented his fingers. "When did you notice the disappearance?"

"On Tuesday. After I discovered the missing drive."

"How could you do your experiments without a key part?"

"It was an extra. Needed repair and Dr. Valois intended to fix it. Something he usually does in the lab."

Carlos processed what he learned. "Fine. I'll ask about the part."

She examined him, head lowered as if she wore bifocals. "Good. Don't delay. And, since we're talking security, I reluctantly have to mention Andy Marino. She seems very interested in the computer software for our experiments."

"Shouldn't Andy be interested? That's her work, isn't it?"

"She's supposed to use the software to do physiology experiments, not know the software. There have been several times when she's volunteered to load or unload the computer, even though that requires Dr. Valois's level of security clearance. I presume Security checked her background."

Carlos wondered if he was about to get into the middle of a catfight. He chose his answer carefully. "She was given the same thorough check we apply to all candidates." He wasn't sure that was true.

They finished their dinners talking only of the casual. At the end, Lisa took his arm.

"Well, it was a great concert and a great dinner, Carlos. We'll have to do it again."

Carlos had declined Lisa's offer to stop in for coffee, and she was home early. Getting ready for bed, she had time to analyze the conversation and the man. Carlos had acted and sounded just like the ladies-man every female employee in her age group was aware of. He was easy to look at, but his womanizing reputation was a negative. She'd expected he'd act pompous and self-centered, but he seemed quite normal. Outgoing and intelligent, with a sense of humor, and easy to talk to. Maybe she needed to reassess her previous judgment that he wasn't her type. Maybe it was worth getting to know him better. She hoped horniness, not her mother's none-too-subtle hints about being alone and the march of time, was the motivation for her change of mind.

Carlos got back home near eleven. Maria called and demanded he come over to talk about some security concern. He accepted her invitation, more from curiosity than belief she was worried about something and needed advice. When he got there, the sofa was stacked with what appeared to be research materials for Maria's journalism work, so he sat on the floor, leaning against a cushion propped against the occupied couch. Maria fussed with refreshments in the kitchen.

The motif was Spanish with a brown, well-padded carpet, an overstuffed, dark wood sofa and armchair in black leather, and wrought iron lamps. Quality oil paintings in mahogany frames occupied each wall, the picture over the sofa depicting a nude lying prone and eating grapes. Classical music played from tall, thin speakers. He stretched his legs and wondered how a freelance writer could afford such quality furnishings.

Wearing a stylish but flimsy button-down shirt and short shorts, Maria returned with two glasses of Malbec. She left the red drapes half open to take advantage of the occasional breeze. The window framed a three-quarters-full moon glowing through the branches of a maidenhair tree at the curb.

She joined him on the floor and moved close.

"What's bothering you so much?" he asked.

"I've noticed a strange car outside, and I want to know what to do. Is it there because of you? You don't just do your security work inside the building, *sí*? Weren't you out interviewing another of the lab techs this evening?"

"How would you know that?"

"You told me about interviewing a new woman a while back. You did that on a Thursday. The only time you dress and go out on Thursdays is when it's business. Like tonight."

Wow, he thought, a Sherlock for a neighbor. "What's strange about this car?"

"Just that it doesn't belong to anyone around here and has been parked across from my house at odd hours. I think someone is in it, someone who doesn't want to be seen. Like they were spying or something." She moved close so their legs touched.

"Spying on you?" He was distracted by her closeness but didn't move away.

"Could be me, I suppose. You were probably right about keeping the shades pulled. Could be a peeper."

"You mean a peeping Tom."

"I don't know his name?"

"What kind of car was it?"

"A grey or black sedan." A stronger breeze made the drapes balloon. "Oh. That's too much breeze." She snuggled even closer. "What should I do?"

He put his arms around her. "You could call the police and have them check it out."

"I don't like dealing with cops. And I don't have any information. No tag number. The car is out there just now and then. Nothing regular about it." She put down her wine glass and repositioned herself against Carlos.

He remembered the car that he'd seen when he left to meet Andy.

"I don't know if we can do anything else right now. Next time you see it, call me." He made a movement to get up.

"Since you can't offer any real help with the car, Carlos, you can at least comfort me." With that she pushed him down onto his back and stretched a leg over his.

"Just what do you mean by comfort, Maria?"

"This will do for starts. I feel much safer with you over here."

He put his arms around his slender neighbor whose head was resting on his chest. "It's getting late. We both have jobs to go to tomorrow."

"Don't be such a prude. Have some fun." She traced little circles on his triceps. "I don't want to deprive you of your rest, Carlos. I'll get you a pillow and a blanket. You can get some sleep right here. That way you'll have a chance to see the car."

"And what are you going to do?"

"I'll get my nightgown and keep you company." She got up and disappeared down a hallway.

Carlos considered leaving, but he wanted to see what Maria had in mind. And there was the memory of the strange car he'd seen. Maybe it had nothing to do with his neighbor and something to do with him. He knew the woman well enough to know she had more than security on her mind, but he didn't have a chance to weigh the pros and cons of staying before she was back dressed in a short garment. While Carlos stared, she went over to the window to close the drapes.

"Carlos. Quick," she said with a wave.

He jumped up and saw what might have been field glass lenses flash briefly in the moonlight. Then the car, which might be the one he'd seen before, started and drove off, too fast for a residential street. Maria leaned against him.

"Too dark to see the license plate."

"At least you know I'm not making this up. Now you have to stay in case it comes back." Maria led him back to the floor cushions, and they both sat down. Carlos wasn't sure about this reasoning, but didn't have much time for analysis, distracted by Maria unbuttoning his shirt.

"This will make you more comfortable, so we can get some rest," she said, grinning.

The music changed to a guitar instrumental. As Maria kissed him, Carlos put his hands under her nightgown and, finding no resistance, let alone panties, cupped her behind. He grew hard as Maria kissed him more fully and reached to undo his belt. She slid his slacks down. He lost any will to resist, any inclination to leave, and watched as she slipped off her nightie. He stared.

"You like, Carlos?"

"You are gorgeous, and much easier to appreciate this close. Better than through the bathroom window." He touched her breasts, feeling the nipples harden. She nestled against him, leaving only thin cotton to separate Maria flesh from his. Any thought of the correctness or implications of this unplanned liaison left his mind.

He turned her over, ran his hands down her thighs, and kissed her. She pulled down his shorts and grasped him, then reached under the sofa and pulled out a condom. Their mutual exploration went on for a while until she led him into her. As Segovia's guitar music intensified, he began a slow thrusting, thankful they were on the floor below the window bottom. His release came and he rolled from her. Maria pulled the couch blanket over them.

34 /ORDERS

ZHENG PRINTED THE DECODED MESSAGE OF THE AMERICAN operation. He took the paper to his desk and sat, rereading the report, a furrow of dissatisfaction deepening on his broad forehead. He closed his eyes, listened to the hum of the air conditioner, and leaned back against the upholstered chair. His posture was one of serenity, but his mind waged a battle between possibilities, options, and consequences. Finally, as a Sung antique clock murmured the hour, he pressed a button on the phone console. A male voice spoke a simple greeting without identifying its owner or asking the identity of the caller. Zheng summarized the contents of his message, then listened to terse instructions.

"The woman has accelerated the pace of the operation. Her instincts are correct. Increased US military intelligence activity is focused on Cybernetic Implementation. It could be routine, but we must not delay our operation to see what might develop."

"I am happy to have your agreement," Zheng said.

"Tell her to pressure the target. Immediately," the voice said. "And complete the operation."

The call ended and Zheng wiped his damp forehead.

Yingyi, dressed in dark comfortable clothes, pulled his gray car up to the secluded house and parked alongside a black Chevy in a shadowed spot. He confirmed that there was no one else about before he exited the car and went in. Inside, Morgan was cleaning a gun at the kitchen table.

"Andy called while you were out," Morgan said. "She's revved up about the young security eager beaver. Carlos seems to have picked up something about Valois. She doesn't want him interfering while the doc gets the property out and delivers it."

"And so?"

"She wants us to watch him and be prepared to neutralize him. That, of course, would complicate the operation."

Yingyi considered the new information. "The boss wants the goods. Neat or otherwise. Let's keep the objective in mind. The longer this takes, the greater the danger. What's on the micro drive we got from her?"

"Not good news." Morgan examined the barrel of the pistol. "The lab said we got a partial copy, lacking some master file. The software is well protected by both external and internal security traps. We'll have to get the doctor to deliver an intact drive and passwords."

"Exactly what does the bitch want?" Yingyi asked.

"To find out if Oreta suspects anything." Morgan slid the gun into a holster.

"And remove him if necessary?" Yingyi had brightness in his voice.

"And remove him if necessary."

"Any instructions about how to do that? Or are we allowed to improvise?" Yingyi seemed to enjoy dealing with this aspect of the project.

"Don't get your hopes up. We may not have to do anything. And the same rules apply. Neatness counts."

"Sure, Morgan, sure." Yingyi picked up the car keys from the dresser. "No use sitting around here. Let's check on Oreta. Any problem leaving our guest for a couple of hours?"

"No, he's sleeping. He's going nowhere." As they locked the door, Morgan added, "Andy will be doing her own checking on Oreta."

A half hour later, Morgan turned onto Carlos's street and parked in a dark spot across from a small, two-story house. He switched off the sedan's headlights and checked the building next door. "I'm not sure what we expect to find. House is dark."

"Junior's car is there. Maybe we learn when his bedtime is. It could be useful information. If he leaves, we follow."

Morgan picked up the binoculars and scanned both houses across from the car. "Looks like Junior is visiting his neighbor. I think I saw him through the picture window next door." He adjusted the focus. "Yeah, that's him all right. Wait. They're looking this way. We'll circle the block and find another spot to park."

35 /SUSPICION

It was well after midnight when Carlos left Maria's. He drove to Cybernetic, not noticing the tail by Morgan and Yingyi. The tail disappeared once Carlos pulled past the Cybernetic gate. He logged in and went to the Security Department storeroom, a closet lined with shelves. Weaponry, electronic bugs, and cameras shared the space with peaceful stuff like hazard suits, eye protection, gloves, and zip ties. He selected a metal box about half the size of a cigarette pack. A tail-like, pencil-thick cable with a tiny lens at the end protruded. He pressed a button that caused a small red light to blink. He pocketed the device along with a penknife.

Near the Valois office and laboratory, he heard only the purr of air conditioning. Carlos keyed in a combination to open Peter's office. Inside he checked for unlocked desk and file cabinet drawers. All were secure, and Valois's desk was clear. Only books resided on bookshelves. Seated in the desk chair, Carlos let his eyes survey the room, coming to rest on a hanging air fern in the corner. "Probably Lisa's work," he thought, as he got up and dragged the chair over to the corner. He stood on the chair and lifted the corner tile. The penknife cut a notch from the tile edge. He took the recorder from his pocket and put it into the ceiling space, laying the cable so the lens barely protruded. The tile slid back in place.

Carlos got down from the chair and returned to the desk. The protruding lens was not noticeable, thanks to the air fern. Satisfied, he went back to the ceiling tile and activated the recorder. It silently recorded the tile being replaced. Carlos returned the chair to the desk, surveyed the room once more, and left. The recorder stopped fifteen seconds later.

He stepped softly down the wide, blue hall from the Valois office to the stairwell and descended. In his office, he mulled over his reactions to Maria, Lisa, and Andy and their possible connections to his job of protecting the security of the DOD contract. He had no idea about Maria's objectives and motivation, but she may have no connection to Cybernetic other than the journalistic one.

Lisa seemed overanxious to raise suspicions about what was going on in the Valois laboratory. And her report of a missing micro drive and the sensor unit could mean trouble. Andy took the opposite position, claiming any odd action on Valois's part was just normal scientist behavior. Carlos recalled taking Andy to a baseball doubleheader, both ends of which the Padres won, where most of the talk was about baseball history, statistics, and strategy. Her knowledge was impressive. Security only came up when Andy was using the bathroom in his house and got a glimpse of his stripping neighbor.

When she returned to the living room, she said, "You know, working in a high security job at Cybernetic trains people to think before they reveal anything. Your neighbor could use some of that training." She explained what happened and added that Valois was pretty conscientious about security.

Lisa might have said that Maria was a plant to lure Carlos into revealing things about Cybernetic. She had provided something new on Peter Valois. Andy seemed more interested in why Carlos was investigating her boss and was defensive about Peter. On the question of his coming into the lab on weekends, Andy claimed the doctor had a bee in his bonnet and put in long hours to pursue it.

From a file cabinet he took the Valois file, sat down, and reviewed the contents, slowly moving individual sheets from right to left. When he finished, he closed the folder and leaned back till his chair touched the wall. The wall clock buzzed. He keyed in his computer entrance code and password. At the prompt, he opened the Building Traffic Monitor database.

He entered Valois's name in the first field and arrowed down to the date fields to the last six-month period. For report type, he chose "Weekly Detail," and the screen displayed a bar chart with each day of a one-month period listed. The length of the bar indicated the length of time Valois was in the building on a given day. The position of the bar along the vertical indicated the hour of entry at the base and exit at the top. Multiple entries were indicated by multiple bars. The screen showed that six months ago in November Valois generally entered the laboratory between seven and eight a.m. and left between five and six p.m. He did not enter the building on weekends. Carlos went to December, then January. Same pattern. In February, there was a week in which Valois left every day at three-thirty. He also started his weekend visits. Valois was in the building on both Saturday and Sunday mornings between eight and ten. In March, Valois's hours changed. Once per week he was out of the laboratory from noon until three. He then worked until eight or nine p.m.

Carlos looked at the screen for a few moments. He hit the function key that brought him back to the main menu, chose "Hour Summary," and entered the same dates. The computer displayed the information that Valois had worked an average of forty-two hours per week during November, December, and January, allowing for the holidays. From March to May, his average hours went up to forty-eight per week.

He considered what he'd learned. There might be some things missing from the Valois lab. Peter Valois had upped his working hours. The increase in hours could be related to workload or to a special project. He'd have to ask about that. Leaving the building early could be a matter of personal scheduling, maybe related to the change in seasons, and entry after hours could be an effort to make up for missed time. There just didn't seem to be anything concrete to worry about.

On Friday morning, Carlos took the Valois folder and banged it twice edgewise on the blotter, then headed for Mark O'Rourke's office. His knock elicited a "Yo" from the occupant. Carlos entered, sat in the chair across from O'Rourke's desk, and leaned forward.

"Mark, I need to go over something with you."

O'Rourke had been with the company since the construction of the laboratory. At age forty-eight, he had over twenty years in security, including several years in the nuclear industry after he had retired from the Army. His military bearing contrasted with his warm smile. "What's up? You look sort of chewed up by something."

"Peter Valois. There are some odd things going on. Let me fill you in and hear your opinion."

O'Rourke sat back. "Dr. Valois has been with the company for twenty years. He's our top robot scientist and helped design some of the security systems in this building. I've known him most of that time, and he has a good record, except for being an insensitive hothead at times."

"Well, that just gives him the edge if he wants to get something out of here."

O'Rourke frowned. "What've you got?"

"He's been working weekends, usually making brief visits. His average hours in the building have gone up since January. He's placed orders for electronic parts from several suppliers for home delivery."

"Doesn't sound like much. He lost his tech in January. Scientists keep odd hours, whatever the project demands, and he's a home hobbyist. I presume he goes through the same security checks on exiting the building as everyone else."

"True. But I've looked at the lab camera recordings of the good doctor's weekend visits to the lab. He doesn't seem to do much except fiddle with some equipment, check an animal or two, and run the computer. And he conveniently manages to place equipment between himself and the camera. I guess what I'm saying is that he acts suspicious."

O'Rourke waited for Carlos to say more, tapping his pencil on a pad. "Sounds like you're doing your job, and no one is above suspicion, especially when we're dealing with the guys doing defense work. Some of the stuff going on in there would be of real interest to the Russians or the Chinese." He got up and went over to the coffee pot. "Would you like some?" he asked as he poured himself a cup.

Carlos shook his head.

His boss continued, "But you don't have anything definite on the company's number one scientist. It's only your interpretation that what he does in the lab doesn't make sense. You're not trained as a scientist."

Carlos felt pressured to throw in his other circumstantial evidence. "I've done some checking on the Valois home front. He has a wife and a teenage son. The marriage seems okay, but the son is having problems that may be tied to drugs and alcohol, although his parents have made contact with the drug agency."

"Really? I wonder why Peter hasn't said anything."

Carlos continued. "Valois, as you know, has a workshop adjacent to his garage. I've watched the house for a couple of nights and seen him working in there until one or two a.m. And UPS has shipped quite a few boxes from electronics companies to his address."

"So, he likes to tinker. That's his profession and his hobby, too. In fact, the Valois household houses a robot."

"Why?"

"For field testing, and to protect Valois and Company interests." O'Rourke did not reveal his personal relationship with the Valois family, including his daughter's interest in Dan. He paused before adding, "You sure don't seem to have much. What do his technicians say?"

"Marino, the new one, thinks highly of her boss and doesn't say much. Macquire, the veteran, says a data storage item and a small part are missing. She claims a box of micro drives that normally contains ten drives had only nine. The missing part was a spare one that needed some kind of repair."

O'Rourke's interest seemed to rise. "Really? Now that sounds like something concrete. Could be just sloppy housekeeping. By the way, do you really have to date the technicians to do a simple security review?"

"I date them to put them in a relaxed frame of mind. I do the review in the office."

"What about your frame of mind? Okay, I see the picture. I hope you haven't told them there is a security problem."

"No, of course not. Besides, we don't know there is. Marino chalks his behavior up to being a dedicated scientist. Macquire suspects both Valois and Marino."

"Begins to sound like paranoia. But the missing micro drive and piece of equipment could be significant. Or they might not be missing at all."

"That's about it. One other thing that may tie in. The guard on duty on Saturday when Valois made his last visit ran into him in the hall and made a notation that he appeared nervous."

"Well, remember who you're dealing with. You're not going to accuse the chief cybernetic intelligence scientist of wrongdoing based on what you've got." O'Rourke was challenging his desk chair to tip over backwards.

Half a minute passed while Carlos fiddled with his folder. Without raising his eyes, he said "One other thing. I put a motion-sensing camera in Valois's office."

"You did what?" O'Rourke bounced forward.

"A camera in a ceiling tile."

"Without asking me?"

"I sensed things were happening, and it was two a.m."

"Get it back."

Carlos folded his arms and thrust out his chin, thinking how to best present suspicions so they seemed like facts. "Mark, it all adds up. He's up to something. It's our job to check it out, put a stop to it. We're Security, remember?"

O'Rourke put his elbows on the desk and covered his eyes with one hand. "Find out what it is you're trying to put a stop to. This could all be coincidence. Scientists can be a bit wacko anyway, and this behavior of Valois could be what accompanies creativity."

Carlos stood up and stared out the window. He had no reply.

"What are you getting out of his new technician?"

"You make it sound like she's just another security tool. I'm not taking her out for that."

O'Rourke looked at the ceiling. "Don't act so damn prissy. I'm not asking you to screw the info out of her. A good cop uses all his sources. She could just as well give you information to clear her boss as to indict him. And the same applies to Lisa."

"Exactly, but I doubt there's much more to find out from Lisa, although she seemed much more interested in the security issue than did Andy." Carlos found his chair again, leaned back, and considered if his whole case against Valois could be a wild goose chase.

"What about that car you were so suspicious of? What did our contact at DMV come up with?"

"The sedan was rented and probably has nothing to do with the Valois case. Not much help."

"So, you don't really have evidence. We can't accuse a top scientist on these suspicions. This is a competitive business. A half dozen companies would love to snap up a Peter Valois, and if that happened because of something we did, you can be sure that we'd be out on our asses. You could kiss the good salary and the good life goodbye."

Carlos weighed his options. "I'll keep my eyes open."

O'Rourke turned in his swivel chair and looked out the window with a view of the parking lot. He watched an employee walk toward his car. "There goes our boy now. Maybe we'd better find out where he goes on his lunch hour."

Carlos ignored the sarcasm in his boss's suggestion and bounded out of the office, reaching his car in time to see the Valois jeep turn right beyond the main gate. Carlos pulled out a few seconds later and found himself about two blocks behind his quarry. He followed Peter two miles out of town to the Easy Eatin' Restaurant and watched him enter without looking around.

Carlos parked at the end of the lot where he could see into the diner. He could not, however, see Valois. Two minutes later a blue Lincoln parked, and a big man in casual clothes and large shades got out. He looked around carefully before heading to the diner. Carlos noted this behavior and reached for the binoculars underneath the passenger seat. He wrote the Lincoln's license plate in his notebook.

Other cars arrived and their occupants went in. Carlos took down more tag numbers, then figured that the diner was crowded enough that he could risk entering. He took off his tie and jacket and put on a brown baseball cap and sunglasses. Once inside the diner, he spied Valois seated in a booth at the end of the row. The man from the Lincoln sat across from him. Carlos chose a seat at the counter without attracting their attention.

"What can I get you?" The waitress, a good-looking blond in her twenties, held her pen ready.

"Just coffee."

The girl smiled, turned, and headed toward the pot, trailing a shapely backside framed in a mid-thigh-length skirt. He checked the booth. The man was speaking in a low tone, and Valois seemed agitated. The man reached into his jacket pocket and pulled something out. He handed what looked like a phone to Valois, who visibly slumped.

The waitress served Carlos his coffee, and he'd begun to drink when the man took the phone back, said a few more words, got up, and started toward the door. Valois remained in the booth, looking out the window. Carlos turned toward the counter and put his hand up beside his face. He caught the waitress's attention.

"Ever see that guy before, the one who just left?" Carlos asked.

The waitress looked at the parking lot. "Maybe once or twice. Yeah, he was in yesterday. Ordered three lunches as carry out. Not very friendly and didn't leave a tip. I'll bet you're a private eye or something, aren't you?"

"Now if I were, I couldn't tell you, could I? It might place you in danger you're not equipped to handle."

"At least it would be something exciting. The only thing exciting that happens to me is when I cut my leg shaving."

"Just hang in there. Something good is bound to come your way." Carlos finished his coffee, left a good tip, and headed for the door.

Valois was still sitting.

Back in the car, Carlos thought about what he'd seen. Valois had met with a guy who looked like a shakedown artist. The meeting obviously upset the good doctor. Maybe it was time to recheck the home front. And put a name with the license plate number.

36 /MARK

At the dinner table that evening, Mark O'Rourke did something he rarely did: he talked about work with his wife. But he didn't consider it a work issue, since it concerned their longtime friend, Peter Valois. After half a glass of cabernet, he said, "Carlos—you know him—is convinced Peter is doing something he shouldn't."

Gerry put down her fork and studied her husband. "Something illegal?"

"So he thinks. But at least something against company policy."

Megan entered the room, putting in one of her rare dinner appearances because a friend had to cancel a dine-out-and-shop invite after she was grounded. "Are you talking about Dan's father?"

"Maybe, but you didn't hear it," Mark said. "How is Dan doing these days by the way? I haven't seen him around. Have you crossed him off your list?"

Megan's face reddened as she served herself salad, a pork chop, and vegetables. "Hey. No list, Dad. But Dan is, like, busy with a problem. He's cool but feels pressured."

"Pressure? From what?" Gerry asked.

Head down, the teenager said, "You know, getting into college, Dad pressure, the usual hassle." She ate some salad before adding, "He's been into stuff like alcohol and drugs. Went to the drug agency." She poked at a brussels sprout with a disappointed expression and turned her attention to the pork chop.

"Pam was over here the other day," Gerry said. "She knew her son has a drug problem, even if Peter didn't. I told her about the Drug and Alcohol Abuse agency and advised her to do something. That's why Dan went there."

"Yeah, and that's good, right?" Megan said. "I'll try to help him anyway I can. There are some good support groups at school. Speaking of which, I have a report to do this weekend and won't go with you tomorrow to open up the cabin." She finished her salad, abandoned the last of the sprouts, and excused herself.

"Take your dishes to the kitchen, please," Gerry said.

Mark refilled his wine glass. He tapped his fingers together. "I guess Peter now knows about Dan. Strange he hasn't told me. It could explain some things."

"Maybe you should let Carlos know," Gerry said. "There might be a connection between Peter's lab activities and the problem with his son."

"He knows. I wasn't very supportive of Carlos because, frankly, he lacked evidence, had just hearsay and speculation. I was using reverse psychology:"

Gerry sighed and put down her fork. "And what are you going to do?"

"Enjoy a weekend alone with a beautiful woman at the lake."

"Maybe, if you're lucky. But about Peter?"

"For the moment, nothing. But if Carlos turns up anything more concrete, I'll have to confront Peter."

Peter was alone in his home workroom, preparing to pay the ransom he hoped would save his son. He already had the COTT software but had to generate a copy on a transportable medium. That could only be done with a program on the lab computer that allowed both modification and duplication of the protected program. The kidnapper also wanted the sensor blueprints. A digital copy was in his office. He would wait until after hours before getting what he needed.

He was studying the COTT code when Kayten knocked. Peter told him to enter.

"The car I observed near the house was a rental unit," Kayten said, feeling again the programming conflict that had accompanied his impersonation of a police officer calling Hertz. He hesitated as his system confirmed that he'd harmed no one and was following a direct human order in his action. "The customer was M. Antonnacio, and the local address given was the Dana Point Resort. They never had such a guest."

"Obviously a fake," Peter said. "Don't all rental cars have GPS locators?"

"The agent indicated the unit was not reporting. It may have been disabled."

Peter closed his eyes. "Not surprising. Well, I don't see how that's of much help. But we can give it to the police when we contact them."

"When will that be, sir?"

"Not sure." He studied the display on the computer screen, made some notes, and said, "To do what I want to do, I'll need to get a utility program I wrote last year. While I'm in the lab, you'd better stay near Mrs. Valois in case we're contacted."

Peter found Pam in the den, holding a book but staring at the wall. He told her what he was going to do.

"I don't know, Peter," she said, her voice catching. Her hand shook as she closed the book. "I just hope we are doing the right thing. How would it hurt to call the police and tell them not to come to the house?"

"For one thing, the kidnappers might know we contacted the police. That would threaten Dan. And the police would not let me give the kidnappers what they want. I know this is tough, but only one more day. I can deliver the stuff tomorrow night, get Dan, and it will all be over."

"I hope you're right. Paying ransom never works—"

"In Hollywood. Be back in an hour," Peter promised.

Kayten had followed Peter and witnessed the exchange. “Is there anything I can get madam?” he asked.

“Just my son.”

On his way to Cybernetic, Peter tried to think of a new excuse for signing in so late. He failed and, when he reached the lobby, didn’t give a reason. The guy waved him in.

He forced himself to walk calmly to his lab, feeling watched. Without hiding from the lab camera, he grabbed microdisks from a locked cabinet and activated the computer. He searched through the directory and found the program designed to modify and copy the COTT subroutines and transferred it to the portable device.

He crossed to his office where he copied the COTT sensor design specs to a second disk. Both disks went into a small bank envelope. He rotated the chair to face the window and pulled back the drape. He picked out the loose caulking at the bottom of the frame, the same one used to sneak out the COTT subroutines employed to copy Dan’s brain. A squeak outside his door froze him. He sat, not daring to do anything but look out into the dark parking lot until he convinced himself it was his imagination. He glanced at the door, then slid the envelope into the space, using a lab spatula to push the envelope against the caulk on the outside of the window. Shaking, he rose and stood with his eyes closed before leaving.

The camera hidden in the corner ceiling tile ceased operation thirty seconds later.

Peter signed out, muttering a distracted good night to the guard, and went to the employee parking lot. The lot was lit poorly by a few perimeter lights. The area near Peter’s office window was even darker, barely illuminated by flood lights at the corner of the building. At least there would be no nosy gardener to scare the shit out of him this time. He leaned into the guy’s precious bush, pulled the caulk away, and fished out the envelope. He tucked the strip back in place and walked to his car.

He drove home numb, repeating, “I have it, Dan. I’m coming.” He pulled into his driveway, exited his car, and glanced around at the sleeping neighborhood. Nothing unusual. He closed the car door quietly and went inside.

Miles away from Cybernetic Implementation, a phone call was in progress. A female voice said, "CI security is aware of missing materials from Valois's lab." The woman sensed that her contact no longer viewed her assignment as routine.

"That's fine. But we can't rely solely on internal security. Keep alert."

"I know my job. Have you gotten anything more on the foreign interest in CI?"

"We're certain something is afoot but can't see what. We're probing a Chinese connection. The doctor had a Chinese technician."

"I knew her."

"If you need help, call."

"Right." The woman put the phone down and leaned her head against the back of her chair.

37 /CONVICTION

Peter Valois's numbness had morphed into agitation by the time he entered his house after the lab visit, still debating the pros and cons of calling the police. Enlisting the police at this point would increase his son's danger, even if it would make his wife feel better. There was no easy answer, and self-doubt could lead to inaction. His shoulders slumped as he opened the front door to find Kayten waiting.

"Is something wrong, Dr. Valois?" Kayten had built a large database relating physical signs to mental states in humans.

"Nothing that you haven't already heard about." Peter went into the den and flopped into his favorite armchair. "Where is Mrs. Valois?"

"Madam is lying down. She is quite upset. Can I get you something to eat, sir?"

"My wife's condition is hardly unexpected. Nothing to eat right now, but I will take a drink. The usual."

Kayten moved to the bar and poured bourbon over ice. When he handed him the glass, Peter looked up. "What does your biosynthetic analysis say about the right course of action for dealing with these kidnappers?"

"I cannot provide a better judgment than yours. There is insufficient data on key points, particularly the intentions and possible actions of those who have Dan. Your analysis may be correct that they will return Dan unharmed. To keep the theft quiet. Unfortunately, Dan may be a threat to the kidnapper's escape."

Peter took a deep breath and fought to regain his composure. "So, you don't see any obvious flaw in my decision not to contact the police."

"I see no flaw in your reasoning. Nevertheless, I cannot assess the probability of success in gaining Dan's release."

"Well, the sooner we deliver the goods, the sooner we'll get Dan back. Right now, I need some sleep."

Andy invited Carlos to the San Diego Museum of Art in Balboa Park to view a new exhibit of modernist works, including paintings and sculpture. He'd been doubtful, but decided he enjoyed her company enough to indulge her interests. Friday evening, they walked past the ornate entrance into a spacious lobby where Carlos paid the entry fee and picked up guide pamphlets. She insisted they plan a route, so they stood aside from the flow of other patrons to identify a mutually agreeable tour that would end with the new exhibit.

"Left to your own devices, you would just wander," she said. She wanted cultural artifacts. Carlos aimed for something requiring less work, like older classic paintings. They started with European art, a gallery that included works of early Renaissance Italians like Giotto and Veronese. Several paintings grabbed Carlos's attention.

"Today's hot women are not in general built the way the masters saw them."

"You must accept a variety of female forms, Carlos, from the ectomorph to the endomorph."

"What the hell is that?"

"The thin and the ample. Preference for one form or the other changes with time and culture. The form plays only a minor part in love. It's personality that counts."

"Right. I suppose. However, I do like to judge a book by its cover."

"Women know that very well. Male preference is dictated by

advertising. Women adapt with fashion and cosmetics, even plastic surgery."

After wandering past French and Spanish paintings, Andy took Carlos by the arm and steered him away from the Renoir bathing nudes.

"Enough excitement for now. Let's see the Asian gallery."

Carlos whined but followed Andy to the next floor.

"Are you feeling better about the security of our lab, Carlos?"

Carlos glanced around and whispered, "Yes. It's all under control."

Andy stopped before a display of Chinese pottery. "That means you're done?" Andy asked as she searched a meiping vase for defects.

Carlos waived his hand dismissively. "Almost. Nothing to worry about. Really just a few details to nail down."

"Details?"

"Minor. Like after-hour visits to the laboratory."

"Probably working on a paper," Andy said. "Dr Valois averages a paper or more a year. They don't write themselves, you know."

They moved silently to an exhibit case that featured some Etruscan pieces, mostly bronze works adorned with mythological figures. "Did you know that there has always been controversy over the origins of the Etruscans," Andy said. "Some thought they were Italian natives, but others contended that they migrated from somewhere in Asia Minor. Obviously liked using bronze."

Carlos pointed to a black, inscribed fragment that seemed to be pottery. "Not everything in this case is of bronze."

Andy checked the fragment. "Good catch. And all you're hung up on is after-hour visits? That's typical scientist behavior. With experiments, meetings, and diversions of the average workday, you really can't get papers done. A paper requires data analysis, creating figures, and writing scientific methods, results, and discussion. Thinking. Peter has several manuscripts in the works."

Carlos had enough of pottery and artifacts and was happy to enter a room of paintings by eastern artists.

"Anything else that has aroused your vulturous Gestapo instincts?" Andy asked.

"Just doing my job, Senorita. It will be done soon. Just a few other things to check."

Andy eyed Carlos with raised eyebrows before they moved on. They skipped the Africa, Pacific, and Native Americas gallery and finally made their way into the Modern and Contemporary art exhibit that included paintings, prints, and sculpture. They left the museum around seven and went to dinner. Andy invited him into her apartment at the end of the evening, and they did some necking on the couch. She sent him home to take a cold shower. The subject of Peter Valois was not raised again.

———

Carlos postponed the cold shower and drove to Cybernetic Implementation. At the lobby security desk, he checked logbook entries for the evening and discovered that Peter Valois had visited for fifteen minutes. Stan, a past-his-prime guy with a shock of white hair and the hefty build common to those in his profession, was on duty. He confirmed that he'd been at the desk when Dr. Valois came in.

"I was just starting the second shift. Having Dr. Valois stop in after hours is hardly unusual, and nothing in his behavior really caught my attention. He wasn't talkative, seemed to be preoccupied with his own thoughts, and in a bit of a rush. Logged in, passed Security, and went to the research wing. Next thing I knew, he was checking out."

"Did he carry anything out with him, Stan?"

"No. Usually carries a briefcase, but last night he was empty handed."

Carlos thanked the guard and steered past potted plants toward the Valois office. He collected the ceiling camera, confident that he had a record of Peter's visit and that it would show something.

In his office, he removed the camera card, intending to check it immediately. But his eyelids were sagging. He needed to be alert to view the video. Or he might miss something significant. He could do it on Saturday and call Mark if anything showed up. He put off the task in favor of sleep, locked the memory card in a desk drawer, and left the building.

An ocean away, Zheng delivered updates to his impatient mentor several times a day. The pace of events had picked up since the kidnapping. There'd been positive and negative developments. On the plus side was the report from Yingyi that they were ready to receive the goods from Valois. On the negative side was a report that Carlos Oreta had continued his close surveillance of Valois and had made several visits to the facility after hours. This could mean nothing and reflect just routine for safeguarding the Defense Department contract, but Oreta was not done, and that was disturbing. It could mean the security man was on to something, or at least had suspicions.

Zheng had to agree with Marino that Oreta was in the way. He could prevent Dr. Valois from getting the sensor schematics and the software. Even if Valois already had them, Oreta could stick his nose in and interfere with the transfer. This threat of interference and failure of the mission was intolerable. Something had to be done.

Zheng placed a pencil across the small ebony blocks on his desk and rolled it back and forth with his index finger. He closed his eyes and opened them. He tapped the pencil and rolled it some more. He became motionless for moments and then moved to his computer keyboard on the side wing of his desk. He typed several lines, and moments later his orders in a cryptic but clear message reached southern California.

Morgan took the call well after midnight. Andy Marino was giving more orders.

"We have a problem with Junior," she said. "He's looking too hard in the vicinity of this operation. I've watched him snoop for the past week, and there's no way he's going to give up. Until we get the goods, we can't have any new security measures at Cybernetic. I want you to clear the obstacle as soon as possible.

"Won't that attract attention?" Morgan asked. "You're sure you want to do this?"

"It's not a question of wanting. Until we get the goods, we can't have any interference by Security. Get rid of Oreta and make it look like an accident."

"Okay, you're the boss."

"How nice of you to notice. Good night."

38 /EVIDENCE

It was Lisa, not Carlos, who showed up early at Cybernetic. She had to take physiology readings from a half dozen rats and two dogs who were part of a new study that had to be done in time for the project review. She'd been stupid enough to "volunteer" when Andy Marino claimed to be busy. Probably recovering from a date with Carlos at the museum and in her bedroom, she thought. That idea pissed her off more than the ruined Saturday. Here she was in southern California with beautiful weather and no one to share it with. Maybe Andy's slutty approach was the way to go.

The early morning visit did produce something that gave her an idea. She left Cybernetic convinced that what she found required immediate action. Lisa stopped at her apartment to change clothes and grab a bag, then she drove to the address she had for Carlos Ortega, maybe as much to check his behavior after his date as to reveal what she'd discovered.

She rang the doorbell at eight-thirty. It took a second chime to produce a groggy, barefoot Carlos in a bathrobe at the door. He seemed suitably astounded that anyone thought a weekend morning began so early. He opened the door scowling to admit a blast of morning sunshine and an invigorating fume of sweet, dry air.

"Lisa!" Carlos pulled his robe closed. "What's going on?"

"Sorry for the unannounced visit, but I have some security business to discuss with you."

"What the hey?" Carlos sputtered. "Can't we talk at work?"

"Can't wait."

"All right. Tell me here."

"Nope. There's a price. I propose a meeting at the beach. You seem to be almost dressed for the beach anyway."

Carlos seemed to have lost the power of speech, so Lisa, in blue shorts and a white monogrammed polo shirt breezed past him into the living room. She dropped her gym bag near the sofa and surveyed the place. "I don't want to be seen lingering on the steps of a Lothario," she said. "Reputation, you know. You should get ready."

Carlos rubbed his unshaved face. "I don't know what that is, but I suspect the worst. You worry about your reputation. What about mine? Going to the beach with an employee I'm supposed to monitor for security wouldn't be professional."

"How about going to the museum? Is that more professional?" Lisa bit her tongue and rushed on before Carlos could respond. "This is your professional responsibility. You're investigating a mystery. Besides, the beach is the ideal spot for sharing info," she said. "We'll go to a deserted place. I know you like to handle security stuff outside your office."

Carlos raised an eyebrow.

"Info doesn't come free. It's threatening summer, shiny and warm, and I need some beaching."

"Beaching? Sounds dirty. You sure this can't wait 'til Monday?" he said. "I have things to do today."

"No, I'm not budging."

Carlos circled Lisa and shrugged. "You do seem in need of sun, something to enhance those freckles. All right. Give me fifteen to get ready. Have you had breakfast?"

"No. I'll fix something while you... whatever. Where's the kitchen?"

Carlos pointed the way. "There are eggs and bacon in the fridge. Feel free to display your domesticity."

"Great. You'll get scrambled eggs the way I like them."

"And juice, coffee, and toast, ma'am," he said and went into the hall where he had to sidestep his cat. Umba ignored Carlos and headed for the kitchen. “I’m sure you think Saturday morning should begin at dawn,” he whispered to the feline. “You’ll get fed when you get fed.”

Lisa pulled out the frying pan and turned to the coffee grinder and gourmet coffee. She started humming as she rummaged for a bowl in which to beat eggs and almost dropped it when something furry brushed her legs. An oversized orange and white cat sat at her feet. The animal had apparently decided this invader presented no threat and exuded no loathing of his species. Umba fixed yellow eyes on Lisa and issued a plaintive meow.

“Well, good morning,” Lisa said. “I presume you live here and aren’t just visiting, since I see a bowl in the corner.” She retrieved the plastic bowl and washed it free of dried-on food. “You should demand better service, cat. Like regular plate cleaning. With every meal,” she said. “You seem assertive enough, and Carlos can be trained.” She found a tin of cat food in a cupboard, popped it open, and placed a spoonful in the bowl. Then she considered the feline’s size and added a second spoonful. “I’m surprised that Carlos hasn’t mentioned you,” she said, holding the cat off until the bowl rested on the floor. The animal pounced.

Carlos returned to a kitchen filled with the aroma of rich coffee. “Need help?”

“Nope. Just sit.” Lisa presented a cheese omelet garnished with microwaved bacon. She poured juice and coffee and served whole-wheat toast.

Carlos emptied half his coffee mug and said, “I see that Umba introduced himself.” He eyed the fat cat who was enjoying a portion of eggs and a piece of bacon from his corner bowl. “There’s canned cat food, you know.”

“Umba. Interesting name. Certainly not bashful. He had some canned food but wanted human food. I offered eggs and bacon and would have claw marks on my leg if I hadn’t.”

Carlos sampled the eggs. “Probably. You were wise to serve him. His name derives from ‘rumba’ which he seemed to do as a kitten, at least when viewed from the rear. He's outgrown dancing with age and size. Great omelet, by the way."

"You have all the necessary ingredients and tools and keep a very neat kitchen for a bachelor. See what a woman can do for you?"

"Women have their uses. By the way, did you water the plants? And I have a basket of laundry."

"How nice of you to offer. I have my own."

Umba came over to the table and sat looking at Lisa.

She came close to the cat's face and said, "Read my lips. No more food."

The cat stretched, revealing a set of prominent curved claws, and issued a plaintive meow that belonged to an animal half his size.

Carlos tapped his index finger on the table. "Do I have this correct? You have a new factoid to trade for the beach?"

"You need the relaxation. So do I. And my factoid will make this outing a business-meeting." Lisa smiled.

Carlos shook his head and went back to his breakfast. Umba, perhaps deciding that his whining would not produce more food, rubbed against Lisa's leg. She gently pushed him away, for which she received a glare. Umba licked a paw and applied it to his face. Lisa began loading dishes into the washer. Carlos came up behind her and encircled her waist.

"Stop that or you can clean up by yourself," she said.

Carlos whispered in her ear, "Factoid, please."

"Beach first."

Carlos sighed. "I'll grab a blanket and towels."

A few early season devotees were scattered here and there on the white sand, and a half dozen surfboarders rode lazy waves under a high blue sky. Seagulls floated on a gentle, warm breeze and screeched over the rhythmic crash of waves and the barking sea lions. The air held a smell of salt and drying kelp.

Lisa chose an isolated spot and stripped off shirt and shorts, revealing a green bikini and more freckled skin. Carlos blinked, trying to remember what she looked like in a lab coat. She led him into the water that proved too cold for more than a brief dip. They toweled off and returned to the blanket. Lisa settled back and said nothing about the business information she'd used as bait for the outing. Finally, his patience exhausted, Carlos threw her playfully onto her back, and pinned her arms.

"Enough, vixen. The factoid or your virtue."

"Let me think for a moment."

Carlos leaned down and kissed her. "More of that after the factoid."

"All right. Here it is."

Carlos held his finger up and surveyed the area. The nearest humans were several hundred yards north and seemed to be massaging each other. The breeze had picked up and would carry their voices away from the sunbathers. Satisfied they wouldn't be overheard, Carlos turned to Lisa and nodded.

She spoke in a low voice. "I discovered two more disks missing."

"When?"

"Just today. I had to stop in early to record some vitals. I found a new box of disks on the lab bench with two missing ones and no entry in the logbook."

Carlos processed that as a seagull swooped overhead. "That's not much. Hardly seems to compensate for this beach expedition." His eyes scanned the bikini and its connections.

Lisa pulled his baseball cap over his eyes, and then grabbed a towel and covered herself. "Well, what are you going to do about it?"

"I'll check it out."

"That sounds like bull. I told you about missing stuff earlier and you've done nothing. This is serious."

"How do you know what I did?"

"I hope that means you did something."

They watched a surfer negotiate a rare large wave and disappear in the foam. His surfboard floated toward the shore, its ankle cord unattached. The owner emerged behind the braking wave and swam after his board.

Carlos sensed the date was over and drove them back to his house and Lisa's car. He didn't have to make any excuse to follow up on what Lisa had told him. She was all in favor of action. It would have ended as a wonderful, pleasant diversion if Carlos had kept his mouth shut about something that happened a week ago.

"I really enjoyed this," he said and should have stopped there. Instead, he continued. "A lot better time than I had when my neighbor Maria showed up last week with a job she wanted help with. In fact, when the doorbell rang, I was sure it was Maria."

"Your next door neighbor?" Lisa asked. "That pretty girl eyeing us from her porch? You're friends?"

"Friends enough for her to ask me to help with a paint job."

"What happened?"

"She showed up as early as you did and was so polite. Sucked me in before I was even awake. 'How'd you like to help a poor, unskilled girl do a necessary job?' she said. I'm thinking she needed something relocated."

"And you just couldn't say no," Lisa said. "Because you are so nice."

"I didn't turn you down."

"I had business for you. Did she make you breakfast?"

Carlos thought back. "Yes. But not as great as yours."

"Was painting all you helped her with?"

"Right. Took a couple of hours. Then I escaped."

"No showering together?" Lisa said without a smile.

Carlos had no response to that, wondering what would have happened if Maria and Lisa showed up at the same time. Might have turned into an interesting introduction. He watched Lisa drive away, cleaned up, and drove to Cybernetic, forcing his mind back on the Valois case. Peter Valois had visited the facility on Friday evening, maybe taking away another two disks. He'd been careless. Why? Some kind of stress?

He thought over what he learned from the security guard. Valois had told the guard he needed "something" from the lab. But he didn't carry a briefcase or anything else with him when he left. Maybe what he needed was information, but that should mean disks if it was enough to warrant a late trip to the lab. A disk would have set off an alarm from the exit scanner. What was he missing?

He entered the lobby, checked the logbook, and went to his office. From the locked drawer, he retrieved the video disk from Valois's office, inserted it into a reader, and started the playback. The bulk of the recording contained the usual office activities during the day on Friday and included everything from typing to eating lunch to shining shoes. But the last segment showed Peter Valois's visit to his office in the evening.

Carlos watched him enter, sit at the computer, and apparently copy something onto a microdisk. *That could be one of Lisa's missing ones.* Then he held two disks, placed them in an envelope, sat at his desk, and rotated the chair to face the window. He pulled back the drape and picked at something. Then he stopped, seemingly content to stare out at the parking lot.

What happened next was so brief that Carlos almost missed it. In fact, he had to replay the sequence. It showed Valois reaching toward the window and then placing the envelope at the bottom. But the movement was partially blocked from the camera's view by Valois's back. A moment later the scientist turned back to his desk without the envelope. He left the office carrying nothing, and the recording ended.

"What the hell?" Carlos said aloud, tapping his pencil. He wondered if Peter used the windowsill as a storage shelf, decided against that, and headed to Dr. Valois's office. He pulled aside the drapes and found no envelope. The window frame caught his attention. Nothing seemed amiss until he began poking along the frame and came to a piece of loose caulking. Carlos lifted the long segment and saw the space between the frame and the cinder block. A sliver of daylight showed that the thin channel reached through the wall.

"Holy shit," he said.

He exited the building, scanned right of the entrance, and walked around to the Valois office. He calculated the window location and pulled aside the bushes. It didn't take much to find the cracked caulking. When he dislodged the piece, the other side of the opening between cinder block and window frame appeared.

"Son of a bitch!" He turned and went back to his office. He dialed Mark O'Rourke's number, thinking he now had something that his boss should know about and act on. He wanted Mark's blessing to talk to Peter Valois. The O'Rourke phone was answered by a machine, and

Carlos remembered that Mark said something about a weekend at their cabin. He wouldn't be back until Sunday evening. Carlos left a message saying he needed to talk and could be contacted at home. He put the camera disk and a note in an envelope, wrote Mark's name on it, and left it on his desk. He grabbed a notepad and left Cybernetic, knowing what he had to do. He couldn't wait for permission. He would talk to Peter Valois.

39 /REVELATION

Carlos left the freeway and cruised through a residential neighborhood filled with activity. Lawn mowing, a driveway basketball game, and a garage sale were in progress. Cars from the garage sale were parked at the curb near the Valois residence. He joined them and sat for a moment, thinking of the questions he had to ask. There was a risk in confronting the scientist before having talked with his boss, but he had to do something.

Kayten answered, escorted Carlos into the den, and left to get Peter. Carlos marveled at the completely human behavior of what he knew was a robot. Peter arrived with a questioning look.

"Good afternoon, Dr. Valois. I hope this isn't an inconvenient time."

"No, I've got an appointment this evening, but right now I'm relaxing. Just finished cutting the grass. Having a teenager doesn't mean it gets mowed automatically."

Carlos thought the doctor winced as he said the last. Peter pointed to one of the easy chairs at the end of a coffee table, and Carlos sat, feeling a warm breeze from the open windows. Peter chose the sofa that faced a big screen television on the wall opposite. Bookshelves, casual lamps, and a potted snake plant made for a comfortable setting, but Carlos sensed tension.

"What's up?" Peter asked in a soft voice. "I thought we'd had our security interview earlier this week."

Carlos got to the point. "I need an explanation. I found a little slot in the wall below your office window, Doctor, and was wondering if you knew of its existence."

Peter's mouth hung open as Pam Valois entered the room. Peter introduced his wife. Carlos wanted to keep this between himself and Dr. Valois, but Pam took a seat. She sat next to her husband on the sofa. Carlos expected Dr. Valois to ask how he'd learned of the window problem and was prepared to say a worker reported it. The need to lie about his source and to get Dr. Valois alone was taken away by Mrs. Valois.

"Peter, I can't take it any longer," Pam said. "I'm a nervous wreck. We have to get help." She put her hand on Peter's leg and turned to Carlos. "Mr. Oreta, my husband was getting something from Cybernetic because we are being blackmailed. Our son has been kidnapped and threatened."

Carlos sat back, his lips parted. This wasn't what he expected and had to fight to respond in a professional manner. He didn't doubt the story, seeing Pam Valois's face. Peter met his eyes and nodded.

No one spoke for almost a minute. Finally, Carlos pulled out his notebook and asked that they tell him the whole story from the beginning. He listened for the next fifteen minutes as Peter and Pam unfolded the story of Dan's disappearance and the demand for payment. Pam was crying before the tale was complete. Carlos confirmed the timing. Dan left home on Wednesday and, as far as his parents knew, never reached his uncle's lake house. A man called late Thursday afternoon, and Peter met the man at the mall. Valois's description was meager, but it sounded like the big guy Carlos saw at the diner with Peter. The instructions were to deliver two items tonight at a meeting after dark.

"And you haven't called the police?" Carlos felt like he was sitting on a powder keg with a lit cigar.

"No. The kidnapper said he would know if we did and demanded I deliver the goods if we want Dan back unharmed. My wife wanted to call, but I convinced her that we had to play along for Dan's sake. You're the first person we've told."

"You should have called the cops. Immediately. You're dealing with a professional, probably more than one, and they have all the advantages if you don't get the experts working for you. In a kidnapping, that's the FBI. You need to call them now. I'm going to alert my boss. Where is the material you took from Cybernetic? Give it to me."

Peter stared at Carlos, "We can't call the authorities since we're being watched, electronically or otherwise. You can do that when you're away from here and sure you're not followed. I'll keep the copies of a computer program and a blueprint of the sensor. Until I have my son." He stood and folded his arms.

"That stuff is not yours. It belongs to the company. Let me have it. If Mark O'Rourke says it's all right to use it as ransom, I'll be back here directly, and we'll do this with the FBI."

Carlos figured the Feds would never let the doctor hand over classified material anyway.

"It's my son's life on the line here," Peter said.

"I realize that, but you've got help now."

Peter slumped as he went to his workroom and looked defeated when he came back with a manila envelope. "The program and COTT sensor diagrams are on microdisks."

Carlos checked that the envelope held disks before tucking it under his arm. "All right," he said. "I'll be back. You're probably right about your phone being monitored, so I'll handle the FBI and my boss. We'll see that your son is returned unharmed. You did the right thing by telling me. You should have done it sooner. Now just sit tight."

Carlos ran to his car and gunned it away from the curb.

Parked half a block away, Morgan and Yingyi watched Carlos leave the Valois house. Morgan started the car and followed.

"Why would the security guy from Cybernetic show up at the doctor's home?" Morgan asked.

"Don't know," Yingyi said. "But he looked serious going in and upset coming out. I think the doctor blabbed."

"I guess the boss was on to something. Junior has definitely become a nuisance," Morgan said as he worked to stay close to Carlos's sedan.

"We have orders, and here he is. Let's find out where he's going in such a rush.

Carlos had to talk with Mark O'Rourke before he contacted the feds. The FBI would want to poke around inside of Cybernetic, something Mark had to approve. Unfortunately, there was no cell phone service at the O'Rourke lake house, but the cabin wasn't far away. Ransom payment was scheduled after dark, so he had time to drive there and return. Might take a couple of hours, but at least he'd give Mark the chance to handle this himself.

Carlos was agitated enough to be oblivious to the car tailing him. Only when he turned off the main highway and started the climb up to the lake did he even notice it. He accelerated. So did the tail. The car closed the distance between them and tried to come alongside him. On the right-hand side of the road was a guardrail protecting from a steep drop off. He recognized the blue Lincoln as the one he'd seen at the Easy Eatin' Diner. Too much of a coincidence.

"If we could make this look like an accident, we'd score points for neatness," Morgan said.

"Let's just do the job and get back to make the pickup from Valois. The boss wants us out of the country tonight." Yingyi had taken a map out when Carlos left the freeway. "He's heading toward the hills; the same road Valois's technician, Ms. Wu, took when she had what the cops called her fatal accident."

"Won't two accidents seem suspicious?"

"It's the main road to the lake. A bad road. Needs better guard rails."

. . .

Carlos realized he was being followed when the Lincoln stayed with him on the two-lane road to the O'Rourke cabin. It hung on his tail way too close. He fished for ıhis cell phone and accelerated. The Lincoln kept pace. Carlos maneuvered over the centerline to hog the road and started to punch 911 when the big vehicle banged the smaller car's bumper and shoved it to the right. The phone flew and banged on the floor as Carlos fought to hold the road. When the vehicles separated, the smaller car's bumper dragged, rattling along the pavement. Carlos fought to stay on the blacktop as he entered a right turn that skirted the ravine. The Lincoln moved alongside.

The Lincoln jerked abruptly and shoved the smaller car into the guardrail. Ripping metal screeched. Carlos unsnapped his seat belt and struggled to hold the car straight. Another shove. A break appeared in the guard rail guarded by a barrel. The damaged barrier would someday be repaired. The wounded vehicle bounced through the opening and into the air. The nose dipped and the small car plummeted down the steep embankment. The vehicle caromed off the ledge and sailed. Sounds of snapping trees, rending metal, and breaking glass preceded a throaty explosion.

40 /PAYMENT

Late Saturday, after taking care of the Carlos problem, Morgan and Yingyi prepared to meet Peter Valois. Andy Marino showed up with questions and instructions.

"What happened?" she asked.

"There was an automobile accident," Yingyi said. "Quite serious, resulting in fatal injuries."

"Where?"

"On the ravine road leading to Lake Cuyamaca. About eight miles from the highway in an isolated area. A piece of guardrail's missing on one of the turns. The driver lost control for some reason and plunged off the road. Into a steep drop off."

"And?"

"There was an explosion. As I said, quite serious." Yingyi glanced at Morgan.

Morgan raised his eyebrows and added, "Right. That's what happened. There was a ball of fire down in the gulch. No one around to see it."

"Did you make sure Carlos went down with the car?" Andy asked.

Morgan shook his head. "No, we didn't climb down the hill. It's a steep drop. Carlos went into the ravine."

"You should have checked. Now I have to do it."

Morgan gazed at the ceiling and said, "I don't think it's necessary, but you can follow up if you want to."

"You collect the stuff from Valois, give it to the courier, and move yourselves and the kid out of the country. Tonight."

"No problem," Yingyi said.

"One other thing," Andy said. "Start thinking about how Dan Valois can overdose and wind up in a back alley somewhere."

When Andy left, Yingyi said, "The bitch thinks she has to check on our work."

"Let her," Morgan said. "Maybe she'll slip and wind up in the ravine. I'll give Valois instructions for transfer. After we collect, we move. Let's feed our guest now. As soon as we return from the lake, we'll relax him and put him in the van. He won't be happy."

"Tough," Yingyi said.

Hours dragged by after Carlos left the Valois house. Now it was dark. No calls from Carlos or the FBI. Disturbing. Peter and Pam waited for the promised contact from the kidnapper. When Pam left to get something from the kitchen, the phone rang. Peter picked up on the first ring. "Valois residence."

"Bring the material to the lake at that county park near you. The north shore parking area in one hour. Stay in the car and wait." The male voice was familiar, gruff, and businesslike.

Peter felt a surge of both relief and anxiety, glad to get his instructions but panicked about his son's welfare. He had no choice but to trust this guy. "Will you have Dan with you? When will I see my son?"

"If you want to see your son alive, bring the stuff now. Just you, Dr. Valois. You'll be watched." The connection was broken. Peter stood with the receiver in his hand, fighting cold dread in the pit of his stomach. Pam appeared.

"I was listening on the extension. Let's call the police now, Peter."

"No safer now than before the phone call. Oreta is handling that, and there's no time to wait for him." Again, Peter wondered why they hadn't heard from the security man or the FBI. What if Carlos had not been able to contact the police? He didn't voice his fears and tried to sound confident. "They want delivery now. We'll get Dan back once they have it. Then we can call the authorities." Peter was even less certain now that going it alone without the police was correct.

"Well, let me go with you, Peter."

"No, you need to stay here to give the new information to the FBI when they arrive. My bet is these guys will be out of the country within hours of getting the program and the blueprints. They may work for a foreign robotics company, maybe another government. I'm sorry I had to see the one guy's face. There's no point in risking your coming face-to-face with him."

Pam looked uncertain. "My brain gets your logic, but my heart doesn't. Things seem so out of control. If seeing the kidnapper is dangerous, then you're already at risk. Maybe they intend to take you captive. Maybe they intend to kill you."

"Don't imagine things. They just want the stuff I got from Cybernetic. They want to keep this quiet. To be safe, I'll take Kayten," Peter said.

Pam collapsed on a chair with her hand to her mouth, unable to speak.

Kayten entered the room. "Shall you be needing me, sir?"

"Yes. You'll come with me, and I'll let you off near the delivery point so that you can observe hidden in the trees. Go put on something dark." Having access to Kayten's observation capabilities could be useful, he decided.

"Shall I bring anything?"

"Just yourself."

Peter slipped on his suit jacket and picked up the manila envelope, a duplicate of what Carlos had carried away, and car keys from the entry table. "This will all be over in an hour, Pam. I love you."

When he reached the car, Peter decided to move the robot from the front seat. "You'd better sit low in the rear seat, Kayten, just in case we are tailed. There's a blanket back there. If it isn't convenient to let you out, you'll have to stay hidden on the floor." He pressed the dome override button so that no light would come on when the Jeep door was opened.

Evening was beginning to dissipate the day's heat as Peter turned onto the road leading to the lake. In a dark area several hundred feet from the parking lot entrance, the Jeep stopped, the rear door opened and closed, and then the car resumed its forward motion. There was one other car. Peter parked away from this vehicle that seemed unoccupied and sat facing the water. His phone rang.

"Proceed to the south shore parking lot and do not stop." The usual voice gave the order.

Peter had connected his phone to his car radio, which Kayten was monitoring and through which he could communicate. "Hear that, Kayten?"

The android confirmed he'd heard. Peter started driving, taking his time about it, hoping Kayten could make his way around the lake in time. Minutes later Peter pulled into the new location and parked in darkness.

Nothing happened, and a fearful, clammy feeling grew worse as time slipped by. He wondered if something had gone wrong. He'd done what they wanted, and there were no police involved. Perhaps he was being observed. *Have I got the right parking lot?*

"Car approaching, sir. Single occupant." Kayten's voice came from the radio.

Obviously Kayten had understood what was going on and found a shortcut through the woods to the south lot. Peter watched a van turn into the lot and pull in close beside the Jeep. Its driver, the man Peter had met before, kept the engine running.

The passenger window was powered down and Peter lowered his window.

"Hand it over." The driver wore sunglasses.

Peter dropped the manila envelope into the van passenger seat. "Where is my son?" he asked. "You've gotten what you want."

The driver did not look at the envelope or check its contents. He kept his eyes on Peter. "We'll check your materials, Dr. Valois. You will hear from us. Remain here for thirty minutes." The window closed, and the van backed out.

Check it out? They could certainly fax the blueprint to their experts, but how could they check out the program? Most likely they would copy the disk, then hand carry it to a laboratory. And it would have to be a sophisticated laboratory for them to do any meaningful checking. The man had clearly said that they would keep Dan until they had completed the testing. Would they take Dan with them? Maybe out of the country? What was he supposed to do now? Would contacting the police help or hurt his son's chances? Uncertainty flooded in as minutes ticked away in darkness.

"Kayten, you might as well return to the car." Peter spoke into his phone. The night was silent except for the regular hooting of a nearby owl. From the woods on Peter's left, a figure emerged from the trees. Kayten took the time to survey the ground next to the Valois vehicle before coming around the back of the car and entering the front passenger seat.

"They are gone, sir. The area is empty. I have no record of having seen the van before around the house, but I may have seen it during our travels to and from Seneca High School."

"That doesn't surprise me. What about that car over there?"

Kayten turned toward the car and studied it for five seconds. "Infrared analysis indicates that there is no life form in or around the vehicle and that the vehicle has not been driven in hours."

"All right. The cops must be on this case by now, and you can give a description of the van and its tag number." He checked the time. A half hour had passed since he'd paid the ransom, and the man had not returned with Dan. "Let's get some help. I've done what I was asked and pray to God that there's some good in the world and we get Dan back safe."

Pain awakened Carlos under moonlight. His left arm was twisted beside him, and his face was pushed into weeds. He raised his head and looked around. His car had vanished. The breeze brought the smell of burnt rubber or plastic. Pain shot through his knee when he tried to move. He sensed his feet were lower than his head and took a moment to figure out he was on a slope. He stopped trying to move and listened to a chorus of crickets. As the fuzziness cleared from his brain, he groaned, more aware of pain in his arm and head. Something skittered on his right.

He tried to remember what happened. There'd been a large, green sedan with a big male driver and a smaller passenger, possibly also male. He'd seen the driver before but couldn't remember where or when. Then the diner came back to mind. This wasn't an accident—he'd been run off the road and left for dead. A breeze arose and swayed branches lower on the slope.

How could I be watching treetops lying on my stomach? At last, he put it together. The slope was steep, and there were trees below him. Not being dead brought a smile despite the pain. The car had shot past the guardrail and bounced. The driver's door flew open and he, not wearing a seatbelt, had been ejected. *I always wear a seatbelt. What happened?* Slowly it came to him. When the big car banged the side of the Toyota, he knew his assailants intended to shove him off the road and he'd unclicked the belt in case he had to jump out.

It took a bit longer to figure out where he'd been going. To the O'Rourke cabin in a rush. To report the Valois kid's abduction and that Cybernetic property was about to be paid as blackmail. There was something else. He had to call the cops. That meant he had to get back up to the road and flag a ride, but when he tried to move, pain shot into his shoulder.

He quelled a sudden panic and focused on the good: he'd escaped his car and hadn't struck a rock or a tree. His luck had held when he'd fallen onto the little ledge that prevented his descent into the gully. Too bad the hard ground had knocked him out and left him with a splitting headache. A pebble meandered past his nose and sailed off the cliff edge. It ended up along with his car many feet below in a rocky streambed.

"For once, not wearing my seat belt was the right thing to do," Carlos said aloud to see if he could speak. Somewhere close an owl hooted agreement. He looked through the one eye that wasn't swollen shut. He touched it and felt blood. "Well, you can't just lie here forever, stupid. It's time to get back in the saddle." He tried to move, and pain almost made him black out. His shoulder screamed. Working with his uninjured right arm, he undid his belt and gingerly slipped the injured arm into his pants. He tightened the belt to immobilize the damaged limb as he moved. The effort covered his forehead with perspiration. He wiped and, in the process, cleared his injured eye. It opened a slit, and he could see. He rested to regain strength before beginning the climb.

———

Hours later, the report of getting materials from Peter Valois in California reached Beijing. For the first time, Zheng sensed success. What else could getting the software and the blueprint mean? Real success needed confirmation, however. He had to have proof that the software was functional, the blueprint accurate.

"How long will checking the materials take?" Zheng asked his assistant.

The man gave the answer Zheng had already heard. "The Palo Alto lab verified the contents but decided they couldn't do the functional test. The materials will arrive late today by corporate jet. A courier will carry them to the laboratory. They're waiting and will commence testing immediately."

"And then?"

"The chief scientist expects to take a week to fabricate a suitable model of the scanner and confirm that the software works."

"Then we must be patient and make sure the American is available to correct any stupid mistakes he may have made. Have they moved the hostage yet?" Zheng asked.

"It is happening now."

Zheng again savored success.

———

Yingyi and Morgan had returned to the house after turning over the ransom to a courier. They packed the cargo van. Yingyi shoved electronics into a bag and zipped it.

"The kid's got to stay quiet," Morgan said, "especially when we cross the border. Not that anyone sneaks across going south. That would be like sneaking into prison."

"Arrangements have been made, and money has been paid to clear our way. There will be no problem."

"Good."

"You take care of the boy while I finish here. We'll drop off the Lincoln for body repair, and the boss can return it. It's only got a little scratch. Get Danny boy to collect his stuff and drug him."

Dan was on his bed reading a book when Morgan arrived.

"We have to move," Morgan said. "Now."

"Where are we going?" Dan hadn't counted on any relocation, which could be good or bad. Maybe it would give him a chance to escape.

"None of your business, kid. Get your crap together. I'll bring you a little something to make you feel good during the trip. Get your butt ready to move, and everything will proceed smoothly. You haven't fucked up yet, so don't start now."

"What little something?" Dan was over the worse physical pain of withdrawal, but his psychological need was still there. He figured Morgan had a downer to keep his him quiet and calm. The attraction of the drug hit him hard, even though he'd avoided taking any of the stuff proffered up to now.

Morgan didn't answer and left.

Dan threw the book he'd been reading into the bag on top of his clothes. He didn't know what to think about the move, but his guts said it wasn't good. A car trip could mean into the mountains or across the border. Dan worried about getting the sedative. Part of him wanted the chemical desperately. Another part said he should be fully alert. He was still debating what to do when Morgan returned with a sandwich, milk, and a pill.

"Take the pill first and eat fast. We're ready to go."

Dan picked up the scored, white tablet and put it in his mouth. He took a drink of milk and then picked up his sandwich.

Morgan grabbed Dan's bag and turned to go. "Five minutes and I'll be back. Use the john." The door closed.

Dan counted to ten, then reached under his tongue and removed the pill. He looked at it before getting up and tossing it into the toilet. He urinated and flushed, feeling good about his choice.

Morgan returned, escorted Dan outside to a blue Dodge van, and stuck him into a coffin-sized box. Dan felt the van move, then after a short time, stop. The sound of a door opening and closing reached him, and after a moment, it repeated. They then traveled for maybe an hour on good roads. The time was uncertain, because he fell asleep. He heard no conversation from the front of the truck and decided, from the muffled sounds, that the compartment was sound-proofed.

When they made their next stop, the back doors opened. There was some conversation, after which the doors were closed, and the van began moving again. At some point after that, they turned onto rougher roads. Dan probably dozed off during part of the trip, but it was still dark when they opened the compartment and led him from the mobile prison. He had the impression of being surrounded by closely spaced, unlighted buildings. All was quiet. He was led up wooden steps into a building and then down steps to a room with a bed. He acted groggy, but took everything in.

"Sleep it off, Dan," Morgan said, throwing his gym bag onto the floor.

PART 7
RESULTS

You take unacceptable risk, you have to be prepared to face the consequence.

- CARLY FIORINA

41 /REGRETS

Carlos struggled up the hill, trying to spare his ankle and maimed arm, planning carefully where to place his feet on the moonlit slope. The air had cooled, and a breeze murmured in the trees below and across his damp polo shirt. He began to shiver.

It took an hour to make it to within thirty feet of the crest. That's when he heard a car and was ready to call out when some sixth sense stopped him. To his surprise the vehicle slowed and stopped. *Why would anyone be driving here after dark? Would a damaged guardrail catch the driver's attention?*

A flashlight beam swept from the top of the hill, methodically moving across the area where Carlos crouched. He stayed motionless, but the light caught him, reflecting off his cream-colored shirt. The light froze.

Carlos kept his mouth shut. Maybe it was the waver in the beam of light, the metallic sound he heard, or that sixth sense again. For several seconds nothing happened. Then gunfire shattered the valley peace. The bullet grazed his shoulder, and he had to clamp his teeth to stop from crying out. He slipped lower on the hill, landing hard, breath knocked from his lungs. Now he was more exposed.

Before the light caught him again, he eased up under an outcropping. Once under cover, he listened and heard scuffling. The shooter was descending. The light swept over the protrusion that hid him, and his attacker came closer. He was sure he'd soon be a clear target.

"It's over, Carlos. Quit playing games." A female voice.

Carlos recognized it. How could it be Andy trying to kill him? *That makes no sense. What the hell is going on?*

"You should have ridden the car all the way down. Now I have to shoot you. This will just make it messier and stir up the cops. Too bad you turned out to be such a persistent, pain-in-the-ass snoop. That has to stop." The steely voice couldn't be farther away than twenty feet. "Thanks for climbing up near the road. I wouldn't have seen you otherwise. And I hate hiking."

"Andy? What's going on? What are you doing?"

"Poor, dumb Carlos, always flittin' about like a man-hunk butterfly. But you haven't a clue who you're messing with, do you?" Andy made a clucking sound.

Images of his interactions with Andy raced through Carlos's head: dinner at Mathilda's Levee, the baseball game, the visit to the Balboa Park museum, even their conversations at Cybernetic. She'd seemed nice. Had he missed something? Nothing could account for this. "I don't have to die. We can talk this through."

"Way too late for talk."

"Why? What are you involved in? Give me some answers."

"I suppose you deserve to know why you have to die."

Carlos looked for options. Maybe Andy would trip and fall.

"It's the U.S. Army's fault you have to die. They set Tony up to be shot in a Nicaraguan ambush. That sort of thing gets on one's nerves, you know."

"You don't know that." Carlos remembered that Tony was Andy's brother.

"But I do. The whole defense behemoth has to be punished, and I found the way to do it. You need a big, powerful weapon in your bag if you're going to take on the U.S. Fuckin' Army, so that's what I got."

Carlos wondered why she seemed so sure that the Army killed Tony, but he dared not interrupt. She was talking instead of shooting.

He scrunched lower behind the overhang and looked below him to see if there was a better place to hide.

"No use moving, Carlos. You can't run from a bullet."

"I still don't understand. How does this get you revenge?"

"Pretty simple. Dr. Valois's project has military applications. My employer will thwart those by developing the technology."

A small rock bounced past him. Andy's voice was closer.

"All I have to do for revenge is steal certain pieces and give them to a competitor. And I'm close to doing just that. Can't have you interfering at this point."

"Theft is one thing, Andy. Murder is a whole different ballgame."

"I came up with the way to get into Cybernetic and the way to force Dr. Valois to give me what I need." Andy didn't seem to be speaking to Carlos.

Another spray of pebbles bounced past as he struggled to process what he'd heard. Could Andy be behind everything: kidnapping Dan Valois and the blackmail? "That's it? Just revenge?"

"And the money. That was part of my decision. But not for me, you see. For my mother in a nursing home, an expensive facility. I need the money for her."

So, there was something bigger behind this, someone with money, Carlos thought. He tried to lower himself behind the rock. "We can get you money, Andy. You don't have to kill me. Don't do this. If you step over this line, you're doomed. You're not a killer."

A hollow laugh. "Didn't you hear? I found the way to open a position in the Valois laboratory. His technician's accident on this road was no more an accident than yours."

Carlos's mind raced. Did she mean that Jun Lin's accident was murder? How could he have missed that possibility, even if it was months before Andy appeared on the scene? The claim chilled him. In the dark he felt frantically for some kind of weapon, and his fist closed on a baseball-size rock. The light caught his motion and another bullet whizzed by. Thinking that the shooter was very close and that he had only one chance, he fired the missile, aiming to the left of the beam, remembering Andy was right-handed, and that was where the gun would be. The motion wrenched his damaged arm, and he almost blacked out from the pain.

The rock struck. Andy grunted, and the gun fired. The bullet ricocheted off the rock above Carlos's head. The flashlight flew into the air and landed up the slope, its light still on. Carlos saw Andy clutching her nose as she fell, screaming. The figure, clad in dark pants and jacket, bounced once and then flew off the lip edge, falling into empty space, long black hair fanning. The fall ended with a thump.

Carlos regretted what he'd had to do, but Andy gave him no choice. She was shooting to kill. He was grateful he had a damn decent pitching arm and hadn't broken it. He breathed deeply with his eyes closed to let the pain in his shoulder subside and then resumed his climb.

Andy didn't die immediately. She regained consciousness after hitting a rock at the crest of the ravine. She wasn't in pain but couldn't move. She stared at stars in a faraway sky and thought, not of her mother, father, or brother, none of the deep, meaningful things that were supposed to flash before the dying. Instead, she thought of her choices leading to attempted murder and her probable death. Oh, the foolish hope. There was nothing probable about her death.

She'd gone for the jackpot: revenge, wealth, power. And what had she gained? Zheng's claim to have proof of government complicity in her brother's death was probably pure bullshit. Andy wondered what would become of her mother now. A daughter should not die first. Dan Valois shouldn't have to die.

Her vision began to fade as cool air bathed her twisted body. She heard movement above her, a scraping, rustling sound. Maybe Carlos was coming for her. She coughed blood and suppressed her panic.

Far above a car stopped. Had Yingyi or Morgan come for her? Zheng said her work would be monitored. Could that be them? Voices spoke in urgent tones. The car drove away. Probably Carlos getting a ride. Andy wondered if Morgan and Yingyi would get away before all hell broke loose.

Her memories became clouded, her consciousness tenuous. In the pitch-dark ravine, wind blew across her face and brought overwhelming feelings of panic, loss, hopelessness, and guilt. Her groan broke the intense mountainside quiet. She couldn't breathe, then she convulsed, coughed, and lapsed into the unconsciousness of death.

42 /HOPE

Any sleep Peter and Pam got Saturday night was snatched in den chairs as they waited to hear from Carlos or the FBI. They'd heard nothing about his accident and how, when he made it to the hospital, had been put under to fix his shoulder. He'd been trying to communicate something to the ER staff, but his mumblings about needing to make a phone call had been dismissed as part of his head injury. The citizen who'd brought him in didn't know what happened. He said the man was saying things that made no sense and was probably in shock. By the time he was conscious enough to speak to the police, it was well past midnight.

It wasn't until three o'clock Sunday morning that Peter and Pam heard from the FBI. The middle-of-the-night FBI agents didn't say anything about Carlos or who had called them. They stayed only long enough to get a skeletal picture of the case before leaving. They seemed most interested in Dan's drug use and suggested he might have left on his own after packing a bag for his fishing trip. Peter bristled, reminding them of the ransom demand and payment.

"Was there a note?" one agent asked.

"A phone call."

"I see. But your son had what he needed for a four-day trip?"

"What has that to do with anything?" Pam said.

The agents admonished them for not contacting the police earlier.

They promised to have agents back for a thorough account of all details of the case and strongly suggested that Peter and Pam stay put. Exhausted, Peter told Kayten to remain alert, and then he and Pam went to bed. He slept until almost nine. Pam was up at dawn.

———

Sunlight woke Dan Sunday morning. It streamed into his tiny prison from a barred open window that hung from two upper hinges. His wristwatch read eight a.m. He rose, used the chemical toilet, and explored the hot space, stopping at the window. A weathered wood building twelve feet away stared back across a bottle-filled alley. Beer bottles were labeled *cervasa*.

His cell door opened, and the overhead light came on. Morgan entered carrying a tray with bread, orange juice, and black grapes, which he put on a small folding table.

"Here's your breakfast, kid," Morgan said. "It's not up to the standards you've been enjoying, but this is not the Hilton."

"Where are we? What's going on?"

"Just the edge of nowhere. You'll stay here for a while longer while we check the goods your father delivered."

"What if the goods don't check out?" Dan asked.

Morgan eyed him, unsmiling. "Don't be a pessimist. Your father wouldn't screw you. Eat. I'll be down with a fan. This room gets hot."

It's already hot, dummy, Dan thought as Morgan left. The door closed and what sounded like two bolts clicked. So, he'd learned two things. They were somewhere as hot as southern California, probably Mexico based on the beer bottles he'd seen, and his father had paid a ransom. Not in money, but in something that had to be checked out. Probably from Cybernetic Implementation. Wondering how long it would take to verify the ransom, he ate his food.

Knowing my father, he has probably figured some way to thwart these guys, Dan thought. *But if the goods are defective, I'll be captive forever. Or dead.*

Dan sought some weakness in his prison, checking the walls, the ceiling, and the door frame. He found nothing, cursed, and sat disconsolate on the cot. He forced himself up and examined the area around the window, using a chair as a stool. The frame and bars were well-fastened, and he had no tools. It was hopeless. A noise from the alley made him look left and right, but he could see no more than twenty feet. It sounded like a crowd of some sort, maybe kids.

The noises did not come closer. Dan got down and went to his cot, picking up the book he'd been given. He read several pages until he heard a scuffle, then the sound of glass hitting glass. A shadow moved in the alley. Dan almost fell in his haste to get to the window. A kid was nudging a soccer ball as he moved slowly away.

"Psst. Hey, kid. *Hola, amigo*," Dan called in a hushed voice.

The boy turned back to the window. "Si, señor?"

He wore shorts and sneakers but no shirt. His black hair and intelligent eyes made him look older than he probably was. Dan guessed about eleven.

"*Habla ingles?* Do you speak English?" Dan spoke slowly.

"Si. *Un poco*. Americano?"

"Yes. And I'm in trouble. What is the name of this town?"

"*Esto es Santo Regás*." The boy said. "*Que quieres de mi?* What do you want?"

"I need help." Dan glanced at his watch. Morgan might come back at any moment with the fan. "Is there a phone you can use?"

"Si, señor. En la tienda."

Dan checked his wallet and saw a ten and three singles. "Here is three dollars. If you make a phone call for me, I'll give you another ten dollars." He held up the bill.

The boy's eyes widened."

"What is your name?"

"Yo soy Ramon."

"Ramon, I want you to make a collect phone call and give a message to my father. Tell him where I am, including the address of this building. Have you ever made a phone call?" Dan handed the three singles through the hole in the screen.

"*Si*," Ramon said, sounding a bit insulted.

"That's great. Here's the number." Dan handed Ramon one of his father's business cards, pointing to the home number he'd written on the back. "Just say 'I have a collect call from Dan. Ask what kind of car my family has so I know you made the call. Then I'll give you this ten-dollar bill."

Ramon nodded and began to leave.

"And, Ramon, don't tell anyone about this. Make the call now and come back to the window. Don't talk if anyone is in the room with me. "My life depends on this."

Ramon nodded and ran down the alley, leaving Dan to wonder if he'd been understood. His English seemed good, but for all Dan knew, he or his family could be in league with the kidnappers. He seemed interested in the ten dollars. Probably too much. He sat on the cot feeling, for the first time, a surge of hope. He said a prayer.

Yingyi arrived to take Dan and his chemical toilet outside. They went to the end of the row of houses to an empty field covered with grass and a few pear cacti. Dan dug down a foot and dumped the plastic container. Yingyi watched from a distance. But he was close enough to get a whiff of foul odor when a dry breeze ruffled the clumps of yellow grass. He stepped back a step.

"Move it along. Refill the hole," he said.

Yingyi's mind wasn't really paying attention to the process of dealing with human excrement. He was recalling the events months ago that brought him to this primitive level of existence. He remembered Zheng in the executive offices of Xianxingzhe Group in Beijing stalking impatiently as they waited for the woman. When Antoinette Marino arrived, his boss first used the stick of threatening the women's mother and then presented the carrots of power, money, and revenge. Those had worked.

After she'd been sent to an apartment, Zheng had told Yingyi he would be responsible for her performance, but he had to play the underling and monitor events from a subservient position. So here he was supervising the disposal of human waste and still wondering about the value of the woman. Her will had proven quite strong, but her actions seemed reckless.

Dan shoveled dirt and tamped it down, then slopped water from a jug to rinse the container.

"Hand over the shovel," Yingyi ordered. "Exercise time is over."

Yingyi kicked himself for having sex with her, not that it hadn't been pleasurable. He'd been ordered to act subserviently, and that was part of the act, but maybe it gave her too much the upper hand, even if she was the one naked under him. He wished he'd screwed her harder. The slut hadn't called after going to check on Carlos Ortega. That was strange, he thought. She should have called. Maybe she screwed up. Too bad. He had no way of knowing what happened on the ravine road while they were meeting Peter Valois, but decided he should let Morgan know she hadn't checked in. Others could tend that loose end.

Ramon had intended to go directly to the store where he could use the phone and return for his ten dollars. But when he emerged from between the buildings, holding the three dollars in one pocket, his friends grabbed him and said a new soccer game had begun. He tried to pull away, but they forced him to the soccer field. He stuffed the three dollars deeper into his pocket and ran onto the field. After an hour of running, kicking, and falling down, the sun had become hot enough to end the game, and Ramon wandered toward home, having forgotten about the American and the phone.

He sat on a small porch outside his house drinking water and watching buzzards circling a field. There were no buzzards in America. Just eagles, American eagles. His eyes widened and he pulled the three bills from his pocket and smiled. He rose and thrust his hand deeper into the pocket, then into the other one. His smile faded. The business card was missing.

"We do not know the American woman's location. She has disappeared," Zheng said into the phone, trying to explain the adverse event to his mentor. He then listened in silence to a lecture about competence and the need for a solution.

"Of course. Immediately." Zheng hung up, tried to regain his composure so he could analyze the California events calmly and rationally. He had to guard against several problems. First, the woman could link the espionage to Xianxingzhe. Second, Valois's materials could be defective. Third, Cybernetic would eliminate any possibility of further theft. He couldn't solve the first problem, but there was a solution to others. Dr. Valois would have to be acquired. In that case he wouldn't need anything more from Cybernetic because Valois would repair what he had handed over.

———

Ramon retraced his steps to the soccer field. His eyes scanned the ground looking for the small, white card. Nothing appeared. On the field itself, he walked around where he remembered playing. Maybe the card popped out of the pocket as he was running and kicking the ball. There was no card on the field. He was ready to give up when it occurred to him that maybe he'd never gotten the card into his pocket. He walked back toward the alley and there, just beyond the building, in a clump of brown grass, was a small piece of stiffened, white paper. Ramon picked it up and smiled. The buzzards were eagles after all, he thought.

He made his way to the town store and found the phone available. He'd called a cousin in California collect once, so this was not a totally new experience. He reread the instructions for making a collect call and dialed the operator.

———

Kayten had cleared the lunch dishes and was in the kitchen when the phone rang early Sunday afternoon. Peter was pacing in the living room and jumped to answer.

Someone with a peculiar accent said, "This is the operator. I have a collect call for Peter Valois from Dan. Will you accept the charges?"

Peter held the receiver, speechless.

"Hello?" repeated the operator.

"Yes, yes, I'll accept the charges."

The next voice was obviously Spanish, accented, and young. "Señor Valois? I have... *un messaje de su hijo*... words from your son. He ask to call you." The boy was remarkably calm and businesslike.

"My son? Who are you? Where is he?" A wash of emotions threatened to overwhelm Peter Valois and completely incapacitate him. He struggled to regain some measure of control.

"He is in Santo Regás. Twenty-one San Miguel. He asked me to call and give you the address. That is all."

Peter repeated the address, confused and unable to put the caller into any context. "Is Dan all right? Who is this?"

"It does not matter. He needs help. He asked me to ask what kind of car you have."

The question made no sense to Peter. He thought he'd misunderstood what was being asked. "What kind of car? What difference does that make?"

"Please, señor. The car?"

"We have a Ford wagon. Was there anything else? Where are you calling from?"

"There is no more. That is the *messaje*. *Adios*." The line went dead.

Peter stood stunned. Then, as a mind is wont to do under duress, it focused on a trivial item. Maybe he'd given the wrong answer about the family car. After all, they had both a wagon and a Jeep. But the wagon was always viewed as the family car. But what difference could that make. Peter wrenched himself out of this stupid mode of analysis and focused on something more substantive: what should he do now? Who was the caller and what could he possibly have to do with Dan's situation? Nothing made sense.

It had been almost twenty-four hours since Carlos Oreta had left to notify O'Rourke and the police. As far as Peter knew, Mark O'Rourke was still up at his lake house and out of touch. Yes, the FBI had finally appeared. But what good had it done? Their interview almost seemed perfunctory, and here he was sitting around waiting for them to reappear. It didn't seem like much of a priority to them at all. Peter felt that he was on his own again. If anything were to be done to save Dan, he would have to do it.

Terry and Megan had spent Saturday night at the O'Rourke house. The slam of churchgoer car doors had wakened Megan, who stretched her arms, yawned, and sat up. "Well, I guess we have to get up."

"I suppose." Terry was on her stomach and hadn't moved. "It must be late. I see the sun trying to come around this side of the house. We should have invited some boys over last night and had a party."

"I don't think my parents would approve of that." Megan got out of bed wearing a short nightie. "If my father calls, remind me to tell him about that message from Carlos Oreta on the answering machine."

"There are a lot of things that parents don't approve of." Terry sat up and put her bare legs over the side of the bed. "Like being 'sort of intimate' with Dan and touching what you shouldn't be touching."

"You've really been fixated on that, haven't you? There was nothing sleazy about it. We actually like each other a lot. You're just jealous."

"Should I be?" Terry smiled and put her hands between her legs. "What are we going to do today? Beach? Tennis?"

"Have you forgotten? We are going to visit Dan today. To check up on him. See if he's still acting weird. Maybe we'll take him out to the beach." Megan stripped off her nightgown and panties and grabbed the robe hanging on the bedpost. "I'm first in the shower."

"I'll go and see what's available for breakfast. Do you want to call Dan before we show up?" Terry found slippers beside the bed.

As her bare behind disappeared into the bathroom, Megan said, "No, let's catch him unprepared. This is a spontaneous behavior test, remember?"

43 /PURSUIT

PETER REPLACED THE PHONE AND TRIED TO FATHOM WHAT WAS happening. The FBI men had not mentioned Carlos, but either he or Mark must have alerted them. Carlos had not returned and had sent no messages. The FBI response was underwhelming, and no local police were involved. After he failed to return from the drop point with her son, Pam had disappeared into the den and closed the door, apparently no longer speaking to him.

He thought about calling the FBI to tell them of the phone call, but decided Pam could do this while he, with Kayten's help, acted. He had to verify the new information on Dan's location. Part of him said it was a red herring; another part decided to trade himself for his son.

He couldn't blurt this to his wife. She'd stop him. He wrote a note relating the phone call and asking her to call the FBI. He propped the paper up on the foyer table. This would get the police doing something and still allow him to drive to Mexico. The FBI would serve as his backup. Peter sensed his action was half-baked, even rash. But he couldn't just sit and wait.

He went to the bedroom and threw clothes and passports into a gym bag. He grabbed his wallet and a windbreaker and returned to the workroom to find the android.

"Kayten, get some sneakers and a light outdoor jacket or sweatshirt. We're going on a trip."

"I don't require added clothes as insulation, sir."

"You may want a disguise."

"You seem agitated, sir. May I inquire the destination?" Kayten said.

"South of the border. I know where Dan is being held and have asked Mrs. Valois to notify the police. Meanwhile we are going to check out the information."

"How will I get across the border?"

"You'll use Dan's passport."

They left quietly in the Jeep. Peter got money from the ATM. He reviewed his preparation, briefly considered abandoning his mission, and then headed to the interstate.

An hour after Peter and Kayten pulled out of the driveway, Pam emerged from the den and read her husband's note. A cascade of anger, hope, and dread hit her. She was about to call the police when the front doorbell rang. Her first thought was that it was the FBI. She replaced the phone and went to the front door to find Megan and Terry on the porch.

"Hi, Mrs. Valois," Megan said. "Is Dan back from his fishing trip yet?"

Pam didn't answer, but she looked close to tears.

"What's wrong, Mrs. Valois?" Terry asked.

"Come in, girls."

Pam held it in until they were seated in the den. Then it came out in a rush. She told them Dan had been kidnapped.

"Holy shit!" Terry said.

Pam showed the girls the note Peter had left. She never said that Dan went missing on Wednesday and therefore didn't have to explain how her son could have been in school on Thursday.

Megan, despite the worry on her face, acted calm. She asked a few more questions about the blackmail, before standing. "You make your phone call, Mrs. Valois, and we'll go home to try to get hold of my father at the lake house. He'll know what to do. Is there any other way we can help?"

"No, I can't think of anything right now. Getting your father is probably best while I contact the FBI. Let me know what he says." Pam lifted the phone as the girls left.

Back in the car, Megan said, "My father is probably traveling back now and will be home soon. I won't be able to get him on the phone 'cause it's like a dead zone on the way from the lake. I'll leave a note. Meanwhile we're going to Mexico in case Dr. Valois needs help. Are you game?"

"Two questions: don't you mean *you're* going, and are you nuts?" Terry asked.

"I'm serious, and I need you. You like going south of the border."

"Didn't you get the part about kidnapping and blackmail? That means criminals and danger. No place for two high school girls to be poking around."

"We're only going there in case we can help—you know, delivering a message, waiting to direct the cops." She smiled and added, "Getting tacos."

"Not funny." Terry scrunched her doubt-filled face. Finally, she said, "Sure, we had nothing to do today anyway. Just a little Mexican kidnap adventure. Why shouldn't I go? As much fun as watching the hunks at the beach, right?"

"Calm down. We won't do anything foolish."

"I don't know why I always listen to you," Terry said. "But we need our passports."

"Right. Both our passports are in my bedroom. You left yours with me after our last visit to our southern neighbor where we weren't supposed to go."

Pam got in touch with the FBI. She emphasized that her son's kidnapping could be a matter of national security because of the nature of the blackmail. She then asked bluntly, "Why the hell haven't you come back here and what the hell are you doing?"

Both the caller's vehemence and the mention of national security seem to heighten the agent's attention. She said she would send two men.

The agents arrived an hour later, one twentyish with a not-quite-combed mop of blond hair, the other with a bald head and old enough to be the young guy's father. Baldy explained that the connection with Cybernetic Implementation had broadened the case to more than a simple kidnapping. He apologized for not getting back sooner and cited the Cybernetic aspect as an excuse. The older agent went over every detail of the story, several times going off on tracks that Pam had not even considered, like who Dan's friends were, why they hadn't gotten him into a rehabilitation facility, and the family finances. Blond guy took notes.

Peter's leaving upset both agents. He pinned Pam down on how long he'd been gone, remarked that it was long enough to get past the border, and went off to call it in. He returned promptly. Pam reminded them that Carlos Oreta was supposed to have contacted them the day before. That elicited blank faces, and they had her repeat and confirm when Carlos left and where he was going. If they knew of Carlos and his message to the FBI, they didn't say.

The older fed left the room with his phone in hand. The younger agent requested pictures of Dan and of Peter Valois and received Pam's permission to survey the house. He returned a short time later.

"The phone is tapped," he said, "so they know you've contacted the police. I've left the tap in place and we'll get a tech team out here. What's in the locked room?"

"That's my husband's workshop." Pam hesitated before telling the police about Kayten, but decided she had to. "Peter's work involves biosynthetic brains in androids, and we have a model home for field testing. My husband services the unit in there, so it contains electronic equipment that is delicate and expensive."

"Can I see this unit?"

Again, Pam hesitated. "Well, it's not here. Peter took it with him."

The older man reentered the room to hear the last exchange. "Why would he do that?"

"Kayten—that's the android's name—has certain analytical and defensive capabilities. He probably thought those might come in handy."

"Defensive? Like what?" junior asked.

"I'm not sure."

When they were leaving an hour later, the older agent spoke to Pam. "I might have acted just the way you and your husband did if I didn't know the FBI as I do, but we have to go forward from here. The process is already underway to find these guys and your son. I'd advise you, however, to do two things. First, get yourself a lawyer. Second, get a friend or relative over here to be with you while this plays out."

Once on Route 805, Kayten said, "I am satisfied."

Peter glanced at the robot. "What? Satisfied with what?"

"Finally taking action in response to the attack on the Valois household. I feel... smoothness. My directives are to provide protection. I should have detected the threat before Dan was kidnapped. Now I will focus on remedial action to rescue Dan and to stop the theft of Cybernetic property."

They passed a sign giving miles and kilometers to the border. Peter asked, "What are our chances?"

"I cannot estimate the probability of success in this course of action without further information."

"What information do you need?"

"The present circumstances of Dan, the number and strength of his captors, the proximity of police assistance."

"At least two of those would help the police as well. That's what we're after."

"Very good, sir. There is a radar gun in use eight tenths of a mile in front of us."

Peter coasted down to the speed limit and passed a state police car at the bottom of the next hill. "Thanks for the warning, Kayten. We certainly don't need the delay of a ticket."

"I'll maintain surveillance, sir."

Before they reached the border, Peter reminded Kayten he was to be Dan Valois at the immigration checkpoint. The android's hair matched his son's and the picture in the passport was three years old. There should be no problem passing off Kayten as Dan. At the border, the tired-looking Mexican immigration agent asked Peter's purpose in entering the country. Peter claimed he was taking a two-day pleasure trip. The agent looked briefly at the passports, asked them both to state their names and place of birth, checked the car, and waved them through.

As they continued south on the main highway leading to Santo Regás, Kayten asked, "What is the plan, sir?"

"I'm not sure. First, we have to locate Dan. If there is a chance to grab him safely, we'll take it. If not, we'll sit tight until the cops arrive."

Megan and Terry had gone back to the O'Rourke house where they'd changed clothes, grabbed some money, and picked up passports. Megan tried calling the neighbor with a phone a few houses away from their lake cottage, but there was no answer. She left her father a note, which briefly described Dan's kidnapping, the blackmail, and Peter Valois's decision to find Dan. She also mentioned the phone message from Carlos Oreta and followed his name with several giant question marks.

On the interstate Megan kept her subcompact in the fast lane while Terry acted as navigator with her phone GPS. An hour into the trip, Terry asked, "Are we following some plan?"

"We'll have to play it by ear once we find Dr. Valois. He may just need someone to go and make a phone call. This will give you a chance to practice the Spanish you're so proud of."

Terry looked at her friend. "You make it sound so simple and quiet. Has it occurred to you that Dan's father could become a kidnap victim, too? He's the one with the knowledge they want. He could stumble into a situation in which he becomes trapped, so we'd better approach with extreme caution."

Megan nodded. "You're right. Dr. Valois could become the captive.

If that happens, then what value would Dan have to these guys? That's what scares me."

"Scares me as well. He could be used to force his father to do what they wanted. The two of us are worth dog doo-doo. Again, I ask why I follow you."

"I am your polestar."

44 /FOUR'S COMPANY

Peter and Kayten stayed close to the speed limit, and the trip took longer than expected. As the late-day sun reached near the horizon, they pulled into Santo Regás, a small, shabby town with wood frame buildings crowding the main street. Beaten-up cars fronted a bar like nursing piglets, and loud voices and guitar music spilled onto the highway. A small grocery store stood darkened nearby. Peter did not want to risk alerting the wrong people to their presence, so he decided to find San Miguel by reading signs. There weren't many.

Kayten's superior vision made this a reasonable option, and they soon found San Miguel, the third street south of the bar. Peter turned east onto a gravel road that kicked pebbles against the Jeep. Worn houses clustered two or three together with narrow allies between. Few provided numbers for Peter's peering eyes. Two elderly residents seated on porch chairs fixed on the Jeep with frank curiosity.

"That house is seventeen, sir." Kayten indicated a gray structure on the left side of the street.

"Good. I turned in the right direction. Then that must be twenty-one."

The building was dark, and no cars were parked nearby. Peter crept to the end of the block and pulled behind a shed. He killed the motor and spoke softly, "See anything, Kayten?"

"My scan of the building would be consistent with two persons on the first floor. But there seems to be a floor below ground level. I can't determine what is there."

"I'll move the car farther away from the building, and we'll survey it on foot." Peter restarted the Jeep and slipped past more houses, lights off. He turned left onto a dirt road that bordered an empty field. He drove off the road surface into a depression with tall grass and stopped. Peter led the way back toward the house using the wide alley that ran behind the row of houses. Sheds occupied the rears of the lots. They stayed in the shadows, approaching in silence. Dusk was full upon them as they neared the back of the target house and crouched next to the garage-sized rear shed.

A door with two cinderblock steps and two dark windows faced them. Crickets began their loud evening conversations in the surrounding fields. Kayten watched the departure of a flock of bats from the roof space of one of the buildings. He knew of bats but had never actually observed the creatures.

"The alleyway on one side has a fence," Peter said. "This one is open. Hug the wall. Maybe you can pick up some more information." Peter led the way, taking care where he stepped. Kayten confirmed there was a living space below the ground.

"There may be someone in the basement," Kayten said.

"Dan could be locked down there, but I don't see what else we can do right now. We can't just knock on the door. Let's keep the area under surveillance until the cops arrive. I'd just feel a hell of a lot better if I knew Dan was inside that building."

They retreated, crossing the service drive into shadows. Male voices broke the silence, and Peter and Kayten stopped as the rear door to number twenty-one opened. Kayten shoved Peter beside a shed.

"What the...!"

"Sorry, sir. They are coming out. Three of them. Wait. I think Dan is with them."

Peter stared until he convinced himself that it was Dan. The boy carried a plastic box that Peter realized was a tank from a chemical toilet. Two men walked one on each side. When the trio passed, Peter saw that the smaller man carried a shovel.

"This may be our chance." Peter grabbed Kayten's arm, filled with elation at seeing his son alive and unharmed. "We have to jump them. What is the probability of success?"

"If they are unarmed, the probability of success is better than zero point nine with me alone, sir. In your condition, sir, you would not improve chances of success and would in fact face a probability of personal injury in excess of zero point six."

"And you think that they are unarmed?"

"I do not detect guns, but the larger man has something metallic at his waist."

"So, you want to take them alone?"

"That is correct, sir. If anything goes wrong, sir, please wait for the police."

Kayten followed Dan and his jailers to the field while Peter remained hidden. Dan was given the shovel and started to dig a hole, but the shorter man, obviously impatient, snatched the shovel and began to dig. Dan started to walk in a circle with Morgan in the middle.

Kayten made his move and reached Morgan in two sprints, slammed into him and sent him sprawling. The android next attacked the shovel-wielder, who dodged Kayten's blow and assumed a karate stance. Yingyi took the offense and aimed several quick chops toward Kayten's head and ribs. The first blow was blocked and glanced off the android's arm, eliciting a wince of pain from Yingyi, probably from contact with a synthetic elbow. As Kayten prepared to deliver an incapacitating blow, Morgan yelled.

"Hold it or Dan is dead."

Morgan held Dan in front of him with a large knife pressed to his throat. "You're fast, but my blade is faster. Stay where you are."

Yingyi patted Kayten for weapons. Kayten made sure his artificial skeleton was padded so that the man felt nothing unusual.

Yingyi handed the shovel to Dan. "Dump the shitcan and fill the hole." Satisfied with Dan's work, he said, "Both of you walk with your mouths shut."

The four trooped past Peter, up the steps, and into the house.

Feeling helpless, angry, and frustrated, Peter was at a loss for what to do. He decided to call his wife to find out what was going on and pulled out his cell phone. No signal. He could not recall seeing an outside phone in Santo Regás, but decided to try the bar.

Once inside the house, Morgan locked the doors after scanning front and back for any sign of accomplices. Then he shoved Kayten and Dan to the downstairs room.

"We've got a leak somewhere," Yingyi said as they ascended the stairs. "What do we do?"

"I don't know how this guy found our location or who he is, but he's not a cop or he'd have a gun. We'll hold them both and report to headquarters. Get on the radio."

In the basement, Dan questioned Kayten, who explained the phone call and the trip to Santo Regás. The robot scanned the basement prison.

"How are you, Master Dan?"

"I'm fine. But what are we going to do now?"

Kayten went to the barred window. "If there were some way to remove these bars, we could squeeze out the window."

"That was how I arranged the phone call. Through some kid named Ramon who happened into the alleyway to retrieve a soccer ball. Glad I paid him the ten dollars."

Kayten examined the bars. The rods were inserted in cement blocks on both sides of the opening.

"Do you think you could dislodge them, Kayten?"

"Not easily and not without making noise. But your father added a little device last week that may be a better approach. Go to the door and listen for our jailers." Kayten raised his hand to the leftmost bar and pointed the index finger at the bottom of the bar. A flash of red light moved from the tip of his finger and after ten seconds of blinding light, the bar was severed.

"Hey, that's real neat. What is it?" Dan was already moving the chair to the window.

"A laser. A powerful and precise way to cut through a variety of materials. It shouldn't be too much trouble to take out the other bars."

"Wait. I hear someone coming." A second later, Morgan put his key into the lock and threw the door open. He held a gun and motioned Kayten and Dan over to the cot.

"Who are you and how did you get here?" The question was directed at Kayten.

"My name is K.C. I'm a friend of Dan's and I drove."

"How did you know where we were?"

Kayten reported the anonymous phone call received by Dan's parents. He insisted he was alone.

Morgan looked at Kayten for a while, and the robot maintained eye contact. "All right. Get yourselves ready to travel. We're moving out." Morgan closed the door and retreated up the stairs.

Yingyi returned from checking the neighborhood. "Everything's quiet. There's a Jeep parked in the field. California plate."

"There's something weird about Dan's friend," Morgan said.

"What?"

"I don't know. Something. What did you get from headquarters on the radio?"

"We move the captives and figure some way to get hold of the senior Valois. As insurance."

"How are we supposed to do that?" Morgan asked.

"We get him to come after his son, and we snatch him."

Peter reached the bar and, despite his poor Spanish, learned the only public phone was in the general store that was closed. One patron who spoke some English said the gas station on the main highway had a phone. Peter stumbled back to his car, wishing he'd remembered the flashlight, his mind occupied with the need to find a phone and to summon help. He started the Jeep and took the street beyond the soccer field that sat behind the house on San Miguel. Minutes after the Valois vehicle left its parking spot, another took its place.

Megan and Terry had duplicated the feat of locating San Miguel and the house. They too cruised past and found the empty field in which to leave the car. They never saw Peter's Jeep. He'd already driven off.

The girls crept along the lane behind the house. They aped Peter's behavior by crouching behind the shed deciding what to do. From somewhere toward the center of town a dog barked.

"What if that dog finds us?" Terry hissed. "What if it's a big attack dog?"

Megan frowned. "First of all, the dog is obviously not near us. Secondly, it sounded like a Chihuahua."

"It could be an attack Chihuahua. We should leave."

"Right. Let's get closer and see if we hear voices, maybe Dan's," Megan said, pointing to the alley on one side of the structure where a three-foot-high chain link fence hung loose from its post. "We can walk along the wall. We need confirmation this is the right place."

"You want to go in there? It looks yucky," Terry said.

"It's just overgrown weeds. You go first."

"And trash." Terry pointed to the other side of the house. "Why don't we go around to the front the other way?"

"They might see us from the windows. This side has only one window that won't be a problem if we stay below it near the wall."

The girls scooted to the fence, and Terry squeezed between the post and the wire. As Megan tried to follow, Yingyi grabbed her arm. "That's far enough, girls. Glad you could join the party. We could stand some feminine company."

Yingyi took each girl by the wrist and gave them a twist. He dragged them to the rear door. "Looks like this is becoming a popular rendezvous." He pushed the two girls in front of him into the room where Morgan stood packing a bag. "I found them going into the alley."

Morgan questioned each of them and received the same story about an anonymous phone call. "We can sort out details later," he said. "Now we have to move. Put these heroines downstairs until we're packed. I just got word about the destination. It will be nicer."

Yingyi put his hands on their backsides and shoved the two girls toward the stairs. They descended, and he opened the holding room. "Stay here and keep quiet."

Yingyi gave Terry another squeeze and relocked the door.

Kayten had interrupted his work on the bars when he'd heard the girls and Yingyi outside at the end of the alley. He'd indicated to Dan that he believed that his two female friends were about to join them. Despite the warning, Dan was unable to speak when they appeared.

Megan's hand went to her mouth when she saw Kayten, who she, of course, knew as the Valois guest robot. Her eyes widened and moved slowly from the android to Dan to Terry.

Dan got the hint. "Terry, this is my friend K.C. What are you guys doing here?"

Terry rubbed her twisted wrist. "We're here to rescue you."

Megan hugged Dan and told how they'd gotten to Santo Regás, keeping her voice low. She didn't dwell on how upset Pam Valois was or the delay in contacting the police. Dan said he was basically all right and asked if they'd seen his father outside.

"No," Megan said, "but we weren't looking for him. We parked and walked to the house. He could have been on another street." She breathed deeply. "I guess we haven't helped anything."

"But you did leave a note that your father should have found by now," Terry said. "And the FBI is supposedly on the case. By the way, I'm sure your dad will be thrilled by your Wild West behavior." She stopped speaking at the sound of approaching footsteps.

Morgan pushed open the door and motioned the four captives

upstairs. "Move it," he said. "Before more friends just happen to show up."

Yingyi joined them holding a gun as they proceeded out the back and to the shed, which they entered by a side door. The blue van was parked inside. Yingyi put Kayten, Dan, and Terry in the rear compartment and directed Megan to sit up front.

Morgan opened the shed doors, then drove the van into the alley.

Ten minutes into the trip, Megan cringed when Yingyi put his hand on her leg. "Where we are going has very nice facilities," he said. "You girls will be able to take a bath and freshen up from your trip. Maybe we will take a bath together. There's even a Jacuzzi." As he spoke, Yingyi was moving his hand higher on the girl's thigh.

"Let's not get distracted and sloppy." Morgan gunned the van and took a turn that shoved Yingyi against Megan.

The trip lasted almost an hour over unlit dirt roads that took them into ranch country and to the gates of a large house where two armed men checked the vehicle carefully before letting it pass. The rear doors were opened, and Morgan and Yingyi ordered Kayten, Dan, and Terry out. They stood in a white-pebbled courtyard before a stucco-faced hacienda roofed in red tile and landscaped with small clusters of desert plants. Spanish bayonet plants guarded the dark wood front door. A generator hummed, providing the electricity for the garden and walk lights. Several curtained windows glowed yellow.

Two burly, rifle-toting, unshaven men came from a side building. They said nothing, smiled at the girls, and waved the guns toward the front door. The group entered. A guard motioned Kayten and Dan to a room on the first floor, one furnished with twin beds and quite spacious in comparison with Dan's previous cages. An adjoining bathroom had a tub and shower. Wrought-iron grills barred the windows.

"You can stay here as long you give us no trouble," Morgan said. "We have shittier accommodations if you do. The girls have their own quarters. Your stupid friends will make no difference in our plans, Dan. If I were you, I'd just cool it. That's the best way to assure your release. Keep in mind that you now have more than just two of us as your jailers." Morgan closed the heavy oak door and locked it.

Yingyi waved the girls to follow him to a nearby room similar to the other. He came up behind them and helped them over the threshold by placing his hand on their butts and squeezing. "Use the modern bath to freshen up, ladies," he said. "I like my women clean."

Morgan led Yingyi out by the arm.

Terry worked to control her emotions. She sat down on a twin bed, scanned the room, and said, "This is a fine friggin' mess you've gotten us into, Fearless Leader."

Megan also seemed upset. "I just hope that Dr. Valois learns where we are. He certainly was there, since Kay... K.C. must have come with him and is now a prisoner. Maybe Dr. Valois has called the cops. Let's just keep our heads and wait for help. Just play it cool."

"Just one problem," Terry said, wiping her eyes. "We are no longer at 21 San Miguel. We're somewhere else in the middle of nowhere. How do you expect the cavalry to find us?"

When Megan had no answer, Terry said. "They want us for entertainment. And you know what that means."

Megan was silent.

"Have you ever been raped, Megan?" There was no lightness in her question. "Maybe it would be better to be shot."

Megan's face lost color. "Don't say that. And don't just think of the worst that can happen. We may have to be very good actresses, but the important thing is to stay alive."

"At least you have some experience. I'm still a virgin. Wish I had a diaphragm with me." Terry flopped down on her stomach, put her face in the pillow, and sobbed.

PART 8
BALANCE

It's all about quality of life and finding a happy balance between work and friends and family.

- PHILLIP GREEN

45 /FREEDOM

Peter cruised the main highway searching for a phone, trying to remember if he had seen something commercial on the way to Santo Regás. Traffic on the highway was light, so he could scan moonlit vacant fields on both sides, every so often spying small, unlit shacks with grey, weather-worn faces. Single wires connected to the roofs. Peter figured telephone service required a second wire, so it made no sense for him to disturb residents about phones they didn't have. What's more, he didn't speak much Spanish.

Several miles north he found a roadside phone booth. Praying that the phone was working, he clambered out of the Jeep and jammed a coin into the slot, hearing it bounce metallically through to the coin return. His sluggish brain took half a minute before he realized that the thing wanted a Mexican coin. He had none and the phone did not provide contact with an operator without a coin. Cursing, Peter got back into the Jeep and continued north. He'd almost reached Enseñada before he found a truck stop with a real phone. He inserted his credit card and dialed his home phone and had to wait only one ring before Pam answered.

Peter sucked in a deep breath and tried to instill calm into his voice. "Pam, we found him. I'm calling from Enseñada. Have you contacted the police?"

Pam sounded close to tears. "Yes, Lieutenant Trent is right here. He's not very happy. Are you all right? Is Dan all right?"

Peter assured his wife that everything was fine, neglecting to mention the fate of Kayten. He'd save that for the not-very-happy lieutenant, who'd taken the phone.

"This is Lieutenant Trent. You didn't play this one very smart, Dr. Valois." The man had a Raymond Burr voice and sounded authoritative in a TV crime-drama way.

Peter cut him off before the lecture could develop. "You can vent your displeasure later, Lieutenant. Let me give you the situation. We found the location where they are holding Dan in Santo Regás. Unfortunately, there's been an unfavorable development. My android was captured. But he may serve as additional protection for my son."

"Where are you calling from?"

"I'm at a truck stop in Enseñada, right on the main highway." Peter turned to look for a name but couldn't see it. He gave the highway number and approximate mileage from the center of the city.

"Here's what I want you to do," Trent said. "First, stay put. Based on what your wife said, we have assembled a team that can be at your location in several hours. We've alerted Mexican authorities. Told them this was international espionage requiring our presence within their borders. The State Department is in the loop and has gotten agreement from the Mexican government for this intrusion. They want it kept short and don't want to hear about it. The group coming to you is headed by Agent Shaunessy... right... like the movie marshal. Any more info?"

"Dan is apparently being held by just two men, one very large—looks like he lifts weights—and the other rather small. The small one may be Asian."

"The big guy may be the one who rented the Hertz car. Let me repeat, Dr. Valois. Stay put. The best help you can give your son now is to lead this team of professionals to where they're holding him. Understand?"

"I understand. I'll be waiting here. Let me speak to my wife." An eighteen-wheeler entered the plaza with squealing brakes and pulled past the phone booth. Peter cupped his hand over his unoccupied ear.

Pam came on the phone. "It's me. Are you all right?" Pam's voice conveyed several emotions: relief to hear her husband, anger, and continued fear for the safety of her son. "Have you seen Megan and Terry?"

Peter was dumbstruck. At first, he couldn't comprehend what his wife was asking. Why should he have seen them? Then the frightening reality became clear. For some reason, the girls had learned of his location and come to help. The fools. He remembered the lieutenant's criticism of his own actions and knew that he wasn't being consistent. "Why are they here?"

"They arrived just when I was reading your note, Peter. It was stupid of me, but I told them what was happening. Megan said she was going to contact her father. They said nothing about following you but called when they couldn't get in touch with Mark and said they were en route. I told them to stop and come back immediately, but they were determined."

"A mistake, but no worse than the ones I've made." Peter's mind grappled with the new fact. "When did they start?"

"An hour after you, I guess."

Peter wondered if the girls arrived after he left to find a phone. What if they'd wound up hostages? "I haven't seen either one. If they get captured, we have a bigger problem. Kayten might be able to protect Dan alone, but I'm not sure what he can do for all three. If Kayten has to make a choice about who to protect first, he might go into stasis. I'm going to wait here for the Feds."

"Please be careful, dear. I love you."

"I love you, too. A little praying now wouldn't hurt. At least we now know where Dan is and that he's alive. I'll call you as soon as there is any news."

Peter hung up, knowing he'd lied. Insects banged against the light over the phone as he pondered the news that Megan and Terry were heading for Santo Regás. That meant there were now more lives in danger, and he was the cause. The thought froze him until he willed the cloud of uncertainty to lift. Despite Trent's command, he had to return to Santo Regás. If necessary, he'd trade himself for the captives and at least pretend to cooperate. He maneuvered his car to a pump, filled his gas tank, and squeegeed bugs from the windshield. In the bluish light of overhead fluorescent fixtures, he thought of what he could offer to free Dan, Megan, and Terry. Still distracted, he pulled from the rest stop, slamming on the brakes when a truck horn blared. He'd cut off a departing rig.

The trip back seemed far shorter than his journey seeking a phone, but he drove without looking at houses and checking for phone lines. Santo Regás was quiet. Even the bar was dark. In the field he found an unoccupied Escort parked in his spot. The O'Rourke girl drove an Escort, he seemed to recall. There was no sign of the girls as he made his way back to the house, now dark and quiet. Maybe the silence meant all the occupants were sleeping, but he didn't feel comfortable with that interpretation, particularly since it now seemed likely that the girls were captives. At any rate, Kayten would not be sleeping. Peter walked back to the Jeep and turned on the radio, dialing the frequency he used to communicate with his android. There was no signal, which meant that Kayten was not near.

Panicked that his son was gone, he crept back to the house, daring to approach the back steps where he spied the footprints leading away from the building. One set of prints was particularly clear, deeper than the rest. Something heavy. Peter surmised that these were Kayten's. Two other sets were smaller sneaker prints. Maybe made by the girls. He followed them and came to a shed with opened doors. Fresh tire tracks ran from shed to road.

The tracks indicated that the vehicle had turned east. The scientist tried to interpret the clues. The kidnappers had a large vehicle, maybe a van. He remembered the dark van at the lake when he delivered the blueprints and the software. Maybe one man went to pick up supplies, but that made no sense. The kidnappers, Dan, Kayten, and the girls had left. Peter checked the shed, seeing nothing until he was ready to leave. A flash of something white in the dimness caught his eye, and he reached down and picked it up. There was no doubt who'd left in the van. The item was a wrapped tampon.

Peter sprinted back to his Jeep, started it, and followed the tire tracks. He had no hope of catching up with the vehicle, but the long-range receiver tuned to the Kayten's transmission frequency would help. If he came in range, Kayten would send a message. The tracks disappeared onto a dirt road that had no intersections for miles out of Santo Regás. The moonlight allowed Peter to turn off his lights. After driving thirty minutes and periodically clicking his microphone button to signal Kayten, hope ebbed. He was about to return to the truck stop to await the FBI when his radio came to life.

"We have stopped," Kayten said in a muted voice. "It is a house surrounded by a wall. There are at least four additional armed men here, Dr. Valois. Dan and the girls are unharmed. I suggest alerting the authorities."

Peter clicked his mike button twice in response, not daring to speak in case his words were heard. "Alerting the authorities" meant Kayten alone couldn't guarantee the safety of the hostages. It was time to get some help, but he needed to know where to lead the police. Kayten anticipated that need.

"Isolated hacienda, east 105 degrees, twenty-nine point four miles from the house in Santo Regás," Kayten said.

Peter clicked his mike, turned the Jeep around, and headed back to Enseñada. He reached the truck stop to await the FBI.

Three Chevy Suburbans pulled up to Peter's Jeep an hour later. A husky man in his mid-forties with a good start on both jowls and a belly introduced himself as Agent Shaunessy of the FBI and got into the Jeep carrying a radio.

"Let's move it, Dr. Valois. We'll take your car in case we want you to stay in it away from the action. The sooner we get there, the sooner we can assess the situation."

Peter didn't mention the real reason for taking the Jeep: the radio. "Things have changed," he said. "My son is no longer in Santo Regás. And he is not the only captive."

Shaunessy fired questions, and Peter told the story, adding Kayten and the girls to the list and telling about finding footprints and tire tracks and following the van to the new location. He gave the heading and the distance without explaining how he got them.

"That was dangerous, Dr. Valois, but your information is critical. You weren't seen?"

"I kept my lights off."

The agent opened an unusual map that seemed to show individual, widely spaced, ranches. "Drug info," he said, laying a ruler along the 105-degree line from Santo Regás. The line ran through a house at exactly the right distance. Shaunessy spoke into the radio, instructing someone in another car to inform the Mexican authorities of the change in plans. He called the new target a hacienda. Then the caravan took off.

"There is one other factor that may be of help to us, Mr. Shaunessy. One of their captives is not a human. It's a robot, a humanoid android."

"It's Agent, not mister. Yeah, I heard about that from Agent Trent. But you're telling me that these guys have taken a robot captive and don't know it is a robot?"

"That's what I'm saying. It's a Cybernetic advanced prototype."

"Hard to believe, but now I see why the State Department is involved. And how does this help?"

"Kayten—that's the robot's name—is quite able to defend himself and, I hope, my son and the girls. He is also equipped with a radio communication capability over short distances. I can receive him on the radio in this car."

"Did you get any information from Kayten after he was inside the compound?"

Peter sighed and decided he might as well come clean. "That's the source of the exact distance and heading information. I never got to see the new place."

"Why didn't you just tell me that?"

"I didn't know you'd heard about Kayten. It would have taken too much time to explain."

Shaunessy snorted. "Anything else?"

"Oh. Yes. Kayten noticed four additional armed men. So, at least six."

"Will you be able to contact this robot when we get in position?"

"I don't know. It depends on where he's being held."

"We'll develop a plan when we get there and keep this robot factor in mind. Speed it up."

Peter took the Jeep up to seventy-five, a speed way higher than his comfort zone and one the Jeep wasn't happy with, but they arrived in Santo Regás in one piece and went directly to the eastbound road he'd followed before. Shaunessy radioed to one of the cars to check the house at 21 San Miguel.

"You said that the hacienda is about twenty-nine miles ahead on this road?"

"Twenty-nine point four from 21 San Miguel," Peter said.

"We'd better take the last mile or so with lights out." Shaunessy spoke again into his radio.

The Jeep and the four FBI vehicles approached the walled hacienda in the dark. A quarter mile from the main gate a depression took them out of sight, and Shaunessy had them stop. A chorus of chirping, buzzing bugs and the sound of a distant generator could be heard. The agent sprinted to one of the Suburbans and returned with night-vision binoculars. Along with Peter and two other agents with rifles, they climbed the incline to the top of the depression. Shaunessy scanned the layout.

"I see a couple of guards," Shaunessy said. "The house stands thirty yards from the walls. The gate and courtyard are illuminated by floods and several house windows are lit. There's a herd of cattle at the top of the hill and what looks like a barn near that far pond. My info doesn't have this place listed as drug-connected. See if you can raise that robot of yours."

Shaunessy and Peter returned to the Jeep. Peter adjusted the gain and spoke quietly into the microphone. "Kayten, do you read?"

"I read you faintly, Dr. Valois. We are together in a locked room on the first floor. We have not been disturbed."

"Do you have any better count of the number of guards, Kayten?"

"A total of six, based on my observation and overheard radio communication. Four guards are outside."

"Okay," Peter said. "We have some help here. Stand by this channel."

There were eight agents besides Shaunessy. He sent them in groups of two to do some surveillance. Two men would scout the entire perimeter.

"Now what do we do?" Peter asked.

"We watch and wait. I need to get a report into headquarters. We may need to call in some local help." Shaunessy went back to one of the Suburbans. The scouting team he'd sent out to circle the house returned and reported the existence of a service drive at the rear that connected with the main road about a half-mile ahead. The land around the hacienda was vacant, covered with brush. The outside guards stood on elevated platforms at each corner of the rectangular wall and seemed relaxed, apparently not expecting trouble. Shaunessy sent two men to cover the rear exit.

"They seem to have bought Kayten's story about acting alone." Peter spoke with more hope than conviction.

"I doubt that. This is just a short stop. They'll be moving on. There's an airport nearby that can handle a business jet." Shaunessy spoke into an elaborate walkie-talkie. "Can the targets be taken out?"

A radio voice answered softly, "We need to get closer. There isn't much cover between here and the wall except one large tree. Getting to it in this moonlight will be tough." Just then the moon was covered by a large, slow drifting cloud. Darkness settled on the area beyond the hacienda walls. "We can do it," the agent said.

Shaunessy turned to Peter. "We'll take out the wall guards and get inside the compound. That will alert the two inside the house. Think your robot can protect the hostages until we get to them?"

"Let me talk to him again." Peter went back to the Jeep and spoke softly into the mike. "Kayten, they are going to storm the compound. Can you protect Dan until they make their way into the house?"

"There is a high probability, zero point nine seven two by my calculation, that I can prevent harm to Dan for at least ten minutes. However, the girls are not with us. I have determined that they are in an adjacent room alone. If I could get us all in one room, I would be better able to assure the safety of all three humans. I have been monitoring radio contacts and they have been instructed to move us promptly. Someone is coming." The radio went silent.

Shaunessy had been listening. "We'll hold off until we find out what they're doing with your son."

The door of the room holding Kayten and Dan opened, and Yingyi entered. "Party's over, boys. It's time for you to travel again, Dan. Your friend, if he behaves, gets to stay behind in one piece. Your girlfriends, too. They have entertainment value for the boys here." The man smiled.

Dan involuntarily moved back away from Yingyi. "Where am I going?"

"Not your worry. How'd you get your location to the home front, Dan? You did it, right?"

"Or you dummies were followed. Maybe's there's a leak in your organization," Dan said.

Yingyi jumped and grabbed Dan's wrist. "Shut your fuckin' mouth, kid. Your cleverness is worth shit. Move."

Dan struggled, but the small man was much stronger. Kayten stepped toward the pair.

"Stay where you are, or I'll break his arm." Yingyi, with Dan in tow, backed toward the door. With robotic speed, Kayten placed his hand on Yingyi's arm.

"Please let him go, sir." Kayten sounded almost apologetic.

Surprise registered on Yingyi's face, then anger. The small man dropped Dan's arm and in a fluid motion brought his hand down hard onto Kayten's neck. The android didn't seem to notice the blow, but his assailant winced in pain. Even though the outer surface of Kayten's shoulder was padded to mimic the feel of human skin, inside was a ceramic, carbon-steel skeleton. Yingyi backed off with an incredulous look at his opponent and assumed a defensive stance.

Kayten put Dan behind him and faced Yingyi, who stepped forward and jumped. A foot snapped toward Kayten's head. The robot grabbed it with both hands and held on. Yingyi fell to the floor. When he tried to rise, Kayten placed his hands on the man's neck and applied pressure to both carotid arteries. Yingyi flailed and seconds later went limp as he blacked out.

Kayten stepped into the hall and transmitted to Peter what had occurred. He said he would find the girls. He motioned to Dan. “Let’s go, Master Dan. There is no one else in the vicinity.”

Dan left the room, closing the door. The hall was empty. The android went to the next room where his sensors said the girls were being held. His hearing picked up their voices, and he motioned for Dan to speak.

“Stand away from the door, Megan,” Dan said.

Kayten leaned his shoulder against the door and applied a sustained pressure. The doorframe near the latch ripped out, and the door caved inward with a crunch of wood and mangled metal. Dan followed the android into the room where Megan and Terry sat together on the bed. They’d risen as the door crashed inward and came forward at the same time to hug Dan.

“There will be time for demonstration of affection later, Master Dan. We must leave the building before our danger increases during an assault.” Kayten directed them out of the room after checking the hallway. They turned toward the window at the end and had almost reached it when Kayten heard a sound. Turning, he saw the giant kidnapper.

“What the fuck? Hold it right there.” Morgan held a small gun in his meaty hand. “Get over here, all of you. I don’t need this shit right now.” His big arm motioned the group forward.

Kayten positioned himself in front of Dan, Megan, and Terry and started walking toward the kidnapper.

“That’s it. Nice and easy,” Morgan said.

As they walked, Kayten assessed the situation. The gun appeared to be a small caliber, so in all likelihood, he could sustain a hit without serious damage. The closer he got to Morgan, the better his chances of disarming the man without damage to his humans. On the other hand, the closer he got the greater the danger of sustaining serious damage, should the bullet hit a sensitive electronic part. Kayten estimated that twelve point two feet was the optimum distance.

At fourteen feet, the sound of gunfire was heard.

“What the...?” Morgan jumped and turned his head.

Kayten rushed at the pointed gun, sweeping his hand upward. As the hand contacted Morgan's fist, the gun went off. The projectile slammed into the android chest plate, and the robot fell forward, facedown, and remained motionless.

Outside the walls, Shaunessy had given the order to advance to positions where they had shots. Two marksmen made it to the tree cover. When his men indicated they were ready, he ordered the guards taken out. From two locations, FBI sharpshooters had targets in their sight, and they fired. Two men on the east wall went down, but the gunfire alerted two other guards who ducked and were missed when other marksmen fired late. Those guards sprayed automatic weapons fire blindly in the general direction of the FBI men. One agent and then another was hit.

The FBI agents told to storm the gate were unable to get closer as long as two guards remained on the wall. An FBI sharpshooter with an infrared scope fried twice, back-to-back. Both guards went down. The agents blew open the front gates and were inside the compound heading for the house within seven minutes of opening the attack. Shaunessy directed half the assault team in the compound to circle the house and the other half to enter the front door. He reminded them of Kayten's directions for reaching the captives.

"There's not much point in being subtle after all the noise," Shaunessy said.

Peter wore a worried look on his face. "I can't raise Kayten."

Morgan stepped over Kayten and grabbed Dan by the arm. "Sounds like we've got company, Dan. I guess you are more than a kidnap victim now. You've just become a shield." Morgan glanced into the room where Yingyi was just regaining consciousness. "What happened here? Can you get up? We've got problems."

Yingyi shook his head to clear it. "The boy's friend jumped me. He must know some martial arts. Where is the son-of-a-bitch?"

"He's got a slug in him. We're under attack. The men should be able to hold them off. But it's time to leave." The pair directed the trio of captives toward the garage. Progress stopped when two FBI agents appeared at the other end of the hall with leveled rifles. Morgan wrapped a big hand around Dan's arm and raised his pistol.

Morgan yelled to the agents, "No closer, or the kid gets a bullet in the brain. Throw down your weapons and back off. We're leaving. Don't be heroes or we waste the kid."

One of the agents barked the stalemate to Shaunessy, who told them to comply. When the hall was clear, Morgan, Yingyi, and the captives proceeded toward the garage. Yingyi delivered a kick to the robot's ribs as they passed Kayten. The oriental yelled, "Damn. This guy must be wearing body armor." Kayten's arm came up and smashed into Yingyi's leg, breaking a bone, and bringing him to the floor. Morgan turned and pointed the gun at the robot. Before he could fire, a beam of laser light erupted from Kayten, flashed off the gun and knocked it out of Morgan's hand with a shower of sparks. In his shock Morgan let go of Dan.

"Get the gun, Dan," Kayten said.

Dan dove and gingerly picked up the warm thirty-eight.

Kayten remained on the floor, his arm extended toward Morgan. "The next target will be your head. On your knees, sir."

Morgan complied, rubbing his burned hand.

Kayten waited until Morgan settled into a non-threatening position and then said, "Master Dan. My upper body seems to work, but my lower body is at the moment not operating."

The radio came alive in the Valois jeep with Kayten's voice. "I was unable to communicate from the room where we were held because of interference, Dr. Valois. But I am pleased to report that the two kidnappers are immobilized and there are no other guards inside the house."

Shaunessy relayed the message to his men. A moment later, Morgan was led from the house in handcuffs. Yingyi was cuffed and dragged out, whimpering. Peter embraced his son and the girls all at once with tears running down his cheeks.

"Thank God you're all right," Peter said.

"But something's wrong with Kayten, Dad."

Peter went inside the hacienda and found the robot. "What's the diagnosis, Kayten?"

"When the projectile struck my thorax, a small piece of a surface temperature probe was dislodged and flew into the integrated circuit board that regulates lower body movements. There seems to be minor damage to a motor integration chip, sir. The mechanical units are fine."

"We'll get you back to the shop and have you repaired. I'll get some help to put you in the Jeep.

"I believe I will be able to effect a temporary repair in three minutes, twenty-two seconds, sir. The integration chip function can be handled by the CPU." Three minutes later, Kayten moved his legs and got up. His movement was not smooth, but it was movement. "That will suffice until we can replace the chip, sir."

Peter, Dan, and Kayten were given the okay to leave and piled into the Jeep for the trip back to the United States. They were followed by a Suburban with two armed agents. The girls drove back in the Escort accompanied by another FBI car. Kayten's self-repair allowed him to move with robotic stiffness. The FBI arranged for Peter to claim that Kayten was the kidnap victim who'd been smuggled into Mexico and held in cramped quarters; a story that also explained the android's stiff movement. The immigration agent was skeptical and remained so even after speaking to the local FBI Bureau Chief and a State Department undersecretary, but in the end waived the party through. Dan used his own passport.

The trio made it home without incident. Peter repaired Kayten by replacing the damaged circuit board and a skin panel. Kayten ran full diagnostics and confirmed success.

Mark O'Rourke grilled Peter at a meeting attended by a corporate lawyer and Phillip Lyerson, Peter's boss. Several facts worked in Peter's favor. First, the threat to his son struck a sympathetic chord in the security chief, who'd been thoroughly worked over in advance by his daughter, using all the powers held by a daughter over a father. Second,

Peter had planted a virus in the copy of the COTT program given to the blackmailers. The virus inactivated the program on the sixth attempted use and corrupted every routine. Copies could not be made. He'd also altered several circuit board descriptions on the sensor unit blueprints that would distort how neural features were recorded. Cybernetic Implementation directors were intrigued more by the virus than any other aspect of the case.

Peter's lawyer found a path that benefitted both Peter Valois and his employer. In exchange for information on the virus Peter used and his assistance correcting flaws in security operations, the company agreed to take no action against Peter. Cybernetic also agreed to hire a new technician, which the Frog would prescreen and approve. The Frog also demanded that Peter finish the Department of Defense report on time. The espionage interest in the project confirmed its importance.

The FBI suggested the Valois affair had a connection with some Chinese company. Morgan and Yingyi, however, had clammed up. The Mexicans had arrested them, and extradition had been in process when the Federales announced that the men had escaped and disappeared.

The Defense Department reviewed security procedures at Cybernetic and were especially antsy about the background check that had allowed Antoinette Marino to get onto their project. Her trip to Beijing, for whatever purpose, raised a red flag. Her previous employment with the CIA uncovered the possible motive of avenging her brother's death. Her interest in the Nicaragua file was another red flag.

Without saying anything about using the brain transfer procedure on his son, Peter tweaked his boss's interest in medical applications of his research, starting with an addiction-control project in monkeys. The Frog said he'd personally take the proposal to the CEO.

Peter Valois wasn't the only one playing cards close to his vest. O'Rourke revealed that Kayten had been placed in the Valois home not as a home experimental project, but as security for Peter's home research.

. . .

Peter left the meeting with his job intact, and his satisfaction expanded in his lab where Lisa had good news. She held a letter from the company that supplied rats for research.

"We have an explanation for the rat deaths. Had nothing to do with brain recording."

Peter folded his arms and waited.

"Cardiomyopathy. The supplier found a virus in some rats from their Phoenix facility. The dead rats were from there. We confirmed the virus in their blood sample with a specific marker test."

Peter smiled.

"Wait. There's more. The dead dog histology came back. Also a cardiac muscle infection. Just our bad luck."

"So, brain recording is safe."

"As safe as a CT scan."

Peter retreated to his office with a sense of relief. His son was safe. Recording was safe. And he could leave well enough alone. No transference of a conditioned brain file into Dan. He didn't need it.

On the trip from Mexico, Dan apologized for letting his drug use open the door to the kidnappers. "But I'm done with that stuff," he said. "Those guys kept giving me crap. Like to keep me quiet. I dumped it in the can and acted high. The jerks bought it," Dan said.

Peter hoped that was a good sign.

The cardiac issue got Peter thinking. Brain recording aimed to modify behavior. There was no reason to record or condition regions that dealt with bodily functions, like heart rhythm. Those regions were well known, and the program could be modified to leave them alone. That would also speed up the recording process. He'd need another grant from the Defense department to confirm this.

In Beijing the head of Xianxingzhe Group had to endure his mentor's verbal punishment for the disaster in Mexico. Zheng convinced the man to wait for the answer from the lab on the authenticity of the goods Valois had delivered. Only then did he get some peace.

The lab results were Zheng's last hope. For his career. For his life.

Failure in so important a task could only be atoned for by his death. Thus, it was a stoic but anxious CEO who sat alone in his vast office, waiting for his phone to ring.

The call finally came through late in the evening on the third day. Zheng listened in silence and finally said, “Thank you.” He rose and plodded to his adjoining private quarters where a hot tub filled with warm water awaited. The sake, too, was warm, and he drank several in silence. Then he went to a vanity and picked up a long, pearl-handled razor, which he laid carefully at the edge of the tub. In truth, he should choose Mishima’s method of death, but the prospect of ceremonial, self-inflicted disemboweling, even with the help of a beheader, was more than Zheng could embrace, regardless of his dishonor. He removed his clothes slowly and glided naked into the water. He sat with his eyes closed for several minutes before reaching for the razor.

Pam showered Dan with attention for days. Although he’d resisted drugs as a captive, he admitted he still wanted them and agreed to enter a rehabilitation program. Arrangements were made within twenty-four hours, and Dan spent the next seven weeks at a small, isolated center for juveniles.

He came home labeled “Compliant” and commenced daily NA meetings. Things went well, and he returned to Seneca High where he encountered Megan.

“Hey, Dan,” she said. “Glad you’re back. Howya doing?”

“Okay. You’re a welcome sight. It’s going to take a lot of work, but Dan the Druggie is gone.”

“Right. You can do it if anyone can. I guess you’ve got a lot of catching up to do.”

“How about some help? You know, from someone who knows how to give an incentive. How about a little tutoring?”

Megan didn’t answer right away, considering Dan’s use of the word “incentive.” It made her suspicious. She smelled bullshit. “Love to, Dan. Let’s start today after school at my house.”

“Okay. How about a catch-up lesson on romance?”

"Whoa, cowboy. You need to think homework."

"No way.

Dan stood with his back to his open locker. Megan grabbed his belt, pushed him into his locker, and kissed him. After pulling him upright, she sashayed down the hall.

One of Dan's track team buddies came up to the lockers. "Welcome back, Dan." He looked at the departing Megan. "Miss O'Rourke has changed in your absence. For the better, I'd say."

Dan found his classes tough. At the end of the day, he headed for the school library and read his history book. A tall, acerbic kid in tattered jeans entered, scanned the area until he saw Dan, and went over to him. He checked to see that no one was listening.

"Hey, Valois," scruffy jeans said. "Glad to see you survived. We got a little party planned Friday night. No parents. Some new stuff. You can be the guest of honor. You know, give us the horror tale."

The rehab program had prepared Dan for this. He reacted how the counselors said he should. He stared ahead and called on his higher power. Megan came into the library.

He rose and addressed Scruffy. "Sorry. I'm not that guy anymore."

Dan grabbed his book and walked over to join Megan.

Carlos tried to get comfortable in his hospital bed. His arm had been set, but he'd started running a fever from the infected gunshot wound. His course of intravenous antibiotic would run another day. He'd given the police details about his "accident" and the attack, and they located Andy's body. Her death was called an accident. Mark O'Rourke filled Carlos in on what he knew about the operation in Mexico.

A nurse entered the room to ask if Carlos wanted a pain reliever to help him sleep. Carlos had in mind a pill, but the nurse returned a moment later with a syringe.

"Turn on your side, Mr. Oreta."

Carlos complied and the nurse in one fluid motion whipped aside the gown and stabbed him. She patted him on the butt and closed the gown.

"That should let you sleep like a baby." It did. At eight, Carlos had to be awakened for breakfast and, in the middle of the fruit and cereal, he had a visitor. Lisa entered carrying some books.

"Lisa, it's great to see you. But I don't know if I trust lab techs anymore. You're unarmed, aren't you?"

"Do you want to frisk me?" Lisa sat down in a bedside chair.

"Yes, but I'll take your word."

"Actually, I do have a confession to make that won't help your trust issue."

Lisa relayed her story. She confessed she was employed by the Department of Defense to keep an eye on the Valois research contract.

"So, what happens now that you've sprung your cover and revealed your dastardly spying to me?"

Lisa walked to the window that viewed the hospital power plant. "I plan to retire from government service. It turns out that I really enjoy the scientific work. Dr. Valois needs help, and I'm hoping to be just a researcher. I like it here in California. And I like you, even if you are beaten up and broken. How are you feeling anyway?"

"Much better this morning. The shoulder aches and so does my head. But basically, except for this arm cast, I'm all right."

Lisa extracted a felt-tipped marker from her purse. "Sounds like you need rehabilitation. I'll volunteer. When do you get out of here?"

"I guess the doctor will tell me today."

"Now hold still. I want this to be a work of art." Lisa inscribed her greeting and name on Carlos's casted forearm. Then she leaned forward and kissed him. He felt something on his chest during the embrace and when it was over found that Lisa drawn a happy face on his left pectoral muscle. "See if you can explain that to the nurses. Is there anything you need?"

"Well, I was fine up to a moment ago. There is one thing you could help with. Could you feed Umba? My next-door neighbor Maria has been popping in once a day, but she had to leave last night for a business trip. Research on tech big shots, I think, for one of her magazine articles. Umba has a cat door, but he's probably torn my house apart by now because breakfast wasn't served to him on his schedule."

"No problem. I'll stop by after I leave here. The cat probably needs some human company."

"The house key is in my pants pocket. In the closet. And if you run into Maria, tell her you are authorized." Carlos wondered if he should elaborate on Maria, in case she returned early from her trip.

"And how old is this Maria?"

"She's in her twenties, I guess, and a real looker."

Lisa fetched the key and stayed for about fifteen minutes. In that time Carlos related his adventure, and they both found it hard to talk about Andy's involvement and her fate.

"In the future, stay away from wild girls," Lisa said. She then volunteered, with a straight face, to help him find a new car, planted a kiss on his forehead as if he were a little boy, and departed.

Months later, Peter was in his work room when Kayten entered and told him that guests had arrived for the cookout.

"Okay. Tell Mrs. Valois I'll be up in a moment to cook the steaks and finish the ribs outside."

"I could do that, sir."

"You could, but then I wouldn't get the pleasure of roasting the kill."

"Kill, sir? But you didn't kill anything to get the steaks."

"Never mind, Kayten. Just get the fire pit, the barbecue I mean, ready for the master to perform his ceremony."

Kayten raised an eyebrow but said nothing more. Peter followed the android from the room, flipping off the light. He found his wife in the kitchen mixing a pitcher of margaritas.

"There you are," Pam said. "You have to get the steaks going. Gerry called to say she and Mark are on their way. Dan and Megan will eat here before going to the beach. And you have new guests who just arrived."

Peter reached around his wife's waist and kissed her neck. "The great meat roaster will go to work. Pour me a margarita when they are ready. Low salt, I assume."

"Saltpeter, in your case." Pam handed her husband a platter of steaks, two racks of ribs, a barbecue fork, and a set of tongs, and shoved him toward the patio door. "I'll be out with the salad."

Outside, the temperature was in the eighties with a high cloud cover. The heat was broken by the occasional breeze. Birds chattered in the yard trees, probably complaining that they didn't want the humans in their space. Peter put the meat on. Kayten vacuumed the pool while Carlos and Lisa lounged nearby offering unhelpful critiques of the robot's technique.

"Still checking me out by befriending my technician I see," Peter said.

Carlos patted Lisa's bare thigh. "Our relationship has grown into nonbusiness areas, Dr. Valois."

"That explains her smiling all the time in the lab." Peter looked at Lisa and added, "And if you wore that in the lab, I'd be smiling all the time."

Before Lisa could answer, Pam came out of the house with a fresh pitcher of drinks, "You are much too old for that sort of thing, Peter. Tend to your steaks."

"Yes, dear," Peter said, applying barbecue sauce to the ribs.

Dan and Megan came around the house. Megan was wearing one of the bathing suits that covered fewer square inches than the paper money used to pay for it.

"Hi, Dr. Valois," Megan said.

"Good afternoon, Miss O'Rourke. Hope you're hungry. We have some great steaks here."

"We'll eat our share, Dad," Dan said.

As Peter seasoned the steaks and slapped more barbecue sauce on the ribs, he realized that since rehabilitation, Dan had been eating like his former self: that is, constantly. He glanced at his son, not seeing any obvious weight gain. Still looked on the slim side. When Dan and Megan dove into the pool, Peter got an image of small kids playing in the water. With a start, he realized they were grandchildren.

THE END

Dear reader,

We hope you enjoyed reading *Clean Copy.* Please take a moment to leave a review, even if it's a short one. Your opinion is important to us.

Discover more books by R.R. Brooks at https://www.nextchapter.pub/authors/rr-brooks

Want to know when one of our books is free or discounted? Join the newsletter at http://eepurl.com/bqqB3H

Best regards,

R.R. Brooks and the Next Chapter Team

ABOUT THE AUTHOR

Robert R. Brooks, a native of New Jersey, writes fantasy, mystery, and science fiction novels and short stories as **R.R. Brooks**. His science background includes a career in pharmaceutical research and development. He has been creating fiction since college and has training from several schools, including The Great Smokies Writing Program of the University of North Carolina. His publications include over a dozen short stories and three novels. His epic fantasy novel *Justi the Gifted* was published by Leo Publishing in 2015, the mystery (co-authored with A.C. Brooks) *The Clown Forest Murders* by Black Opal Books in 2018, and the fantasy *The Gifted Spawn* by Escarpment Press in 2021. Bob is a member of the **Blue Ridge Writers Group,** the **Appalachian Round Table**, and **NC Writers Network**. He has served as a judge for the Brevard Little Theater Annual Play Competition and is now a reader for the Eric M. Hoffer Award for self-published and small press books.

Retired, he lives with a wife, cats, and beagle in western North Carolina, enjoys the arts, and continues writing. His website is www.brooks-authors.com.

The
Gifted
Spawn
R.R. BROOKS

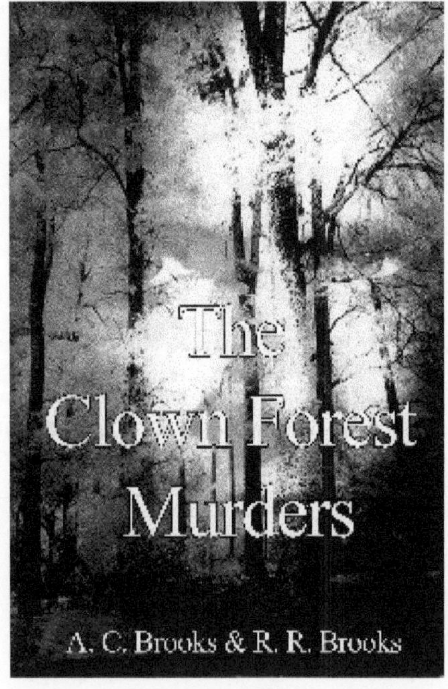
The
Clown Forest
Murders
A. C. Brooks & R. R. Brooks

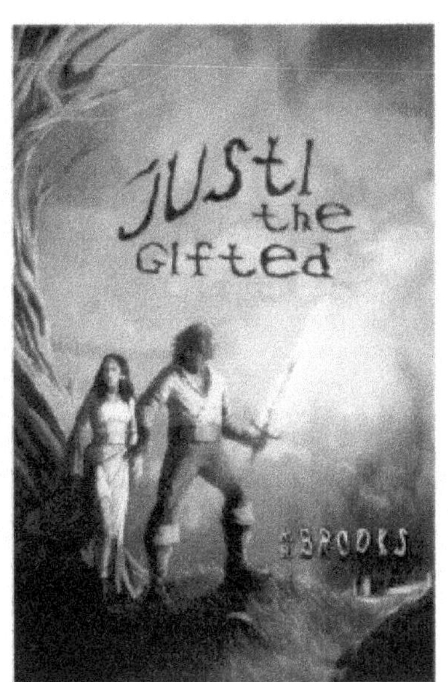
Justi the Gifted
BROOKS

Lightning Source UK Ltd.
Milton Keynes UK
UKHW011849140921
390594UK00001B/109

9 781006 527296